CHARMCASTER

SEBASTIEN DE CASTELL

HOT KEY BOOKS

First published in Great Britain in 2018 by
HOT KEY BOOKS
80–81 Wimpole St, London W1G 9RE
www.hotkeybooks.com

This edition published 2018 by Hot Key Books

A CIP catalogue record for this book is available from the British Library.

ISBN: 978-1-4714-0672-0
Also available as an ebook and in audio

2

Typeset by Palimpsest Book Production Ltd, Falkirk, Stirlingshire
Printed and bound in Great Britain by Clays Ltd, Elcograf S.p.A.

Hot Key Books is an imprint of Bonnier Books UK
www.bonnierbooks.co.uk

CHARMCASTER

THE SPELLSLINGER SERIES

SPELLSLINGER
SHADOWBLACK
CHARMCASTER
SOULBINDER
QUEENSLAYER
CROWNBREAKER

THE GREATCOATS SERIES

TRAITOR'S BLADE
KNIGHT'S SHADOW
SAINT'S BLOOD
TYRANT'S THRONE

To Ralph McInerny.
Some twenty years ago he created a series of cassette tapes
with the preposterously friendly title,
'Let's Write a Mystery'.
He was the best writing teacher I never met.

The Mechanical Bird

DISCORDANCE

Those wishing to become Argosi must first accept that we are neither prophets nor fortune tellers. Our cards hold no magic. We are simply wanderers and the decks we carry nothing more than maps; each suit represents a different culture and each card the structures of power within it. As people and nations change, so too do our decks. These are the concordances and they reveal that which is.

But when an Argosi encounters something new – something that should not exist and yet could alter the course of history – we are compelled to paint a new card: a discordance. Each is both warning and clarion call that every Argosi must heed, for so long as the true nature of a discordance remains hidden, the future will be . . . unpredictable.

1

Desert Lightning

'I totally saw this coming,' Reichis growled, leaping onto my shoulder as lightning scorched the sand barely ten feet from us. The squirrel cat's claws pierced my sweat-soaked shirt and dug into my skin.

'Yeah?' I asked, ignoring the pain with about as much success as I was having stopping my hands from shaking. 'Maybe next time there's a hextracker on our tail, you could warn us *before* our horses panic and dump us in the middle of the desert.' Another thunderclap erupted overhead and shook the ground beneath our feet. 'Oh, and if it's not too much trouble, how about a little heads-up before dry lightning starts crashing down on us from a cloudless sky?'

Reichis hesitated, no doubt trying to come up with a believable explanation. Squirrel cats are terrible liars. They make excellent thieves and particularly enthusiastic murderers, but they're rubbish at deception. 'I was waiting to see if you'd figure it out on your own. I was testing you. Yeah, that's it. Testing you. And you failed, Kellen.'

'You two recall we're supposed to be laying an ambush?' Ferius Parfax asked, kneeling a few feet away to bury something shiny and sharp in the sand. A tangle of red curls whipped around her face while she worked. Despite the strange storm raging all around us, her movements were fluid and practised. This wasn't the first time we'd found ourselves on the wrong end of a hunting expedition.

Hence the need for traps.

Ambushing a Jan'Tep mage is a tricky business. You never know which forms of magic they might have at their disposal. Iron, ember, sand, silk, blood, breath . . . The enemy could have any number of spells to kill you. As if that wasn't enough, you also have to consider the possibility of accomplices – lackeys or mercenaries hired to watch the mage's back or do his dirty work for him. 'This might go faster if you let me help you set the traps,' I suggested to Ferius, desperate to keep my mind off the surprising number of ways I might die in the next few minutes.

'No, and quit watching me.' She got up and walked a few yards away before kneeling to bury another spiked ball or fragile glass cylinder filled with sleeping gas or whatever else she was using this time. 'The fella chasing us could be casting one of them fancy Jan'Tep silk spells to ferret out our plans. That head of yours is too full of thoughts, kid. He'll read you easy.'

That bristled. Ferius was an Argosi – one of the enigmatic card players who travelled the continent attempting to . . . Actually, I still wasn't quite sure *what* they were meant to do other than annoy people. Despite not having much hope of ever becoming an Argosi myself, I'd been studying Ferius's ways as best I could, if only because doing so might keep me alive. It didn't help that she kept insisting I first had to learn to do stupid things like 'listen with my eyes' or 'grab onto emptiness'.

Reichis, of course, loved it when Ferius upbraided me. 'She's right, Kellen,' he chittered from his perch on my shoulder. 'You should be more like me.'

'You mean without *any* thoughts in my head?'

The snarl he gave me was barely more than a whisper, but delivered perilously close to my ear. 'It's called *instinct*, skinbag. Makes it hard for silk mages to read me. Want to know what my instincts are telling me to do right now?'

Another bolt of lightning struck the peak of the dune above us, nearly giving me a heart attack and sending a wave of smoke sizzling up from the sand. Had Reichis and I been better friends, we probably would have been hanging on to each other for dear life. Instead, he bit me. 'Sorry. Instinct.'

I jerked my shoulder, shaking the squirrel cat off me. He spread his paws out and the furry flaps that ran between his front and back limbs caught the wind as he glided down gracefully to the ground where he gave me a surly look. It had been petty of me to throw him off. I couldn't blame him for his reaction to the thunder. Reichis has a thing about lightning and fire and . . . well, pretty much any enemy you can't bite.

'How is this guy doing it?' I wondered aloud. A dry storm in the middle of the desert under a cloudless sky? It made no sense. Sure, the sixth form of ember magic creates an electrical discharge that *looks* a lot like lightning, but it manifests from the mage's hands, not from above, and they have to be able to see the target to cast it.

I looked back up the dune for the thousandth time, wondering when I'd see him coming over the crest, ready to rain seven hells upon us. 'Three days this mage has been on our tail and nothing we do shakes him. Why won't he leave us alone?'

Ferius gave a wry chuckle. 'Reckon that's what comes from having a spell warrant on your head, kid. Whichever cabal of mages implanted obsidian worms in them rich kids can't be too pleased with us going around destroying them.'

Even with more pressing dangers at hand, just thinking about obsidian worms repelled me. They were a type of mystical parasite. Once lodged inside the victim's eye, they enabled mages to control the host from afar. Ferius, Reichis and I had spent the last six months tracking down students from the famed Academy who had no idea they were slowly being turned into spies against their own families – or worse, assassins.

'When did it become our job to save the world from the obsidian worms anyway?' I asked, removing my frontier hat so I could wipe my brow with my sleeve. Despite the dry air, I was sweating profusely; wearing a black hat that was too big for my head wasn't helping. I'd got the hat from a fellow spellslinger by the name of Dexan Videris – payment on account of his having tried to kill me. He'd claimed the silver sigils adorning the band would keep mages from tracking me, but like everything else Dexan had told me, that was turning out to be a lie.

'It ain't *our* job,' Ferius replied. 'It's mine. The whole point of bein' Argosi is to avert the calamities that bring suffering to innocent folks. Since a bunch of idiot Jan'Tep mages assassinating powerful families all across the continent could set off a war, I'd say this situation qualifies.'

The wind picked up without warning and my apparently non-magical prized possession flew from my hand. I almost went running after it but decided not to bother. Stupid thing never fit right anyway. 'It would be nice if just once somebody came along who wanted to *help* instead of everybody trying to murder us.'

Ferius rose abruptly to her feet and peered out into the desert. 'Now that don't look good at all.'

I turned to see what she was talking about. Off in the distance, a wall of sand that must've been a hundred feet high had begun to roil in the air.

'Now we've got to deal with a freakin' sandstorm?' Reichis grumbled. He shook himself and his fur changed colour from its usual muddy brown with black stripes to a dusty beige flecked with grey that matched the approaching clouds of sand and grit. Once it got here he'd be able to pretty much disappear into the storm if he wanted – which he probably would if things went badly. Squirrel cats aren't sentimental.

As the storm approached, I tried to decide whether I'd rather die from being buried under tons of sand, electrocuted by dry lightning or murdered with dark magic. The choices are never pretty when you're an outlaw spellslinger with a gambler for a mentor, a squirrel cat for a business partner and a long line of mages who want you dead.

Oh, and I was fairly sure it was my seventeenth birthday.

'What do we do now?' I asked.

Ferius, her gaze on the thick clouds of sand coming for us, replied, 'Reckon you'd best take a deep breath, kid.'

2

Deep Breaths

Whenever the three of us are about to be attacked – which is a lot more often than I'd like – we each have a job to do: Ferius sets her traps, prepares her weapons and uses those crazy Argosi talents of hers to figure out the best tactics for our survival. Reichis does most of the scouting and uses his keen sense of smell to catch any scent of approaching enemies.

Me? My job is to take a deep breath.

While Ferius is a master of trickery, and Reichis is two furry feet of sharp teeth, claws and a total disregard for the consequences of violence, I've got one and only one skill that matters in a situation like this: a piece of breath magic that relies on quick hands and the twin powders I keep in the pouches on either side of my belt. I might not have a lot of spells, but I've learned to be fast on the draw. Doesn't matter how powerful a rival mage is if you blast him before he performs his invocations. Trouble is, if my hands are shaking or I'm sweating so much the powders stick to my fingers, I'll end up with two charred stumps at the end of my arms and an embarrassed look on my face.

So . . . *Breathe.*

Relax.

Ignore the lightning and the sandstorm. Use the years you spent as an initiate envisioning your spells to picture your enemy at the top of that sand dune, see yourself blasting him right before he can—

A spike of pain that felt like a blast of ice-cold wind stabbed at my right eye. I slammed the heel of my palm over it in a futile attempt to block the sensation. Usually it's my left eye that gives me trouble on account of the shadowblack marks around it (which also happens to be the reason why bounty hunters with spell warrants keep trying to kill me). As if the shadowblack weren't trouble enough, about six months ago my other eye had become home to a *sasutzei*: a wind spirit who'd decided to take up residence there. I was still new to whisper magic, so getting the spirit under control was next to impossible.

'Damn it, I'm trying to concentrate!'

Uncharacteristically, the pain faded away. I took a deep breath and again tried to visualise the moment when I'd lay eyes on our pursuer. My muscles relaxed as I imagined myself pulling the powders, tossing them into the air and forming the somatic shapes with my hands just as they collided, uttering the spell and blasting—

'Ow! Stop it!'

'What's the problem, kid?' Ferius asked.

'This stupid wind spirit in my eye keeps vexing me!'

Ferius came closer, eyes narrowed. 'How long has Suzy been acting up?'

'Suzy' was the name Ferius had given to the sasutzei.

'Ever since this damned mage started hunting us. Every time I think about—'

Reichis cut me off with a low growl, muzzle held high as

he sniffed the air. His eyes glistened with hungry anticipation instead of the much more sensible fear that any sane animal would've felt at a time like this. The corners of his fuzzy mouth rose up in his approximation of a grin. 'Time to fight.'

Lightning struck the sand near the top of the dune again – once, twice, then a third time. Wind from the approaching storm buffeted us, sending sand swirling into the air and turning the world into a hazy mess of grey shadows. One of those shadows appeared at the very top of the dune.

Ferius grabbed my shoulders and pushed me down low into a crouch. 'Wait till he gets close,' she said, her words barely audible over the storm. 'Let the enemy come to us.'

'Stupid humans,' Reichis muttered, but he obeyed for once.

As we huddled there, a slim figure in a long travelling coat stumbled down the dune, face covered against the wind and grit, wearing a beat-up frontier hat not unlike my own. The outfit in itself was rather odd: usually when people come to kill me they like to do it with flair. A four-legged animal – maybe some kind of dog or big cat – limped alongside.

'Hyena,' Reichis snarled, sniffing at the air and baring his teeth. 'I hate hyenas.' He sniffed a second time, then tilted his head quizzically.

'What is it?' I asked.

'Something ain't right. The skinbag and the mutt stink of fear.'

'Of us?' I asked incredulously.

The answer came when the mage reached the bottom of the dune and ran right past us into the deepening storm. A few seconds later four more silhouettes appeared over the crest – men and women clothed in the wide strips of pale linen favoured by the Berabesq, whose lands these were. They wielded curved-bladed swords and flails with spiked balls spinning at the end of their chains, moving with ferocious grace as they pursued the mage across the desert.

'Berabesq Faithful,' Ferius murmured, eyes wide as she watched them pass. Usually most things that come out of her mouth sound like the beginning of a dirty joke, so the awe in her voice was disconcerting.

'What are Berabesq "Faithful"?' I asked.

She watched as the mage fled into the sandstorm. 'For that poor sucker? The worst kind of death imaginable.'

3

The Wind Spirit

'Well, problem solved,' Reichis said, shaking himself. The colour of his fur changed to a jaunty orange with gold stripes as he sauntered up the sand dune in the direction we'd come.

'Wait!' I called out.

The squirrel cat didn't even slow down. 'Nope. If we're not the target, then we got no reason to sit around in this stinkin' desert.'

Normally I'd agree with him. In fact, given how much I hate the desert, I'd be way ahead of him. But something was bothering me – like an itch I needed to scratch but couldn't reach. I looked back at the retreating sandstorm. Both the hunters and the hunted had disappeared from view. 'These Berabesq "Faithful" . . . Why would they be out in the desert chasing down a Jan'Tep mage?'

Reichis gave me the same look he gives crows when they irritate him. 'Don't know, don't plan on findin' out.' He scratched behind one of his ears. 'Gonna find me a bath and soak in it until all this sand is out of my fur.'

'What's he on about?' Ferius asked.

I translated for her.

'The squirrel cat's got a point,' she said, packing up her

traps and tripwires. 'The Faithful are some of the coldest killers you'll ever meet. Magic ain't no different to devil-worship in this part of the world, and the Faithful, well, they've got a nose for it. Once they're done with the mage, you can bet they'll be sniffin' after you, kid.'

That hardly seemed fair. I barely had enough magic for a few paltry breath spells. That was one of the reasons why so many mages were eager to duel me. Now I was going to have a bunch of religious zealots after me too? 'Why does the whole world hate me?'

'Me, me, me,' Reichis mocked. 'Why is it always about you, Kellen? Notice how we never run across other squirrel cats? That's because most of *my* kind have been killed by *your* kind.'

I felt ashamed by that. The squirrel cat almost never brought up the fact that his relatives had died at the hands of a mage from my own clan, but any time I asked if he wanted to talk about the loss of his family, he bit me. Hard.

Ferius offered up a sardonic smile. 'Not everybody hates you, kid. There are entire countries full of people who haven't met you yet.'

'Well, I'm starting to hate both of you,' Reichis grumbled. 'And I'm hungry, so unless one of you is planning to feed me one of your ears for supper, let's get out of this lousy wasteland and find a town with somebody who knows how to make butter biscuits.' The squirrel cat went back to busily – and futilely – picking the sand out of his fur.

'He's right,' I said to Ferius. 'We're supposed to be in Gitabria right now, saving the last remaining victim of the obsidian worms – someone who *hasn't* been hunting us for three solid days. If this mage has got himself mixed up with a bunch of religious fanatics with a burning desire to . . . well, burn people? Then better him than us.'

It didn't sound very noble when I said it out loud like that, but the alternative was way worse. I went and picked my hat out of the scraggly bush where it had landed. 'Let's just get the hell out of—'

Pain. I mean, *pain*.

I rubbed at my right eye to try to get rid of the stinging sensation. 'Quit attacking me, you crazy wind spirit!'

Ferius came over and pulled my hand away, peering into my eye as if she expected to find the sasutzei staring back at her. 'Sounds like Suzy's trying to tell you something, kid.'

'Yeah,' I snapped. 'She's telling me to rip out my own eyeball!'

'I get first bite,' Reichis said, then gave Ferius a snarl just in case she didn't get the message. Unlike me, she can't turn his little chitters, grunts and growls into words, but she's been around him long enough to know his particular culinary proclivities.

'It's all yours once we're done with it, squirrel cat.' To me she said – of course, 'Breathe, kid.'

Since it was becoming clear that the sasutzei wasn't going to let me leave until I paid attention to her, I did just that.

Whisper magic isn't like the spellcraft of my people. Our magic is built on summoning the six fundamental sources of power through the tattooed metallic bands on our forearms. Casting a spell takes carefully worded invocations along with precise somatic shapes to match the intricate mystical geometry we envision in our minds. Whisper mages? They basically just . . . whisper. It's more like begging the spirits than commanding magical forces – which is probably why my people look down on it. 'Okay, Suzy,' I murmured to the sasutzei, 'show me what you've got.'

I let the air ease out slowly from my lungs, using it like a river upon which I sent little wooden boats made more from emotion than thought, each one carrying a message to the spirit. I'm not sure what words I spoke – it's hard to keep track when you're trying so hard *not* to think, but after a few seconds the pain shifted to a softer sensation, like someone gently blowing on your eyelids. When I opened them, I found the world had split in two. My left eye beheld everything before me – the sand dune, the mountains off in the distance; Ferius, standing there patiently; Reichis looking irritable. My right eye was looking directly inside the sandstorm.

'You okay, Kellen?' the squirrel cat asked. 'One of your eyes just went all milky.' His muzzle twisted into a look of mild disgust. 'Don't think I want to eat it any more.'

I ignored him and focused on the visions the sasutzei was showing me. The air that had been so still an instant before was now swirling all around me, sand and dust whipping at my skin, though I couldn't feel any of it. What I was witnessing was further away, deeper into the heart of the storm where the four Berabesq Faithful pushed through fierce winds as they closed in on their prey. The mage looked to be an inch or two shorter than me and even skinnier. If he couldn't destroy them with magic, I doubted he'd be able to defend himself physically. 'They've almost got him,' I said out loud. 'The animal with him, the hyena, it's fallen to the ground. It's not getting up.'

'Good,' Reichis muttered. 'Hope the filthy thing is dead.'

In addition to not being sentimental, squirrel cats also aren't big on sympathy.

I closed my left eye to focus my attention on what was

unfolding inside the sandstorm. 'The mage is trying to pick up the hyena, but the Berabesq are too close – they're starting to . . . Wait . . . He's throwing something at them.'

I watched in fascination as what appeared to be a small wooden box, no bigger than the palm of my hand, fell in front of the pursuers. The instant it hit the ground, it broke open and fire burst out of it, the flames erupting in all directions.

'What is it?' Ferius asked. 'Some kind of weapon?'

'Caged fire, I think. He must be a charmcaster.'

Reichis tilted his fuzzy head at me. 'A what now?'

'A charmcaster. They're like . . .' How do you explain the arcane distinctions between disciplines of magic to an Argosi gambler and a squirrel cat? 'It's like this: a proper mage can invoke spells at will so long as they've sparked the necessary tattooed bands that my people use to create a connection to the raw forms of magic. It's all about energy and will. A spellslinger like me can only do a little bit of magic, so I have to combine it with other things to make it useful. A charmcaster doesn't really cast spells at all so much as bind them to physical objects. Some charms – simple ones like warning locks and glow-glass lanterns that don't require a lot of magical force – can keep working for months or years. Bigger ones—'

'Like freakin' dry lightning?' Reichis asked.

'Exactly. A storm takes a lot of work to bind, so you could only use it once and it won't last for more than maybe an hour.' A sudden twinge of pain in my right eye courtesy of the sasutzei brought my attention back to the visions she wanted me to witness. 'The caged fire didn't work. The Berabesq have the charmcaster pinned down now. Three of them are strapping him down with ropes, but . . .' I hesitated, unable to make sense of what I was seeing.

'What's wrong, kid?' Ferius asked.

Again I struggled to peer closer at what the sasutzei was showing me. 'The way they're tying him down is really weird. They've got ropes around each of his limbs and then they're tying those to each other so that his hands and feet are all outstretched. It's almost like the ropes are forming a circle around him.'

'That's the rite of damnation,' she said grimly. 'They use it to cleanse the earth of a heathen's blasphemy.'

'How?' I asked.

'Slowly, and with a lot of blood.' Her words came out hoarse and gravelly, and were soon followed by the sound of her footsteps in the sand. 'Best we get on with it then.'

I opened my left eye to find her setting off in what was decidedly the wrong direction.

'Is that crazy Argosi going *into* the storm?' Reichis asked.

'Wait!' I called out to Ferius. 'You said the Faithful were dangerous!'

'That I did, kid,' she shouted back, still headed for the sandstorm. 'Then I recalled something *you* said.'

'Me? What did I—'

She stopped then, buttoning up her waistcoat and pulling her hat down lower over her eyes against the wind and sand. 'You forget already? You said you wished that for once somebody would come along to help instead of always trying to kill us. Reckon that works both ways.'

'Are you kidding me? You expect us to put our lives at risk on account of an idle thought I had in the middle of a lightning storm in the desert?'

Ferius glanced back at me, the smirk on her face at odds with the trepidation in her eyes. 'Warned you that head of yours was too full of thoughts, kid.' Then she turned and resumed her steady march into the swirling chaos of the storm, leaving Reichis and I to decide whether to follow or abandon Ferius to almost certain death.

Ancestors, I prayed silently as I jogged after her, ignoring Reichis's threats to let me charge headlong to my own execution without him. *When I come back in the next life, let me carry this one thought with me: next time you meet an Argosi, run away as fast as you can.*

4

Polite Conversation

Even blinded by fierce winds and pummelled by sand flying in all directions, it didn't take us long to find the Berabesq Faithful. By a rare stroke of luck, we even managed to do it without them spotting us first. All we had to do now was keep quiet until we could free the mage.

'Nice weather we're having,' Ferius called out cheerfully to them, completely blowing our cover. 'How about we have ourselves a little picnic and a friendly chat?'

Ferius Parfax has many bad habits. I've never been able to figure out whether these are an unavoidable consequence of walking an Argosi path or whether it's just because she has a terrible sense of humour. Whichever way you look at it though, announcing your position to four Berabesq Faithful in the middle of a charmcaster's sandstorm to suggest a friendly chat is a terrible, terrible idea.

'Totally saw that coming,' Reichis grumbled.

Without so much as a word to each other, the Berabesq came to a joint decision to decline our invitation of tea and polite company. They also settled on a plan: two of them dragged the unconscious charmcaster deeper into the storm, and the other two came for us.

Ferius sighed. 'Nobody wants to engage in a free and open exchange of ideas any more.'

'Thank the squirrel cat gods for that,' Reichis said, puffing himself up. His fur had taken on the exact colour of the sand around us once again, which was smart since it made him almost impossible to see in the storm. But the little bugger has an ego bigger than most countries, so of course he had to make his stripes dark red to show he meant business. 'Come and get it, skinbags.'

The two hunters loped gracefully towards us. The woman was broad-shouldered and slid a sword from the scabbard at her back as she approached. The blade was about three feet long, curved along its length with a tip that ended in a sharpened hook. 'That's a *kazkhan*,' Ferius said. 'Try not to get cut, okay?'

'Why?'

'Because it's sharp, kid.'

'Right. Helpful advice as always.'

'Also,' Ferius went on, 'the Faithful like to coat the inside of their scabbards with a venom from one of the local snakes. Stings like the devil when it gets under your skin.'

Well, I suppose I hadn't really been planning on letting myself be stabbed anyway.

The slender man had darker colouring than his partner and didn't look as if he were carrying a weapon at all until he got within twenty feet of us. That's when I caught the reflection off the metal sheaths attached to each of his fingers that ended in glinting points.

'*Tiazkhan*,' Ferius said. 'Don't let him hit you with those either.'

'Let me guess: poisoned?'

'Strangely, no – at least not with anything that makes you sick.'

'Then what—'

'Ours is a gentle God,' the man called out. 'Even to heathens. So it is that I must offer you a chance at life.' He spoke to us in Daroman, though with a heavy accent. I guess with Ferius and me wearing frontier travelling clothes, we must've looked as much like Daroman herders as anything else.

'May he grant you serenity and peace to all you love,' Ferius called back, an unusual formality to her voice. She does that sometimes: switches from sounding like a drunken gambler to enunciating with the precision and eloquence of a court diplomat.

'And peace, in turn, to you,' the man replied with a note of surprise in his voice. 'Indeed, peace may be cheaply purchased.' He gestured to the ground. 'You need only kneel and bow your head that God may see you are merely lost, and not come here to interfere in His work.'

Ferius gave an apologetic shrug. 'Forgive me, most worthy one, but when I bow, my eyes cannot see the path ahead, and when I kneel, I cannot walk where my heart dictates.'

This too seemed to bewilder the two Berabesq Faithful, but only for a moment. '*Argosi*,' the woman said at last. Well, spat is more like it.

Ferius grinned at her. 'A common and most sensible reaction, faithful one.'

The man grew impatient. 'Ask your questions then, wanderer. We do not seek a quarrel with the Argosi.'

Ferius took a step forward and made a show of looking around. 'You are far from your temples and cities, most worthy ones – closer to the Gitabrian border than your holy places.

What crime has this mage committed that brings you on such a long chase?'

'Heresy,' the two Faithful replied in unison.

Ferius whispered to me, 'It's always heresy with these guys.' She then turned back to the Faithful. 'There are seven hundred and seventy-seven heresies, most worthy ones, could you be more specific?'

The man seemed mildly impressed. 'You know our ways, so I will answer: the crime of witchcraft.' Before Ferius could respond, he held up a hand, the metal points of the sheaths attached to his fingers reflecting the hazy light that permeated the storm. 'Before you ask, of the eighteen forms of devilry, this one is a *forsaken warlock*.'

'Dang,' Ferius muttered under her breath.

'Why is that bad?' I asked. 'I mean, any more than the seven hundred and seventy-six other heresies?'

'The Berabesq hate mages, but most of the time they avoid risking war with their neighbours just for the sake of killing one. A forsaken warlock is someone they've been given permission to execute without reprisal.'

'Clearly *nobody* wants to save this guy,' Reichis said irritably. 'I mean, what kind of filthy reprobate has his own kind telling their enemies to go ahead and kill him?' He looked up at me with what I assumed was the squirrel cat's expression of mild embarrassment. 'Other than you, of course.'

Ferius locked eyes with the Faithful. 'You follow a dark path, most worthy ones. To conduct a rite of damnation without even a trial? What proof have you that this mage—'

The woman started to object, but her partner held up a hand. 'Ease your conscience, Argosi. The heretic was foolish enough to give his name to any who would listen in a town not three days' ride from here.' He gestured nonchalantly behind them to where his fellow zealots had carried off their prisoner deeper into the storm. 'The one we are about to sacrifice is none other than the notorious Jan'Tep fugitive, Kellen of the House of Ke.'

5

The Fugitive

'Okay, I admit it,' Reichis said as we found ourselves squaring off with the two Berabesq Faithful. '*That* I didn't see coming.'

'You've made a mistake, worthy ones,' Ferius said with the same calm, almost jovial tone as before. The Berabesq weren't buying it.

The woman with the sword spoke to her companion in their own language. I had no idea what she said, but the gist was probably something like, 'Hey, let's go kill these filthy heathens, murder our captive, and *then* we can have some nice tea and polite discourse with their decapitated heads.'

'Kneel, beg forgiveness and we may yet let you live,' the man urged as they came for us. 'Our mission is to execute Kellen of the Jan'Tep, not to slaughter misguided travellers.'

'Heh,' Reichis said as he crouched down in preparation to attack. 'This would be kind of funny if we weren't about to get killed anyway.'

The woman swung her curved-bladed kazkhan in effortless arcs. The whoosh of its passage cut through even the roaring of the sandstorm. 'One of the warlock's own people – a mage himself – came to us under diplomatic sanction. He brought offerings and entreaties that we should rid the world of the blasphemer's presence.'

'Which mage?' I asked. 'Who hired you to—'

'Not really the point right now, kid,' Ferius whispered.

'God commands you bow your heads before him,' the woman said, the arcs of her blade taking on a much deadlier pattern. 'He does not concern himself with whether those hands remain attached to your shoulders.'

Ferius gave no ground. 'Forgive me, most worthy one, but it's the two of you who should probably duck right about now.' After a second she glanced at me, looking mildly disappointed. 'That was your cue, kid.'

'What? Oh, right.' I reached into the pouches at my side and took a pinch of each of the powders – not so much that I would blast the Faithful into little pieces, but enough to make an impression. The wind kept shifting direction, which would present a problem if it blew the powders into my own face right as they exploded.

'Any time now,' Ferius muttered.

A gap in the gusting winds finally came, so I tossed the powders into the air. The instant before they made contact, I formed the somatic shapes for the spell with both hands: index and middle fingers aimed at my targets to give the spell direction, ring and little fingers pressed into my palm for restraint, and thumbs to the sky . . . One of these days I really need to find out what that particular somatic shape is supposed to mean. '*Carath*,' I intoned as the first burst of red and black flame appeared and the spell took hold. The twin fires seared the air just inches above our opponents' heads, leaving the scent of sulphur and blood in the air between us.

The two Faithful stopped in their tracks. The man gave me a small, polite bow. 'Your devilry is almost as impressive as your generosity, blasphemer. Had you chosen to do so, you might well have killed us with your first attack.'

'Yeah,' Reichis said, looking up at me. 'Idiot.'

'Now you've seen what we can do,' Ferius said. 'So why don't we all—'

The man ran a metal-sheathed finger from each hand along the outside of the opposite forearm. The sharp metal tips left a scarlet line of blood trickling in their wake.

Ferius turned to me. 'Kid, fire again. Now!'

Fast as a rattlesnake, I pulled powder and cast the spell a second time just as the Berabesq slammed his bleeding forearms together. The air in front of him shimmered. The twin fires of my blast faded before they got within a foot of him. 'We are the Faithful,' he declared. 'Did you think God would command that we hunt warlocks without blessing us with the means to protect ourselves from their foul magic?'

In case I haven't mentioned it before, I'm not much of a fighter. Outside of one pretty decent spell and a few tricks I've picked up on my travels, my usual defensive strategy is to get beaten up a lot and wait for Ferius to rescue me.

'Dang it!' she complained as a volley of her razor-sharp steel cards bounced off the blood shield the Berabesq had summoned. 'Now that's just plain cheatin'!'

'It is by God's hand that we are protected from your weapons,' the woman opposite said, her curved kazkhan blade weaving in a swift figure-of-eight pattern as she approached. 'Just as it is by God's will that your meddling ways end in blood.' With a sudden lunge forward she swung her blade in a horizontal cut that came right for Ferius's neck. The Argosi stumbled backwards – awkwardly, it seemed to me, until she turned her fall into a backwards roll and came right back up to her feet, flinging a pair of steel cards at our enemy. Once again the man with the metal sheaths on his fingers drove the sides of his forearms together and the same shimmering of the air appeared, shielding both him and his partner. The cards dropped to the sandy ground.

Ferius drew the short steel rod from inside her waistcoat. With a flick of her wrist it extended out to almost two feet in length. 'About forty seconds,' she said to me.

'What?'

'The shield, kid. That's how long it holds up each time Fingers over there summons it. Haven't you been paying attention?'

How was I supposed to notice things like that when people were coming to kill me?

'Guess that makes it about thirty-six seconds before my next meal,' Reichis said, stalking along the ground to outflank them. His surreptitious movements would probably have been more effective if he hadn't felt the need to boast.

The broad-shouldered Faithful took another swing at Ferius, who dived once more in a bid to come up behind her opponent. But the swordswoman was too fast, spinning around with her blade, forcing Ferius to back away once again. I had my own problems of course, because whether from random choice or some weird Berabesq gender rules, the man with the steel-tipped fingers was coming for me. He grabbed at my face. I shuffled backwards only to find my boots digging into the soft sand. I had to settle for falling onto my butt to avoid having five gouges marring my features to go along with the shadowblack markings that already weren't doing much for my looks. Fingers loomed over me with an expression that was somehow both sympathetic and disgusted by my inability to present any kind of threat. 'Stay down, boy.'

'Okay,' I said.

Had it been forty seconds yet? It's oddly hard to keep track of time when people are trying to kill you. I decided to take a shot and reached inside my pouches. I may not be much for fisticuffs, but I've spent a lot of time practising using my powder spell from all kinds of awkward positions. My attack was swift, smooth and well-aimed. Unfortunately, it wasn't well-timed. The blast dissipated against the shield barely two seconds before it faded.

Fingers came after me with those claws of his a second time. I rolled away with more speed than either of us expected, and might have felt good about it were it not for the agony of five steel points slicing through the back of my shirt and into my skin. When I got to my feet and turned to face him, my blood glistened along the metal tips of his finger-sheaths.

'Kneel and bow,' he said. 'The next time you see my tiaz-khan they will be holding the remains of your throat.'

I began to retreat, or at least I *thought* I was retreating. Turned out I wasn't moving at all. I was just standing there, unable to convince my legs to get me out of there. Fingers raised his hand for the kill. That should've been enough to get my body moving again. Too bad it didn't turn out that way.

Here's an interesting fact I'd discovered during my year as an outlaw: your brain never really gets used to fear. I mean, sure, you become accustomed to the *idea* of being terrified all the time, but when someone comes to kill you, everything still goes straight to hell.

'You like claws?' Reichis growled from where he crouched off to the side. 'Try mine!'

He leaped at our opponent, limbs outstretched and mouth wide, showing his fangs. Unlike me, Reichis is fast and deadly in a fight. Until that moment I'd never seen anyone evade him, but the Berabesq Faithful sidestepped the attack, spinning around as he did. When he was facing me again, the metal sheaths on his fingers had more blood on them.

'Reichis!' I screamed.

The squirrel cat landed about ten feet away in the sand. He got back up only to have his rear leg give out on him. He unleashed the kind of growl that to most people would've sounded like vicious rage, but I knew it meant he was hurt and scared.

The Berabesq Faithful, apparently having decided Reichis was the greater threat, strode after him. 'Leave him alone!' I shouted. My legs finally obeyed my commands, and I tried to grab the man's shoulders. Almost negligently, he spun around again and backhanded me across the face. The sting of his metal claws on my left cheek was followed by a dribble of blood down to my jaw.

He looked at me through narrowed eyes, a mix of curiosity and maybe even empathy in his expression. 'You would die for the animal?'

I was spared having to answer by the wind picking up, spraying sand all around us and temporarily blinding us both. Our fight had taken us far from the others. I no longer knew where Ferius was, or if my Argosi mentor had finally met an enemy she couldn't outwit. Reichis snarled as he struggled to rise up on all fours and leap at the man's back, but his injured leg kept failing him. It was pitiful to watch.

Ferius says that when things are bad – *really* bad – then all that's left is to decide whether to die on your feet or die on your knees. That's when you become truly free. That's when you can risk everything, because there's nothing left to lose and fear has lost its hold on you.

Ferius is stupid.

'Kneel,' the Berabesq Faithful said. 'The end will be swift, I swear.'

Then again, maybe the Argosi has a point.

'Let's dance, dirtbag,' I replied.

6

The Second Talent

The Second Talent of the Argosi is called *arta eres*, which means 'graceful defence', or as Ferius calls it, 'dancing'. When she fights, it's like watching water swirling at the bottom of a whirlpool: twirling, swaying, always moving, always in harmony with her opponents even when she's beating the hell out of them.

It doesn't quite look that way when I do it.

'You have spirit,' the Berabesq Faithful congratulated me after I'd somehow managed to slide under his arm and punch him in the kidneys. Something to be proud of, all things considered, and all it had cost me was another set of bloody claw marks along my ribcage. Fingers shook his head as we squared off again. 'But you are a heathen and a fool. You sacrifice yourself for what? A warlock you've never met, being brought to justice by foes you cannot defeat. By now he is dead, and you have traded your life for nothing.'

The guy's got a point, I thought. 'Okay, I give up.'

'You do?'

'Sure,' I replied. 'Just as soon as I'm done kicking your ass.'

I slipped left then right, evading Fingers's attempts to skewer me with his metal claws even as my right foot kicked sand up into his face. He ducked and made a grab for me, but by then I was already on his other side. I performed what's called a carry-over, in which you take your partner's elbow and pull them into a new direction to send them careening off to their new partner. In this case, that new partner was Reichis.

The squirrel cat still couldn't quite stay on his feet, but he didn't need to for this manoeuvre. As the Berabesq Faithful struggled to regain his footing, Reichis delivered a vicious bite to his ankle, drawing blood.

'Damned rodent!' Fingers cried out. It was the first decent blow we'd scored since this whole thing began. I think that enraged him more than the pain. Unfortunately he was still bigger than us, faster than us, and more skilled at combat. Before Reichis could get away, the Berabesq kicked him, sending the squirrel cat tumbling over and over along the sand.

Again I ran at our enemy, momentarily forgetting the dance and relying on raw fury to help me land a blow. It didn't. The Berabesq evaded me easily. This time instead of clawing me, he tried to drive those metal finger-sheaths into my side – no doubt to rip out one of my kidneys and present it to me.

All those hours Ferius made me practise country dances saved my life just then as my knee came up reflexively in what's called a 'fancy canter'. No doubt I looked pretty silly, but instead of losing a vital organ I only got stabbed in the thigh. Almost by accident, I drove my elbow into my opponent's face even as I stumbled away. I landed next to Reichis who was, at that moment, trying in vain to launch himself at our opponent. 'Damn leg wound,' he growled. 'Can't jump high enough to get airborne.'

I rolled onto my back and then to my feet. The wind picked up, sending so much sand into the air that I couldn't see the Berabesq any more, and hopefully he couldn't see me either. 'What good would getting airborne do?' I asked.

'I'd show that lousy skinbag the difference between a squirrel cat and a rodent, that's what!'

It's worth noting that, zoologically speaking, squirrel cats are almost certainly a type of rodent.

'I have an idea,' I shouted over the noise of the wind. 'But I don't think you're going to like it.'

Fingers had recovered and was now coming for us again, a little warier than before. That might have been flattering had it not also meant that he wouldn't be falling for any more of my dancing tricks.

'Will I like your idea more than being cut to shreds by a stinking human wearing fake claws?' Reichis asked.

'Maybe, but not by much.' The wind died down just long enough for me to pull red and black powders from my pouches and send my spell screaming towards our enemy. As before, the Berabesq slammed his forearms together and summoned that strange shield of his. But I hadn't been aiming for him. Instead, the twin fires blasted the sand at his feet. In a better world, that would've somehow turned the sand into slippery glass, but the fires the spell creates aren't nearly hot enough to do that. It did, however, distract Fingers long enough for me to execute the main part of my plan: I reached down, grabbed Reichis by the scruff of his neck, and hurled him as high as I could up into the air.

'You dirty rotten—' The rest of that sentence was lost to the gale-force winds that spun him far away into the swirling sands above us. Having perfectly executed that manoeuvre, I then proceeded to the next part of the plan. I dropped to my knees and begged for my life.

Fingers looked down at me, a trace of a gentle smile on his face. 'I would that I could offer you leniency, brave one, but you have struck one of the Faithful, and attempted to hinder our most sacred duty. Mercy is no longer within my power to give.' He brought his right arm back, the now bloody metal claws oddly bright in the haze of the sandstorm.

I clasped my hands together. 'Could I pray? Just for a moment?'

'To worship your heathen gods so close to your death would only tarnish your soul further.'

'It won't take long, I promise!' I bowed my head and spoke very quickly. 'Ancestors, I know I haven't exactly been a model Jan'Tep mage up until now, but if you could see your way to granting me this one last wish, I'd really appreciate it.'

'Cease your prattling and face His judgement with some small measure of—'

'Almost done.' I clasped my hands tighter. 'Ancestors, if you're out there, please send the squirrel cat a strong breeze so he can kill this bastard for me.' I looked up at the Berabesq Faithful. 'See, that wasn't too long, was it?'

The Berabesq's confusion was understandable since he'd probably never seen a squirrel cat before that day and so didn't know what they could do with a little altitude and a strong wind. Too late my opponent figured it out and turned to find a furious, snarling monster swooping down on him from fifty feet in the air. Reichis's paws and back feet were fully extended, his glider wings angled down as he used the wind to strike like a bolt of lightning hurled by an angry god. The Berabesq Faithful got his arms up to protect his face and turned his hands so the metal sheaths on his fingers would skewer the squirrel cat. But Reichis is a slippery flyer; at the last instant he turned, coming round the other side so that even as he flew past the Berabesq, his front claws tore a strip out of the man's neck.

The Faithful roared with indignant outrage, blood from the deep gashes mixing with the sand swirling around us. This time when he turned it was with considerably less elegance than before, slashing wildly with the sharpened sheaths on his fingers. But Reichis was already gone by then, once again borne aloft by the strong winds, into the storm and out of sight.

I jumped back up to my feet, causing the bleeding wounds in my thigh to scream in agony. I pulled powder again and fired the spell. The Faithful was too fast of course, getting his shield up, but this time I'd directed the fires almost straight at each other, closing my eyes tightly against the unbearably bright flash of light. My opponent wasn't so lucky: he'd known his shield would protect him so he'd been staring right at the blast. Now he was blinded by it.

'Coward!' he shouted. 'I showed you the honour of a fair fight and yet you come at me with tricks and deceptions.'

'Sorry,' I said, not bothering to sound sincere. 'But tricks and deceptions are kind of my thing.'

I probably should have kept my mouth shut, because the Berabesq followed my voice and came at me with a series of slashing attacks – any one of which would have got me if his vision hadn't been impaired. But even that temporary advantage faded as the Berabesq blinked several times in quick succession and focused his gaze on me.

Damn it. Too soon. 'Reichis, now!' I shouted.

Fingers spun around, hands held high to grab at an attacker who wasn't there.

'Apologies,' I said, reaching into my pocket and pulling out one of Ferius's razor-sharp cards. It was the four of clubs. Not a particularly impressive card, but it was the one she'd given me the first time we'd ever fought together so it had sentimental value. 'That was another deception,' I informed the Berabesq Faithful as I slashed with the card into his left side, paying him back for the cuts he'd given me.

Not the ones he'd inflicted on Reichis though.

The squirrel cat descended from on high like a spear launched from a tornado. His claws got caught in the flesh of the man's upper back and shoulders. Reichis didn't seem to mind though, and went about the business of shredding his enemy's skin, screaming all the while about eyeballs, ears and tongues.

It's really not a good idea to piss off a squirrel cat.

With the Berabesq Faithful's attention now fully on Reichis, I prepared our endgame. As the man spun around, trying to grab at the squirrel cat, I pulled powder, desperately hoping I'd worked out the timing. Just as the Berabesq was coming back around, I shouted 'Reichis, get off him now!'

He barely paused in his attack. 'Why?'

'Because it's been forty seconds!'

The squirrel cat used his uninjured rear leg to push off from the man's shoulders and leap away. My fingers formed the somatic shapes, my mind envisioned the required mystical geometry, I sent all my will hurtling through the glinting metallic tattoos of the breath band on my forearm, and I spoke the word. I even remembered to breathe first. '*Carath*,' I said.

Despite his numerous injuries and the chaos around us, the Berabesq almost got his forearms back up to form his shield, but by then the twin fires, red and black, had already torn into his exposed chest. He'd have died instantly had I not used less powder than usual. I'd like to think it was thanks to a streak of decency within me, but more likely it was because I'd been shaking so badly that I'd dropped half the powder into the sand at my feet. Either way, my enemy fell to the ground, unconscious, severely burned, but still alive.

'A little help here!' Reichis screamed, drawing my gaze. A patch of his fur had caught on fire.

I ran over and leaped on him, covering his body with mine to snuff out the flames before they could spread. It went out quickly, thank the ancestors, and he and I were left huffing and puffing on the ground, neither of us with the strength to deal with the fact that we looked embarrassingly like we were cuddling.

'You stink,' the squirrel cat said.

'You too,' I replied.

That, in a nutshell, is our relationship.

We couldn't have been lying there for more than a few blissfully peaceful seconds before a voice said, 'Well now, ain't you just the cutest pair?'

I looked up to find Ferius practically standing over us. I don't know how she sneaks up on people like that, but one day I'm going to find a way to make her teach me. 'Come on,' she said, reaching out a hand to help me up. I groaned from the pain emanating from my back, my thigh, and, well, everywhere. 'Those gashes need tending to.' She knelt down to examine Reichis. 'And the squirrel cat's leg's going to want stitches.'

Reichis snarled at her. 'Tell the Argosi that if she tries to *sew me* I'm going to—'

She didn't so much cut him off as ignore him. 'Put the little fella in a sling and start headin' back the way we came, kid,' she said, then strode off deeper into the storm.

'Wait, where are you going?'

'There's still two more of them Faithful out there with that mage. Can't very well let them kill some poor sap just because they think he's you.'

She was favouring one leg and her right arm hung limp at her side. Her black leather waistcoat was in tatters, and blood seeped through her shirt from the wounds across her back and arms. I remembered what she'd said about the painful poison the Faithful used to coat their swords.

'What should we do?' I asked Reichis, but the poor little bugger was unconscious. I took off my shirt and tied it into a makeshift sling, and as gently as I could, I placed him inside it before hanging it over my neck. I looked ahead. Ferius's tracks were already fading under the incessant wind scouring the sand. We'd each barely survived facing *one* of the Berabesq Faithful. Injured as she was, how could she expect to fight off two of them?

'Whoever you are,' I muttered under my breath, as I set off after Ferius, my thoughts on the idiot charmcaster who'd brought all this trouble on us, 'next time, pick someone else to impersonate.'

7

Doubt

The idiot in question was still bound in that strange circular arrangement of ropes. The two remaining Berabesq Faithful were busily and loudly singing prayers while making rather sweeping gestures over their victim's unconscious form. Nearby, the hyena gnawed desperately at its ropes, giving off howls that cut right through to my soul. Though the wind still raged nearby, inside this small area the air was completely calmed. We had come to the very eye of the storm.

I caught up to Ferius just in time to hear her loudly announce her presence. 'Say there, fellas, you mind cutting down that racket?'

Yeah, that's right: she *again* refused to sneak up on them. While that wasn't all that unusual for Ferius, what was surprising was the anger in her voice. That may have had something to do with the six-sided shape in the sand the Berabesq had drawn around the unconscious charmcaster and the metal spikes they'd placed at each juncture in preparation, one had to assume, for driving them into his flesh. I remembered back when I was an initiate, reading about Berabesq religious practices (or 'insane atrocities' as my mother had called them), and thinking how odd it was that a culture that so reviled magic seemed to have a real affinity for esoteric rituals.

The two Berabesq Faithful turned, the first drawing a sword, the other presenting his forearms to his partner who drew two lines of blood along the skin so that he could summon the faith shield they were so fond of using in battle. 'You have bested our brethren,' the bleeding one said, turning to us before giving a short bow. 'Such talent is to be admired.'

I expected one of Ferius's typical snarky replies, but just as she'd done before, she shifted to a more formal way of speaking. 'Talent unguided by truth is an abomination.'

It struck me as an awkward phrase, but the Berabesq Faithful seemed impressed. 'Always the Argosi speak as though wise, and yet do I question your wisdom, for it comes without faith.'

'Care to test *your* faith, most worthy one?' Those last three words came out with a great deal of scorn. Have I mentioned that Ferius loves unnecessarily irritating people?

The second Berabesq, who wielded one of those curved kazkhan blades, took offence. 'What we do here is sacred. It is the will of God. Would you mock *Him*?'

'Right now I mock only you, brother.'

'Enough,' the bleeding Berabesq told his companion. 'The Argosi seeks to delay us in hopes some fortuitous circumstance will aid her cause. Let us finish the ritual and then deal with the heathens.'

A steel card appeared in Ferius's hand, glinting in the hazy light within the eye of the storm. 'It's only a simple test,' she said.

The Berabesq smiled. 'You are foolish to question our faith.' He slammed his bleeding forearms together and again I saw that shimmering in the air as his shield manifested. 'Our devotion protects us.'

'So it does,' Ferius said, then added almost absently, 'That's precisely your problem.'

The swordsman took a step towards us, away from the protection of the shield. 'I will end her blasphemous prattling.'

'Stop, fool,' the other said. 'She tries to draw you away from the shield so that you will be undefended.'

Ferius nodded, then said to me, 'Kid, when that moron comes for us – and trust me, he will – I want you to blast him real good.'

I reached my hands into the pouches at my sides and took a generous pinch of the red and black powders. Reichis looked up groggily from inside the sling across my chest. 'What's happening? Did I miss something?' He turned his head to the scene before us. 'Oh, great. More talking.' He slumped back down and closed his eyes. 'Wake me when something interesting happens.'

'So this is your "test"?' the unarmed Berabesq called out. 'Whether we can be goaded into reckless action? We are the Berabesq Faithful. We are schooled in philosophy and self-discipline even before we learn to read. Our faith isn't some backwards religion, as you may believe. Ours is the most complex and perfect understanding of the universe and its workings. Do you truly believe we can be so easily ensnared?'

'Nope.' Ferius showed off her steel card. 'This here's a simple bet. In a minute, I'm going to throw this card at you. If I can hit you, the charmcaster goes free and we go on our way. If I can't, well, you can bleed three more heathens. That should please God plenty.'

Reichis opened one eye. 'What's that she just said?'

'I think she has a plan,' I whispered.

Please, ancestors, please let her have an actual plan.

The Berabesq Faithful seemed unfazed. 'Perhaps you hope to strike once my shield fades.' He touched his forearms together again and the shimmer in the air renewed. 'It is not so simple, I'm afraid. God protects the faithful.'

Ferius took out a smoking reed from her waistcoat and stuck it in her mouth. 'So I've heard it said.' She pulled out a match and struck it against the edge of her steel card, then lit the reed. 'Only, I've got me a theory about God.'

'Do you indeed?' the Berabesq asked, a contented smile on his face. I was starting to get the impression that maybe these people actually *like* debating religion.

By way of answer, Ferius let out a puff of smoke in the shape of a ring. It seemed to float in place, never quite fading in the strange air inside the eye of the storm.

'Very well,' the Berabesq said, once more renewing his shield. 'I welcome this gamble of yours. Let us see how your Argosi speculations fare against my faith.'

Though Ferius Parfax has no end of tricks up her sleeve, I had a strong feeling her current strategy was to talk our enemies to death. More specifically, try to talk them out of their current intention to kill the mage. That would be a terrible plan.

'Faith is a funny thing,' Ferius began.

Oh, ancestors, she really does mean to do this.

'See,' she went on, 'that fancy shield of yours is only as powerful as your faith, ain't that right?'

'It is God who creates the shield,' he corrected her. 'My faith is merely the conduit.'

Ferius took a puff from her reed. 'Just so. Just so.' She

paused a moment. 'Only, it occurs to me that God might care more about the righteousness of a person's actions than he does how much they pray.'

The smile left the man's face. 'Tread carefully, Argosi, you do not wish to—'

'Oh, I do indeed.' She turned her gaze skyward. 'See, what I think God sees as he looks down upon us is two Berabesq Faithful who've overstepped their own laws, using heresy as a convenient excuse to kill a stranger.' She spread her arms wide. 'I think he's looking down at me and God's saying to himself, "That Argosi there? She's got no horse in this race. She's cut up, beat up, tired, and probably needs a drink. But here she is, putting her neck on the line to keep some poor wretch from being bled to death by a pair of disagreeable zealots."' She looked back at the two men standing in front of the bound mage, then blew out another smoke ring that hung in the air before her. 'That's what I think.'

The Berabesq's expression darkened. 'Then let us test your theory, and be done with this.'

'You sure?' Ferius asked, spinning the steel card in the air, then catching it. 'Because I smell doubt, and I've got a good nose for these things.'

'What you smell is the stench of your own fear,' the Faithful said, and slammed his forearms together once again. 'Now play your card, and reap what follows, for it is known far and wide that you Argosi believe in nothing, and the world will be none the lesser for your passing.'

'What the Argosi believe,' Ferius said, the smirk suddenly gone from her expression, the easy tone gone from her voice, 'is that no God protects bullies and assassins.' She flung the card into the air and it spun through the floating smoke ring, hurtling towards the Berabesq Faithful's shield. It was only in that moment that I realised something: the last time he'd brought his forearms together, the air hadn't shimmered at all.

The razor-sharp card cut deep into the muscle of his arm, drawing a scream of pain from him, followed by a bellow of rage from his sword-wielding companion, who came running towards us, blade held high.

'Anytime now, kid,' Ferius reminded me.

Oh. Right. I tossed the powders against each other and cast the spell. '*Carath*,' I said, and the twin fires struck the centre of his chest. He flew back a good six feet before landing on the ground.

Ferius shot me an annoyed look. 'Did you have to hit him so hard? Between you, me, the squirrel cat, the hyena, that other guy you blasted back there, and now this poor sap, we're going to use up all our medicine.'

'You told me to blast him good!'

'I meant carefully.' She headed off towards the two men, drawing her steel rod from her waistcoat. A flick of her wrist and it extended to its full length.

The Berabesq with the steel card in his arm fell to his knees. 'God has forsaken us!'

She knelt down so they were eye to eye. 'Nobody forsook you, friend. You just doubted is all.' She patted him on the shoulder. 'Doubt is good every once in a while.' Then she slammed the bottom of the rod into the side of his head and knocked him unconscious.

8

The Hyena

In the year or so that I'd known Ferius Parfax, I had on occasion wondered whether – despite her repeated statements to the contrary – she *did* know spellcraft. This was one of those occasions.

'It wasn't magic, kid,' she said before I could even ask the question.

I ran to catch up with her as she walked over to the unconscious charmcaster. 'You took apart a Berabesq faith shield,' I insisted. 'How is that *not* magic?'

She paused for a moment and tapped a finger to her temple. 'Aren't you the one always going on about how brilliant you Jan'Tep are on account of how you can hold that – what do you call it? – "esoteric geometry" in your head so perfectly?'

'Yes, but—'

'"But" nothing. Faith works the same way.' She started walking again. 'Leastways for the Berabesq and their spiritual mumbo jumbo. I gave him just enough doubt to shake his focus is all.'

A *trick*, I marvelled. *Nothing more than a clever Argosi ploy.*

This was how Ferius Parfax got by in a world where she made enemies of just about every powerful person she ever met: tricks and ploys. As she knelt to untie the ropes binding the unconscious charmcaster, I felt a sudden dread spread inside my guts. Ferius was, by far, the most amazing person I'd ever known, but what would happen on the day when she ran out of tricks?

A prickling feeling in the back of my neck made me turn around. Off in the distance, at the top of the dune, a figure dressed all in scarlet stared down at us. I squinted to try to make out any details, but the figure suddenly turned and walked away, over the crest and down the other side. I considered whether I should run after him. The Berabesq Faithful had mentioned a Jan'Tep diplomat had set them on my trail.

'Kid, you wanna free that hyena?' Ferius called out. 'Damned thing's gonna give himself a heart attack.'

'I think I saw someone,' I said. 'It could be the guy who—'

'They look like they're about to kill us?'

'No, but—'

'Then let's deal with the problem at hand.'

Reluctantly, I turned back and approached the animal, who growled as soon as he saw me coming. A second growl arose from my own chest. It took me a moment to realise it was Reichis. The barely conscious squirrel cat tried unsuccessfully to crawl out of his sling. 'Let me at him.'

'Can you talk to it?' I asked.

The squirrel cat paused in his snarling to look up at me. 'You want me to *talk* to a hyena?'

'Yeah. Tell him I'm going to untie the ropes and it would be helpful if he didn't rip my throat out in the process.'

'Sure,' Reichis replied, still awkwardly trying to escape the sling. 'Just let me bite off a few of his parts first to get his attention.'

Okay, new plan. I carefully took the sling off my shoulder and set Reichis down a considerable way away, resisting the urge to say, 'Sit.' I returned to the hyena, moving very slowly and speaking in reassuring tones. 'Listen, my squirrel cat business partner can understand regular humans, so I'm going to assume it's the same for you. We're here to help, okay? I'm going to remove those ropes from you and then you can go to your master, who, I hope you've noticed, we're also trying to help. So don't eat me. Deal?'

The hyena just kept staring at me, but at least it had stopped growling. I knelt and began undoing the elaborate knots. As I removed the last rope, it unavoidably rubbed against the animal's wounded leg. The hyena bit me even harder than Reichis does.

'Ow!'

'Hah!' the squirrel cat chittered. 'Told you never to trust a stinkin' hyena.'

The animal showed us its teeth before hobbling over to where Ferius was removing the last of the ropes from the still-unconscious charmcaster. 'Hey there, fella,' she said to the hyena, reaching out a hand to stroke its fur. In an injustice of cosmic proportions, the beast not only *didn't* bite her, but nuzzled her face briefly before lying down next to its master.

I went over to pick up Reichis, who was still laughing at me. 'Better put one of those fancy healing ointments on that bite, Kellen. Bet you've got rabies now. Also, you—'

'I stink of hyena. I know.'

I knelt down opposite Ferius with the freed but unresponsive charmcaster between us. Again I was struck by the odd choice of clothes for a mage: leather riding pants and boots beneath a long traveller's coat, a swathe of silk that came up to cover his mouth and nose while another wrapped around his head under the frontier hat. From what little I could make out in the strip of tanned, mildly sunburnt skin between the two, the charmcaster probably wasn't any older than me. 'Who is this guy?' I asked aloud. 'And why would he go around using my name?'

Ferius stared at me through narrowed eyes for a moment and then chuckled at me. 'Tell you what, how about you get that silk off the poor mage's face and let some fresh air in?'

I reached for the coverings. The hyena gave a warning growl, and suddenly a hand grabbed my wrist. The mage's grip felt odd – wrong, somehow. I looked down to see two fingers were missing from the hand holding on to me. That explained the vocation as a charmcaster instead of a proper mage – can't do much high magic if you don't have enough fingers to form the somatic shapes.

'Kellen?' a voice said, so ragged and rough that the word came out more as a cough than anything else.

I stared into a pair of dark eyes that were oddly familiar. 'Have we . . .' Before I got the question out, the charmcaster pulled down the swathe of silk covering what I now saw was a distinctly feminine mouth, then she kissed me full on the lips.

'Okay,' I heard Reichis mutter behind me. 'I didn't see *that* coming either.'

The Charmcaster

MEMORY

An Argosi deck is always changing. Our cards are not slabs of stone but pools of water. People, nations, even history itself alters over time, for history is but a tale told to suit the present. Thus must an Argosi be prepared to let go of any card within their deck, for recollection is forever incomplete, and even the most vivid memories must always be . . . suspect.

9

The Charmcaster

It wasn't a great kiss, to be honest. Her lips were rough and chapped from the desert sun and my jaw was swollen from an elbow to the face I didn't even remember taking. The result was that my ability to purse my lips was severely compromised. It's possible I drooled.

Usually when someone uses silk magic to deceive your mind it's either to break your spirit with visions of unimaginable horrors or to seduce you with . . . well, *other* sensations. Neither of those quite matched my current predicament.

'Nephenia?' I asked, pulling away suddenly.

'Of course it's me, Kellen.' She smiled at my confusion. Actually, *smiled* is the wrong word. She grinned – a wild, reckless sort of grin very much at odds with the shy, demure girl I'd known back home. 'Who else would chase you halfway across the continent just to save your life?'

'Save *our* lives?' Reichis growled. '*We're* the ones who—'

The hyena bared its teeth and struggled to its feet, looking even more injured and bedraggled than Reichis.

'Come on, mutt,' the squirrel cat taunted, his fur becoming pure black with dark red stripes. 'I haven't eaten all day.'

The other animal crouched in preparation to attack, only

to stumble when it tried to put too much weight on its foreleg.

'Ishak!' Nephenia cried, wrapping her arms around him. 'You'll hurt yourself!'

'"Ishak"?' Reichis asked. 'She *named* a *hyena*? What's next? Giving royal titles to clumps of dung? Let me at him, Kellen. We can use his hide as an extra blanket.'

The creature struggled to pull away from Nephenia's grip, returning a snarl that was clearly aimed at both of us, even though none of this was my fault. Nephenia didn't seem pleased either. 'What did the squirrel cat just say?'

'He was . . . welcoming your familiar.'

The hyena gave a strange yipping sound that meant nothing to me, but apparently spoke plenty to Nephenia. 'He says you're lying and that the squirrel cat just threatened to turn him into a rug.'

'Blanket, actually. But death threats are pretty much how Reichis greets everybody. You get used to it.'

The hyena made a distinctly chortling sound which seemed to settle Nephenia's ire. 'Well, tell him unless he wants a similar greeting from me, he'd better not—'

'If y'all are gonna wrastle,' Ferius said wearily, 'you ought to know that I'm running out of medical supplies, so you'll have to take care of your own damned wounds.'

I looked over to see Ferius kneeling next to one of the unconscious Berabesq Faithful, slathering ointment from our supply of *oleus regia* over his burns. To say that oleus regia is expensive is like saying diamonds are pricey or mountains are hefty. 'You realise we're all wounded too, right?' I asked.

'I'll be happy to look after your scrapes just as soon as the four of you have decided not to add to them.'

Nephenia's cheeks reddened. 'Forgive our rudeness, Lady Ferius, we didn't mean to—'

'Just Ferius, kid,' she interrupted. 'No "Ladies" around here.'

'Oh great,' Reichis grumbled. 'This again.'

The hyena chuckled, then opened his jaws a little wider and made a strange noise that sounded an awful lot like a mocking version of 'Oh great. This again.'

'A demon!' Reichis said, slowly backing away.

'Ishak! Stop that!' Nephenia scolded the hyena. To me she said, 'His pack have an affinity for mimicry. He doesn't speak other languages, but he can reproduce anything he hears.' As if to confirm this, the hyena swung his head towards Reichis and barked, 'A demon!'

It was a startlingly good impression, which was odd since the squirrel cat doesn't speak so much as chitter and growl; it's the bond between us that lets me hear them as words.

'Shoot the mutt, Kellen!' Reichis shouted. 'Shoot 'em both. Demons, the pair of them!'

'They're not demons,' I informed him, though even I didn't think I sounded very convincing. I mean, let's look at the facts, shall we? The world is a big place, and the odds of running into a girl I'd pined over most of my life out here in the middle of the desert were pretty slim. 'How did you find us?' I asked.

'Tracking spells, mostly.' She extended a finger to trace along the silver glyphs on my hat. 'These things made it incredibly difficult, by the way. Gave me an awful headache every time I searched for you.'

'A headache? These glyphs are supposed to prevent the long line of mages who want me dead from tracking me at all!'

She gave me that sly grin again – the one so unlike the

girl I remembered. 'Then I guess you'd best not kiss any of them, because that's the connection I used to break through the warding glyphs.'

Well, that was some relief at least. Unless she was lying and I was about to get blasted by a silk mage with a lousy sense of humour.

'Anyway, a couple of weeks ago I'd lost your trail. There was a Berabesq city nearby, so I asked around about any Jan'Tep spellslingers passing through. That's when I found out that a delegate from the lords magi of our clan had offered a substantial donation to the Berabesq Faithful in exchange for the apprehension and execution of Kellen of the House of Ke.'

My thoughts returned to the man in red who'd been standing at the top of the dune. 'You're telling me someone from our own clan bribed the Faithful to kill me?'

'You've made a lot of enemies, Kellen.'

Yeah, like, everyone who's ever met me. I guess the despair I felt must've shown on my face because Nephenia put a reassuring hand on my arm. Only, it wasn't that reassuring.

'What happened to your fingers?' I asked.

'An accident.'

Unlikely, for a mage. We tend to be cautious about the parts of our bodies that are crucial for casting spells. I reached over and held up her other wrist. 'On *both* hands?'

She took her hands away and ignored the question. 'As I was saying, a squad of the Faithful was dispatched to hunt you.' She pulled her scarf back up, covering the bottom of her face. With her long coat and the silks hiding both her mouth and forehead, she could've been almost anyone. 'So I went around pretending to be you, thinking I could set them on the wrong path and then lose them using charm spells.'

'Messin' with the Faithful is a bad idea,' Ferius observed. She sounded exhausted, almost sluggish.

'Are you okay?' I asked.

'Just addin' a little nightweed to the bandages for these folks. Make sure they get some proper rest before they decide to come lookin' for us.'

Great. One more thing to worry about.

'The Faithful are unbelievably effective trackers,' Nephenia said. 'I tried everything to shake them, but they just kept gaining on me.'

'So you led them to us?' I asked.

'They would've figured out I wasn't you eventually, Kellen. The only hope for either of us was if I could get to you first so we could fight them together.' She wrapped her arms around the hyena again, gently stroking its fur. 'Poor Ishak nearly died protecting me.'

'Nice story,' Reichis said. 'Only she and the mutt ran into the storm as soon as they saw us.'

'What did he say?' Nephenia asked. When I translated she looked even more irritated. 'By the time I caught up with you there wasn't time to explain and I didn't want to risk you getting killed.' She reached into her coat and withdrew what looked like a tiny iron box, its sides rusted and charred. 'My charm protects me from the lightning, but it would've been just as likely to strike you as the Berabesq.' She tossed the now-dead charm onto the sand. 'Possibly not my best plan.'

Her account made a certain amount of sense. Captured storms were notoriously dangerous to mess around with, and the Faithful had been so close to her that had she stopped even for a second they would've caught her. Of course, that's exactly the kind of story a silk mage would concoct to try to trick me.

'Kellen?' she asked, staring at me intently.

I didn't know what to believe. I was tired and injured and, to make matters worse, my left eye had started to ache. The black markings around it burned like someone had poured acid on them.

My people believe the shadowblack is a conduit through which a demon slowly takes over the body of a mage, but whenever my attacks came, it was everyone else who changed. Nephenia's eyes narrowed into yellow slits and her smile grew so wide her jaw looked as if it were about to come off. She laughed at me – at the way I'd fallen so easily for her pretence. Why would Nephenia be here, hundreds and hundreds of miles from our home? Wasn't it far more likely this was some Jan'Tep bounty hunter who'd been caught off guard by a bunch of religious zealots? Now she was playing me for a fool until she could get a second chance at killing me.

Several things happened at once. The hyena rose to its feet, ignoring the injury to its leg as it snarled at me. Reichis did likewise and started stalking towards the hyena, his fur turned a deep crimson.

Nephenia was staring at my hands. I looked down and discovered that they'd slipped inside the pouches at my sides without me being aware of it. 'Kellen? What are you doing? It's me, Nephenia.'

'Wrong,' I said angrily. 'Her name's Neph'aria now.' I removed my hands from the pouches and made sure she could see the red and black powders I held. 'So who the hell are you?'

10

The Reunion

'Kellen,' she said, eyes narrowed and tone sharp. 'My name isn't Neph'aria any more. It's *Nephenia*. Our clan council took away my mage's name the day they *exiled* me.'

A likely story. My sister Shalla had informed me months ago that Neph was betrothed to Pan'erath and so had the protection of his house. I knew Pan. He'd never have let anyone exile her.

'Let go of those powders, Kellen. Your breath band is sparking.'

She was right. A faint silver-blue glow wound around the tattooed band on my forearm. Nephenia – or the mage pretending to be her – reached into her coat. A charmcaster could have any number of nasty things hidden in there. I was pretty sure I was faster though. *Only at this range I'm likely to kill her.*

The growls coming from the squirrel cat and the hyena kept getting louder. The blood was rushing in my ears. My left eye just kept burning hotter and hotter, showing me visions of fire and death and all the mages who'd come for me before and would surely do so again. The sasutzei in my right eye hit me with an aching cold sensation too, warning me to stop. I didn't know which instinct to trust, but I was sick to death of people trying to trick me or lie to me or kill me. Not this time. Not again.

'Kellen, don't make me—'

Five bright, shining pieces of steel spun through the air to land at our feet in a line, demarcating the space between us. 'All right, children,' an irritated voice said, cutting through all the noise in my head. Ferius stood just a few feet away, the falling sun at her back casting a shadow over us. In her left hand she held her deck of steel cards. 'I figured you could sort yourselves out, but apparently I was wrong.' She drew one of the cards. 'So here's how this goes: the first spellslinger, charmcaster, squirrel cat or hyena to make a move is going to get one of these right between the eyes. I am too tired, too beat-up and too damned sober for this nonsense.'

It took everything I had not to fight back, but I forced myself to take slow, deep breaths until the visions faded and the voices urging me to attack were quiet. Quiet, but not silent. 'How do we know she's not an imposter?'

The Argosi limped her way over to us. 'Show him who you are, girl.'

'He already knows who I am,' Nephenia replied. 'And I'll thank you not to call me "girl".'

'He knows who you *were*. Show him who you are now.'

The frontier hat came off, followed by the scarves covering her head and face. Seeing her now, it was no wonder I hadn't recognised her at first. The skin on her face was dry and deeply tanned from desert travel. The angles of her cheeks and jaw had become sharper. She'd always been slender, but she was almost wiry now. When I was an initiate, I'd learned to memorise images with rigorous clarity – a necessity for envisioning the esoteric geometry of some spells. That's why, even months after I'd left my people, I could have described Nephenia's luxurious, waist-length hair practically strand by strand. But now it was cut short, with unruly dark locks sticking up at odd angles, reminding me more of the fur on her hyena's head than the girl I'd known. I managed to resist saying so. 'You cut your hair,' I said instead, which wasn't so bad until I unnecessarily added, 'I liked it long.'

Oh, ancestors. Why can't I keep my mouth shut at times like this?

The tight line of Nephenia's lips told me that observation wasn't worthy of a response. The hyena opened its mouth and mockingly echoed my words. *'I liked it looooong.'*

'Worked it out yet, kid?' Ferius asked.

I had, in fact, though this had been a strange way to convince me it was really Nephenia. All Ferius had proven was that this girl didn't look, sound, or act like the person I'd known. I guess that was the point. 'A silk mage posing as Nephenia would've pretended to be more like I remembered her, wouldn't they?'

Ferius retrieved her cards from the sand and put the deck back in her waistcoat, then took out a bent smoking reed. She stared at it drowsily. 'The kid finally learns to listen with his eyes. Here endeth the lesson.' With a flick of her wrist, a match appeared between her fingers which she used to light her smoking reed. After a long drag she said, 'I swear, one day you Jan'Tep are going to be the death . . . The death of . . .'

Her words trailed off. She started to sway uncertainly on her feet, like a drunk walking on an uneven street. I hadn't noticed before how pale her features had become since the fight. When she stared back at me, it was as if her eyes couldn't quite focus. She tried to reassure me with one of those smirks of hers, only to then tip forward and fall face first to the sandy ground. I rose to get the pack with our medical supplies, only now seeing just how bad the wounds were on her back. The Berabesq Faithful's blade had done a lot more damage than she'd let on. The deep cuts had soaked all the way through her clothes, and were dripping down her side to turn the golden sand beneath her crimson.

11

The Black Sky

I knew something was wrong with me the moment I took my first step towards Ferius. The blindingly bright afternoon sun had become a black disc that hung in the sky, casting darkness over the desert. The once-golden sand beneath my feet had turned to countless tiny shards of pure onyx. There wasn't a single source of light anywhere, and yet I could see with perfect clarity, as if my eyes could discern the thousands of different shades of black that painted the world around me.

Where am I?

A voice called out to me. 'Kellen?' It was Nephenia, but she sounded as though she were miles away and her voice was echoing along the walls of a distant canyon.

I spun around to get my bearings. Some thirty yards away the desert ended in a ragged coastline that had no business being there. A black ocean swelled with waves that crested high above us. At the shadowy water's edge, a lone figure stood with her back to me. It was Ferius. She seemed to be talking to herself. 'Would've been fine to cross the ocean again, just once more.'

I ran to her, my feet pounding against the onyx sand. Something wasn't right. No matter how far I got, I never seemed to be any closer to her. 'Ferius, it's me!' I shouted. 'I'm trapped somehow. Tell me what to do!'

'Would've been nice to see them again too, maybe talk about things left unsaid, but I reckon the Path of the Rambling Thistle ain't one for looking back.'

Path of the Rambling Thistle? The Argosi gave themselves names like that. Ferius was the Path of the Wild Daisy. Rosie, the only other Argosi I'd got to know, was the Path of Thorns and Roses. I'd never heard of anyone called the Path of the Rambling Thistle.

The faint echoes of Nephenia's pleas tugged at me. 'Kellen, why are you just standing there? I don't know what to do for Lady Ferius. She's bleeding so much. I can't staunch the wound!'

'Nephenia! Where are you?'

Suddenly I heard her voice right behind me. 'Mustn't be her any more,' she said quietly. I spun around and saw her just a few paces away, idly looking off towards the east. Her rough travelling coat and trousers were gone, replaced by the blue-and-silver robes of a Jan'Tep adept. Her hair was long again, down to her waist. She held the strands in one hand and cut away at them with a pair of black scissors, but somehow the hair never got any shorter. 'Got to be someone new from now on,' she murmured. 'Can't be her ever again.'

She couldn't have been more than a couple of feet away from me, but when I reached out to her, my fingers never touched her. 'Nephenia? What are you doing? Who can't you be?'

The apparition didn't turn, didn't seem to notice me at all. Somewhere far away, the other Nephenia called out desperately. 'Kellen, please, don't walk away! Don't you understand? She's dying, Kellen. Ferius is dying!'

'Nephenia! I can't see you. I don't know where I am!'

I got no reply, just Nephenia's sobbing, desperate voice shouting my name over and over, begging me to help her. I looked everywhere for a way back, but the shadowy landscape seemed endless.

A blur of black fur raced past me along the onyx shards. I recognised him immediately. It was Reichis, or a shadow of him, anyway. He stopped to growl at unseen enemies, but I couldn't understand what he was saying. 'Reichis,' I shouted, 'help Nephenia. Show her the oleus regia in the silver jar. She has to heat it up with her hands first or it won't do any good.' The squirrel cat suddenly took off, chasing after things I couldn't see. 'Reichis! Reichis, listen to me!'

He ignored me, scurrying this way and that as he bared his teeth at the darkness all around us. I made a run for him, reaching out to grab hold of him. I would've sworn I was getting closer, yet somehow I was always too far away to touch him. No matter how hard I tried, I couldn't get to any of them. Off in the distance, the shade of Ferius waded into the deep black ocean. I called out to her, but I knew she wouldn't hear.

Surrounded by shadows, alone save for the sound of Nephenia's pleas begging me to help her save my mentor, I finally understood what was happening to me. This was the next stage of the shadowblack. No longer content to terrify me with visions of violence and despair, now it had swallowed me whole.

I was lost.

Lost in shadow.

And Ferius Parfax was dying.

12

The Chains

I awoke in chains and a comfortable bed. How long I'd been there I had no idea, but the injuries I'd taken in the fight with the Berabesq weren't much more than a dull ache now so someone must have seen to them.

Consciousness was a little slow in coming, but I was able to work a few things out. First, I wasn't in a cell but rather a modest guest room with simple furnishings. I must've been on the upstairs floor of the building because I could hear voices – lots of them – coming up through the floorboards. Talking, shouting, laughter; glasses clinking and the occasional creaking of hinges that must've been from a door swinging open and then closed again. A tavern or an inn.

A breeze whistled into the room, and I pushed myself up from my pillow to see out the open window on the wall to my left. Daylight shone through – soft, though, so probably from the late afternoon sun. The air that came with it was fresh, unlike the dry, oppressive desert heat that always brought dust with it. How far had I come?

A pile of curtains lay on the floor beneath the window. Someone had not just opened them, but taken them down entirely to let in as much light as possible. The oil lamp on the small table next to my bed was already lit, which gave me an odd sense of relief. I had vague recollections of screaming my lungs out about being trapped in shadows. Whoever had brought me here had chained me to the bed and yet gone to the effort of making sure I didn't wake up in darkness so I wouldn't panic.

Ferius would've known to do that. Was she still alive?

I tried to get up from the bed, momentarily forgetting the chains. They rattled as I pulled them taut. 'Hey!' I called out, the feeling of being trapped setting me off. 'Get these off me!'

The sound of a scraping chair, just outside. Footsteps. A moment later Nephenia entered the room, her hyena padding silently alongside her. She gave me a searching look. I'm not sure what exactly she expected to find, but finally she closed the door behind her. 'Well, you *look* like yourself, so that's something.'

An odd choice of words, I thought, given that she looked nothing at all like I remembered. Here in these vaguely normal surroundings, so far from the surreal landscape of the desert, the contrasts between who Nephenia had been and who she was now only grew starker.

Stop obsessing over her looks, moron. Focus on what matters. 'Ferius . . . is she—'

Nephenia came to sit at the foot of the bed. 'It's okay. Ferius is alive. The wounds were bad though. She almost . . . Anyway, she's recuperating now.'

Oh, ancestors, thank you. For once, thank you.

I pulled at the chains attached to my wrists. 'Would you mind taking these off me?'

Nephenia's tone was sharp. 'I don't know. Do you plan on abandoning me again like you did while I was trying to keep your friend from bleeding out in the desert?' She stopped herself. 'I'm sorry, Kellen. I shouldn't have said that.'

She came around and knelt at my right side, working a key into the lock holding the chain to my wrist, then unlocking the other side. 'There. You're free now. Try not to run off and . . . Damn it, sorry. I can't seem to stop myself.'

She sat down on the floor next to the bed, her back to the wall. The hyena came and lay down next to her, its head in her lap. 'Two months I've been away from our people, Kellen. I've been robbed twice, nearly killed on three separate occasions. I got food poisoning from fruit that had gone bad in my pack and ended up so sick I would've died from dehydration if Ishak hadn't run fifty miles to the nearest town to steal a canteen of water for me.'

'Why were you . . . ?' I stopped myself. I'd been about to ask her what she'd done to get herself exiled. It felt like the wrong time to bring it up. I was starting to think there never would be a good time. 'I'm glad you're okay,' I said.

She stroked the hyena's fur, then turned to look up at me. 'How long did it take before you stopped being afraid, Kellen?'

'Me? Are you kidding? I'm scared all the time. Hells, I'm scared right now.'

She laughed. 'Of what? Me?' The hyena gave a low growl. Neph patted its head. 'Well, of course, my brave little darling, *everyone's* afraid of you.' In response, Ishak made a chuckling sound and licked her hand.

If I ever tried to pat Reichis's head and call him 'my brave little darling', he'd grab hold of my tongue and shout, 'Call me that again, skinbag. Call me "darling" one more time, I dare you.'

'Come on,' Nephenia said, gently lifting Ishak's head from her lap and rising to her feet. 'You must be starving by now.'

'How long have I been here? And how on earth did you get us out of the desert?'

'With a considerable amount of difficulty,' she replied, leaning back into a stretch. 'Suffice to say, it involved using up every bit of medicine I could find in Ferius's saddlebag, ruining my two best summoning charms to lure your horses back, and three days of walking alongside Ferius's mount, trying to make sure she didn't fall off and you weren't . . .'

'What?' I asked, suddenly self-conscious by the way she was staring at me.

'It's just . . . back in the desert, when you finally came out of whatever had you walking around in daze, I nearly forgot you.'

Great. 'Look, I'm sorry I—'

'No, I don't mean like that. I mean I literally forgot who you were for a couple of seconds. Like there was just some guy standing by himself in the desert.' She shook her head. 'You know what? I'm not making any sense. I was exhausted and dehydrated and a bunch of religious zealots had gotten halfway to ritually murdering me.' She extended a hand to me. 'Let's go. I'm going stir crazy in this place.'

I pushed aside the blankets and rose from the bed. My head was still foggy and I felt a slight chill, but I wasn't going to let either stop me. 'I want to see Ferius.'

Nephenia raised one eyebrow. 'Really? Isn't there something else you ought to do first?'

Being an ungracious idiot, I'd forgotten to thank her. She'd gone through hell to save my mentor, to find me and bring all of us safely out of the desert, and I'd barely expressed the tiniest shred of gratitude. 'Thank you, Nephenia. I mean it. If there's anything I can do in return—'

A smile grew from one side of her face and turned into a chuckle as she gestured towards the opposite wall. I followed the line of her finger to see my reflection in the mirror mounted there.

I was completely naked.

'Just put some clothes on and we'll call it even,' Nephenia said.

Red-faced and suffering the chortling of both her *and* the hyena, I hurriedly dressed myself with the spare set of travelling clothes from my pack. The embarrassment faded when I looked in the mirror a second time and saw the twisting black lines around my left eye had grown. They did that whenever I used Jan'Tep magic, but slowly, almost imperceptibly, over time. Being lost in shadow had made my condition visibly worse than before. I quickly applied the skin-coloured paste I used to hide the shadowblack when we were in cities, flinching every time it touched my flesh.

'Quit primping,' Nephenia said. 'You look more than pretty enough for this place, trust me.'

I put away the tiny jar of paste and grabbed my hat. 'Where are we anyway?'

She held the door open for me. 'You know, I was kind of hoping you could tell me.'

We walked along a hallway with half a dozen doors similar to mine along one side. I assumed Ferius must be in one of them, but Neph went right past them to the stairwell. 'I thought you said Ferius was here recuperating?'

'She is, but apparently Argosi convalesce differently from regular people.'

I followed her to the bottom of the stairs and into a large rustic common room. A dozen rough-looking men and women sat at benches, drinking and talking while a sleepy-eyed bartender sat on a stool washing mugs. Ferius was nowhere in sight.

'She was supposed to meet us here,' Nephenia said, glancing around the room.

I noted the swinging door that led outside. 'What town is this?'

'We're not in a town,' Nephenia replied. 'Actually we're not in anything. So far as I can tell, we're in the middle of nowhere. This tavern sits at an empty crossroads near the border with Gitabria.'

'How did you find this place then?'

She gave a soft snort. 'Lady Ferius. She was so weak I had to tie her into the saddle to keep her from falling off, but every couple of hours she'd rouse herself and shout at me to go left, or right, or cut through some dusty field. We missed three separate towns where I could've found her a proper doctor, but she kept ranting about needing "the universal constant of civilisation".'

'Oh,' I said, finally understanding what this unimpressive wood building really was. Ferius makes them sound so grand, but I've always found them disappointing. 'We're in a travellers' saloon.'

'How is that different from a regular saloon?'

I led her past the bar to the other side of the common room. 'According to the Argosi, in all the ways that matter. Travellers' saloons are secret rest stops on the long roads. They exist all over the continent, though they have lots of different names. In the Borderlands they call them "ramblers' roadhouses". I've never been to any in our own lands, but Ferius says you can find "wayfarers' sanctums" there too. Even here, in the Berabesq territories, they have what they call "pilgrims' respites".'

Nephenia glanced at the men and women carousing in the common room. 'Doesn't look like much.'

'That's because we're not technically *in* the travellers' saloon right now. Come on,' I said, stopping at an innocuous door with three stars scratched into the wood above a small spiral.

The bartender took notice of us. 'Nobody goes in there,' he said.

'That's why nobody ever comes out,' I replied.

The bartender went back to washing his mugs.

'What was that about?' Nephenia asked as we passed through the door and into the darkness beyond. 'Some sort of password?'

'I'm not actually sure, but the bartenders always say the same thing and Ferius always gives the same reply.'

I kept my hand against the wall until we reached rough-hewn stairs that led underground. 'Watch your step. It's supposed to be seventy-seven steps down, but I always forget to count.'

'What's down there, Kellen?'

'If you ask Ferius? The universal constant of civilisation.'

13

The Universal Constant

Nephenia stared wide-eyed at the massive room carved from the rock beneath the saloon. It was probably two or three times larger than the building above. I'd always wondered if maybe these places had first been created as sanctuaries for refugees fleeing the perpetual warfare that once plagued this continent, but they could just as easily have been made for smugglers or thieves needing a quick escape from the local authorities. You could survive a long time in an underground structure like this where it never got too hot or cold, and where the maze of tunnels that led away from it could provide a quick escape. But anytime I asked Ferius what the purpose of the travellers' saloons was, she always gave the same reply – the one she shouted as Nephenia and I entered the cave.

'Gambling, my friends!' She raised a large mug of something I doubted was particularly restorative for someone who was supposed to be recuperating. 'Is it not the finest form of poetry ever devised by civilised people?'

'The universal constant!' others toasted enthusiastically in response.

Two separate bars had been constructed on either side of the cave, no doubt so that the array of drunks never had to stumble too far to get their next drink. In between was a mismatched set of tables of varying sizes and origins, each playing host to a round of cards or dice, along with a few games of chance I didn't recognise.

'Kellen!' Ferius called out merrily from a table where she was playing cards with three other travellers. 'And girl-whose-name-I-keep-forgetting!'

'As I keep reminding you, Lady Ferius, my name is Nephenia.'

'Stop calling me "Lady", kid. I must've told you a hundred times now.'

Nephenia arched an eyebrow. 'Guess I forgot.'

Ishak loped alongside us and greeted Reichis with a low growl. Reichis was perched on Ferius's shoulder, beady eyes focused intently on the card game. He glanced over just long enough to ignore me and bare his teeth at Ishak before turning back to Ferius's cards. 'Come on, Argosi. Let's fleece these suckers. Go all in. All in!'

'You're teaching a squirrel cat to gamble?' I asked.

Ferius grinned, dropping a pile of coins that must've come from at least three different countries into a wooden tray at the centre of the table. 'Little fella's developing quite the knack for it.'

'But how do you even know what he's saying? You don't understand his language.'

'Oh, he finds ways to convey his meaning.'

'*That* card!' Reichis chittered excitedly. He clambered down her arm and grabbed at it with both paws, snarling at her when she didn't let go of it. 'Hurry, before it's too late!'

'All right, all right,' she said, laying the card face up for the other players to see. It was a three of shields – the suit that represented the Daroman Empire. Hardly impressive, I thought, but clearly I didn't know the rules of the game.

'Son of a bitch!' a young woman in Daroman riding gear declared, tossing her own cards face down on the table.

A huge Berabesq man in robes to her right abandoned his own hand next. 'I do not trust this creature. He brings ill fortune.'

'Not to me, sucker!' Reichis said gleefully. He hopped onto the table and began removing the coins one by one from the tray that held the bets to place them onto Ferius's pile. The squirrel cat glanced up at me. 'You and me are definitely playing poker later.'

'What's the point? You already steal anything I have of value every time I go to sleep.'

He glowered at me. 'You take the fun out of everything, you know that?'

'Hey, kid, you okay?' Ferius asked, peering up at me. 'You look a little out of sorts.'

Out of sorts? Her skin was so pale you'd have mistaken her for dead if she closed her eyes long enough. I'm not sure how long she'd been down here gambling, but judging from all the different coins in her pile, I doubted she'd been getting much rest. When she took another swig of her drink, the hand holding the mug trembled a little. That was the last straw for me.

'You think *I'm* out of sorts? Look at you! You're barely able to sit up in that chair! You nearly *died*, Ferius! I was lost in shadow and you were bleeding all over the sand and there was nothing I could do to help. *Nothing!* Do you not get that?'

The other players at the table stared at me, as did several other travellers nearby. I guess I'd got kind of loud.

Ferius waved away their looks of concern. 'Things turned out just fine, Kellen. Now, why don't you go have a seat on one of those couches over there and wait for one of the nice comfort artisans to come along and help you relax.'

'Comfort artisans?' Nephenia asked.

'Prostitutes,' I replied, even though I knew using that term would anger Ferius. Somehow she saw a difference between the two professions that eluded me.

'There speaks a man who ain't never spent a night with a real artisan,' she said, eliciting bouts of laughter from the table.

I felt the sharp sting of my fingernails digging into my own palms. Nephenia tried to pull me away, but I shrugged her off. 'How can you make everything into a joke, you stupid, selfish idiot!'

I knew I'd gone too far even before I saw the expressions of the people around me, which was bad because none of them knew that Ferius had saved my life more times than I could count. In return I'd almost let her die. She pushed her cards away. 'No, Kellen, I guess you're right. This ain't no joke.' She tossed a pair of coins to the Berabesq man who'd taken the deck. 'Deal me out a few rounds, Hedriss. Gotta stretch my legs awhile.' She rose from the table and headed for the stairs leading out of the cave. 'Come on, kid. Let's you and me take a walk.'

I followed Ferius outside, trying my best to stand tall but feeling like an errant puppy waiting to be scolded. The sun was just beginning to set in the west. To the east, darkening clouds settled over a range of hills that on the maps mark the Gitabrian border. We were clearly well out of the desert. There was even a lively stream babbling along a few yards away from the saloon where it passed beneath a small wooden bridge and into a forest of silver-grey trees blossoming with delicate orange-pink flowers.

'Pretty, ain't it?' Ferius asked.

Compared to where we'd been these past few months? It was like I'd fallen into one of those magnificent, peaceful paintings you might find adorning the marble walls of a lord magus's sanctum. 'It's fine, I guess.'

She chuckled, reaching inside her waistcoat – no doubt for one of her smoking reeds. She stopped though, and her hand came back empty. 'Places like this . . . *Times* like this, they're meant to be drunk up like summer wine, kid. You can't taste them if you let fear and anger swell up in your tongue.'

'But you—'

She cut me off. 'You keep sayin' I almost died, Kellen, but I didn't. Dwelling on all the bad things that didn't even come to pass only makes it harder to celebrate that fact. Stop being so scared about yesterday – it only makes you forget to appreciate today.'

Her words made sense of course, and part of me wanted to accept her view of things. But I couldn't. 'All I know is that you *did* almost die.' The last word came out in a humiliating sob.

I always cry after we get attacked, and I guess I hadn't had a chance this time around. Still, I'd promised myself when we came out here that no matter what Ferius said, I wouldn't blubber like some lost child. Like so many other promises, I broke that one too. 'Because of me, Ferius. It's always because of me. You were passed out bleeding in the sand and I couldn't help you because of my stupid shadowblack. If it had been just the two of us out there, you would've—'

She cut me off and did something she'd never done before. She hugged me. The sensation was so odd, as unnatural to me as it no doubt would've felt completely ordinary to someone else. My people don't tend to express physical affection. I tried to push her away but she held me there, arms wrapped around me. 'See, this is what I adore about you, kid,' Ferius said.

'The fact that I'm scared all the time?'

'The fact that nothing scares you more than the thought of lettin' your friends down.'

14

The Game of Cards

Back in the cavern beneath the saloon, Ferius returned to her game. Reichis periodically cajoled her about which cards to play while Nephenia and Ishak watched. Occasionally the hyena would bark or make a yipping sound that meant nothing to me, but which sent Reichis into long-winded explanations of the rules. The squirrel cat now considered himself an expert in the strategies and tactics of card games.

Travellers in garments both familiar and foreign to me came and went. Most devoted themselves to drinking or gambling, others huddled together in quiet corners, negotiating secret arrangements. Some stood by themselves, waiting nervously until a newcomer arrived, then rushing to embrace them in a tearful reunion.

As the hour grew late, a trio of musicians joined us to perform songs I'd never heard before on instruments I didn't recognise. A few people got up and danced in twos and threes or even more while others took their repose on the couches on the far side of the cave where neither the music nor the light from the lanterns quite reached. Young men and women – far too well groomed to have just come from the road – made their way to those on the couches and engaged them in discreet conversations. Sometimes they'd leave together, hand in hand. A fellow with shoulder-length hair, rich in golds and light browns, approached Nephenia. He whispered something to her that made her laugh. Soon they were dancing.

'Something troubling you, kid?' Ferius asked.

'Nothing. I'm fine.'

Reichis hopped over onto my shoulder and sniffed at my neck. 'Jealousy. Smells like regret only more bitter.'

I pushed his head away. 'I'm not . . .'

'Not what, kid?' Ferius asked.

'Nothing. I'm not anything. Just leave me alone.'

A woman who might have been a couple of years older than me, or maybe a couple of decades – it was hard to tell with all the make-up she wore – sauntered over and cooed at Reichis, 'Well, will you look at that? What a handsome, handsome fellow!' She said this to him while putting her hand on my chest, her fingers magically slipping between the buttons of my shirt.

Reichis ignored her, stretching his neck to peer down at Ferius's cards. 'Make the human go away, Kellen. She's bugging me.'

Unaware of Reichis's disdain, she leaned over until her nose was practically touching his, even as her breath managed to somehow tease my neck. 'I'll bet all the ladies ask if they can run their fingers through his fur, don't they?'

The squirrel cat gave her a sniff. 'Kellen, tell her she stinks of three different skinbag men and at least two women. She should really take a bath before—'

'Would you shut up?' I asked.

The comfort girl's eyes went wide right before she slapped me across the face. Despite the shock of the blow, what really struck me was that there was a moment there – just an instant – where I saw genuine hurt in her eyes. Only then did I realise I'd been wrong before and she actually wasn't much older than me. I felt oddly ashamed. 'I was talking to the squirrel cat,' I said, as earnestly as I could.

'Don't take offence, darlin',' Ferius said to the young woman. 'The boy gets cranky when he ain't had his beauty sleep. Now me, I like to stay up late. How about you get us the biggest tray of drinks you can find and meet me up in my room in an hour or three?'

She threw the comfort artisan a coin with all the care of someone tossing a petal from a daisy into the wind. As it spun in the air it flashed with the distinct shine of pure gold and the glimmer of a tiny green emerald embedded in its centre. The comfort artisan caught it neatly in her hand. Even before her fingers closed around it, the smile returned to her face, and a look of curious delight appeared in the slight narrowing of her eyes. 'Why, that sounds just fine, sweetheart,' she replied, her accent suddenly matching that of the Argosi. Somehow that annoyed me – as if I was the butt of a joke.

After the comfort artisan had gone, I asked Ferius, 'What are you doing inviting someone like her up to your room?'

'What? A woman can't have a little company to pass the time? Besides, I got aches in my shoulders and these folks can do wonders with their hands.'

'She's a prostitute. It's reprehensible.' Even as the words came out of my mouth, I realised they didn't sound very good. In my defence, prostitution is a forbidden profession among the Jan'Tep. Of course, so is being a spellslinger.

Ferius shot me a look. 'That girl ain't done nothing to you. Neither have I, for that matter. Let the meanderings of other lives pass you by, kid. There ain't nothing you need to give them, or take from them neither.'

The Way of the Argosi is the Way of Water, I recited to myself. Ferius must've taught me that lesson a hundred times by now. So simple and uncomplicated, yet I was no better at holding on to it than I would be grasping at raindrops.

'You're right,' I said, dislodging Reichis as I rose from my chair. 'I should go apologise to her.'

Ferius caught my arm. 'That girl's smiling right now. She's got more money in her hand than she's probably seen in a month. Leave her be.'

'But she thinks I'm—'

'A rude, foul-tempered, self-absorbed hick who ain't worth her time – which ain't far off right about now. So is this apology of yours to make her feel better? Or are you really just trying to get her to make *you* feel better about yourself?'

Before I could offer up any defence of my intentions, Ferius pulled out a card from inside her waistcoat. It was old and worn, the inks a dark blood-red. I recognised this as coming from the deck of debts she carried with her. 'Here endeth the lesson.'

I took the card. Reluctantly. This deck had different suits from her usual ones; in this case it depicted a pair of vines with sharp, glistening barbs. The name at the bottom read, *Two of Thorns*. 'What does it mean?' I asked.

'It means "be nicer to strangers", kid,' she said, then turned her attention back to the game.

Nephenia stopped dancing and came by to let us know that she and Ishak were going off to find something to eat. I very nearly asked whether her comfort boy was going to join her, but I still had the card in my hand and managed to keep my mouth shut. A small victory in my endlessly failed pursuit of not embarrassing myself all the time.

After the requisite exchanging of growls with Ishak, Reichis declared he needed to wander the rest of the cave so he could study the other games. My strong suspicion was that his real motive was to look for opportunities to sneak a coin or two away from distracted players. He might've taken an interest in gambling, but the squirrel cat's first love would always be thievery.

Ferius must've had the same thought, because she grinned at me and said, 'Always knows how to make himself at home that one . . .' The smile disappeared from her face as she caught sight of something behind me. I spun in my chair as I reached into my pouches. *Not again*, I thought, as my fingertips touched the powders. *I'm not letting Ferius get hurt because of me again.*

There were two of them. They walked towards us, casual as can be. Nobody else even took note of them, maybe because there wasn't much to see. The man wore simple travelling clothes: a worn-out shirt the colour of wheat left too long on the stalk and trousers a shade darker. His hair was grey and short enough that it didn't matter that it hadn't seen a comb in a while. The woman looked much the same, though she carried herself with that sort of elegance some old people have that you can't seem to put your finger on but you know is there all the same.

'Mind if we sit in a few hands?' she asked.

The man dropped himself down into a chair without waiting for an answer. When I looked at Ferius, she had her smile back. 'Always room for new money.'

I let the powders slip from my fingers and back into the

pouches, but I kept my eyes on the old-timers as they were dealt into the game. I suspected they might be Argosi, so I watched their every move closely. It took me almost an hour to figure out what was going on, but eventually I saw that there were two different card games taking place at our table: one between all the players, and another just between Ferius and the old man.

How did I know this? Because I've spent the last year studying the way Ferius Parfax handles cards. I've watched her gamble with them, use them as weapons, or just slide them around her fingers as part of some mindless meditation. What I'd never seen was her bothering to look at her own cards when she gambled. Yet now she was transfixed by her own hand, taking far too long to decide which one to discard when her turn came. The other players paid no heed, except to comment that maybe her lucky streak was finally coming to an end.

'You gonna play one of those cards?' the old man asked. 'Or you figure if you stare at them long enough they'll change into better ones?'

I followed what came next without so much as blinking. That's how I saw that when she finally did drop a card onto the pile it looked ever so slightly thicker than the others. When the old man's turn came and he dropped one of his own, Ferius's card was still there, but the one she'd stuck underneath was gone. They went around like this for a while before I noticed Ferius picking up her mug to take a drink. As she did, I saw her eyes flicker just for an instant to the top of the card now hidden in the cuff of her shirt. The old man had his own trick: he'd slap the table for the dealer to give him another card. When he picked it up, I could see he'd slipped the one he'd got from the discard pile in front so he could examine it in his hand without anyone knowing. Then he'd pat the knee of the woman next to him, and the card would be gone – no doubt left there for her to see. She caught me staring and gave me a wink.

Definitely Argosi, I thought. All this time, while everyone else was playing a form of poker called Brushfire Hold 'Em, Ferius and the elderly couple were exchanging cards from their Argosi decks, conversing silently in that secret language that used cards to say things words apparently couldn't. Then, as abruptly as they'd arrived and without a word of farewell, the couple pocketed their remaining coins and got up to leave.

I'm not sure why, but it surprised me when Ferius spoke up. 'Fancy a drink? They got a case of Daroman whisky here that folks swear makes the dead rise up from the grave just to have a taste.'

The invitation was perfectly innocuous, as these things go, and yet it sounded off to me – inappropriate, somehow. Evidently the couple had the same reaction, because the old man stopped in his tracks. Without turning back he replied, 'It's gettin' late, the wind's blowin', and the world is full of things to drink.'

'Suit yourselves,' Ferius said, then went back to her game, humming to the music and playing cards with a smile on her face as if she were having the luckiest night of her life.

I don't think I've ever seen her look so sad.

15

The Tracker

It drove me crazy, not knowing what had gone on between Ferius and the other two Argosi, so before she could stop me, I ran out of the cave and up the stairs. Outside the saloon, I waited a few seconds for my eyes to adjust to the darkness and then knelt to see if I could spot their tracks. There were footprints everywhere, but I wasn't so much looking for a shape as a pattern.

There you are, I thought. Two sets of footprints, side by side. I followed them along the dirt road, moving slowly, quietly, the way Ferius does sometimes. *Don't walk*, I told myself. *Dance. Glide along the surface of the earth like an Argosi.* I'm pretty sure I looked like a drunk flitting around the road imagining himself a prancing pony.

I probably got about fifty feet before my legs went out from under me and I fell face first to the ground.

'Always said they ought to teach subtlety before they teach daring,' the old man said, looking down at me. 'Fool can't even run proper.'

I tried to push myself up, but my limbs felt weak. Rubbery, almost. Something pinched at the nape of my neck. I managed to reach back and pull it out. My vision had become blurry, but when I held it close to my eyes it looked like a small thorn. I looked up at my attacker. 'You poisoned me?'

'Don't go cryin' to your Jan'Tep momma, now. It'll wear off in a minute or two.'

The woman gave him a poke in the ribs. 'Getting him to stop following us is our right. Taunting him isn't.'

'I'll show you taunting,' I said. Well, I slurred, anyway.

I felt the man's boot rest against my lower back. 'You get up, I'll just put you down again. What did you think you were doing anyway, trying to stalk us with that clumsy *arta tuco* of yours?'

Ferius hardly ever uses the proper terms, but I seemed to recall that arta tuco was the Argosi talent of subtlety. Apparently I wasn't all that subtle. 'I came to find out who you are.'

'To you? Nobody. A breeze that passed you by on a quiet evening.'

'Then who are you to Ferius?'

'Even less than that if she keeps to herself. Something far worse if she doesn't.'

Suddenly the man's boot was off my back, and I saw him stumble. 'That's enough of that nonsense,' the woman said. She looked down at me. 'We're leaving now, young man. You'll do neither yourself nor the Path of the Wild Daisy any favours if you seek us out again.' She led the man away, down the road, pausing to toss something small and shiny over her shoulder that landed an inch from my nose and began spinning on its axis. A coin. Black on one side, silver on the other. Pretty, I thought, though that might've just been the drugs from the thorn talking. I stared as the extrusions on its surface flashed by me, one side looking like a lock, the other a key.

'What's this?' I asked.

'You only wanted to do right by your friend,' the woman replied. 'In return we brought you pain. We can't rightly apologise, for we'd do worse if you tried to follow us again. Let the coin be an easing between us, and a parting.'

The two of them resumed their walk down the road. Something the shadow-Ferius had said by the black ocean when I was lost in the desert came back to me. 'Which one of you is the Path of the Rambling Thistle?'

I could just make out the woman's laugh. 'You see? She told us he was clever.'

'Not that clever,' the old man rumbled, then shouted back to me, 'We both are, *idjit*.'

By the time I got to my room upstairs in the saloon even my sense of curiosity was exhausted. Reichis was already on the bed, curled up and looking none too pleased with me. 'You took off without me,' he growled accusingly.

'You were busy stealing stuff.'

He glared at me with those beady eyes of his. 'Your shirt's covered in dust. Those two Argosi do that?'

I wondered briefly how he knew they were Argosi. Maybe he can smell it. 'It was nothing. I'm fine.'

'You want me to go kill the two skinbags? Just say the word, Kellen.'

Reichis says things like that all the time, but this time he sounded serious.

'What's got into you?'

He turned his muzzle away from me. 'Nothing. Don't care anyway. Go get yourself killed next time for all I care.'

I was too tired for a fight, so I locked the door to the room and wedged the chair under the knob just in case. The oil lamp at my bedside had been refilled, so I closed the window and picked up the pile of curtains from the floor to start hanging them back up. Dawn wasn't far off, and despite my fears of falling back into shadow, I'd probably sleep better without the morning light streaming in. I heard a shuffling from the road outside. When I looked down, I was greeted by the sight of two people strolling along hand in hand. It was Nephenia. The guy with her was the one she'd danced with earlier.

A few unkind thoughts came to me then, but I was keenly aware of the two-of-thorns card in my pocket. Besides, I had no right to expect anything from Nephenia. There'd never been any promises between us. When I'd learned she was betrothed to Panahsi – or Pan'erath as he went by now – I figured that was that. Neph had moved on and so should I. Then I'd met Seneira and for a brief moment I'd let myself believe there might be something between us. That was stupid, I guess. I was an outlaw spellslinger with a curse around my left eye and a spell warrant out for my head. Nobody needed that kind of trouble in their lives.

'Ugh,' Reichis said, sniffing the air and then jumping onto the bed to bury his nose in the pillow.

'What's the problem?'

'Self-pity stinks even worse than jealousy.'

I stripped down to my breeches and got under the covers. 'You know what stinks even worse than that? Squirrel cats, that's what.'

Reichis curled himself up near my chest, taking up more than his share of the bed. 'I'm going to piss under the covers while you're asleep.'

It sounded like a jab, but I've learned to take his threats seriously. This situation required the subtlety of a lord magus and the cunning of an Argosi. Or maybe just the petulance of a six-year-old. 'Of course you're going to piss the bed,' I replied. 'You can't help yourself. Everybody knows squirrel cats have poor bladder control.'

His head popped up and his beady eyes fixated on me. 'You take that back. I have perfect control. *Total* control.'

I shrugged. 'If you say so.'

He stuck his head back into the fur of his chest and grumbled awhile.

I was just drifting off to sleep when I heard Reichis speak again. 'She came into your room to refill the lamp.'

'Huh? Who?'

'Nephenia. She was the one who took down the curtains and brought in the oil lamp to make sure you wouldn't have to wake up in the dark. I can smell her scent on the lamp. She's the one who refilled it. She's the one who's been watching over you since we left the desert.'

'She said everyone took turns.'

'We were too beat-up, and those stupid medicines Ferius carries around kept us too tired to help. It should have been me guarding you, Kellen. *I'm* your business partner, not her. But I couldn't. I was too weak. Nephenia watched over you. Every night.'

I didn't know what to say to that. Reichis sounded . . . fragile. Finally I said, 'Guess you owe me a pair of fresh rabbits.'

He gave a short sniff, then said, 'One.'

'Okay, one rabbit.'

I felt his little body relax against my chest. 'Night. Skinbag.'

'Goodnight, Reichis.'

16

Neither Straight Nor Narrow

I couldn't have been asleep for more than a couple of hours before I woke to the sound of someone calling my name and the itchy sensation of a squirrel cat's tail smothering my face. I groggily pushed Reichis away and looked up to find Ferius in my room, saddlebags already packed.

'We going somewhere?'

She took a seat on the chair by the wall – the same one I'd wedged under the doorknob last night to keep anyone from breaking in. 'Time to move on, kid. You've come out of that shadowblack nonsense of yours, the hyena and the squirrel cat are mostly recovered, and this place is a lot more expensive than it looks. I say we saddle up the horses and see where the road takes us.'

I leaned up on my elbows. 'What about Nephenia? Is she coming?'

'Don't know. Didn't ask.' The way Ferius said it, so completely unconcerned and almost dismissive, made me start to protest. Then I remembered that most times when Ferius gets my back up it's because she's trying to keep me from asking the right questions.

'Who were those two Argosi last night?'

'Argosi?' Ferius made a show of glancing around the room. 'Somebody let Argosi in this establishment? What's the world coming to?'

'I saw you trading cards back and forth with them. What did you learn?'

She clasped her hands behind her head and leaned back in the chair, closing her eyes. 'Boring stuff mostly. A trade dispute here, a new Daroman governor there. Oh, and some Jan'Tep clan or other decided to go to war with their neighbours.'

'What? Which clan?'

'Not yours,' she said. 'Come to think of it, I'm not sure which clans they were talking about. The cards aren't always the most specific means of exchanging information.'

'Then why use cards at all? Why not just—'

'Cos that ain't the Argosi way.'

That was her reply to just about everything – especially this particular discussion. It always ended with Ferius telling me that words only let you describe the details of things, but not the deeper truths behind them. Somehow the cards let the Argosi express both what they understood and what they didn't. In fact, it's not just the cards they exchange or the sequence of the cards; the very means by which they pass them to each other is supposedly a way of conveying important aspects of the events or people involved.

Yeah. It doesn't make sense to me either.

'That last card,' I said, 'the one they gave you right before they left – there's no way you had time to give it back. What was it?'

Ferius gave me a grin. 'Not one in a thousand could've spotted that, kid. Seems like nothing gets by you.'

Actually almost everything gets by me, but the compliment

still brought a flush to my cheeks. I hate the fact that it makes me feel so good when she praises me. I suppose I should be grateful that it's such a rare occurrence – and one that only comes around when she's trying to distract me. 'Quit stalling. Show me the card.'

She pulled her hands out from behind her head and made a bunch of odd gesticulations. 'By the mighty power of iron and ember, of sand and silk, of blood and breath, let the truth be known!' She clapped her hands together.

Nothing happened.

'Are you done making fun of me?' I asked.

'Look down, kid.'

There, on the covers in front of me, sat a card, face down. 'Is it like some Argosi law that you have to mock my people's magic all the time?'

'There ain't much for entertainment on the long roads, kid. A body's got to take what fun she can get.'

Yeah, like the kind you get from drunken gambling and comfort girls.

I picked up the card and examined it. The back was indistinct, the pattern not dissimilar to others I'd seen on Argosi decks. The painting on the front of the card though? That made me catch my breath.

It was beautiful. The style was intricate. Delicate. Ferius is a skilled artist, but this was different. The colours were subtler, full of soft reds and blues and greens. You had to really look at the browns and greys to see how they were differentiated from the blacks. The paint strokes were elaborate too, the lines narrow and fluid as if the artist had simply let the brush flow wherever it wanted. At first I thought the card depicted a bird taking flight from a lush tree full of gold- and copper-coloured leaves growing from thin silver branches. But then I noticed that the leaves weren't natural, but rather painted to be elaborately shaped pieces of metal. The same was true of the trunk and branches of the tree. When I peered closer, I saw that the bird itself was made from metal too, with perfectly articulated wings, feet and feathers.

'A mechanical bird?' I asked.

Ferius nodded. 'Seems to be.'

There was a distinctive geometry to everything on the card – the tree, the bird, even the subtle pattern of the sky and clouds. It reminded me of the designs of certain rugs and porcelain plates that traders would sometimes bring to my city, which helped me finally connect the dots. 'This is Gitabrian, isn't it?'

'Looks that way.'

Gitabria was where we'd been headed when we got caught up in that mess with the Berabesq Faithful. We had a notebook taken from Dexan Videris with an entry for each person he'd infected with an obsidian worm. There wasn't a name for the last entry, but the location was listed as Cazaran, the capital city of Gitabria. 'During that poker game, you told the other two Argosi what we'd been doing and where we were headed next. That's why they gave you this card?'

Ferius didn't bother confirming or denying it, but I was pretty sure I was right.

'So now the Argosi have given you a separate mission in Gitabria as well.' I held up the card. 'Which means they must have either come from there themselves, or got this from another Argosi. I guess we're supposed to go investigate what's illustrated on the card?'

Ferius closed her eyes again. 'Do you need me for this

conversation, kid? You seem to be doing fine all by yourself.'

'But I thought the discordances represent people or events that could alter the course of history – that could change or even destroy entire civilisations.'

'That's the theory, kid.'

'How is a mechanical bird supposed to do that?'

Ferius, eyes still closed, gave me a smirk. 'Welcome to the path of the Argosi, kid; neither straight nor narrow.'

I stared back at the card, part of me admiring the sheer beauty of it, part of me frustrated by the incomprehensible tendency for obfuscation that seemed to be central to the Argosi ways. I got out of bed, glad that I'd remembered to sleep in my breeches to avoid repeating my embarrassment from the day before, and dressed just in time for Nephenia and her hyena to barge into the room.

'Are you two still not ready? We've been standing out there with the horses for half an hour!'

'I thought you said you hadn't told her we were going?' I asked Ferius.

'Of course I'm coming,' Nephenia said, taking the discordance card from my hand. 'Ferius told me all about our mission in Gitabria. We've got to uncover the meaning of this mechanical bird. It's nine days' ride to the capital and we can't lose even one of them if we want to get to the Grand Exhibition in time.'

'The grand what now?' I turned to Ferius. 'Anything else you told Nephenia that you couldn't be bothered to tell me?'

'The charmcaster's right,' she said. 'Best we get ourselves moving.'

I was so furious it was all I could do to remember to grab my bag before I left the room.

Reichis sauntered over with his little velvet bag of stolen trinkets in his mouth so I could pack it for him. 'Should've played poker with you, Kellen. You really are a sucker sometimes.'

'What? Why?'

He didn't answer, but by then he didn't need to. I'd forgotten the most important thing about Ferius Parfax: when she makes you angry, it's always to keep you from asking the right questions. She'd done it twice to me this morning; clearly she didn't want me enquiring about what those two Argosi had done to make her so upset.

Fine, I thought, closing the door behind me. *Keep your secrets, Ferius.*

I'll find the answer myself.

17

The Eight Bridges

Gitabria's capital was unlike any other city I'd seen. Divided in two by a massive gorge, Cazaran's spiralling towers and sprawling avenues flowed out to the very edge of the cliffs. Carved into the two-hundred-foot rock faces, beautifully sculpted homes – palaces, really – looked down upon a fleet of merchant ships in the waters below. Finely dressed couples stepped out from their stone verandas onto wooden platforms that floated up on a system of ropes, weights and pulleys, ending their journeys at one of the eight colossal bridges that spanned the gorge.

'The Cazaran Arches,' Ferius explained. 'Foreign merchants travel a thousand miles just to cross them. The Gitabrians like to say that each bridge is so full of wonders that you could spend every day for a year exploring just one and every night you'd find your heart lighter. Course, that's only because your purse wouldn't be weighing you down. The lords mercantile pride themselves that no one gets across without spending a little coin.'

'What do they sell?'

She pointed to a huge wooden suspension bridge where tall ornate towers rose high above living trees that somehow took root within the deck itself. Dozens of little stalls between them displayed brightly coloured merchandise. 'The Forest Bridge,' Ferius said. 'Exotic fruits and vegetables, delicacies from across the sea, and spices worth nearly their weight in gold.'

The sheer spectacle of it all was enough to entice me, but Ferius turned our attention to a second bridge, this one simpler, more pristine, with marble railings atop its stone deck. Men and women in white robes each bearing a single blue stripe down one shoulder stood on small, individual platforms surrounded by clientele vying for their attention. 'The Arch of Solace. Those folks in the fancy robes will diagnose your symptoms and peddle you a cure for any ailment you got, and probably a few you don't.'

Reichis tugged at my trouser leg. I looked down and saw he was entranced by the third bridge, this one packed with expensively dressed merchants hawking precious stones and jewellery. 'Hey, Kellen? I'm gonna take a little walk, okay? You go find us another horse. Maybe a cart too? Make it a big one.'

I shook him off. 'You are *not* going thieving, Reichis.'

Nephenia seemed to be having a similar problem with Ishak, because she was hanging on to the scruff of his neck to keep him from running off. Apparently hyenas and squirrel cats have at least one thing in common. 'What about the other bridges?' she asked Ferius.

It seemed to me to be an innocuous question, but the Argosi gave her a knowing stare. 'Pretty sure the one you're looking for is over there.' She gestured to a narrower bridge with silver-capped spans linking a complex arrangement of copper-banded ropes. Fewer customers walked along the curve of its arched deck, but those who did looked by far the wealthiest we'd seen thus far. 'The Way of Wonders,' Ferius said. 'That's why you tagged along, ain't it?'

'It's not like I hid my intentions,' Nephenia replied. 'Neither of you bothered to ask me what my plans were.'

'Wait,' I said. 'You were already coming here when you met up with us?'

She nodded. 'The Gitabrians like to bring charms with them on their trading voyages across the ocean. Warded locks, whisper catchers, anything small and intriguing that they can use to sweeten a deal. A charmcaster can make a good life for herself here.' She watched my eyes, and I guess she must've seen something there because she put a hand on my arm. 'I'm not abandoning you, Kellen. It'll take me time to find a patron and secure a permit to set up shop on the Way of Wonders. Until then, I'll do my best to help you and Ferius investigate this mechanical-bird business.'

'Well, that's where we have a problem,' Ferius said, walking the horses along a wide avenue. At the far end stood a huge amphitheatre, the gates already crowded with people waiting to get in. 'The Grand Exhibition is the most likely place we'll find this bird contraption, but they won't let us in without the right coin.'

'Are you serious?' I asked, suddenly irritated. 'You were winning all night back at the travellers' saloon. Now you're saying you spent it all on that comfort artisan?'

'I didn't say money. I said *coin*. Only invited delegates are allowed inside. The lords mercantile give out special mintings to foreign dignitaries or as favours to their friends. Try to get in without one and you'll get pinched by the Gitabrian secret police, and trust me, *those* folks? They make the Berabesq Faithful look like pacifists.'

'So how were you planning on getting us in?' Nephenia asked.

'I'd hoped we'd get here early enough that I might find some over-eager merchant lords on the Bridge of Dice, make a few wagers and see if I couldn't swindle a delegate's coin from one of them.' Again she looked ruefully up at the darkening sky. 'No way I'll find one in time now.'

I smiled, because for once – just *once* – it turned out that I was the one with the solution to our problems. 'Well, let's see what a little Jan'Tep magic can do, shall we?' I began gesticulating wildly in the air, bumping into Ferius in the process. 'By the infinite might of sand and silk, of blood and breath, of iron and ember, let the answer be revealed!'

'Kellen? Are you all right?' Nephenia asked, looking at me intently, as though I were in the midst of some kind of seizure.

Ferius, on the other hand, gave me a mildly amused smirk. 'Not bad, kid, but next time see if you can do it without jostling the mark to distract them.' She reached into the small front pocket of her waistcoat and removed the black and silver coin I'd placed there. She peered at the symbols of the lock on one side and the key on the other, her expression not at all what I'd expected. She seemed troubled by the coin rather than relieved.

'Ferius? I'm sorry, I didn't mean to—'

She tossed the coin back to me. 'Nice thought, kid, but this ain't gonna do us any good.'

'Wait, what?' Then it hit me: *of course* the coin the old woman had given me wasn't a delegate's coin. Who ever heard of an Argosi making your life easier?

'See those fellas over there?' Ferius asked, pointing to a

group of well-dressed Berabesq clerics pushing their way through the crowd in front of the amphitheatre, their leader holding up a coin for the guards at the gate. Even from this distance I could tell the coin was a lot larger than the one I held in my hand, and it gleamed in a way this one didn't. 'The Gitabrians make them from three separate rings,' Ferius explained. 'Each one minted from a different gold alloy that their ships bring back from voyages across the sea. Impossible to forge.'

I felt claws sticking in my clothes as Reichis clambered up my back. Not content to stop at my shoulder, he perched himself on top of my head. His paws started kneading my scalp. 'So . . . pretty. So very, very pretty.'

'Get off me!' I said, setting him back down on the ground.

'What if we wait outside?' Nephenia asked. 'Maybe one of the delegates will leave early and we can trade for their coin. Maybe we'll get lucky and—'

'That's what all them other folks hanging about are hoping, too. Trust me, I've been gambling my whole life and nobody's going to deal you that particular inside straight.'

'Then we try something else,' Nephenia insisted. 'When the exhibition ends later tonight we talk to the people leaving and find out what they saw.'

'They'll *see* what the Gitabrians *want* them to see. The presentations are just a bunch of smoke and mirrors to fool the delegates into bidding up the price for fancy new inventions nobody needs. I'm telling you, girl, I need to be there when it happens.'

The two of them argued back and forth for a while, Nephenia's optimism somehow bringing out Ferius's darker side. I just kept staring at the coin the old Argosi woman had given me. It felt odd in my hand. Whenever I tossed it in the air just so, it would start spinning, and seem to come back down slower than it should. I was so distracted by it that it wasn't until a sudden uproar shook the crowds outside the amphitheatre and guardsmen started running all over the place that I realised something very, very bad: Reichis was missing.

'Ishak?' Nephenia called out.

'They're *both* gone?' Ferius asked.

Oh, crap. A squirrel cat and a hyena at large. That can't be good.

Crossbow bolts struck the pavement about thirty yards away, shot by guards perched in the high towers outside the amphitheatre. The crowds scattered, shouting and screaming as they knocked over food carts and the unfortunate boys and girls carrying trays of drinks for sale. A blur raced along the centre of the avenue, sending panicking citizens stumbling into each other. That's when I saw the strangest sight of my entire life: a hyena, running like the wind, being ridden by a squirrel cat holding up a large, gleaming coin made from three gold rings.

18

The Thieves

'Into the alley!' Ferius whispered furiously, hauling on the horses to get them moving faster.

'What about Ishak and Reichis?' Nephenia asked.

'We can't be seen with them right now. If the secret police connect us with those two fools we'll all spend the next five years in a Gitabrian jail debating whose fault it was. Now come on.'

'It's okay,' I told Nephenia. 'This isn't the first time Reichis has pulled a stunt like this. He and Ishak will find us as soon as they've shaken their pursuers.'

She hesitated, then nodded and followed Ferius into the alleyways. Evidently my confidence was more persuasive than I thought, which was good given that I really didn't feel any. Reichis is an idiot who refuses to keep his paws off things that aren't his and who severely overestimates his ability to get out of trouble.

'How long do we wait?' Nephenia asked.

We were hiding in the alley, watching angry crowds go by. Twice guardsmen came running past us, pausing to ask if we'd seen a strange dog carrying an ugly cat on its back. Ferius made suitably caustic remarks about public servants drinking while on duty. I imagine that would've provoked a confrontation had it not also convinced the guards that she had no idea what they were talking about.

'Those two better find us soon,' Ferius said as the chaos died down. 'The exhibition is going to start any minute now.'

I was anxious for a completely different reason: what if I'd done the wrong thing by hiding with the others instead of going after Reichis? What if he needed my help? His leg was still hurt from the fight in the desert, what if they . . . *Stupid, stupid squirrel cat. He's probably dead and it's my fault for not—*

'Stop, thief!' a voice called out.

I pulled powder and spun on my heels. Someone must've told the guards about us being with Reichis and Ishak earlier. I relaxed when I saw Nephenia letting out a relieved breath and Ferius rolling her eyes. From around the corner Ishak came sauntering towards us, Reichis still on his back, giggling all the while.

'Do it again!' the squirrel cat demanded. 'Do the other one this time!'

The hyena opened his mouth wide and in the frightened voice of an elderly Daroman man shouted, 'They went that way! That way, I say!'

Reichis hopped off the hyena's back and ambled over to me, still holding the delegate's coin in one paw. 'Who wantsh to go shee shome shtupid exhibition?'

'Are you drunk?' I asked, trying to mask my desperate desire to hug him – something I was never, ever allowed to do.

Reichis grinned up at me. 'Nope. Had to make a shtop on the way back.' He reached into his jowls and took out a pair of glittering rubies. He threw one to me. 'Stick this in my bag, would you?' The other one he tossed to Ishak, who caught it in his mouth and presented it to Nephenia, presumably for the same purpose.

'Kellen,' she said, giving me a withering look. 'Inform the squirrel cat that he's forbidden from corrupting my familiar.'

Ishak looked up at her with adoring eyes, then barked, 'Stop, thief!'

A festive, almost celebratory air thrummed through the crowds inside the amphitheatre. Thousands of people chattered while taking their seats along the curved stone benches, calling over men and women bearing wide trays attached to leather straps that went round their shoulders. One of the vendors walked past me and the smells of spiced wine and roasted meats made me dizzy. Boys and girls sat on their parents' laps, pointing and shouting excitedly as foreign delegations paraded into the amphitheatre, proudly displaying their nations' colours and banners.

There was probably more money in this place than in any single country's treasury. Reichis would've been in heaven. Fortunately, after considerable debate, even the squirrel cat had to admit he and Ishak were too likely to be recognised by the exhibition guards.

'Fine,' he'd declared, dusting himself off. 'Me and the hyena have got better things to do, anyway.'

Ishak had let out a short series of excited barks that Nephenia took poorly. 'You will *not*,' she insisted. 'How are we supposed to make a life for ourselves in this city if you and the squirrel cat go off thieving from everybody?'

The hyena's apologetic whine didn't go over well with Reichis. 'Are you kidding me?' the squirrel cat demanded, gesturing towards Nephenia. 'You're gonna let a skinbag get in the way of our new venture? You and me can make a fortune! And Kellen can carry our loot, buy us anything we want.' Somehow, without any agreement on my part, I had become the bagman for a squirrel cat and a hyena.

'Over here,' Ferius said, bringing my attention back to the exhibition. She led Nephenia and me to one of the less densely packed sections. There were sixteen in all, each with its own set of curved stone benches. In front of each section stood a tall structure, about nine feet high, in the shape of a half-shell, the opening facing towards the benches. In each shell a large man or woman holding what looked like some kind of horn or bugle waited patiently. 'Translators,' Ferius explained.

'Translators?'

'You fluent in Gitabrian?'

'Well, no . . .'

She pointed to the woman at the head of our section. I could tell she was Jan'Tep, though actually more likely a Sha'Tep servant since the tattooed bands on her forearms looked long-faded. She made up for it by being bigger and taller than any member of my people I'd ever seen. 'The presentations are in Gitabrian,' Ferius explained, 'but most of the people who come for the event are from other places. So the translators repeat everything in the appropriate language.'

'So you're telling me that all the people in this section will be either Jan'Tep or their representatives?' I glanced around at the other faces. Most didn't pay any attention to me at all, no doubt wondering what I was doing there since I wasn't dressed in the sort of clothes our people wore. They probably figured I was a Sha'Tep servant holding a seat for the head of my household. When someone did bother looking at me closely, their expression made me extremely uncomfortable. 'Umm . . .' I mumbled at Ferius. 'Has it occurred to you that there's a spell warrant out on me? And Nephenia's an exile. What if someone from our clan sees us?'

'No one would dare interfere with us here,' Nephenia said. 'Gitabrian trade laws are very specific. You make trouble for them and you're cut off from all trade. Attempt any military response, and the Daroman or even the Berabesq will retaliate before they let you threaten access to all the trade goods that come from here.'

Which I suppose made Gitabria even more of a safe haven for Nephenia. I doubted it would do me much good, though. I've never known my people to be entirely rational on the subject of what to do with shadowblack outcasts.

A horn sounded, the note surprisingly sweet and pure. 'Saddle up, kid,' Ferius said, pointing to an open seat on the bench. 'You're in for quite a ride.'

19

The Grand Exhibition

It all began with a small man in a long embroidered coat. Bright semi-precious stones stitched into his garments caught the light and gave him the appearance of a glittering peacock taking centre stage. He spoke in a manner so fluid it was almost musical. Gitabrian was a beautiful language, but spoken far too quickly for me to make out where one word ended and the next began. In addition to his oration, the man did a lot of smiling and gesturing, and after a particularly grand bow, he stepped back.

The translators at the head of each section lifted their horns to their lips. They didn't shout exactly, but somehow the acoustics of both the horns and the large shells in which they stood made their voices boom across the rows of curved benches. You could easily hear every word, even as the other translators spoke over each other to their respective sections.

'You are welcome here,' the Jan'Tep woman at the head of our section began. 'You are treasured. You are prized. You are our beloved guests, whether from the brave and noble Daroman empire, the devout and wise Berabesq theocracy, the brilliant and powerful Jan'Tep arcanocracy . . .' She went on like that, mentioning countries I knew well and a few I'd only heard of in passing, some of which weren't even on this continent.

'For one hundred and fifty years the Grand Exhibition has been a place for all to come and marvel at the wonders of other lands, at the ingenuity of those who – though they might not look or talk like us – are nonetheless brothers and sisters in spirit if not in skin. Here you will see what our explorers have found, what they have traded for at enormous expense, and what you, our honoured guests, may choose to purchase and bring back to your own peoples.'

On cue, the man who directed the event stepped forward again. He spoke only for a few seconds, paused, said one last thing, and then stepped back.

'As is our tradition,' the woman at the head of our section said, 'you will also see what we in Gitabria have created this past year. Ours is a culture of exploration, of trade, but also of ingenuity. There is a word in our language which is found in no other: *bellegenzia*. It means the beauty that can only be uncovered through invention.' She gave a slight, theatrical pause that matched that of the lead presenter, then said, 'And oh, what wonders have our contraptioneers wrought this past year!'

The man in the glittering coat stepped forward a third and final time, held out his hands as if in supplication, then suddenly raised them over his head and clapped them together.

It was as if he'd summoned thunder from the clear night sky.

From the wings of the amphitheatre, two contingents of dancers in red silk paraded forth, carrying eight-foot wooden poles connected to each other by similarly red cloth with gold fringes, the entire affair forming a kind of winged mythical beast with a long snout somewhat like that of a crocodile. It was probably best that Reichis couldn't come – he has a thing about crocodiles.

The beast bobbed and weaved, dancing under the elaborate choreography performed by the men and women holding the poles. They crossed each other at the back of the stage, then did so again faster, as if the creatures they bore were about to take flight. Suddenly they ran right towards the front of the stage, towards the audience. The jaws of the twin red silk beasts opened wide, and a clap of thunder and fire roared out. Smoke and flame came from the maw, and I tried to grab Nephenia and Ferius before the flames could reach us. Nephenia shoved my hand away as if I were some annoying child, her eyes still on the beasts. Only then did I realise that what shot forth from the creatures was not flame nor smoke at all, but long red paper streamers that flew through the air in a brilliant display. Something else came along with them: small bundles, each one no larger than a marble, wrapped in shiny gold paper. They fell throughout the amphitheatre, caught by eager hands.

Again the silk monster spewed its strange cargo, and more coin-sized bundles flew into the air. 'These Gitabrians sure do love to put on a show,' Ferius said, idly reaching out a hand to catch one of the gold-wrapped parcels. She unwrapped it and displayed its contents for me. 'Why don't you try it, kid?'

A small round piece of what looked like toffee stared back at me. 'How do we know it's not drugged?' I asked. If that sounds paranoid, trust me: getting poisoned is a lot more common a problem than one might assume.

'Can't imagine that would be good for business,' Ferius

observed, noting all the guests who were greedily eating the contents. 'But if you're scared . . .'

Before I could even attempt to counter that childish effort to sway me, Nephenia had neatly picked the candy from Ferius's hand and popped it into her mouth. She couldn't have sucked on it for more than a second before she stopped, her eyes widening. 'Oh,' she said.

'What? Is it . . .'

Without answering, she looked down at the ground where a precious few gold-wrapped pieces were still being sought after by eager hands. She dived and grabbed one before a large man in mage's robes could get to it. He snarled at her, but evidently the rules of the exhibition stayed his hand. Nephenia ignored him and returned to us, handing the candy to me. 'Try it.'

Not being keen on another accusal of cowardice, I unwrapped it and put it in my mouth, careful not to swallow. The effect was almost instantaneous. Everything around me . . . *sharpened*. Colours, shapes, textures. It was as if I'd been wearing a linen hood over my eyes my whole life and only now could see the world as it was. My hearing was finer, too. More than that, it was as if I could think more clearly, more rationally – like I'd been a dunce before and only now understood the most basic aspects of reality.

'Lucidity,' the translator declared, her voice booming far more loudly than I now thought necessary. I only then realised the exposition's leader had spoken in Gitabrian before her. I could actually remember the exact syllables and pronunciation of the words he'd spoken. Of course, I didn't know what they meant, but all of a sudden the language didn't seem so hard to learn.

'Lucidity,' she repeated. 'Is that not what we all seek? To see clearer, to hear better, to know the world more fully. The Shin Pazhani people who live across the southern sea know their world and more, for they know true harmony. With lucidity comes understanding, and with understanding, peace.'

Already shouts were coming from men and women in all sixteen sections of the amphitheatre. They held up thin sticks, each one about six feet long so it could be seen from afar. The top foot or so of the stick had a crossbar so that various coloured rings could be placed on the stick and counted. Some were blue or green, others gold or silver. As bidders saw their competitors' rings, they changed their own, or simply added more.

'What exactly are they bidding on?' I asked.

'Trading rights,' Ferius said. 'They're bidding for the right to buy the first year's supply.'

'All that money,' I said, 'and they haven't even worked out a price for the thing itself?'

Nephenia, the irises of her eyes radiant, said, 'Imagine how much money the company with exclusive rights to sell these can make.'

Eventually a winner was found, a Daroman who could barely hold his bidding stick up because it was so weighed down with gold rings. There was a kind of gracious applause from those who'd lost the bid, and some fanfare as the men and women holding the cloth dragons made them bow down in the winner's direction. Less than a minute later, the dragons were hung up on hooks high above the stage and the performers were gone. The man in the peacock coat gave a bow, and then he too left.

'That was incredible,' I said.

'You want incredible . . .' a small chittering voice said from beneath my bench. I looked down to find Reichis staring up at me with unnaturally wide eyes. In one paw he was grasping several of the little gold-wrapped bundles. 'You should try one of these Kellen. So good. *So* good.'

'You idiot! You were supposed to hide out in the city. What if someone sees you?'

He snorted. 'These morons? They're all too wrapped up in the show. Ishak and me have been here the whole time and nobody even noticed us.'

I looked over and saw the hyena was under Nephenia's bench, doing a vastly better job than Reichis of staying hidden despite the fact that they'd both disobeyed us. Reichis's brashness was a concern, but it was the way his fur kept shifting colours over and over that really worried me. I grabbed one of the gold-wrapped candies from him. 'How many of these have you eaten?'

The squirrel cat's head swivelled around left and right as if he were waiting for someone else to answer. 'Dunno.' He held up the paw barely hanging on to what must have been half a dozen of the wrapped candies. 'Maybe five?'

'Probably best you take those from him, Kellen,' Ferius said. 'And you . . .' She pointed to the squirrel cat. 'You stay under the benches. You or the hyena try stealing anything and you'll answer to me, understand?'

Reichis banged his paw against his forehead – his version of the way he'd seen Daroman soldiers salute their commanders. 'Whatever you say, Captain.'

Despite the fact that she couldn't possibly know what he was saying, she stuck her finger in his furry face and said, 'I mean it.'

Reichis bared his teeth at her for daring to threaten him,

but his snarl soon dissolved into giggling. 'You have pretty eyes,' he said, staring up at her.

'What'd he say?' she asked me. When I translated, she gave him a smile. 'Well now, aren't you the sweetest little—'

'I'd really like to eat them.' The squirrel cat's head swivelled towards me. 'Can I eat her eyes, Kellen? I'll give them back later, I promise.'

'Uh . . . we'll talk about it some other time.'

'Fine,' he said, then turned to walk away, only to promptly fall forward. It was only Nephenia's fast hand that caught him before he landed face first on the floor. 'She's pretty too,' he said, looking up at her as she cradled him in her arms. 'I always liked this human.' He idly stretched out a paw that had no hope of reaching its target but which I was fairly sure was aiming for one of her ears.

'We should go,' I said, assuming the big event was over.

'Go?' Ferius asked, settling in and turning her attention back to the stage where an entirely new and even more elaborate production was taking shape. 'Kid, that wasn't the exhibition. That was just the opening act.'

20

The Contraptioneer

For the next two hours I sat in mute wonder as a parade of unusual and sometimes bizarre commodities made their way across the stage. Delicacies from places I'd never heard of were overshadowed by beautiful carved tools made from woods stronger than steel, only to have those pale in comparison to cloth goods like a shirt made from a kind of linen that cooled in the presence of heat and warmed when ice was placed against it. These marvels, we were forewarned by the translators, were in excessively limited supplies, and so the bidding started high and only travelled skyward.

'Gimmicks,' Ferius said at my astonishment. 'Most of that stuff is made from materials so exotic you couldn't outfit a household with them, never mind an army.'

'Then why—'

'The Gitabrians like to show off,' she explained, gesturing at the enraptured delegates. 'Most of these people don't need magic candies or shirts that cost a fortune just to save you the trouble of wearing a coat. They come here to secure loads of candle wax or spices, hardwoods or ivory.' She waved a hand dismissively. 'The rest is just spectacle.'

Nephenia wrinkled her nose. 'Forgive me, Lady Ferius, but you reduce the wondrous to something tawdry.'

'Not "Lady",' declared Reichis stridently from his resting spot on Nephenia's lap hidden beneath her coat. He started giggling uncontrollably.

Ferius rolled her eyes. 'I swear, one Jan'Tep is enough to wear on my nerves. Two . . .' She turned back to Nephenia. 'There are maybe a thousand mages worth the name among your people right now, kid. Now that might sound like a lot, but the Daroman army is two million strong. The Berabesq elites – just their elites, mind you, not their regular foot soldiers – are close to a hundred thousand.' She pointed towards the exit of the amphitheatre. 'Gitabria's the smallest country of all – other than the Jan'Tep arcanocracy, of course – but even it's got four million people. All told, this continent is home to sixty million souls.' She pointed back to the stage. 'Now tell me what difference a few warm shirts is going to make.'

Nephenia was dumbfounded by the simple logic of Ferius's arguments, as was I, except for one thing: the card that had brought us here. 'The discordances,' I said. 'You keep saying that they can change the course of history, but they're never more than—'

My very compelling counter-argument was cut off by a flurry of activity on the stage. The men and women in bright costumes left, taking their banners and streamers with them. The various carts and display cases were removed. Even the exhibition leader himself departed. Once the stage was empty, a young man in unobtrusive black clothing rolled out what looked like a massive oval mirror set in a large wooden frame with eight small wheels to allow it to move smoothly across the floor. He placed it carefully in the exact centre of the stage, then tilted it carefully, making several careful adjustments. When he was satisfied, he waved behind it. His hand suddenly appeared monstrously large. Not a mirror, I realised. A magnifying glass.

Without a word, the young man left. The crowd waited, breathless for no apparent reason at the sight of this enormous magnifying glass. Finally a heavy set woman emerged from the wings. She wore an artisan's leather smock over a simple white linen shirt. In her hands she carried a small wooden box, no bigger than one of her palms – which were admittedly rather large. As soon as the audience saw her, the awed silence became punctuated with whispers of words I didn't recognise. 'Janucha . . . Credara Janucha zal Ghassan . . . Janucha Es Maedra Bellegenzia . . . Es Maedra Bellegenzia . . .'

'What are they saying?' I asked Ferius.

'Her name.'

'That's an awfully long name, isn't it?'

'Not for the Gitabrians. They overcomplicate everything. They start with a title, in this case *credara*, which means inventor, or as they like to call it, contraptioneer. That's followed by the given name.'

'Janucha?'

She nodded. 'Then a family name like Ghassan, only there's another word before it that indicates their status within that family. *Zal* means head of the household, in case you're wondering.'

'So her full name is Inventor Janucha, head of the House of Ghassan?'

'Exactly. A little pompous if you ask me.'

Says the woman who goes by 'Path of the Wild Daisy'.

'What about the rest?' Nephenia asked. '*Es Maedra Bellegenzia.*'

'*Maedra* means mother.'

'And the translator said earlier that *bellegenzia* means beauty through invention. So are they calling her the Mother of Beautiful Inventions?'

'Close enough,' Ferius replied. 'Now quiet down. I have a feeling this is what we came to see.'

The inventor, Janucha, knelt down to place the box she was holding on the ground before opening it and reaching inside. When she stood again, there was something in her closed hand. She moved to stand behind the large glass, extending her hand towards it before opening up her fingers. What she held matched the image on the painted card the two Argosi had given to Ferius at the travellers' saloon.

It looked surprisingly small – modest, even – and yet almost impossibly beautiful. The bird was constructed from tiny, precise metal parts, as if someone had tried to make the most complex wind-up toy possible and had accidentally transcended what any of us could imagine.

I guess she really is the Mother of Beautiful Inventions.

The crowd looked on as Janucha played with the bird, gently lifting up each mechanical wing and then letting them fall back in place against its metal body. She turned it around behind the massive magnifying glass so that the crowd could observe the elegant design of the thing. It was truly a work of art, and yet the delegates were no more impressed than I was. I mean, sure, it was pretty to look at, but far more remarkable inventions had already been displayed, and as Ferius had said, none of those was going to change the world.

'Oh hells,' Ferius murmured.

'What is it?' I asked, but then Janucha leaned forward and blew on the mechanical bird, or maybe whispered to it. Suddenly it flew into the air, its wings flapping as perfectly and elegantly as any true creature of the skies. Higher and higher it rose, over the heads of the delegates shouting in surprise, ascending until it circled the very top of the amphitheatre. Finally the bird stopped to perch upon one of the thirty-foot high lampposts that illuminated the interior. No one spoke. They just kept staring at the mechanical creature, which was now too far away to see clearly. Maybe it had all been some kind of trick performed with long strands of thin wire pulled by hidden accomplices. Janucha whistled, a light, musical note. The bird once again spread its wings and took flight, gliding down to land back on the inventor's hand. She beamed at the enraptured audience before giving them a simple, short bow.

The entire amphitheatre, all those thousands of people in the audience, sat in stunned silence. All save one. 'Seven damned hells,' Ferius swore again.

'What's the matter?' I asked. 'It's nothing more than what's painted on the card: a mechanical bird.'

The Argosi just kept gazing at the stage, as if staring at it long enough would enable her to formulate a plan. 'The card is wrong, kid. That's not just a mechanical bird, it's—'

'She's brought a machine to life,' Nephenia said. 'It shouldn't be possible.'

'But you're a charmcaster,' I said. 'You spell objects all the time.'

She shook her head. 'I can put a levitation charm on a piece of metal, sure. I could probably figure out a way to make a wing flap or a head to swivel, but all you'd have is a bunch of bits and pieces that moved when you activated the spell; there wouldn't be any intelligence guiding it to make it fly properly. What Janucha's done . . . I can't even think of what to call it. She's brought forth some kind of . . . miracle.'

Our people, the Jan'Tep, don't believe in miracles. I was about to point that out when Ferius said angrily, 'You're not getting it, either of you. This isn't some wondrous creation or beautiful toy she's made.'

'Then what is it?' I asked.

'A discordance. Something that could set off a war. That damned fool has created a new kind of weapon and she doesn't even know it.'

The Inventor

DECEPTION

Discordances are, by their very nature, deceptive. Every imperfect stroke, each shade of colour a fraction too light or too dark, is a question left for you by the Argosi who painted the card. They are the paths you must pursue as you investigate whether this discordance seeks to bring about peace . . . or destruction.

21

A Mother's Invention

'How could a tiny mechanical bird set off a war?'

My question was lost on Ferius. Her gaze was fixed on the delegates who rose to their feet in droves, stabbing the air with bidding sticks laden with gold rings. They fought for attention, bellowing in their respective languages at the bid takers, at Janucha, and even at each other.

The inventor who had set off all this chaos merely smiled at the audience, the mechanical bird still perched on her two fingers.

'Why are they in such a rush to buy the rights for something that doesn't do anything more than a regular bird could?' I shouted to Ferius over the din, but I might as well have been trapped in shadow again for all the good it did me. Nephenia was chewing her lip, head tilted to the side as she looked up at the bird on Janucha's finger. The hyena was mimicking her pose, which would've looked pretty funny were the situation less tense.

'What's goin' on?' Reichis asked, poking his furry muzzle out from under the coat on Nephenia's lap. 'Is there a fight?'

'Not yet,' I replied.

'Oh. Okay.' The squirrel cat's face disappeared back under the coat.

The cacophony died down almost as quickly as it had begun. Over on the stage, Janucha had raised her hands for quiet. She said something in Gitabrian and a moment later the translators were shouting it to their respective sections like generals commanding their troops to stand down. 'There will be no bids today!' the woman at the front of our section declared. Delegates retook their seats, though they didn't look happy about it.

Over that sullen silence Janucha clapped her hands once again and walked to the front of the stage – a dangerous move given that she was holding the object that the delegates so badly desired to possess. When next she spoke it was in Daroman, the one language that almost everyone knows. 'There can be no bids today, my friends, because there is nothing to sell. I have taken only the first step on this wondrous journey.'

A Jan'Tep merchant in our section stood to shout out his complaint. 'Then why show it to us at all? Did you bring us here to mock us?'

The inventor had to wait for the noise to die down before she could answer. 'I do not seek to offend you, my lord,' she said before switching back to her own tongue, which meant I had to wait for the translation. 'In Gitabria, we live for three simple things: to explore, to trade and to discover beauty.' She bowed deeply. 'Forgive me if I have given insult. Our lords mercantile wanted . . .' She hesitated. 'What I mean to say is that *we* wanted to share this great moment with you.' She held her right hand up high and the bird flapped its wings for balance before settling again. 'This contraption of mine may well be the wonder of an age. Look how small it is! And yet, does it not bring your hearts alive? Do not a thousand questions sing in your mind? What does it mean, the existence of this little bird? What wonders might others devise once silly old Janucha has found a way to repeat this most fortunate of accidents?'

A hush spread throughout the crowd. Even to me it seemed a remarkable admission – that someone so admired, so readily praised, would confess that she didn't yet understand her own creation. It was hard not to be in awe of this Credara Janucha zal Ghassan.

'What a bunch of horseshit,' Ferius muttered.

The cynicism in her voice struck a discordant note against the humility of Janucha's sentiment. 'When did you become such a sceptic?' I asked.

Ferius gestured to the crowds. 'Look at what's happening all around you, Kellen. Look how the delegations are nattering among themselves, figuring out ways to ingratiate themselves with Janucha. You think this is Gitabria sharing their discovery with the world? They wouldn't have brought that contraption out here unless they were sure they could make more of them. The only reason they aren't taking bids today is because there ain't enough money in this whole amphitheatre to buy what they plan to sell. That little contraption is a declaration to all other nations that Gitabria intends to be the richest, most powerful country in the world, and all that's left for the rest is to fight over second place.'

'Look,' Nephenia said. 'She's going to speak again.'

The inventor knelt down and set the bird back in its box, eliciting moans from the audience. When she rose again, she spoke with a regret you could hear even before the words were translated. 'My friends, I sense some of you are disappointed in me. Perhaps in Gitabria itself. I give you my word that more will be revealed at the proper time.' She took a step back, clasping her hands together. 'But let me remind all of you of something that I myself had forgotten until recently. Something our respective countries should value above all other prizes.' She beckoned to someone hiding in the wings on the left side of the stage. A girl close to my age stepped out. She had short dark hair that was a close match for the tone of her skin, and though too far away for me to make out clearly, there was something familiar about her. 'My daughter,' Janucha announced. 'Newly returned to us after two long years. She, my friends, is the great work of my life, not some contraption of metal and gears. Many of you have children of your own. As we stand together at the birth of a new age, let us not forget that the greatest wonders any of us will ever encounter could never be devised by some silly old contraptioneer.'

'What a sap,' Reichis chittered from under Nephenia's coat. Too much sentiment will wake him from just about anything.

Janucha's daughter wandered behind the great magnifying glass and now I could see why she looked familiar. Her name was Cressia and I'd met her at the Academy of the Seven Sands. I was pretty sure that she was the reason I'd been coming to Gitabria in the first place. 'Ferius . . .' I began.

'You reckon she's the one, kid?'

When I'd met her she'd seemed clever, kind and a little mischievous. But she hadn't struck me as coming from a particularly wealthy or powerful family compared to the other students there. Now it turned out her mother was quite possibly the most important person in the world. Cressia was a perfect target for one of Dexan Videris's obsidian worms.

'What's wrong?' Nephenia asked. 'Do you know her?'

'Just a second,' I said, and closed my eyes. I began to whisper softly to the sasutzei. The wind spirit was, on the whole, uncooperative, but she had a particular knack for detecting the ethereal connection between two halves of an obsidian worm. If someone was using an onyx bracelet to control Cressia now, the spirit would see it.

'Come on, Suzy. Show me the thread.'

I felt that subtle sensation in my right eye like a cool winter breeze. But when I looked back at the stage, I saw nothing. No wispy black gossamer filament leading from Cressia back to the Jan'Tep territories, which meant no cabal of mages was using a bracelet containing the second half of the worm to control her.

The tension in my chest relaxed. 'She's clean,' I informed Ferius.

'Will someone tell me what's going on?' Nephenia asked.

'I'm sorry, Neph. It's kind of complicated. I'll explain later, I promise.'

Cressia, still standing behind the magnifier, surveyed the crowd. Her eyes settled on me and she smiled in recognition. I waved back. I'd really liked Cressia when I'd met her at the Academy during our enquiries into the shadowblack plague. Even though she'd quickly seen through my attempts at charm, she'd gone along with my ruse, and, I'd thought, maybe even saw me as a potential friend.

So why is she creeping me out?

It was her smile. When she'd first spotted me in the

amphitheatre, her reaction had been one of pleasant surprise. I couldn't say exactly how it had changed in the past few seconds, but there was something almost . . . leering about her expression now. While her mother kept going on and on with platitudes about children and the need for peace, Cressia herself just stood there, watching me. *No,* I realised suddenly. *She's looking past me at someone else.* I turned around in my seat but couldn't see anything other than the rows and rows of benches filled with delegates. Then a small movement in one of the shallow alcoves along the wall of the amphitheatre revealed a figure waiting there, almost indiscernible from the shadows around him. I squinted, trying to make out his face, but all I saw was the muted crimson of his garments.

'What's the deal, kid?' Ferius asked.

'That guy. I saw him in the desert after our fight with the Berabesq Faith—'

The man in red gave a slight nod. I turned back to the stage and saw Cressia return the gesture. Her eyes came back to me and her smile widened. She winked and then stepped out from behind the glass.

An ice-cold wind bloomed in my right eye. When my vision cleared, the sasutzei showed me an eerie wisp of black thread that twisted and turned from the pupil of Cressia's left eye all the way past the doors of the amphitheatre and into the distance beyond, likely all the way to my homeland.

'*Oh, ancestors,*' I swore.

'Kid?' Ferius asked.

I jumped to my feet, bashing into the people seated on the bench in front of me. Ignoring their outraged reactions, I pushed past the delegates in our row and made for the aisle.

No one but me had been paying attention to Cressia. That's why no one else had seen the tiny blade she'd removed from her pocket and hidden in the palm of her hand as she stepped behind her mother.

22

The Assassin

Despite the slim odds of my reaching Janucha in time, I ran to the wide central aisle that led to the stage.

'Kid!' Ferius called out.

'Get the others out of here!' I shouted back.

Okay, how do I do this?

My first thought was just to scream a warning, but there was no way the inventor would hear me over the noise. By the time she noticed me, the guards at the front of the stage would be too busy beating me into the floor to pay attention to what I was saying. Meanwhile, Cressia's blade was concealed in the cuff of her shirt. Another thought occurred to me: what if she'd only shown it to me so I'd come running and get myself arrested?

My other choice was to try to blast her with my spell. This presented two challenges: first, it's hard to toss powder into the air in front of you while you're running, and second, at this distance it was an even chance whether I'd hit Cressia or end up putting a hole in Janucha's chest. *Which would no doubt please whoever's controlling the worm.*

Shouts and warnings in various languages began to follow me as delegates noticed my passage and debated with themselves whether to jump me or wait for the guards to do it for them. A few probably wondered if maybe they could ingratiate themselves with Janucha by killing her would-be assassin. Not a bad scheme, except for the fact that I wasn't the assassin.

That left me with one final option, which was less likely to hit the wrong people and vastly more likely to get me killed. Halfway to the stage, I stopped and pulled powder. A lot of it. The guards had all settled in front, expecting me to try to rush past them. One of them shouted an order and a group of six of them advanced on me.

This is such a lousy plan, I thought as I threw the powders high up into the air in front of me. They collided about three feet above my head. I focused my will and sparked the breath band on my forearm as my fingers formed the spell's somatic shape. '*Carath*,' I whispered.

Engorged on so much powder, the twin fires looked like bloated red and black snakes as they shot out at the stage. Janucha's eyes were on mine, and something in them surprised me: she wasn't scared. She was fascinated. I could almost imagine her mind working, trying to make sense of a young man who'd seemingly come to kill her only to fire a spell high and wide over her head. I wondered if she might have somehow calculated my true target. It didn't really matter though, because there was no time for her or anyone else to do anything about it. The blast destroyed the supports holding the silk-and-wooden dragon above the stage. The mythical creature landed on Janucha and Cressia, enveloping them in fabric, trapping them underneath the weight of its wooden frame.

The bulk of the guards instantly turned their attention to

the inventor's plight, leaping up to the stage to get her out from underneath all that cloth and wood and then surrounding her in case I tried to fire again. Cressia slipped out from under the dragon and briefly tried to push past the guards to get to Janucha, but had to give up when a second group of guards set themselves to protecting her. Cressia gave me a slight smile. I'm no lip-reader, but I'm pretty sure she mouthed the words 'Shrewdly done, traitor'. For sure the word 'traitor' was in there somewhere.

I enjoyed a very brief moment of satisfaction before the first guard slammed into my chest, knocking the wind from my lungs and driving me down to the floor. Soon other guards were on top of me, and more after them – an avalanche of bodies crushing me. There was nothing I could do about it, so I just kept watching Cressia as her expression changed from surprise to confusion and then finally to horror. Whoever had been controlling the worm inside her had made their attempt to kill her mother, and now, having failed, left her with the mess.

Well, some of it they left with me. The guards were intent on landing as many blows as they could before it no longer mattered, which didn't turn out to be very long since the weight of them piled up on me made it impossible to breathe.

Yeah. That was some plan I'd come up with.

23

The Servadi

I awoke in chains.

Again.

Why does this keep happening to me?

This time there were no windows to let in a fresh breeze, no oil lamps to provide me with light. There was certainly no comfortable bed. I was bound to a stiff wooden chair, breathing air so stale it turned to dust in my mouth. I was in absolute darkness.

'Hello?'

No answer. I'd have worried that I was lost in shadow again were it not for the weight of the heavy chains around my shoulders. My hands were lashed behind my back, and someone had wrapped lengths of sharp wire around my fingers to prevent me from forming any somatic shapes. As if that weren't enough, there was some kind of metal apparatus clamped over my mouth to keep me from correctly pronouncing any incantations.

Apparently they don't take too kindly to suspected assassins in this country.

How long had I been in this place? A day? A week? I'd expected a couple of my ribs to get cracked from all those guards piling on me, but while my whole body was sore, nothing felt broken.

The soft tinkling of a bell outside the room was followed by a door opening. As soon as I saw the growing line of light appear I closed my eyes tightly.

Footsteps. Not heavy, but precise. Defined. Military. Another chair, the legs scraping the floor briefly as it was set down – probably right in front of me. No creaking of the wood, so whoever had just sat down probably wasn't very big. *Which might be useful knowledge if I weren't tied up.*

Hands grabbed at the contraption attached to my face. I heard a click, and then it came free. I swallowed spit that tasted like metal.

'Why do you not open your eyes?' a voice asked. I couldn't quite tell if it was male or female, but the words were Jan'Tep – accented though, so not one of my people. An odd courtesy, I thought. *Or maybe just a way to catch me off guard.*

'You've kept me in the dark for a long time. I'm waiting for you to dim the lantern so the light won't blind me.'

'And why would I extend courtesies to a Jan'Tep spy?' Now I was sure the voice belonged to a woman. She spoke in a flat, disinterested way that said she didn't care one bit for my comfort. And yet, a moment later, I could tell the light had dimmed.

I opened my eyes. My first thought, oddly, was that my captor reminded me of Ferius. I couldn't quite tell her age, though she was at least ten years older than me, but the sharp lines of her face and stern eyes made her seem older. She had dark, curly hair that came almost down to her shoulders. That surprised me. I'd been expecting short hair – isn't that what soldiers and police prefer so that there's nothing to pull at in the middle of a fight? Maybe this was some kind of badge of authority. Maybe she was powerful enough *not* to keep it short.

'Something troubles you,' she said.

Only that I'm chained to a chair in some tiny room who knows where, I don't know if my friends are alive or dead, and there's a creepy Gitabrian staring at me like she can't decide which body part to cut off first.

'I like your hair,' I said. *Ancestors, why do I keep talking about people's hair?* Turns out I'm not very good at talking to women even when they're only there to interrogate and torture me.

'Ah,' she said. 'You are more observant than I expected.'

Seriously? 'I like your hair' makes me sound clever?

She took out a coin from her pocket. It was the one the elderly Argosi couple had given me. 'Where did you get this?'

'Never seen it before in my life.'

'No?' She flipped the coin in the air. It came back down just as any other piece of metal would, which was odd – whenever I played with it, the coin seemed to almost hang in the air for a fraction of a second and then spin as it came down. 'They say that in the right hands, a *sotocastra* – in your language a "warden's coin" – can open any door or lock. Alas, I do not have the touch.' She tossed it in the air again. 'Perhaps because I am neither a coin dancer nor a spy.'

'Neither am I.'

She favoured me with a brief smile, as though the two of us were both in on the joke. 'Is that so? Well, I suppose there aren't many *castradazi* left these days. Since you say the coin's not yours, I suppose I'll hang on to it until I find its rightful owner.'

Crap.

She pulled a small case out from behind the chair. Metal instruments clinked and clanged inside, inviting visions of untold torments that sent a shiver up my spine. 'My name is Servadi Zavera té Drazo,' the woman said. 'I am a minor functionary within the Cazaran security forces. This place . . . well, it has a name, but not one that would give you any solace. Know that it is impenetrable, including by your Jan'Tep sorcery.'

'I feel safer already.'

If she found that funny she betrayed no evidence of it. 'I will ask you certain questions and you will answer them.'

She didn't even have to make it sound like a threat. The links of the chains around my torso were starting to bang together from my shaking. *Stop*, I told myself. *Be like Ferius. The more frightened she is, the more audacious she acts.*

Swagger, as she likes to call it, is one of the seven Argosi talents. Probably her favourite. I quickly worked through the parts of my interrogator's name. Servadi must be some kind of title. Drazo would be the family name, té referred to her status within the family, but since it wasn't zal like Janucha, it meant she wasn't the head of her house. All that left was her given name. 'Nice to meet you, Zavera,' I said. 'I'd kiss your hand like a proper gentleman, only –' I rattled the chains – 'I'm indisposed.'

'*Arta valar*,' she said with a slight smile. 'The Argosi talent for daring. It won't serve you here, I'm afraid.'

I don't think I managed to hide my surprise. She knew a lot about me, and probably about Ferius too, which wasn't exactly fair since I knew almost nothing about her. There was only one way I was going to get any information out of my captor. 'You said you had questions?'

She removed something from her case: a long, narrow object with a sharp end that glinted in the lamplight.

'No, please!' I cried out. So much for my arta valar.

Zavera ignored my pleading and took out a second item: a tiny bottle.

She's going to use pain poisons on me. Ancestors, why do you never—

When she removed the third item – a small notebook – my fear-addled brain finally worked out that the terrifying implement of torture that had very nearly made me piss myself was a pen, and the bottle of horrific poison was just ink.

'You will name for me the lords magi of your clan,' Zavera said. 'You will identify their specialties in magic, the bands they have sparked. You will list all other Jan'Tep mages of whom you have information, especially any details of their lives that they might prefer kept secret.'

'Wait, why would I know—'

'You will provide me with the Argosi path of the woman who calls herself Ferius Parfax. You will name all other Argosi you have met, including their paths. You will list for me all the Argosi discordance cards created within the last seven years and who holds them.'

Why did she want all of this? And why *seven* years? If she thought I had all this secret knowledge, why not ask for all of it? 'But I don't know any of this stuff! Ferius is just a card-playing swindler. I've never met an Argosi!'

All lies of course, but things were getting dangerous and it was time to play to my strengths. 'And while we're at it, do you really think any lord magus of the Jan'Tep would let a failed initiate know their secrets? I'm just a spellslinger, lady. I got stuck in the wrong place and the wrong time and—'

A bell – the same one I'd heard before, though the tinkling pattern was different this time. Zavera's eyes narrowed for an instant, and I saw irritation there. 'Let us begin.' She dipped the pen in the bottle of ink. 'Start with Ferius Parfax. Tell me everything you know about her.'

The bell sounded again, repeating its most recent pattern. It seemed to annoy Zavera, which was good, because it gave me a moment to put several things together at once. It wasn't relief, exactly, but figuring out something the other person doesn't want you to know when they have you at their mercy is strangely reassuring. 'No, Zavera, I don't think I'm going to be answering any of your questions today.'

She looked at me in the way a sleepy janitor might look at the last bit of dust waiting to be swept from the floor at the end of the workday. She set down the pen and notebook and reached into her case. What she removed this time was definitely *not* a writing instrument and its design suggested it could do a great deal of damage to me.

The next time the bell outside tinkled, Zavera ignored it and came to stand behind me. 'You will forgive me, I hope. What I do is for my country.' She reached around and squeezed my jaw so hard my mouth opened of its own accord. With her other hand she reached in with what I could now clearly see was a pair of hooked pliers.

'You really want me to tell you what I know?' I asked, my teeth clattering against the pliers.

Zavera removed the hooked instrument, but kept it close. 'Speak.'

'You're not some minor functionary. You're part of the

Gitabrian secret police. My guess is you might even be their commander. And all those nonsense questions about the lords magi of my clan? That was to distract me from what you really want to know, which is about Ferius Parfax. Oh, and I know one more thing.'

She let the hooked pliers drift up to my right eye. 'What would that be?'

The bell outside the room tinkled a fourth time, more insistent this time. At least, that's what I hoped. 'There's someone in this building with more influence than you and in about thirty seconds they're going to walk through that door. When they do, I'm willing to bet that this little theatre piece of yours is coming to an end.'

Zavera leaned in closer and whispered in my ear. 'You rely too heavily on your arta valar.' She stroked my cheek with the pliers. 'Someone *did* come here demanding to see you. A representative of your own people. I was curious as to why my own government would grant him access to this place, but such diplomatic niceties are beyond me. Nevertheless, this individual is, I sense, rather exceptional, though his taste in clothing is a bit . . . garish.'

Garish? She's talking about the man in red!

When the bell rang again, Zavera dropped the pliers in my lap. 'He was insistent that I leave my instruments here.'

Terror began to wash over me like waves from an endless black ocean. *Damn my stupid, stupid arrogance. Why did I think I could bluff a torturer? Bloody Ferius with her Argosi nonsense. And Reichis, too! He's the one who keeps telling me to be more fierce.*

A latch opened and the door swung open. The light was so bright I could only see the shadows of three figures. Two of them stood with the stiff-backed posture of soldiers, the third was larger. And louder. 'Enough!' declared Credara Janucha zal Ghassan. 'You asked to speak to the boy and I allowed it, but this goes too far, *Servadi* Zavera.'

The emphasis on servadi told me it wasn't a very high title. On the other hand, Janucha was probably severely underestimating Zavera's actual rank.

'Contraptioneer, I was promised two hours with the prisoner.'

'And you may have it,' Janucha replied. 'Some other time, over tea and cake in a very public place with you on your very best behaviour and me watching over you. You'll be paying for the tea and cake, by the way.'

'This Jan'Tep spy attempted to murder you, Credara Janucha. Your value to our nation is—'

'High enough that if I express my displeasure to the lords mercantile they will ship you off somewhere very unpleasant. Servadi Zavera, you are dismissed.'

With what I thought was remarkable aplomb, Zavera gave a short bow and placed her instruments back in her case before turning to leave. She paused at the doorway, and said to me, 'Your *arta precis* is quite good, but it is incomplete.'

Arta precis was the Argosi talent for perception – for seeing what others don't want seen. So I guess that was a compliment. Sort of. 'Hey!' I shouted to her.

'Yes?'

'You still have my coin.' I looked over at the two guards standing in the doorway. 'And somebody better give me my hat back.'

Zavera turned, and smiled in a way that was almost – *almost* – friendly. She reached into her pocket and tossed the coin at me. It landed on my lap next to the hooked pliers. 'Too much arta valar can be a dangerous thing, Kellen Argos. I look forward to our next meeting.'

'Yeah? Well, maybe *I'm* looking forward to . . .'

Oh, ancestors, just shut up when you're ahead. You sound like a squirrel cat.

24

The Credara

Once Zavera and the soldiers were gone, Janucha took the pliers from my lap. She used them to pick up the coin and place it in the pocket of her coat.

'That's mine,' I said. Pushing my luck probably wasn't a good idea, but when you have a squirrel cat for a business partner you get tired of your stuff being stolen all the time.

'A small price to pay, I think, for removing Servadi Zavera from your rather long list of immediate concerns.'

She had a point.

The inventor paced around the room. Sometimes she'd pause and look down at me as though searching for the right way to begin the conversation. Each time she'd briefly reach into one of the pockets of her bulky coat – but not the one where she'd put my coin – before resuming her walk.

'May I see it?' I asked after a few rounds of these dizzying perambulations.

Janucha shook her head. 'The sotocastra is banned in Gitabria.'

'I meant the bird.'

She froze. 'You think I would brazenly carry something so precious on my person?'

'Judging by the way you keep patting your pocket, I doubt you ever let it out of your sight.'

The inventor looked oddly relieved, as if I'd freed her from her own invisible chains. She reached into her pocket and gently withdrew her prized invention.

The bird was even more wondrous to behold up close than it had been at the exhibition. Hundreds of delicate steel feathers adorned its wings. The feet were like ornate bronze sculptures with articulated joints. Janucha placed the bird upon her shoulder and sat down in the chair opposite me. 'Servadi Zavera warned me that the Argosi are particularly observant.'

'I'm not Argosi.'

'No? Then what are you?'

I rattled the chains around my shoulders. 'A prisoner.'

Janucha winced as if I'd struck a blow. 'I . . . regret the treatment you have received at the hands of our secret police. The unveiling of my little contraption has caused something of an unexpected sensation among the foreign delegations.'

'Not that unexpected,' I said. 'You never wanted to show off the bird in the first place.'

Janucha tensed up. The bird had to flap its wings to keep its balance. 'Why do you say this?'

'The translators,' I replied. 'Throughout the presentations they spoke smoothly, but when the uproar began, you started to say something about the lords mercantile and they hesitated.'

'There . . . has been some debate between my government and myself regarding how much to share of my discovery.'

'You wanted to keep it quiet.'

She nodded.

'Because you knew how the delegates would react.'

The inventor chuckled. 'No, never that.' She raised her right hand close to her shoulder and the bird hopped onto her index finger. 'I feared they would laugh at me for wasting their time with such a trifling contraption.'

'I'm guessing you overestimated their sense of humour.'

She sighed. 'Machines. Engineering. These I understand. My husband says the one contraption I cannot decipher is the human heart. I fear he is correct.' She whispered to the bird and thin silver lids slid back to reveal a pair of golden eyes. Janucha's gaze was both adoring and sorrowful as she stroked its head. 'Who would have thought the flapping of tiny wings could raise such a hurricane?'

The Argosi, I thought, but I didn't say it aloud. Ferius says that sometimes it's best to be the silence between the notes.

'The Daroman empire's delegation has demanded proof that I am not using my designs to fabricate weapons,' Janucha went on. 'When they look upon my invention, they do not see its wonder, but rather a sword in the hands of a potential enemy.'

Ferius also says that being silent isn't always the same thing as not speaking. 'And the other delegations?' I asked.

The inventor's expression turned sour. 'I'm told the Berabesq viziers are drafting a decree declaring my little bird an affront to their God. They claim that I consort with demons.'

'People say that about me all the time.'

Apparently Janucha didn't get the joke. She held the bird closer to me. 'Tell me what the Jan'Tep see when they look upon her.'

Finally we had come to the reason for her visit. The Gitabrians must have figured out that Cressia's mind had been taken over. Only one nation on the continent had that power. 'They see a new form of magic,' I replied. 'One my people don't understand. They see a threat to the very basis of what makes the Jan'Tep special.'

'Might they go so far as to kill for it?'

'Without question.'

She looked troubled by the speed of my answer. 'And if obtaining it meant murdering innocents? Would they do that as well?'

Even after all these months, Revian's death was still fresh in my mind. 'Without hesitation.'

Janucha's hand began to shake. The bird, finding its perch no longer stable, flapped its metal wings in search of a more reliable resting place. That turned out to be my shoulder. When those golden eyes peered back at me, it was like looking into the heart of an impossibility. Nephenia had said that with dozens of different charms you could bring about all the physical aspects of the bird, but not the intelligence behind it. Where did that come from?

The sensation of a gentle breeze on my right eye signalled the sasutzei was awake. Perhaps she too was trying to understand it.

'I need your help,' Janucha said at last.

'I tried helping you once,' I said, then gently, so as not to dislodge the bird, I rattled the chains. 'It didn't turn out so well for me.'

She seemed surprised by that, and perhaps even annoyed – as if I'd just demanded an apology. She took the bird from me and placed it back in her pocket. 'Do you know what would happen if your people were to assassinate the daughter of the master contraptioneer of Gitabria? My government would be forced to declare war upon the Jan'Tep!'

'Credara Janucha, in the past twelve months, my people have tried to kill me more times than I can count. Within twelve *hours* of arriving in Gitabria I was beaten, imprisoned and threatened with torture. Frankly, the thought of two lunatic nations going to war with each other doesn't hold nearly as much terror for me as it used to.'

'Young man, if I were to leave this room, I assure you Servadi Zavera would teach you the very meaning of terror.'

Here's another thing most people don't know about fear: while you never get used to it, there's only so much of it your brain can handle. After a while you actually get bored of being afraid. 'Then close the door on your way out, Credara Janucha. The light is interfering with my nap.'

She rose and walked to the door. A sudden chill in my guts told me I'd been wrong about the whole getting-bored-of-being-afraid thing. Not begging Janucha to come back was very nearly the hardest thing I'd ever had to do. But if we started this way – with threats and intimidation – I'd end up as little more than a pawn in these people's games. I had to make sure I left this place free.

Janucha stopped. 'My daughter . . . once the fever left her . . . she told me she had met you before, that you were a friend. Would you stand by as my enemies torment her to get to me?'

'You speak of friendship, Credara. But where are *my* friends?'

'Unharmed. Swear you'll save my daughter and I will take you to them.'

'I require proof.'

The inventor shook her head. 'As you rightly pointed out, we are in a prison right now – a prison my people keep secret for a reason. As I cannot bring your friends here, I cannot imagine what evidence I could offer to assure you of their well-being.'

She turned and peered at me as if she were probing the tiny gears of a stalled clock rather than gazing into the face of another human being. But this too told me something about her. 'You knew before you came through that door that we'd arrive at this impasse, Credara Janucha. Which means you already have something to show me.' Before she could respond, another piece of the puzzle came to me. 'And the fact that you haven't already offered that proof means you don't understand it.'

And who do I know whose messages never make any sense? 'You might as well just deliver Ferius Parfax's message now and get it over with,' I said.

A small smile crept onto Janucha's face. 'She warned me you were annoyingly perceptive.' She came back to the centre of the room and moved her chair out of the way. 'Very well then. Behold the Argosi's message.'

The inventor stretched her right arm out in line with her body, palm up, then placed her left hand on her hip and extended her right foot, the toe of her heavy boot barely touching the floor. She took a deep, uncertain breath, and with that, Gitabria's master contraptioneer – quite possibly the most important person in the world – began to dance around my cramped cell. She swayed to the tempo of a silent tune, stepped and turned and pranced about. Her expression was one of intense and almost endearing concentration.

I vaguely recognised the particular dance, having spent more than my share of nights on the road learning such things from Ferius. The inventor wasn't doing a half-bad job of it actually, though it was a struggle not to laugh now that

I knew what was going on. I let her continue for a couple of minutes before I couldn't stand it any more. 'You can stop now, I believe you.'

She came to a stop in front of me. 'You'll help my daughter?'

'I will.'

The inventor looked suspicious. 'But I haven't finished the dance. The Argosi was very specific on this point: if I failed to perform the entire choreography, her message to you would be incomplete.'

I had to smile at that. 'Master Contraptioneer, I understood everything Ferius wanted me to know the moment you started dancing.'

'Then why would she . . . ?' Janucha's words trailed off. Then she said something in her own language that I was fairly confident was a string of very forceful curses.

'Yeah,' I said. 'The Argosi do that to you sometimes.'

25

The Daughter

It's funny how things work out sometimes. A few hours before I'd been chained up in a cell inside a Gitabrian prison so secret they'd blindfolded me before returning me to the city to make sure I couldn't reveal its location. Now I was inside the palatial home of their most esteemed citizen, seated in a comfortable chair opposite her daughter – by all accounts the person Janucha held most precious in all the world – who was now the one in shackles.

'Hey, Kellen,' she said.

'Cressia.'

She looked reasonably calm, despite the restraints – which I noticed included spelled copper wire. The Gitabrians must've paid a pretty price to some Jan'Tep merchant for it. My people aren't noted for their charity.

'Am I going to die?' she asked.

My instinct was to tell her that of course she wasn't going to die and that I had it all under control. But I'd spent a good part of the last six months trying to get the obsidian worms out of people. Sometimes we arrived too late. Other times . . . well, it was a coin flip if their bodies and minds were strong enough to survive the procedure.

'Well?' she asked.

'I don't know. I hope not.'

She looked away, at the sprawling room that I'd been informed was her mother's workshop. Janucha's home was in the most prestigious part of the city, meticulously carved into the very cliff walls of the gorge beneath the eight bridges. The workshop was practically the size of a barn and chaotically – if somehow methodically – furnished. I counted six different workbenches, each of a different design and clearly intended for a particular type of experimentation. One had tools for working metal, another a large magnifying glass attached to an articulated wooden mount. The room featured both a kiln and a forge. Racks upon racks of exotic metals, small glass tubes, bottles of varying colours and assorted braziers filled every alcove. The walls were covered in pinned sketches of mechanical designs. Some were merely functional, others unnervingly beautiful.

'So,' Cressia said, turning her gaze back to me, 'I guess you're not really a philosophy student.'

On the day we first met, back at the Academy of the Seven Sands, I'd pretended to be a prospective student. After all of her friends had failed to guess my chosen subject (to be fair to them, there hadn't been a right answer), Cressia had suggested philosophy. Because I'd liked her, I'd agreed. 'Actually, that's not really far from the truth.'

'Why do I have the feeling that you and "the truth" have only a passing acquaintance?'

Because I'm an inveterate liar. 'Maybe you're just suspicious by nature.'

That got me a raised eyebrow. 'We barely know each other, Kellen, and yet you sent my mother away so you could come in here alone, knowing I was chained to a chair? In what culture is that considered appropriate?'

She had a point, but, ancestors, was anyone ever going to cut me some slack in this country?

'Cressia, you have something in your eye called an obsidian worm. A man named Dexan Videris devised a means to implant one half in his victims and the other inside a bracelet made of onyx. By means both natural and magical, it acts like a kind of infection, taking root inside your mind. Whichever mage holds the bracelet possesses the means to control the worm. So whenever you get the attacks—'

'But I haven't had any attacks. I'm not—'

'They probably felt like headaches or unusual pains in your eye. You might've thought you had a fever and were hallucinating. Visions. Voices. They're *not* hallucinations though, Cressia. Whoever commands the worm can see through your eyes, hear what you hear. Worse, they can make you do things you don't want to do.'

She bit her lower lip. 'My father says they found a knife hidden in my shirtsleeve. Kellen, I've never owned a knife in my life. How could I have gone out, bought one, carried it with me and then . . . ? What does it say about me that someone could so easily make me . . . make me try to . . . ?'

'It's not your fault. The longer the obsidian worm lives in a person's eye, the more powerful its influence becomes. Most of the people we've found over the past six months succumbed to its control far sooner than you. I'm amazed you held out as long as you did.'

She was quiet for a while, and the awkwardness of me sitting alone with her while she was chained up in this gigantic room with its odd tools and instruments – half of which looked scarier than anything in Zavera's case – made me incredibly uncomfortable. I kept my mouth shut though. She had to come to this on her own.

'You have a cure?' she asked.

'It's more of a procedure.'

'Does it hurt?'

'Tremendously.'

'Is it dangerous?'

'Incredibly.'

She took in a lot of shallow breaths. Even with the darkness of her skin, I could see her face had grown pale. The chains rattled ever so slightly. 'I guess that explains why you wanted to speak to me alone first, right? To give me the chance to scream my head off about this before I embarrassed myself in front of my family?'

'To give you the choice. Cressia, I'm not a doctor. I'm not even a proper mage. Gitabria's probably got thousands of physicians. Maybe one of them could find a less dangerous solution.'

She was blinking a lot, and her eyes didn't look like they were focusing on anything, but still she gave a dismissive snort. 'I forgot what a terrible liar you were.'

'I need you to tell me what you want me to do.'

'Take it out of me of course! Get this thing out now, Kellen!' Her voice rose until she was practically screaming. 'Get it out! Please, get it . . .' Her breathing slowed. She sat there quietly for a while, then shook her head. 'No.'

'No?'

'You tell a good story, Kellen. I mean, this thing about mystical worms and magical bracelets . . . But you know what I just realised? The only thing I really know about you – the one incontrovertible fact – is that you're a liar. You lied to all of us at the Academy. You must've lied or stolen a delegate's coin to get into the Grand Exhibition.' She paused, staring at me as if waiting for a denial. When it didn't come, she asked, 'Is this how you make your living? You travel around looking for marks and tell them that without your "procedure" they'll die or become slaves or something?'

'Cressia, I know you're scared, but this is real.'

'Really? Then show me proof. Take that mirror off the workbench and show me this worm in my eye. I don't have any markings like you have, or like Seneira had. Come on, show me!'

'I can't. Dexan Videris used an obscurement spell to hide them.'

'Oh, isn't that convenient? How would you even know about this mystical nonsense, Kellen? Do the Jan'Tep really let someone who's barely even sparked their breath band call themselves a *mage*? Aren't you really a Sha'Tep? A servant?' She began to sob. 'Why are you doing this to me, Kellen? I was nice to you, back at the Academy. I never did anything to hurt you.'

'You didn't . . . Cressia, I swear, I would never—' I stopped.

'What?' she demanded.

'Nothing, it's just . . . your performance was really smooth.'

My casual indifference horrified her. 'What are you talking about?'

I leaned forward, staring into her eyes, struggling to see some sign of the obsidian worm wriggling around inside. 'I've been spending the last six months dealing with victims of the worm. Some of them slipped in and out of your thrall right in front of me, but I've never seen you take control this seamlessly. A minute ago, Cressia was here with me. Now it's you. I honestly couldn't tell at first. Thing is, though . . .' I held up my arms, which were covered by my shirtsleeves. 'How would Cressia even know I'd only sparked my breath band?'

Even then I wasn't completely certain. Maybe she'd heard about my band from Ferius or Nephenia while I was held in that prison cell. But Cressia – or rather, the person speaking through her – dropped the act. A smile, very slight. Reserved. The way a Jan'Tep is taught to smile. 'Oops.'

I got up from the chair and retrieved the small tray upon which I'd set out the various tools and metallic ink compounds I'd taken from Dexan Videris. Three small braziers melted the inks. Next to each one waited a sterilised steel needle. All that was left was for me to begin working the accompanying spells, and then to inflict on Cressia a cure that would surely feel like torture.

Her head leaned back and she stared up at the ceiling as if bored by my theatrics. 'Go away, Kellen. You're too late. The girl is ours.'

I dipped one of the needles in molten copper. The first step was to counteract the spell that kept the worm invisible. This involved pressing the needle into the skin around her eye until the black markings were forced to appear. From there . . . *Don't overthink it. One step at a time.*

'Run away, little spellslinger. This one is lost to you.'

Despite having gone through this before, I could never shake the eerie feeling that speaking to someone through another person's body made me a kind of accomplice. It set my nerves on edge and caused my hands to shake. 'You might as well get your threats out while you can, because I'm getting pretty good at this. In a few minutes you'll—'

'In a few minutes the girl will be dead.'

I froze. *It's a ruse. They're trying to rattle you.*

'You're lying,' I said.

A self-satisfied smirk appeared on Cressia's lips. 'Well, you've got a great deal of experience with lying, Kellen of the House of Ke, even Cressia knows that. Let's play a game, shall we? I'll tell you three things. Two of them will be lies, and one will be truth. All you have to do is tell me when I've told the truth and that will be the end of our game.'

I brought the needle closer, intent on silencing the voice.

'A pity. She really did like you, you know. Of course, not in *that* way. But I think you and Cressia might have been good friends one day. Had you not murdered her.'

I hesitated, then stepped back. 'Tell me your lies then.'

'Very wise. The first proposition: Kellen, son of Ke'heops, is a true Jan'Tep mage.'

Well, that one was a lie, for sure.

'The second proposition: you are a faithful son of the House of Ke.'

It would be . . . difficult to believe that was true.

'Really? Both are lies? Well then, that only leaves the third proposition: this girl is ours now. Completely. Utterly. While you may have interfered with some of our other investments, this one has had time to grow and now we will collect our profit.'

'And here I thought you said you were only going to tell two lies.'

The smile on Cressia's face widened until it became almost obscene. In that instant I knew I'd made a mistake. They'd wanted this, wanted me to challenge them so they could prove she was beyond my help. 'No, wait, I belie—'

'Too late,' said the voice.

26

The Third Lie

It began as a darkening around the irises of Cressia's eyes, the deep brown turning to pure obsidian. She screamed as black tears the consistency of oil dripped down her cheeks. When the drops fell from her jaw, they evaporated into a shadowy mist. I put the copper-dipped needle back on the tray and took a second one that I dipped in molten silver – the metal used to extract the worm. But as I came closer, the black mist set me coughing uncontrollably, scalding my lungs. I could see the faint beginnings of burn marks on Cressia's cheeks. Even though every part of her shook uncontrollably from the agony, she stopped screaming. 'When the worm has fully . . . settled into its new home,' the voice said, calm and controlled despite Cressia's trembling, 'it begins to feast on its host, and in so doing, develops some rather wondrous abilities.'

'Stop it! I believe you. I won't try to remove the worm!'

Her mouth opened wide, so very wide, and oily black tendrils emerged, reaching for me. I stumbled back to get out of the way. My hands dropped the needle I'd been holding and instinctively felt for the powders at the sides of my belt.

'Go ahead,' the voice said, the words slurred like a drunk's because the black tendrils were making it impossible for her mouth to form the proper shapes.

Her eyes were bleeding black tears freely now, and the room had filled with their shadowy mist, choking me. In a moment I'd have to flee the room and leave her here alone. 'Please, just tell me what you want!' I coughed.

The doors to the workshop burst open and Janucha raced in, followed by a man who looked to be about my father's age, though slender and clean-shaven. 'Cressia! By all that's decent, what have you done to her?'

'Oh, good. Daddy's here!' The tremors shaking Cressia's body increased as the black tendrils emerging from her mouth danced in the air.

'Damn you, stop this!' the man said, grabbing hold of my arm. He was surprisingly strong.

'Altariste, husband, it is not the boy's doing,' Janucha said. Her reaction to all this was the complete opposite of his. She examined everything in the room – the shadowy mist, the black tears down her daughter's cheeks, the tools and liquid metals I'd laid out to remove the worm. She took it all in with an almost perverse dispassion, seemingly trying to calculate the way to her child's rescue.

'Too late, Mummy! Shouldn't have made that little birdy!'

Altariste let go of me and made a dash for Cressia, but the black tendrils slammed into him, tossing him aside. Janucha helped him up. 'Do not do that again, husband.' I would've expected him to rail at her for her lack of response to their daughter's suffering, but instead he nodded and took his place beside her.

'Go away, Mummy,' Cressia said drunkenly, the black tendrils from her mouth waving at her. 'I want to talk to Kellen, not you. Get out before I . . .' The tendrils began to bloat, and I could see poor Cressia's neck expanding as if it were about to split open.

The inventor didn't hesitate, not even for a moment. She took her husband's arm and led him out of the room, backing away as she closed the double doors behind her. She locked eyes with me, and in that moment I understood her message clearly: *If I am denied a mother's rightful fear and fury in the face of my child's suffering, then you had damned well better find an answer to this atrocity.*

'She's gone,' I said. 'Talk to me. Tell me what you want!'

Suddenly the tendrils shrunk, almost withering. Slowly, horribly, they retreated back inside Cressia's mouth. Her throat expanded and contracted over and over as the mages controlling her forced her to swallow the worm's tendrils back into herself. When it was done, she gave a sigh. 'There, now was that really so hard, Kellen of the House of Ke? Can we not speak as friends now?'

'Yes,' I relented. 'Let's speak as friends.'

That earned me a nod of approval. 'First, you will destroy the inventor's abhorrent creation. Crush it. Burn it. Drown the contraption in acids if necessary, but ensure that whatever magic gives it the illusion of life is utterly destroyed.'

'You're wasting your time,' I said, giving the words just a hint of derision. 'I've seen the mechanical bird up close. It's a toy. A few gears and springs cheaply charmed and triggered by specific words Janucha uses to make it seem as if—'

Cressia – or rather the mage controlling her – laughed. 'For a traitor, you are inadequate even at deception.' The hysterics stopped as quickly as they had begun. 'Your second task will be to secure all of the inventor's notes and burn them.' Cressia's eyes darted around the room. 'While you're at it, obliterate this place. It's disgusting.'

She closed her mouth then, and eased back in the chair. Somehow I knew that wasn't the end though. This pause in the list of demands was either for dramatic effect or to test me, to see if I was smart enough to figure out there was more. But I'd finished with Jan'Tep tests the day I'd left my clan. I started for the door. 'Well, if that's everything, I'd best—'

'One final task will be required.'

I turned back. Cressia was smiling, which made what they forced her to say next all the more obscene. 'The inventor, Credara Janucha zal Ghassan, must take her own life.' A pause. 'Or you can do it for her. We don't mind either way.'

'But why? If she swears not to—'

'Even without her research, the inventor could still be compelled by her people to repeat the experiments. Their secret police can be . . . very persuasive.' A slight giggle. 'They might even threaten her daughter.'

'You're out of your mind,' I shouted. It was a dangerous possibility: what if this *wasn't* some grand and carefully thought-out plan? What if the mages controlling the worms were insane and now just playing games with their victims?

'Not only am I perfectly sane, Kellen, what we do – *everything* we do – is for the good of our own people.' Another pause. More theatricality. 'For the good of all peoples actually, even the Gitabrians.'

'Since when do the Jan'Tep care about anyone but themselves?' I asked.

'We care about preserving the natural order. Should Gitabria ascend, either the Daroman empire or the Berabesq theocracy will be roused to respond. Escalation will follow and war will be inevitable.' Cressia's eyes glanced down at her body. 'You care about this girl? Millions will die if her mother continues down this reckless path.'

'You don't know that. She hasn't even—'

'Why don't you have your little Argosi friend explain to you how it works?'

Ferius's words when she'd first seen the mechanical bird came back to me: *'The damned fool has created a new kind of weapon and she doesn't even know it.'*

I considered the mages' arguments, looking for signs that might have slipped through the glib words, that might give me some clue as to their identity. But there was only one real flaw in all of this, and one question for me to ask: 'Why didn't you tell Janucha all this? Why use me as your conduit?'

'Gitabrians underestimate the power of Jan'Tep magic. The inventor's instinct will be to believe that, given time, she can out-manoeuvre us or find some means to disable our spells. You will convince her otherwise. And, should she resist – should her obedience to her masters exceed her love for her daughter – you will do what is necessary.'

There was a depraved intimacy to the words, as though we were co-conspirators setting out our plan. 'I'm not some damned Jan'Tep spy or assassin. You can't expect me to—'

Cressia's eyes rolled back into her skull. Her body began to shake, the jerking motion so severe I worried she'd snap her own neck. Even through this, they made her speak. 'The worm begins to reach into her heart,' she said, the words vibrating from her convulsions. 'It won't be long now.'

'Stop!' I screamed. 'I'll kill you for this! I swear to our ancestors, I'll murder every one of you!'

A trembling, fading laughter. 'Really? A moment ago you expressed outrage at such notions. Besides, we are thousands of miles away.'

'Then I'll find you. I'll—'

'Watch closely now, Kellen, watch as the light fades from her eyes.' A pause. 'Almost there. Time to say goodbye.'

'Wait! Wait, please! Make the worm stop! You get nothing if she's dead!'

The shaking halted, and I could see Cressia's eyes again, though the irises were still as black as coal. Her chest was pumping like bellows. 'Then . . . let us both . . . ensure . . . the girl lives. Convince Janucha of our determination. Ensure the inventor does what is right, and thus prevent the deaths of the many rather than the one.'

The black fled from Cressia's eyes and the lids slipped closed. Her head fell back. The trauma must have left her unconscious.

It took me several seconds to remember to breathe. My hands shook. My whole body began to shiver uncontrollably as the horror of what my own people had visited on Cressia replayed itself over and over in my mind.

It's too much. I can't do this any more.

I wasn't some heroic mage like the ones in the stories I'd grown up on as a child. I wasn't even an Argosi like Ferius. I was just a seventeen-year-old outcast, trapped inside the machinations of great nations. 'Why me?' I cried out, so loud that I was glad there was no one to hear me sobbing. 'Why in all the hells are you forcing me to be part of your damned plans?'

Suddenly Cressia's head came back up and her eyes opened wide. She grinned, her teeth blackened from the oil of the worm's tendrils. 'Because you are a turncoat, Kellen of the House of Ke. It is only fitting that we should bind you to our service for the benefit of the very people you betray at every turn.'

The eyes closed again as she slumped back into unconsciousness. I watched her, searching for any sign that this was another ruse, but she was asleep this time. This last piece of theatrics had been to ensure I understood their command over Cressia was absolute. There would be no word shared between her and Janucha that they could not hear, nothing she could see that they would not see, and nothing she did without their express consent.

They were in control now.

27

The Alloys

Janucha and her husband were waiting in the hall for me as I left the workshop. Nephenia rushed past them, her hyena close behind. 'Kellen, are you all right?' she asked. 'I heard you screaming and then . . .' She hesitated, but not in the way people do after being afraid you'd died. More like when they're slightly embarrassed for you.

Reichis, perched on the flat crown atop an arched window that looked out onto the gorge, confirmed my fears. 'We all heard you blubbering.'

Reflexively I reached up to wipe at my eyes, which only made things worse.

Cressia's father stepped forward. 'Forgive me,' he began, then proceeded to butcher my name. 'Magizier Kellen fal Ke té Jan'Tep, is it?'

'Just Kellen is fine.'

'Ah, yes, as you say. I am Credaro Altariste té Ghassan. I must apologise. When I entered the workshop . . . what I saw unnerved me. I overreacted.'

Janucha took his hand. 'You are a father, Altariste, one whose love for his daughter overtook him. There is no shame in this.' She sighed. 'Let there be one of us at least who is guided by the heart and not always the mind.'

The smile Altariste gave her was as much one of admiration as affection, and made me feel as if I were spying on someone's private moment. Fortunately, Janucha put me out of my misery. 'We heard the demands they made of you. No doubt these mages believe this information will cause me to act rashly. They will find I am not so easily beguiled.'

'My wife possesses the greatest mind of our generation,' Altariste declared. 'Hers is a genius that comes not once in a hundred years.'

I wasn't entirely sure that geniuses were any less prone to being manipulated, but I let that go.

'If these fools believe they can command the death of Gitabria's master contraptioneer then they are truly mad,' he added.

I got the sense he might have gone on at length had Janucha not interrupted. 'No, husband. Lunatics do not have the capacity for such finely tuned levels of control over the world around them.' She turned to me. 'Have you any confidence that the ones who possess this onyx bracelet would honour their agreement, if I were to fulfil their requirements?'

'You cannot—'

She cut Altariste off. 'We are merely exploring what is possible, before we decide what is not! Well?' she asked me. 'What do you believe of these mages of yours, Kellen?'

The way she implied a connection between myself and the people hurting her daughter wasn't lost on me. 'I wouldn't trust any of them, Credara Janucha. I've spoken with these mages through the obsidian worms before. They're ruthless and arrogant beyond measure.'

The inventor tapped at her temple. '*Arrogant*. Arrogant is good. Might we perhaps goad them to honour their agreement simply to prove their strength? If you were to imply that failing to do so would be seen as an admission of weakness?'

Ishak gave one of his little barks – an odd noise for an animal that was related more closely to the great cats than to dogs. Nephenia looked down at him, her expression thoughtful.

'What did he say?' I asked.

Altariste stared at me as if I'd lost my mind. 'What would an animal—'

'Ishak says it's the mechanical bird they want,' Nephenia said.

Altariste looked sceptical, but Janucha began pacing excitedly around the hallway. 'Ah, ah ah,' she muttered.

'One of their three conditions was that we destroy it,' I reminded her.

'Yes, yes. They made a great many demands, didn't they? Negotiation is a part of every trade, and they have ensured their opening bid requires something Gitabria could never allow. The lords mercantile would lock me in a cell before they let me destroy my work, let alone take my own life. Yet with all these demands, they leave out the obvious prize: my little *bellegenzia* bird.'

'Because they know we would refuse,' Altariste said angrily.

'Before, of course. But now, with my very life at stake? Everything I could ever do for our people? Perhaps they believe I would become desperate and offer them the bird.' She turned to Nephenia and me. 'Could these mages truly be so conceited as to believe they could—'

Nephenia nodded. 'They will believe that given the bird and enough time they could use silk and iron magic to work out its properties.'

'Interesting,' Janucha said, then repeated the word twice more. 'This gives us something to consider. Insight to work with.' She smiled at Nephenia. 'It is fortunate you were here to provide it.'

'Ishak's the one who figured it out,' Nephenia corrected, grinning as she patted the hyena's head. 'He's clever that way.'

Great. Her familiar's a strategic genius. I looked up at Reichis sitting on his perch atop the window, utterly disinterested in the conversation. *Whereas my squirrel cat business partner mostly just bites me and steals my stuff while I'm asleep.*

Altariste put his hand on Janucha's arm. 'You cannot be giving this serious consideration. Your invention is the pride of our people, the future of our country!'

'No, husband, my contraption was a mistake. A beautiful, miraculous mistake. A hundred times I have tried to repeat the experiment. Each time I have failed, destroying the very metals themselves in the process. The next hundred attempts will end no differently. My designs are flawed. Every one of them.'

'Now it is you who are being illogical, my love,' Altariste said. 'You just need more time. Your discovery will be Gitabria's glory for a thousand years.'

'Alas, it is not time that binds us.' She removed the mechanical bird from her pocket and held it out for our inspection. 'You've shown yourself to be clever, Magizier Kellen – can you discern the second flaw in my country's great ambitions for our future?'

I might have, had Nephenia given me time. 'It's the metals,

isn't it?' she asked, peering closely at the avian contraption. 'Even setting aside the question of how you've given it the will to act on its own, gears and springs wouldn't account for the way it moves. You've been hiring charmcasters to bind the necessary spells onto each mechanism, to make it move, or fly or sing. But ordinary materials of this size can't hold on to a spell.' She held out a hand for the bird. Janucha placed it carefully in her palm. 'These alloys, I've never seen anything like them . . . Am I right that there are five different ones?'

Janucha smiled at me. 'She is clever, this one. She is full of . . . What was it Servadi Zavera called it? Arta precis? Perception?' To Nephenia she added, 'An excellent skill for an inventor. Perhaps you should become a contraptioneer.'

Nephenia beamed. 'I would certainly like to learn some of your techniques if you would allow me, Credara Janucha.'

Reichis jumped off the window arch and landed on my shoulder, sniffing at my face.

'Don't say it,' I warned him.

'In any case,' the inventor went on. 'You are correct. The mechanisms are constructed from the *alción mistivae.* The "exquisite alloys", as you might call them, are forged using methods my people have forgotten, out of rare metals that no longer exist.' She led us to a cupboard just outside her workshop and unlocked the door. As she opened it, dozens and dozens of broken mechanical birds clattered to the stone floor. The metal surfaces looked worn down. Rusted. 'With each failed experiment, the alloys perish,' she said.

Altariste looked troubled by his wife's admission. He knelt and carefully began returning the fragile corpses to their grave inside the cupboard. 'What little of the alloys remains is so rare that it is illegal for anyone but a contraptioneer to possess them.'

'This is the second flaw,' Janucha said, taking the bird back from Nephenia. 'Even if the errors in my designs were found, there simply aren't enough of the raw materials to make more than a few tiny miracles like this one.' She kissed the top of the bird's head. 'You are certainly no cause for war, little one.' She began to place it back in her pocket. Reichis's claws scraped against my shoulder as he launched himself at the bird.

'Stop!' Altariste shouted, horrified, but by then it was over. Janucha had swiftly placed both her hands over the bird and successfully kept it from Reichis's claws. The squirrel cat slid inelegantly down the stiff leather of her coat.

'Reichis! What the hell are you doing?' I demanded.

Without explanation or a trace of shame, the squirrel cat sauntered out of the room.

'I suppose he *is* a predator,' Janucha said, her expression curious as she watched him leave.

'Credara Janucha, I'm so sorry. I don't know what came over him.'

'No harm was done,' she said, secreting the bird away in her pocket. 'You understand now why my work is no threat to anyone. Tell me, is it worth offering those who are tormenting my daughter that which they secretly covet?'

'Neither the lords mercantile nor the secret police would allow it,' Altariste warned. 'Nor will they tolerate the murder of a child of Gitabria by those who would extort from us that which we do not wish to sell.'

'Forgive me, Credaro,' Nephenia began. 'I mean no offence, but would your government truly risk war over the life of one girl?'

Both the inventors were silent for a moment, as if Nephenia's question had crossed some line into the political affairs that separated us from them. 'My husband is correct,' Janucha said. 'We are a nation of traders, not soldiers. But we are also a nation of mothers and fathers.' Her expression turned grim as her eyes sought mine. 'The very instant my daughter dies, Gitabria goes to war.'

28

The Painted Card

All right. This isn't so complicated.

Somewhere, likely thousands of miles away, a cabal of mages was slowly killing Cressia. I just had to find them, knock them around a bit and break the onyx bracelet they were using to control the obsidian worm. Oh, and preferably before she died and two nations went to war.

Easy. You can do this.

No, you can't. Where the hell is Ferius?

I spent the better part of an hour looking for my Argosi mentor, only to find her outside on the stone veranda overlooking the gorge. She stood with her back to me, a thin brush in hand and Reichis on her shoulder. The two of them were peering down at an easel.

'You're painting?' I asked incredulously.

Neither of them so much as spared me a glance. 'Shh,' Reichis hissed. 'Busy.'

It said something about my life that being shushed by a squirrel cat wasn't even the most embarrassing thing that had happened to me that day. I ignored him and focused my ire on Ferius. 'I can't remove the obsidian worm from Cressia's eye,' I informed her. 'Whoever's controlling it is threatening to—'

'Lemme take a wild guess,' she interrupted. 'Those Jan'Tep mages will do all kinds of terrible things to the girl unless you do equally terrible things to the inventor. Meanwhile the lords high whatever of Gitabria are thinking up ways to make a bad situation worse.'

Here's what I hate about Ferius Parfax: one day she lectures you about not being kind enough to other people, the next it's as if she barely notices they exist.

She dipped her brush into a tiny jar of paint. 'You try askin' Suzy to find them mages for us?'

'She can't. The black threads only appear when the obsidian worm is awake and I don't think Cressia will survive another attack.'

'Which will force the Gitabrians to declare war.' Ferius sighed even as she continued her painting. 'Some days I really do believe this whole world is determined to destroy itself just to spite me.'

'So what are we going to do about it?' I asked, approaching the easel to see what was so much more important than murder and warfare. Reichis glared at me as if it were *his* work I was interrupting. Ferius ran her brush in quick, light strokes across the surface of a playing card held in place with small wooden clips. There wasn't room for me to get close enough to see the whole card, but when her brush passed along the edges, I saw the colour change from indigo to a deep azure. The effect was almost hypnotic. After a few more strokes, she set down the brush and took another from inside her waistcoat, this one even smaller – the size of a toothpick with no more than a dozen short strands of what looked like clipped horsehair glued to the end. She reached over to the veranda's flat stone railing where the rest of her little jars were arranged and unsealed one that was black as night. Reichis had to readjust himself to keep from falling off her shoulder. After dipping the little brush inside, Ferius returned to the card. Her strokes were quicker now, tiny flickers near the bottom edge as she wrote words I couldn't see.

'Why are you making another discordance card?' I asked.

'Because my gut tells me that little metal bird isn't the real danger here.' She took a step back to survey her handiwork. 'Well, it's rough and rushed, but Momma always did say that vanity was a chain that bound the truth in illusion.'

I tried to wrap myself around that – both the unintelligible sentiment and the notion of Ferius having a mother. 'Show me,' I said.

She moved aside and what she revealed took my breath away. The lines on the card were fluid and graceful – achingly so. The figure depicted wasn't pretty, yet the rendering made her arresting. The colours of her tools, the subtle shadows cast by the golds and pinks of the sky in the background, all of it was perfect. Even the clothing seemed to take on the textures of linen and leather, of copper buttons and a brass buckle on the belt. The title of the card, written in a script both elegant and dramatic, was 'The Contraptioneer'.

'You think Janucha herself is the discordance?'

Ferius nodded, still carefully assessing her work.

'And *this* is your idea of "rough and rushed"?'

She turned to me, her expression concerned. 'You think it's no good? I could start again, but that would—'

'You used too much blue if you ask me,' Reichis offered sagely.

'Are you mad?' I asked Ferius. 'It's a work of art! I don't think I've ever seen anything more beautifully done.'

Something very strange happened then. Ferius Parfax, Argosi wanderer, gambler and inveterate braggart, blushed. 'It ain't all that.' Before I could comment on this odd behaviour, she picked up the card by the edges, blew on it, and held it out to me.

'What am I supposed to do with it?'

'Make your way to the Bridge of Dice. Towards the northern side of the bridge there's a tent with an all-night card game. Play for a while, and when you spot an Argosi, slip them the card.'

'How would I even recognise them?' I asked.

She raised one eyebrow at me. 'All this time around me and you still can't spot an Argosi?'

'In case you've forgotten, *you're* the only Argosi I know, except for Rosie, I guess, and the two of you have nothing in common. I don't know anything about those other two from the travellers' saloon, but then, they don't look or act like you either.'

That seemed to annoy her. 'Then just stand around until one of them recognises *you*.'

'What about Cressia?' I demanded. 'If she dies—'

'If the Argosi have any information on those mages, they'll give you a card in return.'

'And if they don't?'

'Then this whole place goes to hell.' She pressed the card into my hand. The paints were already dry, but they felt oddly warm to the touch. Ferius looked tired. Weary. I realised then that she still hadn't fully recovered from the wounds she'd taken in the desert. 'Kid, there's a lot going on here that we don't understand. I can't deal with that *and* find somebody to spread the word of what we already know. If things go south . . . Just take the card, okay?'

It wasn't a command, nor even an instruction, really. It was more like a plea, and not once in all our travels have I seen Ferius Parfax beg for anything from anyone. 'Okay,' I said, sliding the card into my shirt pocket and putting my hat back on. 'Come on, Reichis. Looks like we're going gambling.'

29

The Bridge of Dice

We arrived at the Bridge of Dice early that evening to discover that gambling wasn't its only enticement. Reichis and I walked past all kinds of entertainments, from musicians and dancers to troupes of actors performing outrageous plays. Some of these involved very little clothing and would've been grounds for arrest in the Jan'Tep territories. Reichis took one look and decided that humans were even uglier when naked.

The bright colours all around us were mesmerising. Ingeniously designed lanterns hung from poles along the bridge, their light shining down on hundreds of metal discs embedded in the deck that made you feel as though you were walking on stars.

Crowds of revellers strolled, danced and caroused with each other as they travelled from one end of the bridge to the other and back again. Sometimes they gave money to the beggars who juggled or performed tricks with swords or torches to attract attention. We passed one old fellow who flipped coins high up into the air, sending more and more of them spinning after each other without ever letting a single one fall. When he caught me watching, he smiled, but a second later his eyes narrowed. He let the coins come tumbling down into his hand, one by one. Something about his stare made me uncomfortable.

'Hoi, castradazi!' he called after me as Reichis and I walked away. A quick glance back told me he was following us.

'I don't speak Gitabrian,' I apologised, picking up my pace.

'Castradazi! Hoi, castradazi!' he repeated. A few steps later I felt his hand grip my arm. I spun around to give him my most threatening glare. He was depressingly unperturbed.

'You're doing it wrong,' Reichis said, opening one eye unnaturally wide and snarling at the man, flecks of spit dripping from his lips.

'Castradazi,' the beggar said again. Apparently even Reichis wasn't sufficiently intimidating.

'I don't speak your language,' I said in Daroman. 'I don't know what that word . . .'

Wait a second, where have I heard it before? Then I remembered back at the prison when Zavera had taken my coin from me. One of the words she'd used to describe it had stuck with me. 'Castradazi,' I said out loud.

'Zia, zia! Castradazi,' the beggar repeated. He was as thin as a rake but his brown toga-like garments were clean and he certainly didn't look like he suffered from any of the ailments that often afflicted those forced to beg in the streets. Still, he seemed awfully concerned with getting something from me.

'I can't help you,' I said, holding up my hands to show I didn't have what he wanted. 'No castradazi.'

In response, he folded his arms across his chest and stared at me as if he knew I was a liar.

'Look,' I said, 'I *had* a castradazi, but I don't any more. A crazy person from the secret police took it from me, and then when I asked for it back Janucha grabbed it and . . . Why am

I rambling on at you in Daroman when you clearly don't understand a thing I'm saying?'

The man glanced around as if to make sure no one was watching, then reached into the folds of his toga. His hand came back with a small coin, silver and black with the symbol of a lock on one side and a key on the other – just like the one Zavera and later Janucha had taken from me. The old man pinched it between his two fingers and held it up to me. 'Castradazi.'

I began to get annoyed. I doubted this guy was Argosi, which meant he couldn't help me find the mages responsible for Cressia's torment. 'Look, I swear to you, I don't have any—'

The man waved his coin in front of me in a lazy figure-of-eight pattern, his eyes searching me all the while. Suddenly he stopped, and held his coin up to Reichis's face – his left cheek, to be precise. 'Castradazi,' he said confidently.

It took me a second to work out what had happened. I sometimes forget that squirrel cats are incorrigible thieves. 'Reichis?' I asked quietly. 'Is it possible that you only pretended to jump at the mechanical bird in Janucha's hand when in fact you were using it as a distraction to pick her pockets?'

'What? Of course not. You know me, Kellen – honest as the day is long. I'm so honest it's almost criminal.'

I stared unblinking into the squirrel cat's eyes. For some reason this always throws him. Reichis's composure lasted about three seconds before he started giggling. 'Okay, fine.' He reached a paw inside his jowls and pulled out the little silver and black coin. 'Saw the inventor playin' with it. Then that Altariste guy asked where she got it and she told him she'd taken it from you. I figured it was only fair that I take it back.'

'And return the coin to me when, exactly?'

He scrunched up his muzzle. '*Return* it?'

I held my hand out and again stared into Reichis's eyes until he dropped the coin in my palm.

'Castradazi,' the man in the toga said with what sounded like considerable relief. He put a hand on my shoulder.

'You want my coin?'

'*My* coin,' Reichis corrected.

The thing had caused me nothing but trouble. I had half a mind to give it away, when a voice behind me said, 'Castradazi ain't what the fool *wants*. It's what he thinks you *are*.'

Even the man in the toga jumped. 'Argosi,' he muttered afterwards, sounding more irritated than anxious. I turned and found myself face to face with the old man who'd come to the travellers' saloon to give Ferius the mechanical bird card. He'd replaced his rough travelling clothes with a long brocade coat trimmed in dark blue over a silk shirt with the same elaborate inlay I'd seen on the wealthier Gitabrian lords strolling along the bridge.

'Are you in disguise?' I asked, glancing around.

'Why, didn't you recognise me?'

'Well, yes, but—'

'Then I guess I ain't wearin' a disguise. Idjit.' This was the second time he'd called me that. I was fairly sure he meant 'idiot'.

Reichis chuckled. 'Heh. Idjit. I like that. *Idjit*.'

'Durral, don't you start on the boy now,' a female voice called out. Over on the other side of the bridge, the woman who'd been with him at the saloon leaned against the railing, looking out at the gorge. She wore a long black coat embroidered with delicate silver leaves over a green pleated dress.

With her hair pinned up so elegantly she fitted right in with the Gitabrian ladies walking by.

Durral took her injunction as a reason to glare at me. 'Enna's got a soft spot for strays. Runs in the family. I see you've met Savire.'

The man in the toga shook his head. '*Castradazi* Savire.'

'Whatever,' the old man shot back. 'Don't know why Gitabrians need to hear their job title every time you say their name.'

'At least he doesn't refer to himself as the Path of the Rambling Thistle,' I pointed out.

'He's got you there, Durral,' his partner added, still looking out over the gorge.

'Just you keep watch for them secret police and leave me to my business, Enna.' He turned back to me. 'Castradazi means coin dancer, in case you're so thick you haven't figured that out yet.'

'Durral . . .'

He glanced back at the woman at the railing. 'You wanna scold me all night or maybe keep us from gettin' arrested this time?'

The man in the toga – Savire – rolled his eyes at me. 'Argosi,' he said.

'Argosi,' I replied back.

He laughed and clapped me on the shoulder.

'If you two comedians are done,' Durral said, 'then maybe we can get on with this.'

'Get on with what?' I asked. 'And what's a coin dancer?'

Savire – who'd been remarkably patient up till now – took this as a sign it was time to resume our one-word conversation. 'Castradazi,' he corrected, and again flipped the coin in the air, his eyes going all foggy as it spun on its own for a few seconds before falling back into his palm.

'That coin he's holding is a *sotocastra*,' Durral explained. He tapped the one in my hand. 'Just like yours.'

'The one you gave me outside the saloon,' I pointed out. 'Why?'

'So you'd end up here of course.'

'Here?'

He sighed. 'Sands and sorrow, give me strength. Here. On this bridge. In this city. On this night.' He pointed to Savire. 'To meet him.'

'I came here because Ferius . . . Wait, back at the saloon while you and her were playing cards, did you tell her to send me here tonight?'

Durral gave me the sort of smile you put on when the impression you're going for is the exact opposite of what a smile is supposed to mean. 'You're a genius, kid. Now, can we get to business?'

'Fine.' I reached into my pocket for the card Ferius had given me.

Durral grabbed my wrist and squeezed it hard. 'Not here, idjit. Not yet.'

I tried to pull away, but the old man had a strong grip. Reichis gave him a growl.

The woman – I guess Enna was her name – came and put a hand on Durral's shoulder. 'Don't push the poor boy. Look in his eyes. He's carrying the weight of the world in there.' She gently prised his hand from my wrist and then looked up at me. 'They won't kill the girl just yet, Kellen.'

'How do you know?'

'Because you don't torture someone to cause pain. You do

it to create fear. They're trying to terrify the girl's mother into giving them what they want.'

'Then shouldn't we be finding them first?' I asked.

'Just trust us a little while,' Enna said, squeezing my hand. 'You're here for a reason.'

'Which is . . . ?'

Durral nodded to where the man in the toga waited, watching our exchange. 'Savire needs to see you flip the coin. Make it dance.'

I had no idea what that meant, but I did as I was told. The coin spun up into the air, but didn't float for anywhere near as long as Savire's had. The coin dancer shook his head at me. '*Dazi*,' he said. Apparently our conversation was now reduced to half a word. He held up his own coin between two fingers and tapped it against his forehead, then against his chest, and finally against my hand. 'Castra *dazi*.'

'He's telling you that to make it dance you need to use your mind, your heart and your hands.'

'How?'

'How should I know? I'm an Argosi, not some old weirdo who wanders around peddling obscure philosophy and treating coins like they were sacred artefacts.'

Given everything I knew about the Argosi, that statement was pretty funny. Even Reichis chuckled. 'Heh. Stupid Argosi.'

Durral grabbed the coin from my palm. I thought he was going to show me how to make it float, but when he flipped it in the air it just fell right back down the way it had done for Zavera. 'I ain't got the knack for it. Can't tell you how it works exactly, but it's like some folks have the touch – they can wake the spirit that lives inside the metal.' He handed it back to me. 'That's how you make the coin *dance*, and when it does, you can use its abilities.'

'Like what?'

'Depends on the coin. There used to be loads of different ones. Sotocastra like this one to open locks, *orocastra* to help you find water or gold.' He nodded to the man in the toga. 'Castradazi like Savire here used to be folk heroes. Some years back the lords mercantile decided they were tricksters and thieves, sent the secret police after them. Now there aren't but a few left, and probably even fewer of the coins.'

Altariste had said something about the metals needed to make the bird – that no one except for contraptioneers was supposed to possess them. I held up my coin. 'This is what Janucha's been using in her experiments.'

'Could be,' Durral said, 'but if you ever want to find out for sure you'd better show Savire here that you can flip the damned thing!'

The old man in the toga seemed to understand more than he'd been letting on, because he motioned for me to watch, and began flipping his own coin over and over. At first I was distracted by the way it would hang in the air for a second, then two, then three, but then I realised I was focusing on the wrong thing: what I needed to do was pay attention to the *way* he flipped it.

The old man placed the coin on his thumb just so, and twitched his whole hand just a bit before flicking it – almost more on a curve than straight up. He picked the coin out of the air and then gestured for me to try.

While I'd pretty much washed out as a mage among my people, the one thing I'd always been good at was mastering somatic forms. It wasn't just determination and practice on my part. I'd enjoyed the feeling of it – the *art* of making your fingers move so swiftly in such complex patterns. In its own way, it kind of *was* like dancing.

I stopped trying to emulate the other man's movements and just let my hands do the work, feeling the shape of the coin, its weight and the way it rolled across my palm.

Okay, we've been properly introduced now. Let's see if we can dance.

When I flipped the coin this time, it hung in the air, spinning awhile before ever so slowly beginning to fall. Savire grabbed my wrist and pulled my hand underneath the coin. Its descent stopped entirely. It floated there above my palm, no longer spinning but turning on its axis as if suspended from a string.

'Castradazi,' Savire said, though this time in a hushed, almost awed voice.

The day my parents had counter-banded me had taken away any hope I'd had of becoming a mage. I'd figured all my practice at somatic forms – the one thing I was really good at – had gone to waste. So even though all that was happening right now was that a coin was floating a few inches above my palm, I felt better than I had in a long time.

'Okay,' Reichis said, tilting his head as he watched. 'I want my coin back.'

The man in the toga covered my palm with his. He wrapped his fingers around my hand and turned it until we were locked in a handshake. He spoke to Durral in Gitabrian.

'He wants you to tell him a lie,' the Argosi said.

'Like what?'

'Like anything. Nobody ever teach you to lie, kid?'

It's pretty much all I learned from my people actually. 'The

Jan'Tep brought the seven forms of magic to this continent,' I said with absolute confidence.

Durral smirked at that. Savire just watched me. An itch started in the centre of my palm where the coin was pressed between our two hands. The sensation grew stronger and stronger until it was almost unbearable. I tried to pull away but the old man wouldn't let me. Instead he said something to Durral.

'Now tell him the truth.'

'What? Why would . . . ?' The discomfort was getting to be too much for me. 'We stole the oases from the Mahdek,' I said loudly. 'We took their magic from them and pretended it was ours.'

The pain disappeared as if it had never been there in the first place.

'Sotocastra,' Savire said.

'*Soto* means both "to open" and "to speak the truth",' Durral explained. 'In anyone else's hands that coin is just a dead hunk of metal. But a castradazi can use it to unlock doors or tell if a fella's telling the truth or not.' He gave a sniff as if the thing were beneath him. 'Course an Argosi don't need no coin to do those things.'

'How many other kinds of these coins are there?' I asked.

'Used to be there were twenty-one different sacred coins, if you believe the old castradazi stories. They've been outlawed for years now though, so you'd be lucky to find a coin dancer with more than one or two.'

The man in the toga said something else, and then Durral frowned.

'What did he say?' I asked.

'He says the art will be gone soon. Says he's old and ready to move on.'

'Can't he teach someone else?'

'*Dazigenzia,*' the old man said to me, squeezing my hand even harder.

'The dance isn't taught,' Durral explained. 'It has to be discovered.' To Savire he added, 'Which is nonsense, by the way.'

Savire ignored him, using his grip on my hand to pull me closer before kissing me first on one cheek then the other. That earned him an angry hiss from Reichis, who promptly leaped from my shoulder to the lantern post above. 'Creepy skinbags.'

'Name,' the man in the toga said to me in heavily accented Daroman. 'You *name*?'

'Kellen,' I replied. Then I remembered the way Gitabrians constructed their names, and tried to recall what Altariste had called me. 'In your language I guess I'd be Magizier Kellen fal Ke té Jan'Tep.'

He shook his head vigorously. 'No. No. *Castradazi* Kellen.' Then he turned my hand over so my palm was facing up. When he removed his own, there was no longer a single coin in my palm. Now there were five.

'Well, I'll be a tumbleweed rolled clear across the ocean!' Durral breathed. He turned to the woman keeping watch. 'Enna, you ever seen *five* of these before?'

She smiled at him but stayed where she was. 'Still an excitable little boy under all that bluster, ain't you?'

I held the coins up closer to see them better. Each was a different size and colour – from a glittering orange copper, to a blue so deep it was as if someone had found a way to mix steel and sapphire together. They tingled against the skin of my palm, each one vibrating in its own unique way. Savire closed my fingers over the coins. 'No . . .' He struggled, searching for the word. 'No show, Castradazi Kellen. No show.'

'But what am I supposed to do with them?'

He exchanged a few more words with Durral, who translated. 'He says the kids here don't want to be coin dancers any more; they want to be contraptioneers or explorers or merchant lords. He's tired of the secret police coming around looking for his coins, so now these are yours. Says you gotta keep 'em safe. Take them away from here.'

I looked down at the little metal discs. Had I seen them on any other day, I would've thought them rather plain and probably not worth very much. Now it felt as if I held a treasure horde in the palm of my hand. The old man looked at me expectantly, and I remembered that Gitabria was a trading nation. 'I . . . I don't have much money,' I said, reaching for the small pouch of my own coins. 'But I can—'

'Practise,' Savire said, then he tapped me three times: on the forehead, the centre of my chest and finally on the hand holding the coins. 'Practice is pay.'

With nothing more than a toothy grin and a wave of his hand, the castradazi turned and walked away.

'Wait,' I called to him. 'I don't know what the other coins do! You haven't told me how to—'

'Practise,' he said without stopping.

I considered running after him, but Durral grabbed my shoulder. 'Let him be, kid. This is how it is for his folk.'

I felt a strange kind of awe at this gift – and not just for the coins themselves. I was keenly aware that without Savire's kindness and Durral's machinations to bring me here, I would never have known they existed. 'Thank you,' I said to Durral.

The Argosi shrugged. 'Just had a feelin' about you. Saw how

your hands moved back at the saloon and Enna reckoned you might have the touch for it.'

'Thank you,' I repeated. 'I mean it.'

'Well, you might want to save all those thank-yous for someone else.'

He led me by the elbow across the bridge to where Enna waited, no longer looking out at the gorge or watching the bridge for police. Her eyes were on me now. 'You know the Argosi Way of Water, Kellen?'

'Sure,' I replied, 'it means . . .'

A sinking feeling came over me. The Way of Water means a lot of things: balance, never interfering in the path of another, and providing fair exchange in all trades. But it also means something else: making restitution when you've done wrong to another. Balancing the scales. Durral and Enna, the Path of the Rambling Thistle as they called themselves, had just led me to a gift that was already more precious than anything I'd ever owned. So how do you balance that?

'Let's take a walk across the bridge together,' Enna said.

30

The Forest Walk

Cazaran's Forest Bridge spans just over three thousand feet as it crosses the gorge. The only reason I knew this fact was that it was the first thing Enna said to me as she led me there.

'Beautiful, isn't it?' she asked as we walked between rows of thirty-foot trees that grew from roots deep inside the thick deck of the bridge itself.

It was, and I said as much.

'And a pleasant evening,' Enna went on. 'Air's warm, breeze is soft, and the company, well . . .' She patted my arm. 'It's not so bad, is it?'

'No, ma'am.'

'So nice to be in the presence of a proper gentleman for a change,' she said, stepping away to give me a little curtsy. She held out her hand. 'Now, I believe you have something for me.'

I took the discordance card from my pocket, but found parting with it wasn't easy. I had trouble reconciling the delicate painting with Ferius's swaggering personality. Letting go of it felt like giving up a chance to better understand my Argosi mentor.

'Oh,' Enna said as soon as she took it from me. She held

it between both her hands and a terrible sadness found its way to her otherwise inscrutable expression.

'What's the matter?' I asked. 'What does the card mean?'

The Argosi slid the card into the sleeve of her coat. 'It's fine, Kellen. Just fine. I miss her painting, that's all.'

She took my arm and we resumed our walk. I found it hard to break the silence between us, but a question had been plaguing me since the travellers' saloon. 'Ferius is your daughter, isn't she?'

'Durral and I are her foster parents,' she admitted. 'Found her when she was just a little thing. Her own blood, well, like so many of the Mahdek, they wanted to get their revenge on the world. Can't blame them, of course, but it's a sure path to a short life.'

'What was she like? Ferius, I mean.'

'Angry, mostly. Angriest child you've ever seen. The minute she learned how to make a fist, she beat a boy bloody. Stole herself a throwing knife when she was seven. Practised every second she thought we weren't watching. You ever see her use a blade? I mean, like a proper Shan sword or a Tristian rapier?'

'Never seen either,' I replied.

'She was fast, boy. Oh, was she ever fast! Could've made her living walking across this continent killing for money. She wanted to, you know. Thought the way to make peace with her dead was to send as many Jan'Tep after them as she could before some mage or other got to her.'

'So what happened?'

'Durral saw something in her. Wanted to make her his *teysan*. Ferius, though, she didn't take to it. I mean, sure, she wanted to learn the talents. The tricks. Begged us to teach her all the forms of arta eres and arta tuco. I warned against it, but Durral's always had a soft heart.'

'Really? Because I think maybe he left it somewhere.'

She gave my arm a little squeeze. 'Now don't you start. Anyway, Ferius went on getting in all kinds of trouble. Every time she ended up in a jam, me or Durral would have to get her out of it. But she hated having debts. Kept trying to give us things – things she'd stolen. So Durral, he started giving her the pledge cards. You know what those are?'

'The ones with the blood-red ink? Ferius says they carry an Argosi's debts.'

She nodded. 'Wasn't too long before she had a whole deck of them. Still nothing changed. So much anger in that girl.'

'But Ferius is the least angry person I've ever met! She never fights when she can avoid it, never hurts anyone more than necessary. Four Berabesq Faithful nearly killed us in the desert and she used up all our medicine saving them!'

At first Enna didn't respond to my defence of Ferius, but then she stopped, and looked up at me. I saw the first hint of tears in her eyes. 'It makes me happy to hear that, Kellen. It is a very fine gift. Thank you.'

Her words carried a finality to them that told me she wanted to stop there, but I couldn't let it go. 'If Ferius was so violent before, what changed her?'

Enna opened the first few buttons of her coat. She pulled the neckline of her dress down to just above her breastbone. The scar was old, but not fully healed. It couldn't have been more than an inch from her heart. 'Durral got to me in time,' she said. 'But it was awful close.'

'That's not possible. There's no way that Ferius would do something like that.'

'Says a boy who's never seen a mother and daughter go at it. Tell me, if Durral showed you a scar like mine and told you he got it when his son lost his temper, would you believe him?'

'I guess so, but—'

'She didn't mean to do it,' Enna went on. 'Truth be told, it was my fault as much as hers. I wanted to prove to her that no matter how quick you think you are with a blade, there's always someone just a little faster.' She chuckled. 'Turns out I was the one who needed to learn that lesson.'

'Is that why you won't talk to her? I know she misses you. I saw it in her face at the saloon, and then again when she sent me here with the discordance card.' The more I talked about it, the more excited I got, or maybe panicked. 'Let me take you to her right now. Or if you can't come, I'll bring her to you. You could see her again, just let her know you aren't angry with her.'

'Are you done now, son?' Enna asked, not a trace of meanness in her voice. I knew then that nothing I said was going to convince her. She pointed towards the end of the bridge ahead of us. 'How far you reckon we have to go?'

I glanced back to see how far we'd come. 'Maybe another seven hundred feet?'

'Sounds about right to me.' She took my arm again and resumed our walk. 'I've enjoyed meeting you, Kellen, more than, well, more than most. But when we reach the end of this bridge, for all that I might wish it otherwise, I'm going to say goodbye to you. Chances are this will be the last time you and I ever see each other.'

'Why? What did I do?'

'Nothing at all. But I'm an Argosi, and we walk our paths alone.'

'But you and Durral—'

'Durral and I happen to be on the same path. Have been for close to forty years now.' She gazed off towards the Bridge of Dice where we'd left him. 'One day, our paths will diverge and I'll have to say goodbye to him.'

'Why? Why would anyone want to live that way? Always giving up the people you care about?'

We'd reached the end of the bridge. Enna almost stepped off then stopped herself and turned to me, taking my hands in hers. 'You came here tonight because you want to find those mages so they don't kill that poor girl and start a war. Those are fine things to want, Kellen, but are you willing to pay the price?'

'You think I don't already know I could get killed?'

She shook her head. 'Any fool can throw away his life. I'm talking about something bigger. The way of the Argosi . . . It's not just a bunch of fancy cards and tricks, Kellen. We follow our paths because they take us where we need to go so we can protect the people we love from the terrible things that sneak up on the world when no one's watching. War. Oppression. Genocide.'

'You mean like the Mahdek. Like what my people did to them.'

She nodded.

'Then why didn't the Argosi prevent it?'

'Because we aren't grand mages, Kellen. We're not kings or emperors. We don't have armies. Just our cards and a few tricks up our sleeves. Sometimes we fail because we're on the wrong path.' She reached out a fingertip to flick away a lock of hair that had fallen over my left eye. It fell right back into place and that made her smile. 'Sometimes we're on the true path but someone comes along who makes us want to stray from it.'

Too late I understood what this was all about – why she and Durral had gone so far out of their way to be nice to me. I pulled away from her. 'You brought me here to tell me that Ferius is going to leave me?'

'No, don't you see, son? That's the problem. The minute Durral and I saw Ferius standing outside that saloon with you, we knew. We *knew*. She'll never abandon you, Kellen. She'll keep trying to defend you from all the people who want to hurt you. She'll keep trying to teach you even when the learning won't take inside that head of yours, even if it means giving up the Path of the Wild Daisy.' Enna put her hands on my shoulders. 'You have to be the one to walk away from *her*.'

Fear and anger competed for space inside my chest. 'You're wrong. Me and Ferius and Reichis, we look out for each other!'

With that soft, patient voice of her she asked, 'How many times has my daughter nearly died saving your life, Kellen? You said yourself that she prefers peaceful ways. How many times has she had to commit violence to protect you?'

Too many times to count, I thought, but I didn't say it out loud. I couldn't bring myself to. I took the castradazi coins from my pocket. 'Is that what this is? Some kind of *payment* to make me leave? Is that how it works – the Way of Water? You decide Ferius has to be rid of me so you give me some coins in return?'

Enna looked stung by my words. 'That's not our way, Kellen. You ought to know that by now. You really want to find those mages and stop a war?' She reached into her coat and took out a card that she handed to me. 'This is the price you have to pay.'

I took the card from her and stared at it, transfixed by its ugliness. It depicted a road so covered in twisting black markings it looked as if the entire card had been soaked in ink. The title at the bottom read, 'The Path of Shadows'.

'This is where the path leads, Kellen. This war – and make no mistake, that's what's coming – needs someone to walk a road too dark for the rest of us.' She briefly put a hand against my cheek. 'You know my daughter better than almost anyone else alive. You know the Path of the Wild Daisy means everything to her. That's why you have to be the one to decide.'

'Decide what?'

She took away her hand and tapped the surface of the card. 'Whether you'll walk this awful road yourself, or make Ferius walk it for you.'

With those words the Path of the Rambling Thistle turned away from me.

And I was left alone.

The Path of Shadows

THE PATH

To be Argosi is to accept one's path without knowing its destination. We take to the road regardless of whether it leads us into brutal heat or bitter cold, through blinding light or unrelenting darkness. We know the journey is perilous. We know the end comes sooner than we would wish. Still the path calls to us, and that is what makes us Argosi.

31

The Cure for Anger

Reichis could tell something was wrong the moment I returned to the Bridge of Dice. He tried to distract me with endless nattering about squirrel cat philosophy as we walked aimlessly back and forth across every one of Cazaran's eight bridges. Just a few days ago I'd marvelled at the sight of them. Now they seemed petty and garish.

Reichis started racing around the merchant stalls, popping his head up behind their tables and warning me that he was about to steal something and I'd better start running. When even that failed to get a rise out of me, he decided sterner measures were necessary and returned to hop up on my shoulder.

'What are you doing?' I asked irritably when the squirrel cat started patting my head with his paw.

'I'm . . . comforting you,' he replied. 'Isn't this what humans do to reassure each other?' His batting of my head intensified. 'Is this better?'

'Stop it.'

He sniffed at my cheek. 'You're angry with *me*?'

'No. Just angry. At everything.'

I felt the fur of his cheek tickle mine as he grinned. 'You know what I do when I'm feeling angry?'

'Murder things?'

'Exactly! Let's go find some—'

Someone shouted my name and the sounds of footsteps followed. I turned to see Nephenia running towards us, her hyena loping alongside. 'Kellen,' she said again, sounding mildly infuriated. 'Finally!'

'How did you find us?' I asked. Cazaran wasn't exactly a small city.

Neph tapped a finger on the sigils of my hat. 'By giving myself a headache, thank you very much. Do you have to wear that thing all the time? No, don't answer that. We have more urgent things to discuss.'

'What?' I asked.

'Just . . . let me catch my breath.'

The hyena gave a quick series of yips and barks.

'Ishak says Cressia woke up an hour ago asking for you,' Reichis informed me.

'Why would she ask for . . . Oh, hell.' In all my previous encounters with the obsidian worms, the attacks never came closer than a day apart. There was no way Cressia could survive another brutal assault so soon.

'It's okay,' Nephenia said. 'They're just . . . talking.'

'Talking?'

'Negotiating. Janucha is trying to see if she can come to some kind of agreement with them. I was only there for the first couple of minutes before I realised I should come find you.' She hesitated a second. 'Kellen, the mages don't seem nearly as sadistic as you described them. The way they talk is more pompous and arrogant than cruel.'

'They probably think they're close to getting what they want from Janucha.' Gitabrians are supposed to be master traders. Maybe she could find a reasonable accommodation with them.

Yeah. Probably not.

'Why are we standing around here?' Reichis growled, his fur changing to black with red stripes. 'Wake up that stupid wind spirit in your eye and let's hunt them down!'

'How?' I asked. 'Even if the sasutzei can find the threads, those mages are thousands of miles from here.'

'How do you know?' the squirrel cat asked.

'Because the mages . . .' I was about to say 'because they told me so', when I realised how stupid that sounded.

'I don't think they can be that far,' Nephenia said. 'Janucha was quizzing me on Jan'Tep magic. She thought she could devise some kind of copper or silver barrier to lessen the mages' connection to the obsidian worm. I told her silk spells are the only means of controlling something with your mind, and nothing weakens silk magic except—'

'Distance,' I said, interrupting her.

Damn it. Why hadn't I figured this out before? Silk magic was like sound: in theory it kept on going forever, but it faded more and more the further it travelled. I'd just assumed the worm had become more powerful because it had lived inside Cressia for so long, but even if that were the case, the mages sending their will needed to be closer to have such perfect control over it.

'Kellen, are you okay?' Nephenia asked.

I was too angry to answer. This was why the mages had taunted me the whole time they were tormenting Cressia: to keep me so wound up and convinced everything was my fault that it wouldn't occur to me to question whether they might be lying about their whereabouts.

Ancestors, but I was sick of being manipulated.

I lifted Reichis off my shoulder and deposited him on the ground so I could concentrate. 'Okay, Suzy,' I whispered, my eyes closed tightly. 'It's very, very important that I find the thread between Cressia and the bracelet that's got the other half of the obsidian worm.'

Nothing, of course.

The reason the Jan'Tep don't study whisper magic is because my people don't trust forces that can't be controlled. They especially don't like spirits that you have to repeatedly beg for help in the hope that eventually you'll say something that sparks their interest. 'This is a good cause, I swear it. Innocent people are being hurt and this whole country could fall apart if we don't put a stop to it.'

Still nothing.

'Maybe the spirit needs to be near Cressia before it can see the ethereal connection?' Nephenia suggested.

I couldn't answer because I needed to keep my attention on the annoying, useless wind spirit that was all too happy to give me headaches when it suited her but never actually helped me when I asked. 'Look, I'm trying to do the right thing here! You think I *want* to go chasing after mages who'll probably kill me?'

I felt the barest hint of breath on my right eye when I used the word 'mages' – light as a feather, almost an expression of curiosity.

'The mages? *That's* what piques your interest? You do realise I haven't got one tenth of the magic of any Jan'Tep who—'

A stabbing pain – like an icicle being driven into my eye. 'Ow! Stop it!'

The feeling subsided, though it didn't leave entirely. I should've figured it out sooner: the sasutzei despised all things Jan'Tep.

Except me, hopefully.

I opened my eyes. My vision always gets a little hazy when the spirit wakes. The first thing I saw was Reichis staring at me with his lip curled. 'Your eye's gone all milky again, Kellen.' He turned to Ishak. 'This is why squirrel cats don't invite spirits to live inside their eyeballs.'

'Come on,' I whispered under my breath to the sasutzei. 'I need this. Just once I need to *do* something. You hate mages? Me too. So let's go do something about it.'

It seemed like nothing at first, but then I looked back at the bridge and there, barely visible in the dim light, floated a twisting black thread that began far off on the other side of the gorge – right where Janucha's home was carved into the cliffside. I spun around, my eyes following the thread. It seemed to go on forever, winding along avenues, turning here and there like the lazy drawing of a bored child. But there was a definite direction to it: deeper into the south-eastern part of the city.

'What do you see?' Nephenia asked.

'A trail,' I said, and then took my first step along the path of the black thread to where I knew my enemies would be. *I've got you,* I thought.

Nephenia held me back. 'Shouldn't we try to find Lady Ferius? She left not long after you did, but if you have something of hers, maybe I can use it to—'

'No,' I said, removing her hand from my arm. 'The moment

those mages cut off the connection, the thread between the obsidian worm and the onyx bracelet will disappear. We have to do this now.'

Besides, I thought to myself, *I'm going to have to get used to doing things without Ferius.*

32

The Black Thread

That night we sped down streets and alleyways and squeezed through the narrow gaps between buildings as we followed the black thread's winding route across the city. More than once we found ourselves backtracking when the filament split in two. We'd follow one only to find it looping back on itself and fading away only to then become visible once again a few yards away.

'Why can't you just give me a straight line?' I asked the sasutzei.

No reply was forthcoming.

'It must be the amplifying forces,' Nephenia said, pointing up at a nearby minaret atop a tall building. It stood perhaps a hundred feet high and was capped in bronze – an architectural style popular with the Gitabrians. 'I bet the thread is going around the top, isn't it?'

I nodded. 'It circles around and then splits in two, one going north and the other south.'

'When you're making charms, you sometimes use bronze as an intensifier to keep silk spells from fading too quickly. The building materials they use here are drawing the ethereal thread that connects the two halves of the obsidian worm –

increasing their strength even as they wind around them. That's probably one of the reasons why the mages have so much control over the worm here.'

That made a kind of sense, though the specifics of what she was talking about were beyond me. 'I don't remember you being an expert on charm theory when we were initiates,' I said, jogging ahead to where the thread took a sharp left turn off the avenue only to then float up the side of one building and over to another.

Nephenia held up her hands. The last two fingers of each glove had been removed and sewn over. 'The day after this happened I knew I'd need a way to make a living outside of our homeland. I'd always been pretty good at charm-casting, and since I couldn't form the somatic shapes required for the high magics any more, it was the obvious choice.'

'I'm sorry,' I said, stopping so we could catch our breath.

'Don't be. I figured out in my first week that self-pity was no defence against the outside world, and looking back can get you killed.' She grinned at the hyena and reached down to scratch its head. 'Besides, if I hadn't been forced to leave home, I never would've met Ishak.'

The hyena barked a reply.

'Yes, dear, of course you're right; our partnership was fated.' She rolled her eyes and whispered conspiratorially, 'He's terribly superstitious.'

'Hah!' Reichis said, as if this represented some kind of victory for squirrel cat kind. 'Stupid hyenas.'

I got us going again, worried that the sasutzei might get bored if I waited too long and stop revealing the thread to me. I kept glancing at Nephenia though, struck by the confidence in her movements – the way she held her chin up just a little, as if daring the world to get in her way.

'I guess we've both changed a lot, haven't we?' I asked.

She looked as if she were about to reply, but then bit her lip.

'What?' I asked.

'Nothing. You're tracking the thread. Now's not the time.'

'I can do both. What were you going to say?'

'It's just, I don't think you *have* changed, Kellen. I mean, you've got your spells and your skills. You lead this insane life, but underneath it all?' She laughed. 'Just look at what you're doing: striding off to duel some mage who you know – you *know* – is going to be way more powerful than you. I bet even now you're trying to devise some trick or ploy so that you can scam your way to victory. Being here with you now? It's just like that day I came to the oasis to watch you duel Tennat.'

Only this time we could all be killed. But her words had struck a chord in me. 'Am I really no different?'

'Hey,' she said, putting her hand on my arm, 'I didn't say it was a bad thing. It's who you are. A ridiculous frontier hat and a few scars haven't changed that.'

'I could say the same thing about you, you know. Exiled charmcaster or not, you're still the same person underneath.'

She stopped me there in the middle of the street. 'No, Kellen. I'm not. It's important that you understand that I'm not the girl you knew.'

'I didn't mean to—'

'No, listen to me. Before I was exiled, I did some things that . . . I had to make a choice. I had to decide whether to hate myself for what I'd done, or believe that this was exactly who I was meant to be. No apologies to anyone. You want to know what makes us different?'

She removed one of her gloves and reached a finger up to the twisting black marks around my left eye. I flinched. '*That's* what makes us different.'

'The shadowblack?'

'No, the way you let it make you feel – as if you're broken somehow.' She held her hand in front of my face. 'You see a girl with missing fingers. I see my hand.' She put the glove back on. 'When I look at your face, I see my friend. But when you look in the mirror I bet all you see are shadows.'

I don't think her words were meant to make me feel small, but that's exactly what they did. Bad enough I had to go around with a curse hanging over me, with spell warrants out for my head and people telling me I had to get used to the idea of being alone. Now it was my fault because I didn't share Nephenia's cavalier attitude about life?

I should've kept my mouth shut. I still carried around the card Ferius had given me with the two of thorns imprinted in blood-red ink – a reminder not to hurt other people without cause.

'I guess you're right,' I said, picking up the pace. 'We *are* different.'

'Hey!' Nephenia said, grabbing my arm. 'Just because I'm not the same girl you remember, doesn't mean the person I am now isn't worth knowing.'

'I don't doubt that,' I said.

She took my hand. 'And just because you're still the same schemer who thinks he can trick the whole world, doesn't mean I don't want to know you better. You don't have to act like you're all alone even when I'm right here with you.'

'Oh, great squirrel cat gods,' Reichis muttered to Ishak. 'Please keep me from puking.'

I was about to remind him of an assortment of embarrassing things I could bring up about him when a blast of ice-cold wind chilled my right eye. 'What?' I demanded of the sasutzei. We couldn't have found the mages yet because the black thread continued far off into the distance.

I heard a soft thump behind me, then another. Nephenia's hand fell out of mine and I saw her fall to the ground. 'Neph?'

I knelt down to see what was wrong. She was breathing, but unconscious. I tried shaking her but nothing roused her. Reichis and Ishak were in the same state. The sound of approaching footsteps brought me to my feet, and too late I understood the sasutzei's icy wind. She hadn't been trying to tell me we'd found the mages. She'd been warning me that someone had found *us*.

Someone who wanted me alone.

33

The Man in Red

It was the first time I'd seen the man in red up close. The experience didn't agree with me.

He was only a little taller than me, but a lot broader in the shoulders. Leather straps wound around the red silk covering his upper arms to trace the lines of his muscles. Every inch of him was covered in crimson silk except his forearms. Six metallic tattooed bands glistened in the darkness.

'Who are you?' I asked. I kept my hands at my sides where they could quickly reach my powders if things went badly. *Who are you kidding*? I thought. *When do these things not go badly*?

He didn't speak, but he did smile. That was even more troubling, because his face was covered with a red lacquer funeral mask like those the Mahdek placed on their dead to ward away demons. Somehow the rigid surface of the mask altered its shape in response to the wearer's expression. Right now the lines of the mouth were twisting up into a hideous grin as the ridges of the eyes narrowed.

He hadn't answered my question, though, which was unusual. Jan'Tep mages tend to favour elaborate, long-winded death threats. The red mage, however, kept silent. He walked a few yards away and knelt down to the cobblestones. With his index finger he traced a circle around himself. Wherever his finger went, a trail of red sparks followed, leaving a glimmering ring all around him.

Show-off.

'You want to duel me, is that it?'

My opponent stood back up and folded his arms across his chest, evidently waiting for me to draw my own circle. Having only ever sparked my breath band, I couldn't work any of the types of magic that would make a spell circle useful. But over the past year of being attacked by mages, thugs, hextrackers and bounty hunters, I'd come to learn that the most precious resource before a fight is time. Time to think. Time to plan.

I reached into the pouch on the left side of my belt and took out a handful of black powder. I slowly let it spill from my hand, turning so it formed a dusty ring around me. When I was done I looked at him with as much false bravado as I could muster. 'It's customary to set terms before a duel.'

The red mage offered no reply. That in itself set the terms: if he won, he could do whatever he wanted with me. If I won . . . Well, we both knew that wasn't going to happen.

Think, damn it. Ferius says every trap has an escape. You just need to find it.

'May I have a moment to meditate?' I asked.

Again I received no reply, but since he didn't immediately kill me, I took that as a yes.

Okay, I need a plan. A devilishly clever plan. No . . . wait . . . I'm looking at this backwards. I need to know his plan. Why would he go to the trouble of a duel when he's obviously more powerful than I am?

He'd used a silk spell on Neph, Reichis and Ishak to put them to sleep. He'd have to divert a portion of his concentration to it to keep them unconscious. So why not use something simpler like iron binding magic? That way they'd be restrained while forced to watch as he blew me to pieces. Why did he want to keep this private so badly?

The red mage dropped his hands to his sides and I just about jumped out of my circle. He gave a twitch of his fingers to let me know he was tired of waiting.

He really doesn't like me, I thought, seeing how the lines of his mask twisted and turned into an expression of both fury and hunger. That wasn't an uncommon reaction of course. Proper mages resent spellslingers for giving magic a bad name. Someone who'd sparked all six bands would have an especially big grudge against someone like me.

All of that left me with roughly seven possibilities to explain my situation. Six were terrible and meant I'd be dead in the next few seconds. One was still pretty awful, but there was a chance – just a chance – that I might survive it.

I decided to test that theory by pulling a pinch of red and black powders from my pouches, tossing them into the air without warning and forming the somatic shapes with my fingers. '*Carath*,' I said, breaking about three hundred years of Jan'Tep duelling tradition.

The red mage brought his own index fingers together and turned his hands in opposite directions, invoking an ember shield that barely even glowed as the red and black fires of my spell met their end against it. He retaliated by bending all four fingers at the second knuckle and then flicking them open. The tattooed grey band on his forearm sparked and the spell we call the iron wave struck me in the centre of the chest with the force of a battering ram. I was knocked back several feet. The breath fled my lungs and my ears rang as if someone had stuck a very large bell over my head and hit it with a mallet.

But I wasn't dead, which meant I was right.

The mage wanted to show me how tough he was, but without actually killing me. 'You're here to delay me, aren't you? To keep me from tracking down your employers before they finish getting what they want from Janucha.'

The expression on the red lacquer mask became one of benevolent amusement as the mage gave a slight nod.

It was that look as much as anything else that made me say something very stupid. 'What's it like being an errand boy for cowards who torment innocent girls because they're too scared to fight their own battles?'

This was one of those times when I would've been better off heeding the two of thorns card in my pocket that warned against insulting strangers. The brows and ridges of my opponent's lacquer mask took on a distinctly pissed-off appearance. He hit me with a bolt of ember lightning that hurt much, much more than his previous spell.

It took me a minute to force myself back to my feet. Being partially electrocuted isn't great for your balance. My only consolation was that I had confirmed three important facts.

First, your bosses clearly don't want me dead yet.

With considerable effort I stumbled back into my little circle. Once I was reasonably certain I wasn't about to fall down again, I gave the red mage my best smile. Something wet dripped down my chin. I think I was drooling. 'Guess it's my turn,' I said, sounding like a drunk with missing front teeth.

The mask's upper lip curled as the red mage gave me a look of utter disdain.

Second, you really don't like me.

With a dismissive wave he gestured for me to take my best shot.

And third, we both know without a shadow of a doubt that I haven't got a chance against you.

That last part was my only hope. Enna was right when she said that no matter how dangerous you might *think* you are, there's always someone out there who's a little *more* dangerous.

I just had to become that person.

34

The Trickster

There's a sad truth about magic: the guy who's got more of it almost always wins. It's not like being strong, because a strong man can still be slow. And it's not like being fast either, because a quick opponent might still make stupid mistakes. Casting a proper spell? It takes power, speed, precision and a mind disciplined enough to envision complex esoteric geometries. The reason why Jan'Tep mages are so convinced of their superiority over everyone else is because for the most part it's true. My job was to make that fact irrelevant.

'Watch carefully,' I told my opponent, reaching into my pocket and taking out one of the castradazi coins. It had a pleasant weight to it, but more importantly the edges were thin, almost sharp. 'In just a moment I'm going to make this coin disappear.'

My opponent's fingers clenched just a fraction before he relaxed them. A trained mage rarely does this because tense finger muscles aren't good for spellcasting.

This guy must hate me even more than I thought.

I tossed the coin in the air with my left hand a couple of times before I got the motion right. Even now I couldn't help but feel a tingle at the way it floated in the air, spinning slowly on its axis as it danced a foot above my palm. I reached into my right pouch with my free hand and took a pinch of red powder. I held it up for him to see. 'Now, I know what you're thinking, friend. You're thinking, even if he could cast that fire spell of his with just one hand, what difference would it make? No matter how much of an explosion he puts into the spell, it's never going to get through a proper ember shield. But watch carefully . . .'

I closed my right hand around the powder and pulled my arm back as though I were going to throw it at him. With barely a twitch of his fingers he brought up an ember shield. *Okay, fast hands. Fast hands,* I repeated to myself. In a single smooth motion, I dropped my left hand into the black powder pouch. As the coin began to fall, I grabbed a pinch and threw it in the air while my right hand tossed the red powder. My fingers formed the somatic shapes and I uttered the invocation just as the powders collided together.

'*Carath.*'

Here's the thing about shield spells: there are a lot of different kinds. Why? Because different types of energy and matter are repulsed by different kinds of barriers. The reason I'd rattled on about fire and explosions was because I wanted the red mage to invoke an ember shield. They're great against energy-based attacks, but less so against physical objects. So while he thought I was using the coin to distract him, what I was really doing was using it as the weapon.

The explosion did nothing of course – barely more than a flash of red and black flame that mostly singed my face because I hadn't actually used the spell on it. Instead I'd made the coin the focal point, channelling the breath magic into it and sending it flying at my enemy. It passed through his ember shield like a rock through rainwater, the spinning edge slicing through his silk garment and burying itself a half-inch deep into his flesh.

He tore at it, grunting from the pain. This might make me a bad person, but the sound was sweet to my ears. 'You like that?' I called out. 'Well, here's another.'

I tossed a second coin into the air and pulled the same stunt with the powders. The shimmer of an iron kinetic shield flared up, which was fine with me since this time I just let the coin fall and used red and black fire on him. Kinetic shields, as you might imagine, aren't particularly good at stopping fire.

I had to give this guy credit – he was fast. He dropped the first barrier and got an ember shield up just in time to keep from being burned alive. He got singed for his troubles, though, and growled in rage. Before he could use his own spell against me, I pulled my third act. 'Watch the pretty coin now!' I said as I threw it into the air. I pulled a great deal of powder and shouted '*Carath!*' as loud as I could.

The barrier the red mage summoned was a particularly impressive one – resistant to both kinetic force and energy. Neither coin nor flames got to him. In fact, nothing happened at all. I'd tossed the powders too far away and they hadn't collided.

The mage's mask contorted itself with a mixture of rage and joy as he realised what had happened.

'Wait,' I said, holding up my hands. 'One more trick, please! It's a really good one.'

'No,' he replied, his voice spell-masked to sound like it came from everywhere and nowhere at once. At least I'd finally got an actual word out of him. His hands formed the somatic shape for lightning, and as he drew on his ember and iron bands, I crossed my arms in front of my chest and waited.

Proper mages accuse spellslingers of being little more than frontier carnival magicians – the type who use petty tricks to simulate magic because they have none of their own. Well, the secret to fake conjuration is to fool the audience into watching the wrong thing. In this case, the red mage had been so concerned with my coins and with the bolts of fire, that he'd failed to notice the real trick: he'd missed the trail of black powder that had passed through his shield and got all over his chest. The instant he sparked his lightning spell, the powder caught fire.

He screamed as the flames ignited all over his lovely crimson silk garments. I found it pleasantly musical. It's possible I've been spending too much time around a certain squirrel cat.

'Told you it was a good trick,' I said as he stumbled around, batting at the flames. I quickly grabbed for every rock on the ground I could find. There are any number of Jan'Tep spells that could put out a fire, but it's hard to make them work when your opponent is pelting you with stones.

A sudden gust of wind spiralled around him, and the fire disappeared. Turns out some people *can* cast a dismissal spell while being hit with rocks. The shimmering of his bands lit up the darkness. Most Jan'Tep spells only use one or two of the bands. I mean, it just doesn't take that much magic to kill someone. The red mage, though, was sparking iron, ember, sand and blood. I couldn't even guess at what horrors he planned to unleash on me.

I pushed him too far, I realised too late. Whatever injunction his employers had given regarding my life, he was about to ignore it.

Between his two hands an oozing, blood-coloured force began to writhe. It was like watching a squirming creature emerge from a fire. Red sparks spun around it like flies on a corpse.

'No, please,' I said, backing away as fast as I could. 'I have something you want!'

I didn't, but it couldn't hurt to try.

His hands extended out towards me, and with a slow but sickening anticipation, the foul thing he'd brought forth reached out for me. Even if I'd sparked the bands necessary for summoning a shield, I didn't have a clue which one to use against his creation.

Sometimes at night I imagine myself dying. Burning. Drowning. Freezing. Being eaten alive. I've thought about them all in the hope that when the day finally came, the end wouldn't be so frightening. Turns out it was all a colossal waste of time, because now that my death was here, I was so afraid I couldn't so much as raise my hands to protect my face.

No tricks were going to save me now.

No trick did. Instead I was knocked aside as someone stepped between me and the red mage's spell.

It was Nephenia.

35

The Box

No cry of pain erupted from her mouth as the foul spell struck her. There was no spray of blood from her body. I thought at first that the hideous, oozing creation the red mage had summoned was burrowing inside her, tearing her apart from within. It was only when I rolled back up to my feet that I saw Nephenia's face. She didn't look like she was in pain or even scared.

Shock can do that to a person – make them unaware that they've been hurt. It's like they don't realise what's happened until a couple of seconds later when their heart stops beating and their legs fall out from under them. My eyes went to the spot where the spell had hit her, expecting to find a gaping wound. Instead I saw a rusted iron box. Trapped inside was a roiling mixture of darkness and light from the red mage's spell. Nephenia shut the lid and took two steps towards him. 'You used silk magic on me?' she demanded, her voice filled with a rage I'd never heard from her before. 'You put me to *sleep*?'

The Nephenia I'd known when we were initiates had been gentle, almost withdrawn. The charmcaster I'd met in the desert had been full of joy and recklessness. The woman before me now was just plain furious.

'Stay back,' the red mage said, his deep voice echoing all around us. 'I did not come for you.'

If that was supposed to make her feel better, it clearly didn't. Her expression only grew more incensed. Her hands shot forward. 'Too. Damn. Bad.'

The box flung open as it struck him. His own creature slithered out and started to attack him. Mages are especially vulnerable to their own spells, and most – even a lord magus – would be done for. This guy, though? He managed to get his hands to form the somatic shapes for three different dismissal spells, causing his own creation to burst into its component forms of magic and then fade to nothingness. By then Nephenia had already reached into her coat and removed a small wooden whistle. She blew into it and I heard a shriek so loud I thought my ears would burst. It was evidently much worse when you were directly in the charm's path, because the red mage slammed his hands over his ears. The lines of his mask twisted into an expression of pure agony.

Nephenia moved in close and punched him in the face – an impulsive attack rather than a wise one. She grunted in pain as her knuckles came back bloody from their collision with his lacquer mask. 'Are you going to help?' she asked me, more irritated than hurt.

'Sorry.' I got up and pulled powder from my pouches, but by then the red mage had somehow put up another shield that protected him from Nephenia's charm. He struck out at her with a hastily constructed lightning spell. The sparking blue tendrils grabbed hold of her, binding her tightly as they sent jolting shocks through her. 'Stop!' I shouted, and fired my own powder spell.

The red mage easily dismissed my attack, but then with a

twist of his right hand he banished the lightning spell. Nephenia fell to the ground next to me, her body still shaking. When the mage looked down at her, the lines of his mask twisted into an expression that was hard to recognise at first. *Despair.*

His hands came up, fingers twisted into somatic shapes I didn't recognise. Before I could get between him and Nephenia, his forearms crossed, the bands for silk and sand touching one another. They sparked so brightly that I was left blinded. I blinked furiously, trying to clear my vision. By the time I could see again, he was gone.

In the ensuing silence my own breathing became deafening. I went to Nephenia and knelt down to check her pulse. Her hand shot out and grabbed my wrist. 'Nephenia?' I asked. 'Are you—'

'I'm alive,' she said, though she didn't sound particularly happy about it. She pulled herself up, refusing my help. When she was standing again she locked eyes with me. 'Never use a sleep spell on me, Kellen. *Never.*'

'Why would I . . . Neph, I can't even spark my silk band. Why would you think I'd—'

She shook her head and it was as if her whole body shivered in response. 'I'm sorry.' She turned and reached down to pick up the iron box only to toss it away. 'Bastard.'

'Me?'

'*Him* of course! Do you have any idea how hard it was to make a netherbox?' With the toe of her boot she kicked the remains of her wooden whistle. 'And now my shrieking charm is busted too.'

That, of course, is the problem with charmcasting; anything you make with any real power either wears out over time or breaks after its first use. Still, I knew that couldn't be what had so enraged Nephenia. She caught me watching and said, 'I just hate silk magic, that's all.'

I let it go. Dense as I am sometimes, even I could tell this wasn't something she wanted to talk about. Not to me anyway.

Nephenia went to where Ishak and Reichis lay and knelt beside them. 'They're alive, but they're more vulnerable to sleep spells than we are.'

The hyena stirred, and his head came up to lick Nephenia's face.

'Where is he?' Reichis demanded sleepily. 'Did I kill that stupid mage?'

'Almost,' I replied, coming to sit next to him. 'You'll get him next time.'

'Got that right,' the squirrel cat growled. He reared up on his hind legs and toppled almost immediately. 'Just gonna nap here awhile first.'

'They'll need time and rest,' Nephenia said. She was watching me carefully as I retrieved my castradazi coins from the ground and checked my powders. I guess she knew what I was going to say next. She didn't look pleased about it.

'I'm going to need a favour, Neph.'

The problem with being attacked by vastly superior mages is that they make you late for important appointments like hunting down other mages.

Dissuading Nephenia from following me hadn't been easy. She'd assumed I was somehow trying to be noble and therefore convince her to stay behind so that I could venture into danger alone. It's funny how little people know me sometimes.

The simple truth was this: while the red mage had knocked

me around a lot, he'd been toying with me, never using his full strength. When Nephenia had attacked him, he'd instinctively struck back with lightning that was much worse than anything he'd used on me. She was in rougher shape than she let on. Reichis and Ishak could barely even walk on their own. Someone needed to get them back to Janucha's home and take care of them.

So why didn't I go with them? Why not abandon this obviously doomed attempt to track down the people responsible for this mess? Because I had no choice. Until now, the ones controlling the obsidian worm had been a step ahead of us. There was no way they'd predict we might defeat the red mage. Even if he could warn them in time, I was willing to bet they'd expect me to go back with the others to recuperate. This was my one chance to surprise them. I had to press that advantage before they could alter their plans.

Now all I had to do was find the damned black thread again.

My heart kept racing in an attempt to convince me that I really ought to be running away. I forced myself to relax just enough to attempt a little whisper magic. 'Come on, Suzy,' I pleaded, 'show me the path to the onyx bracelet. Help me find those sons of—'

A blast of air hit my right eye – this one burning hot.

'Ow! Stop attacking me all the time!'

The sensation was gone as quickly as it had appeared. The sasutzei wasn't trying to hurt me – just warn me off my present course of action. In her defence, the rest of my body was likewise concerned. 'Look,' I whispered furiously, 'I know that guy got the jump on us, but I'll be more careful this time.'

Nothing. No blast of hot or cold air, no reply at all. I tried a hundred whispers to cajole her into helping me, but none of them worked. Either the mages had broken their connection to the obsidian worm, or the sasutzei had simply decided not to show me the path.

Anger roiled inside my gut, rising up in my throat. I felt like someone was grabbing me by the lapels and shaking me, laughing in my face all the while. If I wanted to attempt whisper magic again, I'd need to calm down.

I didn't even try.

The skin around my left eye had begun to tingle, like a fingertip tracing a line along the winding markings of the shadowblack. Usually when the attacks come, they bring a sudden, burning pain. This time was different. It was almost playful. Beckoning me. Inviting me. A contrary sensation arose in my right eye as the sasutzei roused itself, hitting me with short blasts of cold as it tried to warn me off. I ignored it.

I opened myself to the shadowblack for the first time. 'I bet you know the way,' I said aloud. 'Show me.'

The glow of oil lanterns along the street faded from view. So too did the slivers of light from the windows of the homes on either side of me. Even the stars above me flickered off one by one until I found myself shrouded in darkness. The city itself disappeared, leaving behind only a desolate landscape unfit for the living. I looked down to find the cobblestones beneath my feet were gone and I now stood upon black sand.

I was lost in shadow.

The overwhelming sense of solitude was like being smothered beneath a thick blanket of sorrow. The warning blasts from the sasutzei withered away. Whatever the shadowblack was, whatever my grandmother had chosen to band me with as a child against all the laws of my people, I had taken my first willing step inside it.

'Show me,' I said again.

Though there were no roads in this place, the shadows at my feet gathered and thickened, twisting into a path. I had no reason to trust the shadowblack, and yet somehow I knew it would lead me where I wanted to go. It was as eager to find the mages as I was; it knew what I would do to them once I found them. That was the real reason why I'd sent Nephenia away with Ishak and Reichis – the one I couldn't bring myself to say out loud.

Enna had been right when she'd given me that card on the bridge. There was a price to be paid to put a stop to the conspirators who had so quickly brought two nations to the brink of war. It was a price someone like Ferius – someone who'd fought and won against their own darkest impulses – should never have to pay. It was a price I wouldn't allow any of my friends to pay.

Someone had to kill the mages.

Not try to stop them.

Kill them.

It had to be me.

36

The Tower

I walked in shadow until my soul couldn't take it any more. Without a sun or moon or sky of any kind, there was no way to keep track of time. I knew only that with every step I felt sicker. More hollow.

Though the landscape wasn't that of Cazaran, still I saw people there. Shadows of people, anyway. They muttered to themselves, staring into the distance at things I could not see. They spoke of longing, or consuming dread, or terrible shame. They whispered their deepest and darkest secrets, but I closed my ears to them, afraid their sorrows would swallow me whole.

I felt myself begin to sink into the onyx sand. 'Let me go,' I begged the shadowblack.

The skin around my left eye blazed, as if the markings themselves were angered by my plea. Just as the pain became unbearable, I found myself released. Bright lights blinded me, a thousand pinpricks stabbed at my eyes. I was on my knees, staring up at the stars. My surroundings were only dimly lit by a half-moon, yet for the first few seconds I had to squint from the intensity of it all.

I struggled to my feet. It was still dark, so I couldn't have walked for more than a few hours. There were new scrapes along my arms and shoulders that must have come from stumbling into the edges of buildings, and a cut on my cheek that I couldn't explain. When I brought my fingertips higher – to the skin around my left eye – I was sure the markings had grown again.

I was in a narrow alleyway and had to walk to the street to get my bearings. There were fewer lights here than in the centre of the city. A patchwork of unremarkable storehouses and dull little supply depots dotted the sloped terrain that led up to a tall arch and a wide road beyond.

The eastern trade route, I thought. *I must be in the warehouse district.*

The slapping of sandalled feet against the cobblestones forced me to duck back into the alleyway. I waited and watched until a man in simple merchant's clothes walked past me towards a tall, unguarded grain tower. He looked like a perfectly unassuming trade delegate, probably from the Seven Sands. Only, I'd been around those people. Folks on the frontier tend to walk with a sort of wide-legged stride, almost a strut. The man before me carried himself with a good deal more formality, as though he were walking past admiring throngs rather than along an empty street.

If there's a surer way to identify a Jan'Tep mage from a major house, I haven't found it yet, but I had to be certain.

I dug in my pocket and took out my castradazi coins. I still didn't know what each did, but right now that wasn't important. I chose one of the coins at random and threw it at a brass-rimmed barrel sitting outside a supply shed just after the would-be merchant passed by. The clang gave him a fright. When he spun around I saw the tell-tale glow of sparking bands beneath his shirtsleeves.

Got you.

I waited for him to reassure himself that it was just the sort of random noise you hear around buildings that tend to attract rats. Once he resumed his march, I retrieved my coin and padded softly behind him. I was moving in a passable imitation of the way Reichis stalks a rabbit. I probably looked pretty ridiculous, but if anyone saw me I'd have bigger problems to deal with than public humiliation.

The mage in merchant's clothes walked to a solitary grain tower. It didn't look like much to me, but he circled it carefully before stopping at the door. I hid in the shadows of the building opposite and watched as he performed a series of small, precise gestures that ended with his palm an inch or so from the door where he drew a small circle in the air. A series of clicks was accompanied by a glow that emanated from the centre of the door. A second later, it opened of its own accord and light streamed out. The mage began to step inside but then stopped, turned, and stared right at me.

Crap, I thought, my fingers longing to reach for my powders.

Every instinct screamed at me to run. That's not unusual though – my instincts are cowards. But a minuscule sensible part of my brain reminded me that I was standing in complete darkness whereas the mage's eyes had just been hit with the light from inside the door. Chances are he was completely night-blind right now, and would be for at least a few more seconds.

I started counting in my head, which is actually a pretty bad way to keep time when you're nervous. For just an instant the mage's bands sparked again, but then he turned and entered the building.

I let myself breathe and listened for the sound of his

footsteps. I could just begin to hear him walking upstairs when the door began to close itself. It moved so slowly that I wondered why he hadn't pushed it closed before heading up the stairs. Then it occurred to me that I hadn't seen him touch the door at all. Doing so would almost certainly trigger an alarm spell or, more likely, do something unpleasant to the would-be intruder.

Move, I told myself. In a few seconds the door would be closed and I'd have lost my chance. *On the other hand, if he's not already at the top of the stairs, he'll see you coming in.*

It's moments like these when you really need to dig inside yourself for some deep well of courage, determination, or just a reckless disregard for your own well-being. Lacking any of those things, I thought back to Cressia's eyes rolling up into her head as oily black tears dripped down her cheeks and the worm's tendrils flowed out from her mouth, pushing her body to the very edge of death. With that memory firmly in mind, I took two quick breaths and ran for the grain tower. Slipping past the door just before it shut, I entered the lair of my enemy.

The ground floor was a dusty mess of tools, buckets, barrels and broken-down carts. The stairs I'd heard the man climbing wound up in a circle that ran along the outer wall of the tower, vanishing into a gap about twenty feet up where the next floor began. I waited at the bottom of the stairs, listening until I could hear the faint sounds of voices above. I closed my eyes and whispered to the sasutzei, 'I know you're angry with me, but if you could just tell me where they're keeping the onyx bracelet, it would be a big help.'

Nothing. I couldn't even feel the subtle wavering breeze of her presence.

Apparently Suzy and I were done.

Okay, I thought. *Simple plans are the best: run up the stairs, kick in the door and blast them before they can get a shield up. From there it's just a matter of making sure everybody's good and dead, then find the bracelet.*

I reached into my pouches to touch the powders – a habit I'd got into whenever I needed to make sure I was ready for a fight. My hands came out with grains of powder stuck to the fingertips. I was sweating. This, I've learned the hard way, is my body's way of telling me when I'm about to execute a terrible plan.

If life were at all fair, Ferius would be here with me and we'd be following *her* plans, which were invariably stranger – but ultimately better – than my own.

Well, Ferius isn't here, I reminded myself. *You're alone. Maybe that's how it's meant to be.*

I walked as quietly as I could to the other side of the room. A ladder bolted to the wall travelled up to a hole in the second floor that had to be at least twenty feet from where the voices were coming from. I reached up and grabbed one of the rungs, testing it to make sure it wasn't rotten all the way through. A broken leg makes for a lousy companion when you're trying to get the jump on someone.

The rung felt solid enough. I took my first step, then my second, slowly but surely making my way up the ladder. I stopped just before the hole in the ceiling above me. I couldn't see any light, which I took as a good sign. I kept climbing until I was high enough to step off onto the first floor. The boards creaked, but not so much that someone would've heard it over the sound of their own conversation.

When I surveyed my surroundings, I found I was at the end of a short corridor with small rooms on either side. Over near the stairs, light seeped from under a crack beneath one of the doors.

This is it, I thought, fighting and failing to stay calm. *The onyx bracelet is in there. The bastards who killed Revian, and will just as happily kill Cressia if it suits their purposes, are waiting for you even if they don't know it yet. Waiting to see if you're more than just a dumb kid with a powder spell.*

Among the Jan'Tep, the duel is a sacred thing. How else do you keep any semblance of honour among a people who can use magic to murder their enemies in their sleep? I had grown up in that tradition, believing that to attack a fellow mage without warning was not just craven, but utterly and irredeemably damning to the soul. But if I gave the people in that room a sliver of a chance, they'd kill me without a second thought. After all, I wasn't a proper Jan'Tep mage. Just a spellslinger.

Was I ready to do the same? To end their lives without so much as a word of warning?

I slid my hands into the pouches at my side. My fingers came out dry.

Damn right I was ready.

37

The Quick Draw

I hadn't made it two steps when a gloved hand clamped hard around my mouth. Before I could so much as twitch, my assailant's other arm was around my throat. 'Foolish little spellslinger,' the voice whispered, so quiet I might've imagined it. 'Did you think you could enter a mage's lair unnoticed?'

I should have struggled, tried some ingenious move to throw off my opponent, but I froze. My tongue tasted bitter as all the fear I'd pushed aside in my rush to attack came down on me like an avalanche.

The arm didn't tighten though. It just held me perfectly still. 'Well, child, where are all your Argosi tricks now?'

Good question. *Think, damn it.* Ferius says that when you can't think your way out of a jam, it's usually because you're trying so hard to figure out what to do that you forget to pay attention to what's going on around you. *Okay, so what's happening here?*

The voice had been menacing. Terrifying. But also elusive somehow. My opponent wasn't choking me, yet I couldn't move my head to see anything but the top of the glove. The leather carried a trace of something else . . . the faint scent of ash from a fire or . . . *smoking reeds.*

Very slowly, I reached up my right hand just over my head and felt behind me. My fingers touched the brim of a hat. 'Damn it,' I mumbled into the glove.

Ferius Parfax chuckled softly, then let me go. She nodded to one of the nearby rooms. I followed her inside, angry and yet so relieved to see her that I almost forgot where we were. 'Why are you here?' I asked.

She reached out and put a hand on my shoulder. 'Where else would I be, kid?'

My mouth was unusually dry all of a sudden. Before I could say anything she took her hand away and put a finger to her lips. 'Stay quiet,' she said. 'I ain't taught you how to whisper properly yet, so just let me do the talking, okay?'

Ferius was watching me, waiting for a sign that I understood. I nodded my assent. She did likewise, as though we'd just struck some kind of bargain. 'You were headed in there ready to murder those folks, kid. I saw it in your eyes.'

I felt both ashamed and annoyed by that. Who was Ferius to accuse me? I was only doing this because *she* wouldn't – because *her* parents had told me it was my job to do the dirty work so she could stay on her path.

'I'm not sayin' you're wrong,' she said softly. 'Just want to make sure you're willing to live with the consequences. You don't know who's in there. Are you sure you can kill a stranger?'

A stranger? Whoever was wearing that onyx bracelet had tortured and killed more than once. I'd been there when they'd used Revian as the anchor for an ember spell that burned his family alive, only to then make him turn that same magic on himself. They hadn't shown him an ounce of mercy, any more than they would Cressia.

Whoever was in that room? They weren't strangers to me any more.

Ferius must have seen something in my gaze, because she gave a slight nod. 'Okay, kid. Let the cards fall where they may.'

We stepped back into the corridor, moving as silently as we could on the creaky boards. At the end of the corridor, she reached into her waistcoat and drew her deck of razor-sharp steel cards. She put a hand on my shoulder to signal for me to wait, then she set herself two steps back from the door. I hadn't quite mastered the art of kicking in doors yet.

I pulled powder from my pouches – more than was safe. I'd probably come away from this with some nasty burns, but I wasn't taking any chances. If the red mage was in there, I couldn't afford to let him get a shield up in time. Ferius was watching me, waiting to make sure I was ready. I locked eyes with her and nodded.

She leaned her back against the wall for just a second, then drove forward, raised one leg and slammed the heel of her boot into the door barely an inch from the lock. The door burst open with an ear-splitting crack. For barely a second it hung off one hinge before crashing to the floor.

I stepped in front of Ferius. With the precision and reflexes that came from months of practice I tossed my powders into the air. Even before they collided my hands had taken on the somatic shapes. As I uttered the first syllable of the invocation, my eyes adjusted to the light. I counted three figures in the room, seated close enough together that one blast would take them all and finally bring an end to the obsidian worms.

'*Ca—*'

The incantation died on my lips. The powders clashed together and a flash of red and black flame blinded us all for an instant before fading into nothingness. I was left standing there like an idiot, staring at my enemies, and one in particular who I'd recognised just in time to stop myself from murdering her.

'Shalla?'

38

The Delegate

My little sister looked up at me with a hint of a smile. 'Brother!' she said, and leaped up from her chair to hug me, as if three seconds before I hadn't been a hair's breadth from turning her to ash.

'Shalla?' I hadn't seen my sister in over a year – not since I'd left the Jan'Tep territories. Well, that's if you don't count the times she used spells to make her face appear in a patch of sand or a bowl of water from hundreds of miles away. She usually went to all this trouble for the sole purpose of expressing her disapproval over some new embarrassment my being an outlaw had caused our family.

'Of course it's me, silly. Who else would it be?'

Good question, I thought, unsure if I could trust her and yet unable to stop myself from returning her embrace. Silk magic is effective for deceiving the eyes and ears, but it's less reliable with the other senses. The girl in my arms certainly gripped me with the determined affection Shalla showed when she wasn't irritated with me. She *felt* like my Shalla. The scent of her hair, so much like our mother's, reminded me of home. But if this *was* my little sister, then that begged a question: 'What in the names of our ancestors are you doing here, Shalla?'

She let go of me and took a step back to strike an unmistakably condescending and self-righteous pose. *Okay, this is definitely Shalla.*

'I'm our clan delegate to Gitabria, *obviously*.'

'Wait . . . You're the what? You're only thirteen years old! How could they—'

'I'm *fifteen*, silly. I'm two years younger than you, and my birthday comes two weeks before yours.' Her face lit up in a smile. 'Which means we missed your birthday! We must celebrate together!'

Her unbridled enthusiasm left me speechless. Not so the others in the room.

'Enough of this nonsense!' the older of the two mages said. Layers of silver-and-grey robes stretched around his belly as he pounded a heavy fist against the table. 'This wretch is a traitor to our people!'

The younger man – the one dressed as a merchant who I'd followed inside the tower – spoke with less exuberance but equal hostility. 'Lord Magus Hath'emad is correct. This one is shadowblack. It is our duty as Jan'Tep to end his life.'

'Don't be ridiculous,' Shalla said. 'Kellen is my brother.'

'Then I'll happily deal with him myself,' Hath'emad declared, pushing himself to his feet with no small effort. Grey and gold shimmered about his forearms as he drew on the magics of iron and sand.

Before he could speak his invocation, a steel playing card embedded itself in the wall less than an inch from his face. 'Reckon we'll all get along better if you keep a civil tongue, friend.'

The card was still vibrating, fluttering against Hath'emad's cheek. 'Perhaps I *was* hasty, Argosi.' He stepped away from the wall, holding his hands up, palms out to show he wasn't about to cast a spell. 'Dal'ven? You kill them.'

Without hesitation the younger mage took on the shape of the second somatic form of lightning – hardly the most powerful variant of ember magic, but certainly the quickest. The moment the final syllable of his incantation passed his lips, blue and white tendrils of energy came for us. I dived in front of Ferius. It wasn't from any courageous impulse on my part, simply that she was more likely to be able to take him out before his spell killed one of us. Besides, I'd been hit by lightning spells so many times I had to be building up some kind of resistance by now, right?

Ferius caught me in her arms. 'You're a sweet kid sometimes, you know that?'

'You were supposed to throw something at him!' I replied, a little embarrassed. But oddly not electrocuted.

I turned to see the tendrils of Dal'ven's bolts halted just a few inches away. The sparks threw themselves against an invisible barrier keeping them from us. 'That will be enough of *that*,' Shalla said, her right hand slowly pushing outward.

The muscles in Dal'ven's fingers tensed and the copper sigils of the ember band tattooed around his forearm flared. Being undermined by my little sister didn't appear to agree with him. 'Do not think to command me simply because your father is clan prince.'

'Oh, I wouldn't dream of it,' she replied. With nothing but a twitch of her own fingers, the barrier pushed the lightning back towards its source. 'There's a much simpler reason why you ought to obey me.'

Dal'ven's face was already slick with sweat and his brow

furrowed as he struggled to keep his own spell from shocking him to death.

'I warned them not to send a precocious child as our delegate,' Hath'emad growled. He placed his palms against each other as though he were about to shake hands with himself. He twisted them together and the iron band on his forearm shimmered. A simple spell we used to call the fettering magnet when I was an initiate. *But why? All it does is create a connection between two spells . . . Oh, hell.*

'Ferius!' I shouted. There wasn't time to explain that Hath'emad was about to bind Shalla's shield to Dal'ven's lightning and kill her with it in the process. If I tried firing my powder spell into the mix to stop him, I'd end up creating an explosion that would kill all of us.

'On it,' Ferius said. Though she seems to take pride in her ignorance of magic, she has an uncanny knack for guessing people's intentions. Hath'emad was halfway through the invocation when a second steel card lodged itself in his mouth.

He spat it out. Blood came with it.

'Awgothy bith!' he swore. Well, I think that's what he said. It's hard to talk when your tongue is bleeding that profusely.

'Now what did I say about keeping a civil tongue?' Ferius asked.

Hath'emad was gesticulating furiously, several of his tattooed bands sparking, but without noticeable effect.

'Hey, kid,' Ferius said. 'You don't suppose enunciation is important for spellcasting, do you?'

The air between Shalla and Dal'ven sizzled as she forced his ember spell back on him. 'Come now, my lord,' she said idly. 'I'm not even a proper war mage. Just an impudent girl. Isn't that what the two of you keep reminding me?' I don't know why Shalla insists on taunting her elders, but she's been doing it since the day she uttered her first coherent sentence and shows no signs of slowing down as she gets older. 'Surely one of you two great and powerful mages is prepared to teach me a little lesson in magic?'

Dal'ven's eyes had grown so wide you could see the sparks of his own lightning reflected in them. 'Enough!' he said, dropping the spell. 'I yield.'

Shalla looked disappointed. 'Oh, all right.' She turned back to me. 'Now, brother, let's talk about your birthday.' She tapped a finger against her lower lip and frowned. 'Gitabria is such a gauche little country. I'm afraid we won't be able to celebrate as we should, but still . . .' She spared a passing glance at the two mages behind her. 'One does what one can with the resources available.'

How do you reply to that kind of insanity? She'd always had that effect on me – like a whirlpool that draws everything around it into its own swirling miasma of confusion.

For a moment there, it almost looked like we'd get through this without bloodshed – well, except for Hath'emad's tongue. But then Ferius said, 'Kid, you're paying too much attention to the forest. Don't miss the trees.'

I thought she must be referring to Dal'ven or Hath'emad, but neither had moved so much as an inch. Then I looked back at Shalla and noticed something odd. All this time, she'd kept her left arm at her side, the sleeve of her gown covering her wrist.

Ancestors, please, no. 'Shalla,' I said, my voice sounding cold even to me, 'hold up your right hand.'

My sister saw where I was staring. 'Don't be like this, Kellen. We'll talk tomorrow when you've—'

'Hold up your right hand, sister. Now.'

She raised both hands, in fact – as close to an act of submission as I'd ever seen from her. The sleeve of her shirt slid down her arm. 'Brother, there are things you don't know. Things you *need* to understand before—'

Sometimes I think maybe I'm two different people. One of them is a whiny Jan'Tep boy, desperate for all the things he'd wished for as a child: to be safe; to wield the high magics of his people; to be with his family. But the other Kellen? He's an outlaw – an outcast older than his years and sick to death of the unconscionable ways his people use their magic. It was the outcast who saw the onyx bracelet around his sister's wrist and reached inside the pouches at his side for the powders that would blast her from existence.

39

Sibling Rivalry

The problem with threats is that not everyone waits for you to finish them. In fact, some people don't even let you get started.

The powders weren't even out of my pouches before everything went to hell. Dal'ven and Hath'emad were already lighting up the room with the glow of their tattooed bands as they brought their hands up to form the somatic shapes of a pair of particularly nasty spells. Their invocations turned to howls of pain as Ferius's steel cards sliced into the flesh of their palms.

Dal'ven recovered a lot quicker than I would've expected and sent a burst of iron magic spikes that should've skewered her right where she stood, except she wasn't standing there any more. With that uncanny tactical awareness of hers, Ferius had already launched herself into a shoulder roll the moment she'd flung the cards. She went under the mage's spikes and came up right behind him, the edge of a razor-sharp steel card resting against the ball of his throat. 'You tried to kill me just then, friend. Most places on this continent that gives me the right to make sure you never cast another spell. I'd prefer it if you were to come to that conclusion on your own, but I'll let you decide.'

A few feet away, Hath'emad's bleeding hands shook as he fought to calm himself enough to attempt a counter-attack. The outrage and contempt in his eyes was something to behold. Ferius kept her card on Dal'ven's neck while she gave Hath'emad a tolerant smile. 'Really, old man? You think I haven't worked this out? You reckon I went to all this trouble without a plan for dealing with you?'

'A thousand times will you die, Argosi,' he declared, still lisping a little from his bleeding tongue, but doing an impressive job of enunciating his threats. 'You will scream. You will beg. Even as I—'

'Hold that thought, master mage,' she interrupted, then turned her gaze to me. 'Kid, I told you before: this is your decision to make, but make it one you can live with.'

Shalla was watching me, making no effort to protect herself or hide the bracelet. Her expression wasn't so much concerned as curious – as if she were wondering why it was taking me so long to solve a simple problem. 'Brother, are you quite all right? You appear unwell.'

Absurd as it sounded, the question was sincere. The thing about Shalla is that she loves me. She always has. How could something so simple and pure be housed within such callous self-interest? How could she so willingly participate in the torture of Cressia – a girl who'd never done her any harm? How could my sister support the attempted assassination of Janucha, in an effort to ruin the hopes of an entire country?

Because Shalla is the worst of all of them. Those were the words my uncle Abydos had spoken to me on the day he tried to get me to help him counter-band her and take away her magic. *'I've tried to get her to change,'* he'd said, *'but she is a perfect replica of Ke'heops in female form, only she will be stronger than he ever was . . . She'll be the worst tyrant our people have ever seen.'*

'Kid,' Ferius said, 'you've got about three seconds to make a decision here.'

Shalla shot her a contemptuous glare. 'You must be mad, Argosi, to think my brother would ever harm me.' She reached out and took my arm. 'No matter what nonsense he believes.'

She always did think she knew me better than I knew myself. But she was wrong. She had no idea how much I longed to throw off her hand and toss the powders into the air; to see the look on her face when they collided and I said the word. I might have less power than Shalla, but I was sure I was faster. I could outdraw her. I could *end* her.

Without warning, the shadowblack took me. The room, the tower, the whole city disappeared for me. I was back in the place of onyx sands, where all was darkness and yet I could see with perfect clarity. The people in the room were gone, replaced by otherworldly versions of themselves. Shalla shifted between two different beings: one who smiled with cruel delight as thousands upon thousands of men and women dangled from strings attached to her fingers. The other was pleading with someone off in the distance behind me. 'Please, don't make me do this,' she cried over and over.

'Kid?' The voice belonged to Ferius Parfax, but not the one I could see standing alone on the shadowy beach staring out at an endless black ocean. 'Kid, you gotta come back now.'

Why did it matter? I was alone here, as were the rest of them. If I just stayed in this desolate place, maybe the world would forget about me. Maybe I wouldn't have to hurt my sister.

'Kellen, don't!' Shalla screamed from somewhere far away just as a blast of icy-cold air in my right eye shocked me to my senses. Suddenly I was back in the room, the dim light from the lanterns blinding me.

That's not the lanterns, I realised too late. *It's the flash of my powders!*

Black and red flames had just begun to flare and my hands were aiming the somatic shapes right at my sister's heart. I could feel the one-word incantation of the spell vibrating on my lips, too late for me to stop. It was the look of sorrow on Shalla's face that struck me with a force as raw as iron magic and let me turn my hands just enough to save her. The blast that tore through the tower's outer wall was big enough to ride a horse through.

A wisp of my sister's hair, the gold burned to black, floated between us. 'Who . . . Who are you?' she asked. The question sounded curious. Genuine. As if for a second she really hadn't recognised me.

Ferius looked equally confused, even as she kept her eyes darting between the two mages to make sure neither attempted an attack. 'Kellen,' she said slowly, as if my name was unfamiliar to her. 'He's Kellen.'

'No,' said Hath'emad, his fingers holding a binding shape. 'He is not.'

Unnatural grey light from the iron band on his forearm spun out into gleaming strands that whipped around our throats, holding us immobile. The lord magus stepped out from the wall and examined his handiwork before walking over to Ferius. He carefully removed the steel card she'd been holding to Dal'ven's throat. Then he came for me.

Hath'emad took the card between his thumb and forefinger and placed its cutting edge at the ridge of my left eye. 'His name is Shadowblack.'

40

The Shadowblack

After what I'd done, you'd think my sister would've been content to watch Hath'emad slice my eye from its socket. Instead she grabbed his arm, hauling on him without effect. Her slim figure next to his bulk made it look as if she were trying to climb a tree. 'I am the chief delegate of our clan.' Shalla gave the words as much authority as her quavering voice allowed. '*I* will decide what to do about my brother.'

'No,' the big man said. 'I am done taking orders from a child.'

Something profound had changed in Hath'emad. He stared at the black markings around my eye without a trace of anger or viciousness in him, only determination. This wasn't about hatred for me any more, but rather a sacred duty to rid the world of what he saw as an imminent danger to his people. Hath'emad was the hero now, and I was the monster.

The pinch of the card's edge began to bite into the skin near my eye. Ferius was still trapped by the mage's iron binding. Dal'ven watched her, slowing his breathing in preparation for what I had no doubt would be very unpleasant spells to use against her.

'Lord Magus Hath'emad,' Shalla shouted, 'you *will* heed my

words.' Light flickered from the sigils on the tattooed bands for iron and ember around her forearms, but the sparks died just as quickly.

'Terror is hard to swallow, isn't it?' Hath'emad said, his gaze still on me. 'It sticks to the throat, choking off our incantations. Makes our hands shake until they can no longer form the somatic shapes. With experience, it gets easier. But experience is what you lack, little girl. So no, I will not heed your words. I will be leading our mission in Gitabria from now on.'

'My father—'

'The new clan prince has not shown himself to be sentimental.' The edge of the card dug deeper into the markings on my skin and I felt a drop of blood begin to slide down my cheek. 'If he were, don't you think he would have lifted the spell warrant against his own son?'

Don't show fear. Show them arta valar. I briefly considered one of Reichis's usual retorts, but this didn't seem like the time to talk about eating people's eyeballs.

'Hey, kid,' Ferius called out.

I couldn't even turn my head to see her. 'Yeah?' I asked, with all the casual indifference possible for someone whose voice is barely a squeak.

'I ever show you my favourite summoning spell?'

Her question made Dal'ven throw up his hands to conjure a shield against an attack that wasn't coming. 'Don't be a fool,' Hath'emad said. 'This is what the Argosi do: they talk and talk and talk, hoping to use their words to delay and deceive. They have no magic.'

Ferius made a 'tut-tut' sound. 'You know, the kid says that all the time, and I keep having to prove him wrong. Like this, see?' She pursed her lips and let out a piercing whistle so loud I thought my ears would rupture. It carried through the hole in the outer wall to the street outside. A second later we all heard the tower door, followed by heavy boot heels running across the lower floor and then up the stairs. Lots of boot heels.

'That there,' Ferius said casually, almost seeming to rest against Hath'emad's binding spell, 'is a contingent of the Gitabrian secret police. They have a more respectable name, I'm told, but make no mistake, they have a nasty disposition – especially towards spies and assassins who sneak into their country and try to kill their favourite contraptioneer.'

More than a dozen men and women crowded outside the room. They wore leather armour covered in thin copper-coloured plates I'd never seen before. About half bore tall shields covered in sigils that I recognised as wards against spellcraft. Others gripped long iron tubes with both hands, aiming them at the mages.

'Those funny sticks are called fire lances,' Ferius said to me. 'They kind of do what your little powder spell does, only the results ain't quite so pretty.'

Hath'emad dropped the steel card and stepped away from me, his left hand conjuring an iron shield spell that wrapped around him while his right drew on ember magic. Without so much as a word of warning, a young woman twisted the two halves of her fire lance in opposite directions. A blue spark at their meeting point was followed by a deafening roar of thunder. Smoke and fire exploded from the front end of the fire lance.

My eyes blinked back tears and my ears rang. I felt Hath'emad's binding spell slip away, and turned just in time to see a hole in his chest that let the lantern light behind him shine right through before he fell to the floor.

The fire lances and spell-shields moved aside to let a figure come through the smoke and enter the room. I saw the dark curly hair draping to the black epaulettes on her uniform before the early morning sun entering through the hole I'd blasted in the wall illuminated her features. 'Visitors of the Jan'Tep territories,' she began, 'I am Servadi Zavera té Drazo. It is my privilege to formally welcome you to Gitabria, and my duty to inform you that you are now my prisoners.'

It was an impressive entrance. Ferius didn't seem to care. 'Damn it, Zavera,' she said, shaking off the last effects of Hath'emad's binding spell. 'We had a deal.'

The Gitabrian spymaster – for I was certain that's what Zavera really was – ignored Ferius and went to stand over the mage's smouldering corpse. 'We agreed no *unnecessary* deaths. Perhaps you should have persuaded the mage not to attack us.'

'Those fancy shields of yours would've protected you from his magic and you know it!'

Zavera looked around the room, barely taking notice of me despite our previous acquaintance. 'I allowed you the first opportunity to deal with the conspirators, Argosi. I'd hoped to avoid intervening and thus setting off what will no doubt be a series of arduous and long-winded diplomatic exchanges with the Jan'Tep arcanocracy. As you have failed to fulfil your part of the bargain, you can hardly hold me to mine.'

Shalla, in a remarkable display of poise given the unhealthy pallor that had come over her face, spoke in tones that conveyed only the mildest disappointment in what had transpired. 'Servadi Drazo, I am Magiziera Shalla fal Ke, delegate of the Jan'Tep—'

'I know who you are, magiziera.' Without even deigning to look at Shalla, the spymaster reached out a hand and grabbed my sister's arm, raising it up and almost lifting her off the floor. Zavera removed the onyx bracelet from Shalla's wrist and tossed it to me. 'I assume you know what to do with this?'

I caught it in the air and examined it only briefly before placing it on the floor so I could crush it under my boot.

'Kellen, don't destroy it!' Shalla called out to me.

I rested my heel against the bracelet. 'You think I'd *ever* allow this foul thing to be used again?'

'You don't understand! The Gitabrian girl has had the worm inside her too long. If you shatter the bracelet, the shock could kill her. Use the bracelet to draw out the worm from her eye instead. There's less risk to her and it won't be nearly as painful.'

I knelt down and retrieved the onyx bracelet. The part of the obsidian worm that had been split from the one in Cressia's eye slithered inside the glimmering stones as if it were swimming in oil.

'Kellen, please trust me. Not everything is the way it appears. You know you can just as easily destroy the bracelet after you've cured the girl.' Without waiting for any reply from me, she turned back to Zavera. 'I am the Jan'Tep delegate, servadi. Our two peoples share long-standing diplomatic traditions. You cannot arrest me without first severing my status as their representative, which requires prior notification to the councils of lords magi. How do you think the Jan'Tep will respond when they learn you took me prisoner like some street urchin caught stealing bread?'

Zavera signalled to two of her officers. They brought forth a pair of thick copper shackles wound in layer upon layer of thin spell wire and clamped them around Shalla's forearms. 'You are not being arrested, *delegati*. Merely detained in a guest house we reserve for those of your lofty rank.'

'No,' Shalla whispered. 'Please, don't take me to Notia Veras.'

'You Jan'Tep,' the spymaster said, finally allowing a measure of disdain to break through her otherwise implacable expression, 'you think you are so very special because of your little magics. Always threatening. Always looking down on my people. What is it you call us? "Tinkers and traders"? Perhaps we are, but we are also explorers and scientists. Those things we understand least compel us most to seek out answers. Those bands you have imprinted on your arms as children, they are wondrous. Beyond our ability to comprehend or reproduce. That is why we have worked so very hard to find a way to counter them.'

Dal'ven, kneeling by Hath'emad's corpse, looked up with a desperate panic in his eyes. Nothing horrifies a Jan'Tep mage more than the prospect of being denied their magics. Still, I had to admire his defiance when he shouted, 'Those foul restraints will not long hold me, Gitabrian! This I swear: you will suffer more than you imagined possible once I am free.'

Zavera turned to Ferius. 'You see the kind of threats I am forced to deal with?' She sighed. 'Still, the lords mercantile long ago warned me that service to one's homeland required sacrifice.'

'Don't,' Ferius warned. 'The boy's all talk. Just a lot of hot air, that's all.'

'*Hot air*? An apt choice of words for an Argosi. After all, what follows the Way of Wind? Ah, I remember now.' Zavera's hand whipped past Dal'ven's neck. 'The Way of Thunder, is it not?'

I hadn't even seen her draw the blade from the cuff of her coat. Blood began to gush from Dal'ven's throat, spilling down his robes to pool on the floor.

'No!' Ferius shouted. 'I said no more killing!' She launched herself at Zavera.

The guard next to me started to raise up her fire lance. I rammed my shoulder into her and pulled powder in the hope I could use the blast to distract the others while Ferius took out Zavera. I was just about to toss them when the spymaster shouted, 'Drop the powder or she dies!'

I turned and saw something that froze the blood in my veins.

Since the day I'd first met her, I'd witnessed Ferius Parfax square off against mages, soldiers, bully-boys and just about everything else you could imagine. I'd seen her outnumbered and out-powered. The one thing I'd never seen was someone get the drop on her.

Zavera had one arm wrapped around Ferius's neck. In her other hand she held a blade so thin it looked like a long needle. The tip was pressed against Ferius's temple. 'The master contraptioneer of Gitabria was most insistent that I not break anything of yours that she could not herself repair,' the spymaster said without a trace of ire. 'I would prefer to keep my word.'

I let the powders drop to the floor.

The spymaster let go of Ferius. I could see the twitch of my Argosi mentor's hands that meant she was about to make a move. Apparently Zavera did too, because she dropped the needle and drove her fist into Ferius's lower back, right at the spot where she'd been so badly injured in the desert, then slapped the edge of her hand into her throat. Ferius dropped to the floor, gagging.

Zavera pulled back her foot, ready to drive it into Ferius's stomach, an eagerness in her eyes that told me once she started, she wouldn't stop.

I said something stupid then. 'She's not like you.'

The spymaster looked over at me, foot still raised, mild curiosity in her gaze. 'No?'

I shook my head. 'No matter what you do to her, Ferius won't come after you. She won't try to hurt you or get retribution for what you've done.'

'And you, spellslinger? Will you one day seek me out and get revenge for what I've done to your mentor?'

I breathed in, slowly, and closed my eyes. I thought back to where every person in the room had been standing. Zavera, Ferius, Shalla, the officers with spell-shields and the ones with fire lances. I worked out who was close to me, who had a weapon aimed at me, and what I'd need to do to get one good shot in before they got me. When I opened my eyes I said, 'Touch her again and I won't wait that long.'

'Kid, don't,' Ferius coughed.

I kept my eyes on Zavera, who looked not in the least bit afraid of me. 'A killer then,' she said, and stepped over Ferius to walk towards me.

Shalla absurdly rushed to me, the copper restraints around her forearms banging against my wrists as she took my hands. 'Please, brother, don't do anything foolish!' She dropped to her knees and cried even as she clung to me. 'I don't want you to die, Kellen!'

Zavera chuckled at this, and either came to her senses or decided whatever she'd been planning to do to me could just as easily wait until later. 'Now, now, magiziera,' she said, grabbing Shalla by the shoulders and hoisting her to her feet.

'Let us retain as much of our dignity as we can. You, after all, are the chief trade delegate of the Jan'Tep people. Do not weep and wail like a street urchin caught stealing bread.'

'They're taking me to Notia Veras,' Shalla said to me. 'Get word to our father, Kellen. Please. You don't know what they do to mages there!'

The spymaster smiled at me as if we were old friends. 'Our business is concluded for now, spellslinger. I imagine Credara Janucha zal Ghassan would be most grateful if you could make all speed to her residence and free her daughter from the creature your people put inside her. On the other hand, if you would prefer to challenge me . . .'

I put up my hand, still holding the onyx bracelet. 'I'll help Cressia.'

Zavera nodded, and led her squad out of the building, hauling Shalla along with them and leaving me feeling like even less of a human being than I had before this had all started. It wasn't as if I hadn't wanted to put up a fight for Shalla. It's just that I was too busy sliding the card she'd snuck me into the cuff of my sleeve.

The Crowned Mage

THE GAZE

Be wary of the discordance cards you place within your deck. There are others besides the Argosi who paint symbols of change. Their purposes are not ours and the cards they create can be dangerous. Gaze too long upon them and you may soon find something staring right back at you.

41

The Missing Question

It occurred to me, as Ferius and I spent the better part of the early morning hours stumbling our way through the warehouse district on the way back to the city centre, that every time one of my brilliant plans fell apart, someone handed me a card as if to say, 'I told you so.'

The Mechanical Bird. The Contraptioneer. The Path of Shadows. The Crowned Mage.

I was getting sick of discordance cards.

'That ain't no discordance, kid,' Ferius insisted, handing me back the card. For about the tenth time she tried taking a drag from the smoking reed hanging from her mouth that she still hadn't lit. Even that small act made her wince. It hurt when she walked; it hurt when she tried to take a deep breath. Not even that perpetual swagger of hers could hide how badly she was injured. Watching her pretend for my sake that she was okay made me feel even worse. If I hadn't messed up in that tower – if I hadn't let the shadowblack take me over for the brief second it took to ruin everything – Ferius would have kept the situation under control. She wouldn't have had to signal for the secret police. She wouldn't have almost been beaten to death by that crazy Gitabrian spymaster. Enna's words on the Forest Bridge echoed in my mind: '*How many times has my daughter nearly died saving your life?*'

'M'fine, kid,' she mumbled. 'Quit starin' at me like I'm a glass vase teetering off a table.'

She hadn't even turned to look at me so I had no idea how she could tell.

Since making a fuss or trying to get her to rest wouldn't do any good, I turned my attention to the card itself. 'How do you know it's not a discordance?'

She answered with a question of her own. 'What do you see?'

A gleaming crown held aloft by a pair of wooden hands; the six symbols representing the principal forms of Jan'Tep magic floating around it like fireflies. At the bottom of the card, in black ink, the words *The Crowned Mage*. I didn't bother telling her any of that of course, since she'd just respond with some nonsense like, '*Don't describe the card . . . Tell me what's missing.*' Some conversations with Ferius you can pretty much just have by yourself.

We stepped onto the wide deck of the Arch of Solace. I briefly hoped Ferius intended to get medical treatment from one of the physicians standing on their little platforms as morning crowds vied for their attention, but given that she kept snorting at them as we walked past, my optimism soon faded. *Focus on the card*, I told myself. If nothing else, it would keep *me* from passing out from exhaustion before we arrived at Janucha's home and I could get that damned obsidian worm out of Cressia's eye. *Okay. What's wrong with this card?*

The image itself was beautifully rendered: the crown painted in metallic gold inks, the flickering symbols coloured to match those of the Jan'Tep form of magic they represented. The wooden hands holding the crown were perfectly formed. There was nothing odd or abstract about the card. In fact, if anything it was *easier* to interpret than the other discordances I'd seen. Those always had vague aspects to them – lines that weren't quite straight or colours that weren't quite right, like the painter hadn't been sure of . . . *Oh.*

'There you go,' Ferius said, still looking ahead.

'There aren't any questions.' Now that I'd said it out loud, it seemed even more obvious. The card was almost glaringly precise in its depiction of the crown and the scene around it.

'And what are the Argosi all about?' Ferius asked.

Questions. Every encounter I'd ever had with an Argosi always raised more questions than answers. 'Okay, so it's not a discordance. Chances are it was made by someone in the Jan'Tep territories. So why would my sister, in her last act of freedom before being carted away by the secret police, choose to give me this card?'

Ferius smiled for the first time since we'd left the tower. 'See? Now that's a good question.'

Occasionally I find her enigmatic ways endearing. This wasn't one of those times. 'Fine. Since you're in a mood for questions, how about this one? Did you know Shalla was in that tower?'

'What's that, kid?' Her attention was suddenly drawn to an apothecary's stand in the middle of the bridge. 'Say, you think this fella might sell smoking reeds?'

'Don't change the subject. You got to that tower before I did – and I'd like to know how, precisely, since I was following the black threads that you couldn't have seen.'

'That's cos I've got something even better.' She rapped her knuckles on the top of my hat. 'A brain in my head. You should try usin' yours more often.'

Her condescension didn't mix well with my frustration. 'What's that supposed to—' I stopped myself. Yet again I was about to fall for Ferius's favourite trick of aggravating me until I forgot the question I needed answered.

I glared at her. She grinned back at me. 'Guess that one won't work on you no more.' Her right hand slapped the underside of the brim of my hat, causing it to flip in the air and land right back down on my head. 'Ah, kid. I could make such an Argosi out of you. I swear, the world wouldn't know what hit it.'

'Really?'

She nodded, the smile becoming something more serious. 'What we do, Kellen, this wandering life, following the Way of Wind? Searching for discordances that could change the world – hopefully for the better, but sometimes in a direction so much worse it keeps me up at night just thinking about it? Well, there aren't a hundred people on this continent who can do what we do.'

'And you're saying I'm one of them?' Even before Enna had tried to convince me I could never be Ferius's teysan, I'd pretty much given up hope. 'Most of the time it seems like you think I'm doing something wrong, or thinking something wrong, or that I'm just built wrong.'

She patted me on the cheek with a gloved hand. 'You're all of those things, Kellen. We all are.' She turned and set off towards the apothecary's stand. 'But you keep trying to be better, and in my book, that's not nothing.'

I let her walk a few steps before I said, 'You're right.'

'I'm always right, kid. Wouldn't still be alive if I wasn't.'

'I meant earlier, when you said that trick wouldn't work on me any more. It won't.'

That made her stop. 'Then ask again, Kellen.'

'Did you know it was my sister in that room? You got there before me, and I've never known you to walk into a situation without knowing what's waiting for you. Did you know Shalla was there?'

'Sounds to me like maybe you already know the answer, kid, so ask me the real question.'

I hesitated. I wasn't sure which answer I could live with. Either Ferius had been taken as much by surprise as I had, and so wasn't the person I thought she was, or she *had* known, and had let me walk in there ready to kill my own sister. Ancestors, I'd come within a fraction of a second . . .

When I didn't speak, Ferius turned and came back to me. She held out her other hand. For a second I thought she wanted me to take it, but when I looked down I saw traces of powdered green leaves. I'm not much of a botanist, but any Jan'Tep initiate would recognise nightbloom, or, by its more common name . . . '*Weakweed?*' My hand went to my mouth, reflexively wanting to scrape any remnants off my tongue. My people have an instinctive fear of the stuff as it inhibits our ability to work magic. 'When you grabbed me in the darkness, I thought it was shock and fear that gave me that bitter taste, but it was you! You shoved weakweed into my mouth!'

She wiped off the traces of powder on her trouser leg. 'Don't beat yourself up over not catching on sooner. It's common enough for your tongue to taste something bitter when you're scared.'

'Beat *myself* up? *You* poisoned me right as I was about to enter a room full of mages!'

She snorted. 'Hey, remember that time you spiked my hooch? Let's not get all high and mighty about a little poison between friends. As to those two bumblers in that room? You can find half-penny mimes on the Bridge of Dice scarier than either of them.'

'But you asked me . . . you *forced* me to be prepared to murder someone in cold blood!'

'Hot or cold, it's all red when it leaves the body.'

'You *knew* it was Shalla in there! Why would you do that to me?'

Ferius's expression softened . . . saddened. She looked almost stricken by my words. 'I had to know, kid.'

My own blood was boiling. 'Had to know what?'

'How dangerous you are.'

'We've been travelling together for a year! You've seen me fight people. You've seen me ready to kill people befo—'

She shook her head. 'Not like this. Not the way you've been getting lately; walking into a room ready to end a life without being in immediate danger, without a trial or proof? You just up and decided whoever was in there was guilty and you were the one to execute them.'

I was suddenly painfully aware of another card sitting in my pocket: the Path of Shadows that Enna had painted. 'They *were* guilty. They were the ones controlling the obsidian worm!'

Ferius let out a sigh so weary it sounded as if she could barely hold herself up any more. 'We don't know much of anything yet, Kellen. We never do. An Argosi tries to live by the Way of Water, passing through life without causing harm to any, leaving the world in balance. But some people and events can't be ignored, so we follow the Way of Wind and seek out discordances. Only when we're sure – far more sure than you could've been in that tower – do we walk the Way of Thunder and take action against others.'

'So I failed your little test.'

'It wasn't . . .' The words drifted off. She nodded. 'Yeah, kid. You failed.'

'So all that stuff about how me being one of those hundred people on the continent who could become an Argosi – what was that? No, you know what? It doesn't matter. Because a few minutes after we entered that room, the weakweed wore off and I got lost in shadow again and nearly killed my sister.'

'Funny, she didn't look dead to me.'

'Yeah, but I—'

'You really think you could've stopped yourself if your heart was half so full of darkness as you think it is?' Ferius bent at the knees just a fraction so we were eye to eye. I'm almost as tall as she is so I find this habit particularly annoying, but she does it regardless. 'You were a normal kid once . . . well, normal as any Jan'Tep can be, anyway. Then it all got taken away from you and now you spend every minute of every day looking over your shoulder. You think that comes without a cost, kid? You're angry and you have every right to be. That anger doesn't make you a monster, Kellen. It doesn't make you special neither.' She reached out and took my hand. 'You know what does?'

I thought back to what Enna had shown me – the scar from a blade that had nearly taken her life. 'The fact that I don't let the anger control me?'

Her eyes softened for just a moment, then she smirked and gave me a gentle slap on the cheek. 'Nah, kid, you got a terrible personality. But you got excellent taste in mentors.' She turned and took a step only to stumble off balance. It was only by the sheerest luck that I got to her in time to catch her before she would've fallen to the ground. For the next few seconds she just held on to me. I could hear the wheezing in her breath. I felt her heart beating way too fast. 'How could you let Zavera defeat you?'

I wished I hadn't said it out loud. I'd promised myself all the way here I wouldn't bring it up. Whatever the answer, it wouldn't do either of us any good. Ferius righted herself and straightened her hat before she set off for the end of the bridge and the platforms that would take us to Janucha's home. 'See, now that's *not* a good question.'

Let it go, I told myself. 'But how did she—'

'Zavera whooped me because she's a better fighter than I am.' Ferius said it the way you might note the time of day or the fact that one fruit seller's pears were a penny more a basket than another's.

I had to jog to catch up to her. 'What happens if you have to fight her again?'

'Then I guess she'll whoop me again.'

The bitter taste in my mouth wasn't from weakweed this time. 'How can you be so cavalier about this? Zavera could have *killed* you, Ferius! She *wanted* to! I saw it in her eyes.'

'Nah, she couldn't've killed me, kid.'

'Why not?' I demanded, becoming more and more infuriated. 'Give me one reason why she couldn't have just kicked you to death right in front of me!'

Ferius stopped, and I wondered if maybe I'd pushed her too far. Then she turned and put her hands on my shoulders. 'Because you wouldn't have let her.'

I don't think I've ever seen her cry before, but there were tears in her eyes. She pulled me close and for only the second time since I'd known her, hugged me.

'Ferius, what's—'

'Don't ever kill for me, okay, Kellen? Just promise me that. I know how bad you want to protect your friends, but don't you ever walk in shadow for me.'

'I won't,' I promised, because I couldn't stand the hurt in her voice.

But I'm pretty sure I lied.

42

The Onyx Bracelet

'Are you ready?' I asked Cressia.

For a girl who'd spent the last two days in chains, terrified of the twisting creature living inside her eye and all the terrible things it could do to her, Cressia's poise was remarkable. She arched an eyebrow. 'That's the third time you've asked, Kellen. Are *you* ready?'

In theory I was. The flames of three different braziers kept the metal compounds in a molten state. The required needles were cleaned and ready. Though I knew the two breath spells by heart, I'd practised them anyway just to make sure exhaustion didn't cause me to drop a syllable at the wrong moment. Unlike most parts of my life, this was an area where I actually knew what I was doing.

Sort of.

The inclusion of the onyx bracelet in the process complicated matters and added to my nervousness. So too did the presence of Janucha and Altariste, who stood a respectful distance behind me and yet I swear I could hear doubt in their every exhale. While the inventors had some experience with charmcasters like Nephenia – who also insisted on watching – the esoteric workings of the obsidian worm seemed absurd to their scientifically bound ways of thinking.

'Are you gonna puke?' Reichis asked. He was perched on top of Ishak, sitting like a frontier rider astride a horse. The hyena didn't seem to mind, but Nephenia sure did.

'It's unseemly,' she whispered to her familiar. He gave her a dismissive yip in reply.

'Hah,' Reichis said.

'Ya'll want to shut yer respective traps awhile?' Ferius asked. 'Can't y'all see the kid's tryin' to concentrate?'

You want to know what's hard? Removing a disgusting, slithering, esoteric monstrosity from someone's eye. Doing it when you're exhausted and can't count all your bruises any more doesn't help. But having an audience watching you? That's definitely worse.

'Okay,' I said, taking the silver needle in hand and dipping it into the spelled copper solution melting over the brazier on the tray. 'Okay. Okay. I'm sorry, Cressia, but this is going to—'

'Stop telling me that.' She looked back at me with more sympathy than I could possibly have deserved. 'I think this may hurt you almost as much as it does me, Kellen.'

Not damned likely, I thought, but what I said was, 'That's what comes from being a philosopher, I guess.'

She chuckled, not because it was funny, obviously, but because she was incredibly brave.

'Is there no alternative to this barbaric ritual?' Altariste asked for what must have been the fifth time. I had my back to him, so I couldn't see for sure, but I'd have bet all the money I had that his hands were twitching with a desperate desire to drag me away from his daughter.

Janucha began to reassure him but it was Cressia who cut him off. 'I am Étuza Cressia fal Ghassan,' she said, 'daughter of a nation of explorers. We travel the world unfettered and fearless, and whether in life or in death I *will* be free of this thing.' Her gaze returned to me. 'Now, Kellen. *Now.*'

Truth be told, I could've used a few more minutes to settle my nerves, but Cressia had made her choice so I did as she asked. With the onyx bracelet around my left wrist, I used the thumb and forefinger of that hand to hold her eyelid open.

The first problem was to draw the worm out. I did this with a mixture of breath spells and, of course, the burning-hot needle whose tip I now pressed against Cressia's eyeball. The trick – *what an inexcusably casual word for something as awful as this* – was to make contact with the silver without actually piercing her eye. All the while I had to alternate between two different breath spells – one to keep her eye from burning and the other to cause the copper compound on the needle to forcibly summon the worm.

Simple.

Cressia's whole body shuddered as she screamed so loudly I thought my ears would bleed. Black oily tears began to drip down the dark skin of her cheeks, unleashing a hissing sound that could be heard even over her cries of agony. Slowly, resisting all the way, the obsidian worm began to crawl out onto the needle. Cressia stopped screaming, but her shaking got much, much worse. Ferius came behind and held her head in place.

'She's dying!' Janucha shouted, her stoic demeanour breaking at last. 'The procedure is killing her!'

She wasn't wrong. Shalla had warned me that the worm

had been in Cressia too long; the shock of removing it might destroy her mind. That's where this revolting ritual – which at least I'd performed a few times over the past six months – turned to something new.

You will leave her, I said silently, pouring my will into the onyx bracelet on my wrist. *Your place is inside the bracelet.*

The worm continued its slow progress along the needle, but something didn't feel right.

'I don't think she can take much more of this,' Nephenia warned. 'You have to get it out faster, Kellen.'

Even as the creature oozed from her eye, Cressia's breathing became shallow and laboured. 'He is killing our daughter!' Altariste yelled. 'We have to put a stop—'

'Don't interfere,' Nephenia said. 'You have to let him—'

'Get out of my way, damn you!'

An altercation broke out behind me. Altariste and Nephenia were in some kind of struggle. I heard a bark followed by a cry of pain. I think Ishak must've bitten him. Then a thud and a yipping sound, and then Reichis's distinctive growls as he threatened to kill Altariste any number of artful ways if he tried to kick the hyena again.

It was all going to hell very quickly.

Cressia's whole body convulsed. I could see her pulse in the vein on her neck. It was racing far too fast. The worm resisted the summoning and my control began to slip. 'I can't do it!' I cried out. 'It's not—'

'Kellen,' Ferius said. She'd spoken so quietly it was surprising that I'd even heard her. 'Look at me now.'

I did, and the first thought that came into my head was, *How can she be so calm?*

'You got this, kid. The whole history of your life and hers

brought you together. Here. Now. Every bad day you survived, every tough choice you've had to make, they made you both who you are. You hear me?'

My will was stripping apart like strands of rope holding too much weight. 'It's too strong!'

'I ever tell you what the word *Argosi* means, kid?'

'Wha– What?' I stuttered, barely hanging on. The inside of the onyx bracelet swirled as the other half of the worm writhed and twisted. It was suddenly so heavy that my wrist began to drift down.

Ferius gave me one of those smiles of hers that make it seem as if the sun itself came out just to shine down on her teeth. 'It's an old Daroman word. Means "wandering hero". Ain't that a thing?' She locked eyes with me. 'That's what you are, Kellen. You're an Argosi. Don't matter what me or anyone ever tells you. Your name is Kellen Argos. Let me hear you say it.'

'I'm . . . Kellen Argos.'

'You didn't ask for any of this. You'd have travelled the Way of Water, not making trouble for anyone, but the Way of Wind brought you here, to this place and this brave girl who needs your help right now. Even though you're scared, the Way of Thunder made you strike against that thing in her eye. Now it's time for the fourth way. Make your will unbreakable, Kellen. Show them all why we call it the Way of Stone!'

Sweat poured down my forehead and tears down my cheeks. My hands shook so hard that it was all I could do to keep hold of the needle. If I could have spoken I'd have told Ferius that she was wrong. I didn't have the Way of Stone in me. It wasn't my will that was unbreakable. It was something else.

I looked into Ferius's blazing green eyes, almost blinded by the faith I found there. Whatever else happened to me, however many people tried to tell me otherwise, I *was* her student. Her teysan. And no matter what it cost me, I would become the person I saw reflected in her eyes.

I reasserted my will through the onyx bracelet. The worm resisted me, its own bottomless strength pulling back. *Mine,* it said to me. *This body is mine. Alive or dead, it will ever be so.* A moan broke through Cressia's chattering teeth, then turned into a kind of hissing sound. *The death rattle,* the creature said. *She dies now. Will you kill her to be rid of me?*

No, I replied silently. *But you won't hurt her any more.*

Slowly, agonisingly, inexorably, the end of the obsidian worm slipped from Cressia's eye onto the needle. *No!* it pleaded. *I will die without her!*

Inch by inch, the creature slid along the silver needle towards its other half in the bracelet. Cressia stopped thrashing in Ferius's arms and her breathing began to settle.

'Keep it up,' Nephenia said from somewhere behind me. 'You've almost got it!'

I realised then that I could no longer hear the sounds of fighting. Oddly, I couldn't hear anything else either. The room had become completely silent, and the light itself began to disappear, replaced by . . .

'No!' I screamed.

Too late.

The skin around my left eye burned with a gleeful heat. The obsidian worm gleamed like a twisted beam of black sunlight. It stopped its progression towards the onyx bracelet and reared up, bloating in size, drawn by a new voice, to a new home.

To me.

Come, little one, said the shadowblack. *There is so much fun to be had . . .*

43

The Vessel

The obsidian worm slid right past the onyx bracelet to wriggle underneath the sleeve of my shirt. Coaxed by the shadowblack, the creature travelled along my arm to the top of my shoulder before slithering up my neck. I batted at the worm with my hands, but here in this place of shadows my fingers passed right through it. When it slithered along my jaw to the ridge of my left eye, terror overwhelmed me, and I opened my mouth to scream. What came out was laughter.

Who are you fighting, little spellslinger? Never before had the shadowblack spoken to me.

Stop, I answered back. *I don't want this!*

The worm will be a fitting addition to our family, Kellen. A useful tool for me, and I promise you'll hardly know it's there after a while.

Desperately I summoned all my will and turned it against the worm, forcing it to stop. The creature hesitated, its tiny head weaving back and forth blindly. Dozens of tiny slits that took the place of eyes opened and closed like the mouths of hungry birds waiting to be fed.

Hurry, little one, the shadowblack urged. *Why let yourself be trapped in the cold stone of onyx when what you really want is so warm and plentiful in here? Come and feed and feed and feed.*

The first tentative brush against my eyelash sent a shiver through me. Again I resisted, fighting back with everything I had. It did no good. Even my will seemed insubstantial in this place. In my mind, I screamed over and over, but all that came from my lips was a single word. 'Welcome.'

The worm was about to burrow into the soft jelly of my eye, but instead of the burning pain I expected, I felt a sudden sharp cold. Stranger still, the sensation had come from my other eye.

Enraged, the obsidian worm reared back, bloating until it was the size of a python. An angry black mist came from the slits where its face should have been. I flinched, anticipating the scalding pain from those tiny droplets of black oil, but they froze and fell as a frigid cloud of white smoke poured out from my right eye. The worm grew even larger, hissing as it did, but the cloud began to whirl around it like a slow-moving tornado, becoming more solid as it shrieked at the creature.

The sasutzei, I thought dumbly.

No, the shadowblack shouted inside my ears. *She mustn't be allowed to do this!*

The wind spirit reared up as it blew against the obsidian worm with the force of a hurricane. The creature hissed and more black oil emerged, winding into the wind spirit's cloudy form, tearing a squeal of pain from her.

Kill her! the shadowblack urged the worm. *She is weak here!*

The two creatures coiled around each other like twin snakes, each trying to crush the other first. The screams became louder. *She's dying*, I thought. *Dying for me.*

'Suzy!' I called out. 'Tell me what to do!'

Even as the two creatures snapped at each other, their ethereal forms striking so fast I could barely follow, I heard a single word come from the sasutzei. '*Whisper*,' she said.

For once I understood.

I poured my will back into the onyx bracelet even as I stopped fighting against the worm itself. Instead I spoke in soft breaths, using the magic that Mamma Whispers had first shown me back in the Seven Sands. *You don't need to fight*, I told the obsidian creature, cajoling rather than commanding. *Those mages made you as much a slave as the girl. Inside me your captivity would be absolute.*

I reached the limits of my will. It wasn't enough. I had to go further. I had to let go of everything but the one thing that mattered. For the first time, I understood what the Way of Stone meant: to be unbreakable, a thing must be pure. I left behind my fear, even my anger. The worm wasn't my enemy. I didn't *have* enemies. Such concepts were meaningless. The obsidian worm was simply a lost creature, torn from itself, worthy only of pity. *Be whole again*, I whispered. *Be free of the machinations of others.*

The shadowblack raged inside me, but I ignored it. Stone doesn't listen to such things.

The swirl of black and white began to slow, the writhing creatures within shrinking as their strength waned, disentangling when they became too small to fight. Suzy drifted back into my right eye and fell silent. The obsidian worm slid down my cheek like a tear, falling from my jaw to land on my wrist. It crawled into the onyx bracelet and disappeared into the stones, becoming one with its other half.

44

The Debt

I must have blinked a hundred times before the blurriness faded away and Janucha's workshop reappeared. Having spirits and curses living inside your eyeballs can't be good for your eyesight.

The sensations and sounds that had been lost to me in shadow returned one by one. First I heard Cressia letting out a series of wracking coughs. She settled back in the chair, the chains still holding her in place. The last drops of black oil slid from her eyes and the tears of a normal girl took their place.

Janucha and Altariste practically knocked me over running to their daughter, the father wrapping his arms around her as the mother looked to me with a question in her gaze. I nodded, and Janucha began removing the locks of the chains. Only when her daughter was free did she allow herself to cry.

Cressia looked at me as if I were a stranger. They all did. Each time I fell into shadow, the world seemed to forget me a little more. 'You're Kellen,' she said at last.

I nodded.

She favoured me with a weak smile. 'I thought you said it

was going to hurt. Do Jan'Tep boys never scratch their knees or stub their toes?'

At that precise moment I was crumpled up on the floor, which I felt was a poor position from which to argue the point. I rose to my feet and promptly fell over again. Ferius caught hold of me. Someone kissed the back of my head. It turned out to be Nephenia, which surprised me. 'Not bad for a spellslinger who only ever sparked one band,' she said, hugging me from behind.

Reichis came over and clambered up to my shoulder, then he bit me. 'What did I tell you about getting into fights without me?'

'It was Suzy that did most of the fighting,' I said, trying to feel the sasutzei's presence. If she was still there, she was dormant again. I guess even wind spirits get tired after a while. I couldn't blame her if she'd decided to leave. It would be too bad though; I was just starting to get used to having her around.

'Give me that foul thing,' Altariste said to me, reaching for the onyx bracelet. 'We will destroy it once and for all.'

I started to remove it, but a subtle breeze in my right eye – barely noticeable at all – stopped me. Apparently the sasutzei *was* still around. 'The worm wasn't entirely responsible,' I told Altariste. 'The creature was taken from its natural habitat, cut in half and implanted in Cressia. It belongs back in its own home.'

Ferius let go of me, making sure I could stand on my own before she said, 'Guess that means someone's going to have to take it back there some day soon, don't it?' There was something both sardonic and . . . amused in her expression.

It took me a moment to figure it out. 'Give me the damned card,' I said finally.

She grinned and gave me one of her crimson debt cards.

'Is this what it means to be Argosi?' I asked. 'You nearly kill yourself trying to do the right thing and you still end up with more debt?'

She clapped me on the shoulder. 'Why do you think I gamble and drink so much?'

'I'd like to speak to Kellen,' Cressia said, rising unsteadily from the chair. She turned to her parents. 'Alone.'

With some reluctance and not a few warning glances my way, they left the room. *Ancestors,* I thought, *I nearly died trying to rid their daughter of the worm. What harm do they think I'm going to do to her now?*

When we were alone, Cressia came to stand before me. I'll admit, I kind of expected an outpouring of gratitude. Instead she held out a hand, palm up. 'I believe you have something of mine.'

'What?'

She gestured to the card I was holding. 'That is my debt to pay.'

'Cressia, you don't understand how this works.'

'I don't?' She shot me a look that made it clear any expressions of gratitude or declarations of heroism were now behind us. 'Is it especially complicated? The card represents a debt to take the worm back to its home in the Seven Sands and find a way to free it where it will not harm anyone else. Or have I missed some subtlety to this matter that only a great Argosi like yourself would understand?'

'No, that's pretty much it.'

She took the card, then slid the bracelet from my wrist and put it around hers. Despite her bravado, I saw her shudder. 'I will travel back to the Seven Sands and complete this task. Then we will have an end to it.'

I was stunned to silence by her dauntlessness and the way honour and duty came so naturally to her.

She gave me a smile. 'You know, my friend, you look much wiser when your mouth is closed.' Suddenly she embraced me in a hug that took the breath from my lungs. '*Thank you*, Kellen.'

It was awkward at first. Part of me kept wondering if she was about to kiss me, which was stupid because I'd learned from her friends at the Academy that I wasn't her preferred gender. But my people aren't affectionate by nature, so everything like this feels . . . strange. I think Cressia must've sensed this somehow, because she just kept holding on, as if waiting for me to get the hang of this. Finally I did, I think. It's possible for a second there that I hugged my friend fully without any of the nonsense that usually goes around my head at times like that. It was a remarkably pleasant experience.

Something changed, though, and I felt a slight tension in her even as she still held on to me. She whispered in my ear, 'Don't trust my parents.'

I tried to pull away but she didn't let go. 'I love them. They are the finest people I have ever known. But something has changed in this house. Zavera, the head of the secret police has been here several times since my return. This creation of my mother's . . . I believe there is more to it than they have told you.'

'What do you know?' I asked.

'I cannot say with any certainty. I . . . I misspoke when I said something had changed inside my home. It is my entire country that seems to be changing.'

The doors to the workshop opened and Janucha entered.

'Forgive me, but I must insist my daughter sees a proper . . . That is, she has wounds from the worm's passing. I would like one of our healers to see to them.'

Cressia let go of me. 'Of course, Mother.' She gave me a playful punch on the arm. 'These Jan'Tep – far too prone to expressing their feelings if you ask me.'

45

The Reward

I badly wanted to talk to Ferius about what Cressia had said, but the moment I stepped out of the workshop, Altariste grabbed onto me like the mast of a ship in the midst of a storm. 'There is no greater gift – none – that you could have given me,' he declared. 'Name your price, name any service I or my wife can render to you, and it will be done. On this I swear a father's oath!'

Despite the fact that he was smothering me, his ebullience was endearing. 'You don't need to—'

'Get Janucha to end her experiments,' Ferius said, cutting me off as she came striding into the hallway.

Altariste looked surprised, but then chuckled as though convinced Ferius was only joking. 'My friends, I may be a poor contraptioneer compared to Janucha, but I assure you, my inventions have brought me considerable wealth over the years. If such things are beneath you, let me persuade my government to help you.' He turned back to me. 'Your charm-caster friend has told me something of the life you've been forced to lead, the dangers you face. Though I am not one for politics, my government values my services. I could press them to use their influence with your people to have this . . .

What did she call it? A "spell warrant"? Diplomatic overtures could be made requesting that it be removed.'

The inventor's proposal brought a sudden rush of hope to me. Trade with Gitabria was important to my people, as it was to every nation on the continent. What if he or Janucha could . . . but they couldn't. The lords magi of my clan would never concede their right to have me killed. My people would rather starve to death than allow a foreign country to interfere with their business.

My expression must have revealed my deflation. 'Or if not that,' Altariste went on, 'I could design something to make your travels easier. You've seen the fire lances? I've been contemplating a new kind of device, one that would be smaller, lighter. Another tool with which to surprise your enemies.' His gaze went skyward as if he were already making plans, idly patting my shoulder as he spoke. 'I could create such a wonder for you, my lad! Yes, already I—'

'He doesn't want a weapon,' Ferius said, again speaking on my behalf. 'Kellen wants Janucha to stop her experiments. Don't try to replicate the mechanical bird. Convince her to tear up the designs.'

Altariste looked despondent. 'Ask for anything within my power, but this . . . my wife's research is vital to our country.'

Ferius got in his face. 'See, now that explains a lot. At first I figured maybe you were dumb. I mean, you're clever, obviously. Those trinkets and contraptions can't be too easy to make. But even a clever fella can be still dumb, like when he discovers fire and can't figure out that it might be used for something more than cooking a meal. But that look you got when I asked you to stop the experiments . . . that's not the look of someone who thinks he's just making curious inventions. It's the look of a man who knows precisely why his people want this particular one so badly.'

'You summon ill thoughts on a joyous day, Argosi,' a voice called out. Zavera entered the hallway and came to stand between Ferius and Altariste. 'A child has been delivered from the evil of our enemies. Can her parents not be given a chance to celebrate?' She turned to Altariste. 'Go, Credaro. Be with your daughter. I will negotiate an appropriate reward for these friends of Gitabria.'

The inventor, freed from whatever sense of obligation had driven him to seek me out in the first place, practically jumped at the chance to leave. Soon we were alone with the spymaster of Gitabria.

'He does not understand your ways,' she said to Ferius.

'And you do?'

Zavera's eyes narrowed, and she gave Ferius a cold stare. 'You Argosi fascinate me, you know that? When I was a girl, I wondered what it must be like, to develop such remarkable talents. Defence, eloquence, persuasion . . . I forget the others. And then you . . . what exactly? You wander the world, using your abilities to enact your will as you see fit, tilting the balance here, destabilising a culture somewhere else. All without any form of rank or chain of command. It must be nice to do whatever you wish without ever having to serve any cause greater than yourself; to face no consequence when your choices prove disastrous.'

'Nice speech, sister,' Ferius said, reaching into her waistcoat and taking out a smoking reed. 'But next time save the poetry and just say what you came to say.'

'Wait, what about Shalla?' I asked. 'When will you let my sister go?'

'Soon. I must first question her to ensure there are no further Jan'Tep agents hiding in my country. After that is done, I will release her. In the meantime, she will be my guest at Notia Veras.' Zavera held up a hand to me. 'And before you ask, no, I will not harm the girl. This is a diplomatic matter between nations. I am not here to start a war.'

Ferius gave a snort. 'Then maybe you ought to tell Janucha to leave her experiments alone, because that's what's got everybody up in arms.'

Zavera's upper lip curled. 'Mine is a small country, Argosi, with a small population. Our people are peaceful, their pursuits noble. They love art and beauty, they explore far lands and trade with any who wish to do so. The Gitabrians turn their minds to invention, to creation. They know little of intrigue or war. They don't understand violence.' She inched closer until she was nose-to-nose with Ferius. 'They have me for that.'

I've always found it remarkable that Ferius not only stands up to intimidation, but can seem completely oblivious to it. She lit her smoking reed and took a puff from it. 'See? More speeches. More poetry. The words you're looking for are, "Hey, Argosi. Get the hell out of my town."'

Zavera turned to me and gave a small bow. 'You have the thanks of the people of Gitabria. Your name will forever be spoken with admiration and gratitude.' When she stood up again, she smiled at Ferius without a trace of mirth. 'Now, Argosi, get the hell out of my town.'

'See? Not so hard.' Ferius reached up a hand and tipped her hat to the spymaster. 'Evening, servadi.' Then she turned and walked down the hall to the stairs, leaving me to follow.

*

'What was that all about?' I asked Ferius as we stepped out onto the stone veranda.

She leaned on the railing and stared out at the gorge. Her smoking reed slipped from her hand to slowly drift down to the ships below. 'That woman really sets my blood to boiling. Can't say for sure why, but she surely does.'

'So what now? She just told us to get out of the country and we still don't know why that mechanical bird is so important.' I hesitated before asking my next question, in part because it felt like a slight to Ferius. 'What makes you so certain that a war is coming?'

'Because it is.' She reached into her waistcoat for another smoking reed but her hand came away empty. 'Darn it. Should've asked Altariste to whip me up some smoking reeds as a reward, seeing as how we're not likely to get anything better at this point.' She let out a long breath, which made her wince in pain. She took a deck of cards from one of the pockets inside her waistcoat and handed it to me.

'These are just your regular deck,' I said, a little disappointed. 'The ones with the shields for the Daroman and the chalices for the Berabesq and such.'

'Those are the cards that matter,' she replied. 'For all the nonsense of discordances and such, what you're holding in your hand is what tells us that war is coming.'

I riffled through the cards, noting the images of different roles within each culture. Instinctively I lingered longer on the suit of spells of course, because those represented my people. But each suit had its own set of names and structures. General of Shields was one of the face cards of the Daroman suit. Beggar of Chalices was one of the Berabesq cards. I'd never really spent a lot of time just looking at Ferius's Argosi deck. Something about it had always bothered me.

'What do you see?' she asked.

I couldn't quite put it into words. It was almost on the tip of my tongue, as if my brain knew but couldn't find the words to describe it. In a way the cards reminded me of the powders in my pouches – inert on their own, but whenever I put them together . . . 'It's not because of some event,' I said suddenly. 'This war you and the other Argosi think is coming, it comes from the very structure of each of our cultures. It's as if the way our countries work, they almost can't help but be in opposition to one another.'

Ferius nodded. 'Leave tinder out in the sun long enough and all you need . . .'

'Is a spark,' I finished for her. 'Then that's—'

She tapped the top of the deck. 'Pick a card, kid. Any card.'

I flipped it over and there was the mechanical bird. I wish I knew how she did those tricks. 'How's that for a spark?' she asked.

Ferius left me there while she went to pack our things. Apparently we were done with this country. The only question left was what I was supposed to do about my sister. It's not like I really trusted Zavera's promises, but after all Shalla tried to do in Gitabria, was she truly expecting me to intervene on her behalf?

I took the false discordance card that she'd given me out from my pocket, trying to discern why it had been so important to her. Looking at it now, I could almost see why Ferius disdained it so. I mean, it looked perfect – in some ways more so than the Argosi cards I'd seen – but there was a coldness to it. A kind of perfection that seemed arrogant rather than pure. Staring at the crown, held aloft by those wooden supports carved to look like hands, a tightness rose in my chest like smouldering resentment. *No,* I thought. *Not resentment. Anxiety. Like when I misbehaved in front of one of the spellmasters and they'd send me home to my . . .*

I thought my vision was starting to blur and feared the shadowblack was taking me over again, but the world stayed as it was. Well, most of it anyway. The light on the card shimmered unnaturally. The lines of the illustration became more defined. I nearly dropped the thing over the railing into the gorge when I saw a hand reach down and take hold of the crown. The perspective shown in the card changed, as if I were right inside it and had begun to look up. Then, despite how impossible it was, I watched as my father set the crown upon his head.

'You always were impressed by tricks,' Ke'heops said. 'I thought you'd appreciate this one.'

46

The Crowned Mage

The eyes were what bothered me. To see your father's face come alive in a card is disconcerting on its own; watching the lines warping to conform to his features, the colours retaining the simplicity of their original paints and yet shifting subtly here and there to take on the most infinitesimal changes of light against his high cheekbones and stern jaw. But for all that, it was the way his eyes stared out at me, *seeing* me, that made the breath in my lungs turn cold and my own flesh feel thin and brittle – as if *I* were the one made of paper instead of him.

Let it fall, I tried to command my hand. *Toss it into the gorge or crush it underfoot. See how he likes that.* But I couldn't. Try as I might, seeing his face in that card . . . I couldn't even think of a way to describe it, but then the word came to me unbidden: unmanned. The sight of my father *unmanned* me.

'You betrayed your sister,' he said.

'I . . .' *Stop. Don't let him control the conversation.* 'Shalla came here as a guest of the Gitabrians and instead conspired against them, and used the obsidian worm to torture a girl who'd never done anything to her or to you or to anyone else.' Somehow the truth of that lent strength to my voice and certainty to my next conjecture. 'You commanded her to commit these crimes.'

'Crimes?' he said the word as though it were foreign to his tongue. 'What do you deem a crime, Kellen?'

'She broke their laws! She's the Jan'Tep delegate and now the Gitabrians will forever know our people as oath-breakers and—'

My father's eyes narrowed as he looked through me. 'You speak of oaths, of laws, of crimes. Tell me, Kellen, what oaths have you made to your sister?'

'What? None. Why would I—'

'And what laws have you seen written governing your relationship to her?'

'What are you talking about? There are no "laws" between two siblings. Why are you—'

'No oaths made, no laws written, so then you owe your sister nothing?'

'Of course I . . .' The chains of his logic wrapped around me. Once again my father had gotten the better of me.

Ke'heops looked down at me – a remarkable accomplishment considering his face was nothing more than the black lines and simple colours on a card. 'The oaths that bind us the most are never spoken, Kellen. They aren't made of promises and vows. They simply *are*. The laws that matter – the laws we must follow – need not be written down. They are in your blood. And the only crime you should care about is the one you know in your heart you committed when you let foreign soldiers lay hands upon Shalla. You let them imprison the sister who loves you, who defends you before your people no matter all the foul things you've done, no matter what you've become.'

What began as a pit in my stomach turned to stone, growing and growing, becoming harder and more painful with each passing second. Ke'heops might as well have cast an iron spell against me. I can't imagine it would have hurt more. Despite that, despite how I had never forgotten when he'd tied me down to a table and spent five days counter-banding me, imprinting reversed sigils into the tattooed bands on my forearms and forever denying me access to all but one of the magics that defined my people, despite all that, still I asked, 'And what is it I've become, Father?'

For the first time since his face had come alive in the card, he hesitated. The lines of black ink on the card forming his jaw tightened. He said nothing, though we both knew the words he longed to speak. *Traitor. Outlaw. Enemy.* All these and more I knew were on the tip of his tongue. That he didn't shout them at me with a fury that would have torn the card in half told me something I probably should have figured out a lot sooner. 'You need something from me,' I said aloud.

That broke the silence between us, and my father changed as he always did at times like these. No longer was he the parent infuriated at his child's failings. Now he was the head of my household, the prince of my clan. The man who believed with the surety of iron and the weight of a mountain that he had the right to command me. 'The Gitabrians will have taken Shalla to their secret prison. They are known to have devised a set of cells through which our spells cannot pierce, and within which our magic is rendered inert.'

'I've been there.'

The shape of his head on the card tilted a fraction. 'You

have?' A shiver of a smile appeared on the simple lines of his lips. 'Good. That will make things easier. You will make your way to this prison, and use whatever means available to you to free Shalla and assist in her escape from the city.' He paused just a moment, and the black line of his smile flowed into the curl of his upper lip. 'You may even use those *tricks* you're so fond of.'

I let that slide, partly because doing so would annoy him, but more so because it was irrelevant. 'By the time I get there it won't matter. The Gitabrians are exiling her from the city as soon as they finish interrogating her. You'll have your daughter back soon enough without my help. It should please you that you won't owe me any favours.'

I waited, fully expecting a rebuke over my presumption that anything I did for Ke'heops would create any sort of debt between us. For a long time nothing happened, and I thought the spell that had brought the card to life must have broken somehow. Just as I was about to put it away he said, 'And here I thought you were clever, but it seems even that one quality was simply another trick.' He didn't wait for me to disagree. 'Whatever Shalla's diplomatic status, to the Gitabrian secret police she is a spy and an attempted assassin. They will torture her until they are sure she holds no more secrets, and then they will execute her.'

'They wouldn't dare to—'

'Exactly what sentence did you think would be passed upon a foreign agent? Worse – a saboteur? The Gitabrians care about nothing so much as their little toys and inventions, and Shalla's attempts to interfere with them are a capital offence.'

The first drops of a cold sweat formed on my brow at the thought of what they might do to my sister – at what a people famed for their contraptions and devices might be able to construct for the purpose of inflicting pain. 'You said it yourself, she's our people's delegate and the daughter of a clan prince. Harming her would be an act of war!'

The chains of self-control deserted my father. 'You insipid child! Your sister committed an act of war! You think the council of lords magi will admit she was there with our blessing? We had no choice but to declare her a rebel and disavow her activities.'

'So you're going to let her rot to avoid embarrassment?'

'To avoid war.' His eyes narrowed. 'Do not look at me that way, boy. Whatever nonsense the Argosi woman fills your head with, *this* is the way diplomacy is done. *This* is the price nations pay to maintain the peace.'

'Maybe next time you could maintain the peace by not sending my sister to spy on them, to use the foulest magic I've ever seen to torment a girl barely older than your own daughter!'

'Are you really so blind? Do you think so little of your sister? Shalla wasn't the one who abused the obsidian worm. She took the bracelet away from that overzealous fool Hath'emad who sought to end our problems too quickly. And Shalla *volunteered* for this mission. She practically demanded it!'

'But why? Why would she—'

'To protect you! Kellen, she knew there was a chance you'd end up in Gitabria, collaborating with that Argosi as she systematically destroyed the onyx bracelets and stole our best chance to secure our people's future. If any other patriotic clan mage had gone they'd have killed you on sight!' He went silent for a moment, and I could almost feel the card momentarily thicken as he took in a long breath and then let it out again. His composure returned and he repeated his command from earlier. 'You will find Shalla, you will free her. You will do these things because otherwise your sister will suffer and die at the hands of our enemies.'

'The Daroman empire. The Berabesq theocracy. And now even a peaceful merchant country. When did Gitabria become our enemy, Father?'

'They are not Jan'Tep, Kellen,' he replied, as if that explained anything. Seeing my confusion he added, 'Thus are they all enemies to our people.'

His cynicism – his absolute certainty that the world was divided up not into different peoples and cultures but simply into family and enemies galled me. But it did something else as well: for the first time since he began speaking to me through the card, that small shred of inquisitiveness, of insight, that I manage to make use of every once in a while, came back to me. 'You lied, Father.'

Again the card went still, and again it seemed as if the spell had broken, but this time I wasn't fooled. 'You said the reason Shalla led the mission into Gitabria was because she demanded to do so.'

'She did,' he said.

'Perhaps, but the great and mighty Ke'heops would never let sentimentality affect his plans. You *wanted* her to come here and fulfil your wishes while trying to protect me.'

'And why would I do such a thing?' he asked, though he didn't seem very interested in the answer.

'Because you knew whoever came here would likely be caught. They'd be interrogated and eventually reveal everything – including things you'd want kept secret. So you sent Shalla because you also knew she's the only member of our clan for whom I'd risk my own life.'

The lines on the card shifted again, and for the first time my father's smile was something other than mocking. It may even have been proud. 'Perhaps you're still a little clever after all.'

47

The Prison

'You sure you want to do this alone?' Ferius asked.

I looked through the gap between the trees to the relatively small, relatively innocuous grey stone building and tried not to shiver. I'd already given up on not sweating. 'I'll be fine,' I said unconvincingly.

Despite having spent a couple of unconscious days in Notia Veras, I'd had no idea how to find it again. Part of the condition of them releasing me into Janucha's custody had been that I be blindfolded on the trip back. Fortunately Ferius had used the subtlety of her arta tuco to secretly follow the contraptioneer the day she'd come to see me just in case things didn't go well and she'd have to break me out. It was strange to think how many layers Ferius had to every one of her plans. Me? I was lucky to have even a vague idea of what I was doing next.

Reichis skittered down from the branches of a tree. 'Kellen won't be alone, idjit. He'll be with me.' He'd taken to calling people idjit ever since our encounter with Ferius's father. I was careful not to tell the squirrel cat that it made him sound like a backwater cowherd.

Ferius didn't wait for me to translate. 'I know you'll be

with him, ya dumb squirrel cat. I'm worried about you too!'

'We'll be okay,' I said. 'Reichis is the best scout out of all of us and whatever traps they keep in there probably aren't made to deal with a small animal.' He growled at me. 'Which is why that spymaster is going to feel real stupid once she realises you were the one who engineered the entire escape.'

That seemed to mollify him. 'Anyway,' I went on, 'the more of us there are, the greater the chance of being discovered. It's better if only two of us go.'

'So why does it have to be you?' Nephenia asked, annoyed. 'What makes you better qualified than Lady Ferius—'

'Still not a "lady",' Ferius corrected.

'Oh, that's it,' Reichis chittered. 'I'm not sitting here for another round of skinbag salutational etiquette.' He climbed back up the tree, scrambling higher and higher until he reached the top and launched himself into the air. 'See you on the inside, loser!'

'You asked why I have to go?' I said to Nephenia. 'Because I'm the only one who can understand the damned squirrel cat.' With that, I took off at a loping run towards the back entrance of the prison.

Gitabrians have a pretty interesting way of building prisons. Actually, they have pretty interesting ways of building *everything*. I guess this is because they travel so widely: they pick up tricks from other cultures and combine that with their infatuation for invention to come up with ingenious solutions. For example, I hardly encountered any guards at all on my way through Notia Veras. This made sense given that Zavera was probably pretty paranoid about her little secret prison. Also, there were more than enough locks and traps to ensure anyone without a warden's coin would never make it inside. Fortunately I just happened to have one.

No, I thought, correcting myself. *Those two Argosi, Enna and Durral, made sure you had one.* If Ferius's plans had as many layers as an onion, I couldn't imagine how many her parents' schemes must have. It would have been nice if they'd bothered to explain any of them to me.

I held my five castradazi coins in my hand as I made my way through the halls of Notia Veras. I'd already figured out how to use the warden's coin to open several different locks. The key – so to speak – was holding it just right so that whatever strange property the metal held caused it to almost magnetically grab hold of the inside of the locking mechanism. Then you had to work by feel until you were turning each tumbler one by one. Breaking in was an oddly satisfying experience.

The next parts? Not so much.

Gitabrian traps and alarms are positively florid in their complexity. I entered one passageway, only to find the walls were made entirely of brass. I must've stepped on some kind of mechanism, because a second later the walls rang like massive bells, the reverberations going back and forth between them, over and over until not only were my ears in danger of bleeding, but I fell to the floor. Every time I tried to back get up, I'd just fall down again. Something about the frequency of the vibrations was messing with my sense of balance. Worse, while the sound seemed confined to this hallway, there was still a chance it could be heard elsewhere, which would bring guards. I was starting to really despair when I noticed one of the coins in my hand was vibrating at exactly the same rate as the walls. On a whim

I stuck it in my mouth and clamped down hard on it with my teeth. Almost instantly the awful clanging in my ears stopped. Somehow the metal of the coin created a kind of counter-reverberation in my skull, and the cacophony of the brass walls disappeared.

Figuring out the bronze passage got me to the first set of cells. They were empty, except for one that contained a slender man whose first few words convinced me he really did belong there and letting him go would likely get me killed. Followed by the rest of Gitabria, if his boasts were to be believed.

Deeper inside the prison I found a set of six-foot high wheels that turned from the flow of a little river that ran across a narrow channel cut into the floor. The hallway it led into was completely bare, but the metal sheen of the floor made me suspicious. So, too, did the fact that the closer I got to it, the more I felt the hair on my head start to stick out.

'Is that silver?' Reichis asked, suddenly at my feet. As he got closer to the edge of the silver section of floor ahead of us, his fur started to rise up in the air, pulled by the same force at work on my own hair.

'How did you get here?' I asked.

He gave the squirrel cat equivalent of a shrug. 'Even prisons need sewer tunnels.'

That explained the smell. I didn't bring it up, though. For his part, Reichis shook his fur, sending liquid and particles of things I didn't want to imagine streaming into the air. 'Been searching this place,' he said. 'It's bigger than it looks on the outside.'

'Did you find Shalla?'

He looked up at me, tilting his feline head. 'Shalla?'

'Yeah. My sister? The person we came to rescue?'

'Oh,' he said, as though it was the first he'd heard of her. 'I was looking for stuff to steal.' He sat back on his haunches and waved his front paws in frustration. 'Nothing. Not a thing. You'd think a place where they bring criminals would have lots of good stuff. I mean, what do they do with all the trinkets they find on the thieves?'

'You're thinking of a jail,' I said.

'What's the difference?'

'A jail is where you take someone when you catch them, and a prison is where they go after they're convicted. Completely different places.'

Reichis stared up at me as if he thought I might be making fun of him. 'Are you serious?'

'Yeah, why?'

He shook his head. 'You skinbags really like to overcomplicate things, don't you?' The squirrel cat turned his attention back to the silver floor. 'Bet this is worth a pretty penny though. All we have to do is dig some of it out.' He extended the claws of his right paw and reached out to it.

'Reichis, don't!'

The moment he tried to scratch it he was sent flying through the air. His body hit the wall behind us with a thud before he tumbled to the ground. I ran to him and picked him up. His fur was sticking out wildly, making him look like a puffy flower. Oddly, he was completely clean now. 'Reichis, are you all right?'

He looked up at me, his eyes unfocused. 'That was different,' he said.

'What happened?'

'Lightning,' he replied, his voice filled with awe. 'These

Gitabrian skinbags have dominion over lightning. We must bow to them, Kellen. They're clearly gods!' It's possible he hit his head when he slammed into the wall.

I looked back at the wheels turning just outside the silver passageway. 'They aren't gods,' I said. 'I think somehow those wheels are generating some sort of build-up of energy. When your paw touched the floor, it passed into you.'

Reichis crawled up to my shoulder and shook himself off again. 'Well, I hate lightning, so *you* step on it next time.'

I went back to examine the heavy wheels. 'If we could stop these from turning . . .' I put my weight against one of them, but even though the flow of water that made it turn wasn't very strong, the wheel itself was far too powerful for me to hold back. It must have had something to do with all the little gears they were connected to. 'Okay,' I said, 'how come the wardens can get by here?'

'Because they're gods?' Reichis suggested. 'They just command—'

'They're not gods,' I insisted.

'Hey, don't take it out on me just because you're upset that the Gitabrians are better at magic than your people are.'

'They aren't,' I said, though I really wasn't sure at this point. 'What they do is different. Anyway, I doubt the wardens are mages.'

Reichis tapped a paw at a spot on the wall. 'Well, then maybe they stick a key inside this opening.'

I stared where he was pointing. There was nothing there, just bare wall. 'I don't see anything.'

'What, are you blind?' He tapped the spot again. 'This little spot here is clearly more worn than the rest of the wall, and the shape and size is like a lock.'

Not knowing what else to try, I started spinning the sotocastra coin. 'Show me.'

The squirrel cat pointed with a claw at the spot on the wall and peered into it. 'Simple three-tumbler lock, but it's way too deep inside for me to pick.'

I still couldn't see any difference on the surface, but when I spun the coin above my palm a little further back from the wall, I started feeling that subtle tug, as if it had latched onto something. It took a few minutes, but eventually Reichis claimed all three tumblers had turned. The wheels started slowing down and after a few more revolutions came to a stop.

I plucked a hair from my head and carefully touched it to the silver floor. When it didn't shock me, I started through the passage.

'Hey,' Reichis said, when we got to an intersection on the other side. 'I haven't explored this part yet. You think maybe down here is where they keep the good stuff?'

'We're looking for my sister, remember?'

'Oh . . . right.'

When I looked back and saw he was still sitting there, staring down the other hall, I asked, 'What are you doing?'

'It's just . . .'

'What?'

'Well, it's not like your sister's going anywhere, is she?'

Ancestors, I thought, going over to grab him and stick him on my shoulder before setting off towards where I hoped to find Shalla. *If I ever need to be rescued by a squirrel cat, please make sure it's not somewhere with shiny objects.*

48

The Cell

We found Shalla at the bottom level of the prison. Evidently she was considered a lot more dangerous than the few other prisoners we came across, which really said something. She even rated an actual guard all to herself. Reichis offered to deal with him, but I wasn't sure I could trust the squirrel cat not to kill the poor bastard who, after all, was only doing his job. Of course, blasting the guy with my spell probably wouldn't make him happy either.

I saw he had a fire lance with him – the sort I'd seen other Gitabrian secret police carry back at the tower. That might be a problem.

'Hello,' I said.

The guard stood up, his left hand reaching for his mace. 'Who are you? How did you get here?'

'I'm an outlaw,' I admitted. 'And I'm here for a jailbreak.'

'I thought you said this was a prison?' Reichis chittered on my shoulder.

'Shut up, stupid.'

The guard's face took on a fierce expression. I think he was more outraged that he thought I'd called him stupid than he was over me coming here to break out a prisoner. 'Best you kneel, son. Let me put the cuffs on you and then we can find the servadi to see what this is all about. I'd rather not have to kill you.'

'Me too,' I said. 'So it would be helpful if you could just let me put the cuffs on you instead.'

His jaw tightened. 'So be it. Fair warning was given, and my conscience is clear.'

He hefted up his fire lance and aimed it at me. Reichis leaped onto the end of it, knocking his aim way off. When he twisted the two halves, the blast went off to the side. I pulled powder from my pouches and tossed them into the air between us. '*Carath,*' I intoned, my fingers forming the somatic shapes.

I hadn't used much powder so the twin red and black fires didn't burn through the leather armour covering his chest. The shock of it did make him stumble back hard enough to bash his head into the steel bars of Shalla's cell. The look of surprise lasted only a second before his eyes fluttered closed and he sank to the floor.

'Better get the cuffs on him quick,' Reichis advised.

'Why? I just knocked him unconscious.'

The squirrel cat sniffed. 'He's just stunned and closing his eyes to make you *think* he's unconscious while he tries to regain his wits.'

Wow. You can't trust anyone these days. Anyway, Reichis was right. I barely got the guard's cuffs on him before he started thrashing at me. He was a big man, so even handcuffed he was a bit of a threat. That's where Reichis took over. 'Listen, skinbag,' he snarled in the man's ear. 'It's been days since I drank human blood, and I'm getting thirsty.' He reached out a claw to very gently touch the corner of the man's eye. 'Hungry too.'

The guard couldn't understand him of course, but I guess he got the gist of it because he stopped trying to shake us off. I managed to push him into an open cell nearby and lock it using the warden's coin. It really was remarkable, all you could do with this thing. No wonder the secret police weren't fond of the castradazi.

When I was done, I returned to Shalla's cell.

'You really didn't need to go to all this trouble,' my younger sister said. Her cell had reasonably nice furnishings, all things considered, and Shalla, seated in a chair, reading a book, managed to look as if she were lounging in her private sanctum instead of wallowing in prison waiting for the guards who'd escort her to what would surely be slow torture followed by a swift execution.

'Is this the part where you pretend I didn't save you?' I asked.

She shrugged. 'Oh, I suppose now's as good a time to leave as any.' She rose from the chair and gave a scathing glance at the walls. 'Do you know, they seem to have infused the walls with some of that Gitabrian copper that prevents magic from working? It's really rather annoying.'

'So we're agreed that I *did* save you?' The point felt important to me.

'It's not really a rescue until I'm out of the cell, wouldn't you agree?' She gestured towards the door's locking mechanisms, of which there were two. The first was a regular lock near the centre of the bars, and another was high up – a rotating cylinder combination lock near the ceiling. 'The guards informed me that both locks have to be opened at once or else a glass tube inside the locks breaks and a fast-acting poison gas is released.'

I motioned for Reichis. He sauntered over, sniffed at Shalla before giving her a brief snarl, then clambered up the bars to start turning the rotating tumblers on the lock at the ceiling while I set to work using the sotocastra coin on the one in the door. 'Ready to turn the last one,' he said, far sooner than I was.

A couple of minutes later I was ready to flip the last tumbler in mine. 'Count of three?' I suggested.

'Sure. Three.' His claw turned the last cylinder and it was only by sheer luck that I managed to flip my own lock's tumbler in time. 'Remind me to explain how counting works some time,' I said.

'Whatever.'

I held open the door for Shalla, who actually took the time to dog-ear the page of her book before setting it down on the small cot and leaving the cell. 'I admit, that was a *little* impressive,' she said.

'I do my best,' I said.

'I meant the squirrel cat.'

49

The Confession

With a new moon lighting the way, the three of us escaped back into the woods and then along the trail where we met up with Ferius, Nephenia and Ishak. The three of them had kept abreast of the few patrols in the area and picked out the best route for us to get back to the city gates, where we'd send Shalla on her way. Given that for once nothing had gone wrong and no one had been hurt, I'd expected everyone to be overjoyed.

The moment we were in relative safety, Shalla turned on Nephenia. 'You should know, exile, that in deference to my brother's presence I've decided not to kill you.'

'Wait, what?' I asked. 'What are you talking—'

'I'd be within my rights,' Shalla went on, ignoring me. 'You may have . . . *persuaded* the council to be lenient with you, but no one would blame me if I executed you here and now.'

The way she said 'persuaded' gave the word a distinctly salacious implication.

'You'd be within your rights to try,' Nephenia said, reaching into a pocket of her coat. 'But perhaps not your right mind.' Ishak's growl added a note of menace to her words.

'What in the name of sand and sorrow is the matter with you Jan'Tep?' Ferius asked me wearily. 'Seems anytime two of you get together, *somebody's* got to threaten murder.'

I got between Shalla and Nephenia. 'Nobody's killing anyone! What the hell is—'

'Too late for that,' Shalla said. 'Mouse girl here is a murderer.'

'What?'

'Oh, hasn't she told you?' Shalla rounded on me like an advocate about to deliver her final argument before the court. 'Shall I perform a testimony spell for you, Kellen?' The glyphs of the silk band on her forearm shimmered to life. 'Would you like to fill your mind with visions of the condition in which we found the corpse of Eld'reth?'

Eld'reth? That was the name of Nephenia's father.

'Would you like to see the pieces of him that had to be collected from the walls of his sanctum after her spell was done with him?' Without asking my permission, Shalla did just that.

'Stop!' I said, reeling from the visions of blood and charred human flesh she put in my mind.

'If we're going to all this trouble,' Nephenia said, 'perhaps I should demonstrate the spell itself.'

'Okay, this is getting interesting now,' Reichis chittered, wandering over to stare up first at Shalla then Nephenia. 'I think they might just kill each other.'

Try as I might, I couldn't even begin to wrap my head around the idea that Nephenia had murdered her father. The words she'd spoken when we'd been following the black threads came back to me with a disturbing new clarity: '*I'm not the girl you knew,*' she'd said. '*I did some things that . . . I had to make a choice.*'

'Now you know,' Shalla said triumphantly. 'You know what she is.'

I wondered why it was so important to her to ruin Nephenia in my eyes – why Shalla always had to seed distrust against anyone who wasn't part of our family.

'I *am* a murderer,' Nephenia confessed, her chin held high. 'A fact you should keep in mind the next time you threaten me.'

My sister smiled, her hands relaxed by her sides. 'Come on then, mouse girl. Show me.'

Ishak bared his teeth but didn't growl. Somehow that made him scarier.

Reichis – usually keen to see violence – scampered up to my shoulder and snarled at all of them. 'You better pick which one you're going to help kill the other, Kellen, because these lunatics really are about to fight.'

'She already told me what happened,' I lied.

'Don't fight my battles for me, Kellen,' Nephenia snapped at me.

'Either pick a side or let's get out of here,' the squirrel cat insisted. 'One of them's going to make a move any second now!'

'Please,' I begged, 'both of you, just let me—'

'Shh . . .' Shalla said quietly. 'I'm concentrating.'

The pair of them were facing off now, closer than any sane Jan'Tep mage would stand for a duel because they'd end up within the blast of whatever assault spells they cast against each other. With no other solution in sight, I was about to throw myself between them when Ferius said, 'The problem with too much focus on the destination, girls, is that you miss a lot of the scenery.'

I hadn't even seen her hands move, but in each one she held a steel card, the sharp edge glimmering in the dim light of the street lantern. They were positioned a hair's breadth from the corners of Shalla and Nephenia's mouths. 'The first one of you tries to utter one of your Jan'Tep incantations is going to get their tongues sliced up real good.' Without shifting her eyes, she said to me, 'Kid? One day you are going to explain to me just what it is they put in the water where you come from that makes folks so homicidal.'

Nephenia was the first to back away, which was good, because I'm pretty sure Shalla was just arrogant enough to believe she might be able to outdraw Ferius Parfax. It took a few seconds, but eventually my sister decided she had better things to do than get in a mage's duel in the middle of a foreign city. 'I withdraw my prerogative to render judgement on the exile,' she said, then, because she's Shalla, she added, 'For now.'

She started to walk away, and I thought maybe that was it – my sister would leave the city and return to our homeland – but she gestured for me to follow. 'A word, please, brother? There's something you should know about my mission here before you decide to commit another act of treason.'

Not knowing what else to do, I followed Shalla a few dozen yards away. Even though we weren't in hearing range of the others, I saw her fingers flicker a somatic shape as she whispered a word, then took my hand. It was a silencing spell that would make it impossible for anyone to eavesdrop on us. Knowing Shalla, she'd probably added the second form of the spell, that would confound anyone trying to read our lips. 'You're on the wrong side, Kellen,' she said at last.

I almost laughed at that. 'This again? After all this time, you still can't come up with anything better than "just do what Father wants and don't ask questions"? Or do you have some new offer to make me? Father's forgiveness perhaps? A chance to go home? Shalla, I'm not Jan'Tep any more. I don't want to be.'

A trace of hurt came to her eyes when she looked up at me, but she quickly banished it. 'Are you done?' she asked. 'Or do you need to rant and rage against the unfairness of the world a little longer before you listen to what I have to say?'

It is a distinctly unpleasant experience to be upbraided by your little sister, made worse when she tries to make you feel like you're a pouting child. Especially if it works. 'Tell me,' I said.

She looked around at the streets with their beautiful geometry and the almost unearthly lighting of the street lanterns, their positioning and illumination calculated with mathematical precision by Gitabrian artificers to give perfect clarity to the evening setting without offending the eye. 'They're brilliant, these Gitabrians, aren't they?'

'*That's* what you wanted to tell me?'

She ignored me. 'They love invention, these little men and women with their numbers and their theories. This nation of tinkerers, of pot-makers.'

'If that's all they were, you wouldn't be here spying on them.'

Shalla nodded. 'You're right – I wouldn't.' She squeezed my hand. 'Kellen, I came here to uncover what the Gitabrians are planning with this new invention of theirs – this combination of mechanical genius with frontier charmcasting and whatever final piece gives the machine life.'

'Janucha's not trying to—'

'Don't be naive! Sooner or later the contraptioneer will use this new ability of hers to design weapons for her people. She will create machines of war.' Shalla hesitated a moment, then, even though we were within a quieting spell, still she whispered what came next. 'They could destroy us, Kellen.'

There was such certainty in her voice, such a sense of foreboding, that it took me aback. 'That's . . . Shalla, the Gitabrians don't want war. They're explorers, like you said. Traders and tinkerers. They invent new things because it's what they love to do, it's how they think, how their culture works.'

She looked up at me with an almost indulgent smile. 'I forget sometimes just how idealistic you are, Kellen. And how gullible.'

'That's too bad, because I never forget how manipulative *you* are, Shalla.' I pulled my hand away from hers, breaking the spell. 'If you have proof, show it, otherwise this is just another game you're playing . . . Or worse, one that our father is playing through you.'

I was only a few steps away when she called to me. 'Kellen!'

I turned back just in time to see her tossing something at me.

'Since you like coins so much.'

I caught it in my hand. Almost instantly I felt that distinct quality of the castradazi coins. But what was Shalla doing with one? 'Where did you get this?' I asked.

'They told you there were only a few of them left, didn't they? Well, I put a little sympathy spell on this one. I was intending on using it to find out what the Gitabrians were up to, but then you led the secret police to me and I was captured.'

I held up the coin. 'What do you expect me to do with it?'

'Find out where it leads. Uncover what the contraptioneer is hiding. Maybe then you'll finally accept what I've tried to make you see ever since we were children.'

'Which is?'

Her hands traced a sigil in the air. An obscurement spell formed around her and she faded from view. 'Don't trust anyone who isn't family.'

50

The Mountain

We followed the coin or, rather, I let its strange vibrations direct me and the others followed. Mile after mile we walked, yet long after the moon had reached its zenith, still the coin continued to pull me onwards.

'Where do you think it's taking us?' Nephenia asked.

Ferius gave a snort, wiping the sweat from her brow. 'A better question is how far? For all we know, this fool's quest your little sister sent us on could be leading us across the sea.' She chuckled. 'Actually that *would* be a pretty good prank.'

'Kellen, I will kill your sister if this turns out to be a prank,' Reichis warned, sitting atop my right shoulder. 'Do you have any idea how long it's been since I had a bath?'

I sniffed. 'Pretty sure I do. Now would you shut up about baths so I can concentrate?' I held my hand out in front of me so that the coin could wiggle and vibrate along my palm to indicate which way to go.

'Is *that* where all this talk of bathing is coming from?' Nephenia asked, staring down at Ishak. The hyena gave a barking laugh, to which Nephenia replied, 'And no, I'm not going to abandon our efforts to prevent a continental war just to find you butter biscuits.' She turned to me. 'What exactly *are* butter biscuits, anyway?'

'Something you don't want greedy, gluttonous animals to acquire a taste for.' The coin seemed to be drifting along my palm in a westerly direction, up the initial slope of a hill, so I headed that way.

'You really don't understand the concept of "business partners",' Reichis observed.

Ishak barked. Or maybe yapped. I still couldn't distinguish between the sounds the hyena made. Reichis seemed to have no difficulty. 'Her too?' The squirrel cat gave Nephenia a withering glance. 'They really are a useless species, aren't they?'

'Why is he looking at me that way?' she asked me, then looked down at Ishak. 'And what did you mean, "She's no better"? What was *that* supposed to mean?'

I explained Reichis's – and apparently Ishak's – assessment of our mutual qualifications as business partners.

'You are *not* my business partner,' Nephenia told the hyena. 'You're my familiar. It's an ancient and time-honoured pairing of two souls, not some shallow business transaction.'

The hyena yapped at her for several seconds, then Nephenia punched me in the arm. Hard. 'Ow! What was that for?'

'For letting your squirrel cat introduce these ruinous ideas into my familiar's head about "partnerships" and "equitable relationships". Do you realise Ishak's now telling me he wants us to work out a formal contract?'

'Wait until she hears about the clause he wants on freshly killed meat,' Reichis whispered into my ear. He started chortling. 'That hyena's *way* more demanding than me.'

'Don't think I can't tell when you're mocking me, squirrel cat,' Nephenia warned. 'In case you're unaware, there are all kinds of unpleasant charms I can attach to a living being.'

Reichis spun around on my shoulder so he was facing her, the sudden snarl telling me he was baring his teeth at her. 'Tell the bitch that she's going to need to charm her eyeballs with a location spell so she can find them in the morning.'

'Two Jan'Tep exiles, a squirrel cat and a hyena walk into the middle of a war,' Ferius said. She stopped walking and shook her head. 'Sounds like the beginning of a joke, but I'm pretty sure none of us are going to be laughing once things get ugly. So could you children *please* stop nattering at each other? I'm trying to save the world here.'

'Sorry, Ferius,' Nephenia said.

'Can't do much with apologies, girl.' The comment came out terse and a little scathing.

Nephenia's jaw tightened, but then she took a deep breath. 'You're right, so tell me how I *can* help.'

Ferius took hold of my hand, holding it up. I opened my fingers and let the coin do its thing. Once again it spun, tilting on its axis towards the hill ahead of us. 'See where the coin's aiming us? If there's anything up top that hill worth more than a stray goat, then chances are there's going to be either people watching for strangers along the way or devices to alert them someone's nearby – or worse, traps.' She let go of my hand. 'I need to get us up there without running into any of those things, which means I need the four of you to go where I go, do what I do, and above all else, keep your mouths shut for more than five seconds at a time.' With that she took off up the hill, striding past the rest of us, mumbling all the while about why Argosi were meant to travel alone.

Nephenia's hand touched my arm. 'She seems worried, Kellen. Do you think she's—'

'Being afraid is the price an Argosi pays,' I replied, following Ferius up the hill.

I just wished it was the only price.

I was limping by the time we reached the top. Ferius had been right about traps. She spotted tripwires and pitfalls that ranged from simple yet elegant to incredibly complex. Most of these we got by, and for a brief time I thought I was getting the hang of identifying traps. That changed when I nearly impaled my foot on a set of spikes buried just under a path of soft earth. Had Ishak not barrelled into me from behind I would've speared more than just the edge of my heel on them.

There were sentries and patrols too, of course, which confirmed that we were onto something important even as they made it vastly more difficult to find out what exactly it was. My spells weren't much help in dealing with them, since setting people on fire isn't a good way of sneaking into a place. Fortunately, Nephenia had brought a couple of ingenious little bells that acted as confusion charms. Other than Reichis forgetting to cover his ears and finding himself incessantly heading the wrong way, we got by most of the guards without too much of a problem.

Once Reichis recovered his sense of direction, he scouted ahead of us, using the trees that grew along the slope of the hill to spy for any other guards or traps we might not be able to see from the ground. Ishak sniffed along the path, sometimes warning us away from patches of blue and green moss that Ferius said were poisonous even if they just touched your skin. Apparently someone really didn't want visitors.

The first orange-red glow of morning was creeping over the horizon by the time we neared the top. The coin was beginning to settle itself in my palm. It vibrated even more than it had before, but now the pull seemed to come from everywhere. Our destination, whatever it was, was close at hand.

'On our bellies now,' Ferius whispered as we neared the top. She had us crawling on elbows and knees. Twice we had to back up to go around a patch of poisonous moss, making our progress feel dangerously slow.

'What's wrong?' I asked, when she stopped us just shy of the summit.

'Nothing,' she replied.

'I mean, what do you see?'

She shot me an annoyed look. 'Nothing. That's the point.'

The rest of us, ignoring her previous instructions, crawled over to her She'd been right: there was nothing there other than the uneven ground of a wide, flat summit probably three hundred yards across. 'Could the coin have been wrong?' Nephenia asked. 'Or maybe your sister really was sending us off on a wild goose chase?'

'Doubt they'd post that many guards around a mountain with nothing to recommend it but poison moss,' Ferius said. 'No, I need someone to take a look-see.' She turned to Reichis. 'Can you do it real quiet like?'

He gave a low, soft growl. 'Kellen, did the clumsy, unwieldy human just ask if *I* can move silently?'

'Just do it,' I said. 'This could be important.'

'There are some bushes ahead,' Ferius said, clearly unaware

of her personal jeopardy at this point. 'Tell him to stick to those if he can.'

Reichis crawled up right in front of Ferius, getting nose to nose with her. 'Stop. Telling. Me. How. To. Do. My. Job.'

I started to translate but Ferius waved me off. 'I get the idea.' To Reichis she said, 'Well then, squirrel cat, what are you waiting for?'

I gave him a warning glance in the hope he'd get the message that this was the wrong time to get into a pissing match with Ferius. He must've decided to take pity on me – or at least defer his outrage until a more convenient time – because he started making his way silently across the ground ahead of us. He got about ten yards before he froze. A second later he disappeared.

'What happened to him?' I asked, rising to my feet and ignoring Ferius's prior injunctions.

She dragged me back down. 'Stay where you are. He knows what he's doing.'

'You didn't seem to think that twenty seconds ago.'

Every nerve in my body was screaming at me to get up and run over there. Reichis could have fallen into some kind of trap. He could be hurt. I felt Nephenia's hand on my arm and she motioned to Ishak. The hyena was sniffing the air but didn't seem concerned. 'He's got a very acute sense of smell,' Neph said quietly. 'If Reichis were hurt or scared, Ishak would catch it from his scent.'

The hyena's apparent confidence in his olfactory abilities might have been reassuring, if Reichis didn't make pretty much the exact same claims and I weren't dead certain he was lying most of the time. A sudden movement caught my attention, and the squirrel cat appeared from one of the bushes ahead of us and ran back to our position. 'By all seventeen squirrel cat gods,' he chittered.

'I thought you said there were nine?'

'Nine what?' Ferius asked.

'Never mind. What did you see, Reichis?'

'This mountain ain't a mountain,' he replied.

'What are you talking about?'

He looked like he was struggling to find the words. 'It's *like* a mountain, and I'm pretty sure it's natural, but it's hollow.'

'You mean, like a volcano?' I'd never actually *seen* a volcano before, but I'd read about them.

'A damned inactive volcano,' Ferius swore. 'Gitabrians are all so darned committed to building things and inventing things, it never occurred to me they might actually use the natural landscape for something.'

'Yeah, but for what?' I asked.

'Come on,' Reichis said, returning to the top. 'There aren't any guards or traps up top.'

The rest of us followed, warily, still on our hands and knees just in case. We only had to go a few feet before I could see the rim of black rock ahead of us. Almost the entire summit opened up to a massive cavern below. Once we made it to the edge, we could see what was hidden inside – what the Gitabrians hadn't wanted us to see. Maybe what they didn't want their own people to see.

The inside of the volcano had been turned into a massive workshop. A good hundred and fifty feet below us were huge racks of tools next to workbenches the size of houses. Dozens of men and women – blacksmiths and labourers, from what I could see – tended forges and shaped metal while a cadre of contraptioneers and their assistants assembled machines. Massive machines. Seventy-foot-long armoured bodies with sweeping metal wings and extended articulated necks that ended in terrifying steel skulls with rows of spiked teeth. They looked like monstrous versions of the silk and paper creatures used at the exhibition to spout the gold-wrapped candies to the crowd, only whatever these things spouted, I doubted it was sweet.

'Dragons,' Nephenia said. 'They're building mechanical dragons. But . . . those metals they're using . . . they must be alción mistivae – the sacred alloys that Janucha used to construct the mechanical bird. She and Altariste said they were all but gone.'

'Look,' Ferius said, pointing to open shafts far below us. Even from here we could see the veins of metal exposed in the rough cavern walls. 'This whole place must be a mine for the lost metals.'

'Janucha lied to us?' I asked.

'Maybe she doesn't know,' Nephenia said. 'But if the Gitabrians have been building these all along, then they must believe she's close to recreating the experiment.'

Ferius started easing herself away from the rim of the volcano towards the long journey we'd need to make back to the city. 'Hey, kid, you know the difference between a tiny mechanical bird and a massive iron dragon?'

'What?'

'A little metal and a whole lot of dead bodies.'

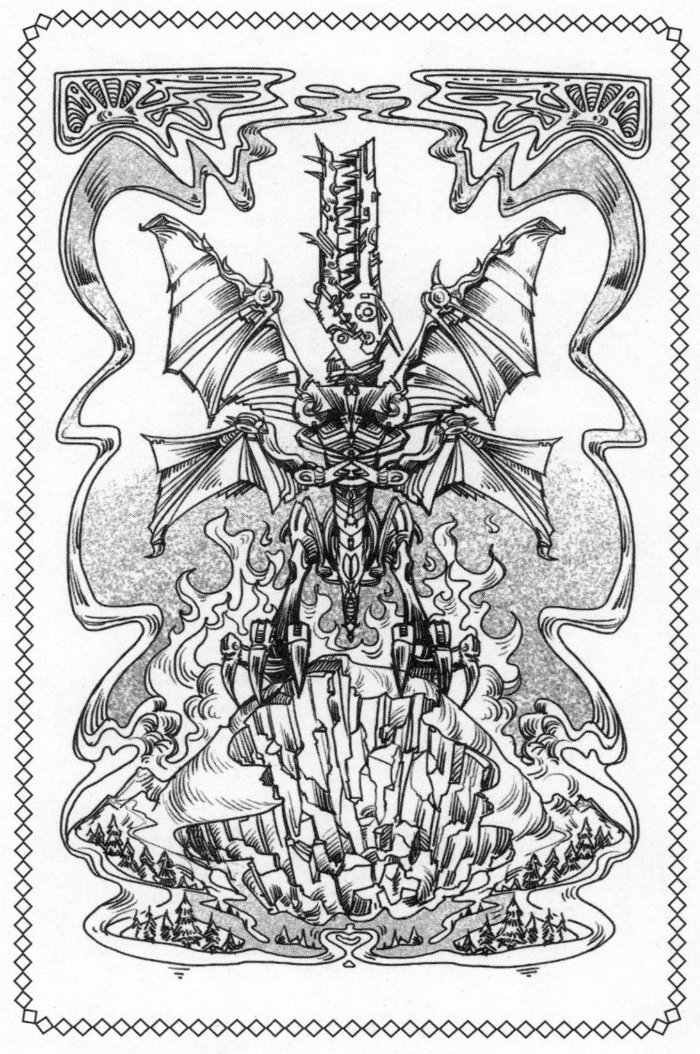

The Mechanical Dragon

THE TRUTH

When the nature of a discordance has been uncovered, then does the work of the Argosi truly begin. Guide the discordance if you can. Destroy it if you must. Should all your efforts fail, should the talents and tactics of the Argosi prove insufficient to contain the threat, then will you learn the most painful truth of all: just because you can see what's coming, doesn't mean you can do anything about it.

51

The Spies

We hid in a cave about a quarter of a mile from the mountain. Evading the patrols and sentries would be too risky in broad daylight. Reichis grumbled, Nephenia and her hyena slept, and I sat there shaking from the cold while Ferius Parfax painted another card.

'How can you do that?' I asked, watching as her brush travelled in smooth strokes across the surface of the card. 'There's barely any light in here.'

'You blind, kid? There's tons of light.'

'We're in a cave, Ferius. If it weren't for what little was coming from the entrance, it would be pitch black in here.'

She leaned towards me to show me that her eyes were shut. 'Then just imagine some more.' With that she turned back to her card and resumed her work.

'You're painting with your eyes *closed*? How is that even possible?'

She chuckled. 'Kid, I was painting Argosi cards blind by the time I was eleven years old.' She dipped her brush into one of her little glass jars. 'It's easier, actually.'

'Easier? How?'

She drew a single curved line on the card, then pulled the

brush away. 'There's a lot that goes into making a discordance card. Painting something, well, that's the easy part. It's imbuing it with what you know about the subject, what you suspect might be happening, colouring it with evidence and shading it with uncertainty, that's what's hard.'

Colouring with evidence and shading with uncertainty. No wonder so many people can't stand the Argosi. The discordance cards, on the other hand, were finally beginning to make sense.

I sat with my back against the cave wall and closed my eyes. I pictured myself holding all the discordance cards I'd seen together as if they made up a single hand of poker. One of the few benefits of having spent my childhood training to be a mage was a particularly good recall of images. Try casting a spell without the precise esoteric geometry in mind and you'll soon learn the reason for the old Jan'Tep saying 'A forgetful mage is a dead mage.'

Individually, the discordance cards were just a bunch of enigmatic pictures, cryptic symbols and unseen allusions. Together they told a simple, if tragic, story. The Mechanical Bird: a wondrous discovery. The Contraptioneer: the genius with the ability to turn that discovery towards whatever purpose she chose. The Path of Shadows . . .

When Enna had given that card to me, I'd thought it represented my destiny. Maybe she had too, but the Argosi aren't fortune tellers. I understood now that what the card really signalled was that all of us – maybe the whole continent – were being driven by fear and uncertainty down a road that led into darkness. For all the talk of exploration and invention, the fact that Gitabria afforded its secret police so much power meant the nation itself was far less secure than it pretended.

The Crowned Mage – even if it wasn't a proper discordance – told me what would come next. The Jan'Tep clans, fearing a newly militarised Gitabria, would for the first time in centuries unite behind a single ruler. Darome, Berabesq, even the Seven Sands would make preparations as the idea of war changed from an occasional threat between belligerent nations to an inevitability for the entire continent.

The cards vanished from my mind as I opened my eyes. 'Ferius?'

'Yeah, kid?'

'If Janucha solves the flaw in her design . . . If she can bring those iron dragons to life . . .'

Ferius paused in her painting. 'Seven kinds of hell, kid. Seven kinds of hell.'

'So will you . . . ?' I stopped myself. *Will you kill her to prevent it?* Even asking the question would force her to step too close to a line I knew she didn't want to cross. 'Forget it,' I said.

'See? That right there is why we've got to make you a better poker player.'

'What do you mean?'

'So you'll learn that no matter how bad your hand looks, all it takes is the right card to change the odds.' The sound of her brush moving across the surface of the card resumed. 'Now, you mind, kid? All that fretting you're doing is blockin' my light.'

I got up and headed deeper into the cave to get some sleep. 'You know that nothing you say ever makes sense, right?'

Her laugh was small and bright, and as it reached my ears it made even the darkness shimmer. I stopped for a second, holding on to that laugh. It contained everything I loved about Ferius Parfax, and everything about her that made me crazy.

The Path of the Wild Daisy.

How I wished I could walk that path with her.

I found the others nestled against the cave walls. Reichis and Ishak seemed to be in unconscious competition over who could snore the loudest. I came perilously close to stepping on Nephenia, who lay on her side, apparently able to sleep despite the echoing cacophony.

I lay down and covered my ears as best I could. I wasn't optimistic about getting any rest, but that turned out not to matter because a moment later I heard Nephenia say quietly, 'You two are a lot alike, you know.'

I pushed myself up to a sitting position. 'Who? Me and Ferius?'

She sidled up next to me. 'I'm serious. All those questions you ask her, the little things that bother you . . . I think they're important somehow.'

'Well, that's depressing, because her answers are unintelligible rubbish most of the time.'

Neph's shoulder was close enough to mine that I felt her shrug. 'That's what I thought at first. I just assumed the Argosi were eccentric. But when I listen to the two of you bickering—'

'We don't "bicker".'

'Fine. When you're having your profound and entirely composed philosophical discussions, it . . . it's like there's something there, underneath the words. Lady Ferius—'

'She's not a lady.' *Great. Now I'm doing it.*

Neph slapped my hand lightly. 'Would you mind not interrupting all the time?' I would have been annoyed by that except she left her hand there. 'Everything the two of you talk about feels *right* somehow, like I'm hearing someone describe a painting that I know is there but I can't see myself yet.'

A chuckle escaped my lips. Nephenia tried to pull her hand away to slap mine again but I held firm. 'You're starting to talk like her now.'

A pause, then a squeeze. 'That might just be the second nicest thing you ever said to me, Kellen.'

Something in the sound of her voice, the touch of her hand on mine, made me want to be closer to her. A lot closer. 'What was the nicest?' I asked. I remembered of course. Back in our city at the oasis I'd said she would one day figure out she was special, but until then she could just trust that she was special to me. Funnily enough, those had been Ferius's words, not mine.

Neph shifted a little closer. 'If you want to kiss me, Kellen, either ask me or just do it and live with the consequences. Don't play around at the edges hoping I'll do it for you.'

So much for that plan, I guess.

I would have kissed her then, I think, or at least tried. Unfortunately, that precise recall that comes with a mage's training? Sometimes it brings memories you don't want. Unbidden, the image Shalla had put in my head of Nephenia's dead father came to me so clearly it was as if his corpse were right there with us in the cave. Despite the near-perfect darkness, I could've sworn his blood was dripping down the cave walls in front of me. I heard a slow exhale of breath, and for one brief, panicked instant, I thought it had come from the ghostly cadaver. It was just my imagination, of course; the sigh had come from Nephenia.

'I murdered him,' she said.

'How did you know I was—'

She let go of my hand. 'You went cold, Kellen. It doesn't take a genius to figure out why.' She went silent for a moment, then said, 'Go ahead and ask, if that's what you want.'

Everything felt very dangerous all of a sudden – not that Neph would attack me of course, but rather that whatever happened next could change our relationship forever. Not that we had a relationship exactly. 'I don't need to ask,' I said finally, reaching out to find her hand once again. 'I already know what happened.'

'Tell me.'

Ever since we were kids, Nephenia's father had been stern. No. Not 'stern'. A bully. That wasn't it either though, was it? Because whatever cruelty I'd witnessed as a child could only have been the barest hint of what Nephenia and her mother had to endure. Before I left our people, Nephenia had told me how important it was that she earn her mage's name so that she wouldn't be forced to live like her mother – a servant to her father's whims. 'It got worse,' I said. 'After you passed your mage's trials. You thought things would be better, but they only got worse.'

She didn't reply. She didn't need to. Months ago Shalla had communicated with me through a spell she'd devised and told me that Panahsi's grandmother had promised Nephenia protection if she agreed to marry him. 'When your father found out about the arrangement you made with Pan's family, he got angry. He . . .' I stopped.

What am I doing? She's never brought this up, so keep your mouth shut.

But Nephenia spoke, her voice sounding ragged, as if she'd been screaming for days. 'He used a silk spell on me. He put me to sleep.'

Her anger over the red mage's spell suddenly made a lot more sense. 'Did he . . . ?'

'I don't know. There wasn't any . . . I don't know if he did anything to me, Kellen. I think that was the whole point.' I felt her hand starting to shake. 'From the time I sparked my first band I'd been casting wards around my bed every night. It was the only way I could sleep in that house. My father was never a strong mage, but he had friends. He had one of them break my wards that night.'

So she'd know he could get to her any time he wanted.

There were a dozen questions I almost asked. Did you tell anyone? Did you go to the council of lords magi? Did you try to run away? Did you, did you, did you? But I knew the answers already. My people don't tolerate crimes of violence, but a father simply putting a sleep spell on a disobedient daughter? The head of a Jan'Tep house has the right to keep order within their home.

'I murdered him,' Nephenia said, her voice flat.

'You were protecting yourself. You were just—'

I felt, rather than saw, the shake of her head. 'No, you don't understand. I didn't wait until he attacked me. I played the good girl for weeks until I was sure he believed I'd learned my lesson. Then, when he was alone in his sanctum, I killed him. No threats. No warnings. It was murder.'

I weighed her words like a magistrate at trial. 'If you'd waited, it would have been too late. Neph, he would have—'

She went on as if she couldn't hear me. 'My mother turned me in. I'm not sure why. I guess she'd been living with his abuse so long that my refusal to do so was a slap in the face to her. A week later I was condemned to death by the council of lords magi.' Her voice deepened. '"An attack on the head of a Jan'Tep house is an attack on the entire clan."'

'Did . . . Did my mother or father intervene?' It was a stupid question, but I couldn't help asking it anyway. I still wanted to believe some decency existed in my parents.

Nephenia shook her head. 'It was Pan. He went to the council and threatened to abandon our clan if they executed me. He's the most promising mage they have other than your sister. His grandmother has a lot of influence among the council, and eventually they relented.' She tapped three fingers against my palm. 'After they cut off two fingers from each hand, they exiled me into the desert. Since there was a decent chance my wounds would get infected or I'd die by some other means, the clan had technically fulfilled my execution.'

Ancestors. I couldn't imagine what those first days must have been like, unable to cast any healing spells, trying to staunch those wounds while staying alive on the road. 'I'm sorry, Neph,' I said.

'Don't be. I'm not.'

'What do you mean?'

She moved herself around so we were sitting facing each other. 'I told you before, Kellen, I had to make a decision. I could either be the girl who lived with the shame until bad luck or my own stupidity got me killed, or I could become who I am now.'

'And who is that?'

'Someone who doesn't apologise for who she is'. Despite the darkness I saw her hand reach out to touch the skin around my left eye. Even prepared, I still flinched. 'That's what makes us different, Kellen. If they found a way to resurrect my father and my crime was wiped away, you know the first thing I'd do?'

'You'd go back and kill him again,' I said.

'Damn right.'

All at once I understood why Nephenia had kissed me when we'd first seen each other in the desert, and why she hadn't since then. The reason she hadn't told me about her father before wasn't because she was ashamed of it, but because it wasn't any of my business. She'd told me now, not because I'd asked, but because she wanted me to know her better. That left me with a choice – one that meant I had to let go forever of the memory of a shy, demure girl who just happened to have the same name as the woman sitting across from me.

I took her hand and shook it. 'My name is Kellen. It's nice to finally meet you, Nephenia.'

I think she might have let out a sob then, but it was hard to tell because Reichis and Ishak – though I suspected they weren't actually asleep – were snoring even louder than before. Nephenia pulled me into a hug. 'You know, for someone who's absolutely terrible at talking to girls, sometimes you say just the right thing.'

I think I was getting the hang of this hugging thing, because for once it felt completely natural. I was actually kind of enjoying it until Nephenia suddenly drew away from me.

'What did I do?' I asked.

'I felt something in your trousers.'

Oh, ancestors. This is really not how I pictured this going. 'I'm sorry, I didn't mean to—'

'Not that! I mean something in your pocket is heating up.'

Now I could feel it too. For an instant I feared that the

powders I keep in the pouches on either side of my belt had mixed together. I dug into my pocket and yelped as I felt the source of the heat. When I dropped it on the ground between us, we could both see the small coin glowing with an angry red glare against the darkness of the cave.

'More of your coin magic?' Nephenia asked. 'Did you somehow trigger a spell?'

'That's not my coin; it's the one Shalla gave me. But why would it be doing anything now? The charm on it was supposed to lead us to the mountain.'

Suddenly Nephenia reached down and grabbed the coin in her fingers, sucking in air between her teeth at the pain, and ran past me towards the entrance. I followed close behind, nearly tripping on the uneven ground. The second Nephenia was outside she hurled the coin as far as she could. It disappeared somewhere off in the trees. 'Lady Ferius!' she called back into the cave. 'We have to run!'

'I don't understand,' I said. 'What does it mean?'

The look she gave me was as unsettling as it was urgent. 'You can put more than one charm on an object, Kellen. Heat isn't part of a navigational spell. It's a by-product of a tracking charm. Someone's using the coin to follow *us*.' She turned back towards the cave. 'Lady Ferius, we have to go now!'

Ferius appeared at the entrance of the cave, eyes narrowed as she peered past us into the forest. 'Bad news, kid. They're already here.'

I turned to stare at the expanse of trees gleaming like copper pennies from the reflection of morning light on the dew of their leaves. Slowly, the glow changed colour as a different light – one very much like that of the coin – began to radiate from the forest. A figure emerged some hundred yards away, his body clothed in red silk, his face covered in a crimson lacquer mask that shone like a blood-red sun.

The red mage had found us.

I had just enough time to hear someone shout, 'Run!' before a bolt of ember magic set the trees on fire.

52

The Betrayal

Branches and brambles whipped at my face and arms. Panic turned every stinging sensation into the first prickle of fire before it burns you to a crisp.

I hate being a coward.

Ferius and Nephenia ran alongside me as the three of us fled. Our only hope was to stay ahead of the red mage long enough to reach the city, where attacking us would risk further exposing the Jan'Tep presence in Gitabria. Ferius took the lead, guiding us along trails I couldn't even detect until my feet were already on them. She was as quick and agile as a gazelle, leaping over rocks and bushes, never looking down, her eyes always searching for the next path. Nephenia and I followed as best we could, huffing and puffing in time with each other. 'What about Ishak and Reichis?' she asked breathlessly. 'I can't see them.'

'The critters know how to take care of themselves and they can track us easy,' Ferius replied. Without warning she pushed Nephenia and me down a sloping path between the broken remains of a boulder. Off in the distance Cazaran's eight bridges came into view. They might as well have been a mirage in the desert. We were still miles away when a blast of what had definitely been ember magic turned a tree ahead of us to ash. Once again we were forced to change course.

'Damned mage isn't hunting us,' Ferius said, taking up the lead again. 'He's herding us!'

'But where?' Nephenia asked, eyes darting around. 'There's nothing—'

'The patrols,' I said, suddenly realising why he kept making us turn. 'Ferius, I think he's forcing us towards one of the Gitabrian patrols so we'll get caught.'

She came to a sudden halt and it was all I could do not to crash into her. She turned back, towards the sound of our enemy's footsteps. 'Reckon you're right about his plan, kid.' With a shake of her hand she fanned out a dozen of her sharp steel cards. 'I was gettin' tired of running anyway.'

My hands were shaking as I slid them into the pouches at my side. Nephenia reached inside her coat where she kept her few remaining charmed objects. I doubted any of it would do us much good now.

The red mage appeared over the top of a ridge, moving without any discernible haste. In fact, when he saw we weren't fleeing any longer, he hesitated, stopping some twenty yards away. When he spoke, that strange breath spell of his made his words echo all around us, the reverberations masking his voice. 'You should run,' he said.

Ferius idly shuffled her steel cards, sending them spinning through the air between her two hands. 'We're fine right where we are.'

The lines of the mage's red lacquer mask altered slightly, the shapes of the eyes narrowing. 'As you wish. They will have you in minutes regardless.'

'Who are you?' I demanded, though I knew I wasn't going

to get any better an answer this time than on my previous attempts. 'Why do you keep coming after me?'

'Ask your father,' he said, coming closer until he was less than ten feet away.

I had a moment of wondering if the man in red might be Ke'heops himself – some kind of perverse joke he'd played on me. But this guy wasn't tall enough to be my father.

'Well, kid?' Ferius asked.

'What?'

'Do as the man says: ask your father.'

It took me a second to figure out what she meant. I reached into my shirt and took out the card Shalla had given me. It felt stiff and lifeless in my hand. I drew on the breath magic from the only band I could spark. A spell like the one used to create the card was far beyond my meagre talents, but igniting it was a less daunting prospect. It still wasn't easy, though, and the process was a lot slower than I'd expected.

Just when I thought I might be close, the red mage said, 'Enough.' With a flick of his index and middle fingers and the utterance of a single syllable, the card went flying from my hand. Why did this guy feel the need to keep showing off?

The card flipped end over end. The mage's hand twisted a fraction and suddenly the card froze in the air between us. With a final invocation, he brought it to life. At first the crown remained still, but then I heard the clack of boot heels against a marble floor drifting out from the card. A moment later my father's hand reached down and took the crown. As before, the perspective of the image shifted and I found myself staring at my father's face. He looked irritated.

'I specifically instructed you against this.' He didn't seem to be talking to me.

'He should know who put him here and why,' the red mage replied.

'Very well.' The blue and black paint strokes of my father's eyes found me. 'Come then, Kellen. Rage. Shout. Whimper. Do all the things you do whenever you feel the world has wronged you.'

'Ain't the world that wronged him this time,' Ferius said.

My father didn't even bother looking at her. 'Don't bray at me, woman. My son would never be in this situation had you not taken him from his family. For that crime alone I should—'

I stepped closer to the card. 'Don't ever talk to my friend like that again,' I said. I probably should have backed that up somehow, but I doubted there was any threat I could make that would give my father pause.

Nephenia hauled me out of the way. Evidently she'd decided one of us should attempt diplomacy. 'Lord Ke'heops,' she began, far more respectfully than I could've managed, 'you mustn't delay us. We've found evidence that the Gitabrians are—'

He cut her off. 'The mechanical dragons. A little theatrical perhaps, but no less dangerous for it.' Again he ignored her and spoke to me. 'Now they need only find a way to repeat the process of bringing the machines to life and this nation of tinkerers will become an unstoppable military force.'

'But if you already know what we've found . . .' I stopped, unable to complete that thought because another had wormed its way into my soul. 'You *want* the Gitabrians to catch us. This was your plan all along.'

'What?' Nephenia asked. 'But why?'

'Now that he's used us to find out what the Gitabrians

have been hiding,' I replied, my gaze still focused on the smug expression painted on my father's face, 'he needs Zavera and her troops to catch us – no, make that, to *execute* us – so they'll believe the information is contained.'

Nephenia gestured to the red mage. 'But what about him?'

'He's only here to keep us from escaping. He'll disappear right before the patrol arrives.'

The flowing lines and bold colours on the card shifted, and my father looked almost proud of my deductions. *Almost.* 'By now the Gitabrians know their hidden factory has been found. They'll put the contraptioneer in hiding until she solves the puzzle of her failed experiments. You must put the secret police off the scent of my own agents until they can deal with the inventor. Think, Kellen! Your deaths will save our people. Your sacrifice will avert catastrophe!'

I did something then that I'd never done before: I laughed in my father's face. 'The clan prince's crown must be too tight for your head if that's what you believe. The second the Gitabrians capture us, I'm going to tell them *everything*.' I reached out for the card. 'And this is the first piece of proof I'll give them.'

The red mage raised his hand. His fingers took on the somatic shape for a spell I barely had time to recognise before a hurricane's worth of wind blew me backwards without affecting anyone else. *Damn, I wish he'd stop using breath magic on me.*

'Enough,' my father commanded. 'Kellen will not reveal us. Nor will the Argosi.'

'Are you out of your mind?' I asked, but then I saw the expression on Ferius's face. 'You can't *agree* with this?'

'She understands what you do not,' Ke'heops said. 'The

Argosi fear the destructive potential of the mechanical dragons to destabilise the continent as much as we do. She no longer has the means to prevent the Gitabrians from bringing their foul inventions to life –' he leaned forward as though he were about to step out of the card and shake hands on the deal – 'so she will keep silent, and allow me to do what must be done for the greater good.' The black circles of his eyes swivelled to me. 'As will you, Kellen, because it is your duty as a son of the House of Ke.'

'*Duty?*' Nephenia demanded, her eyes blazing. Apparently she was done with diplomacy. 'My father used to talk about duty – every time he beat my mother! Every time he—'

'*You* do not speak to *me* in such a fashion, murderess. I have no need for the Gitabrians to find you alive.' He signalled to the red mage. 'The spell she used on her father – cast it on her now. Bind her to him forever in the lands beyond the grey passage.'

My hands were pulling powder so fast I think I might've actually out-drawn the red mage were it not for the fact that part of me wanted so badly to blast the card instead of him.

'Stop!' the mage said, summoning a shield I couldn't get past. 'Lord Ke'heops, I will place a mind chain on the girl to keep her silent. On all of them if need be. Let me deal with this matter and be about my mission.'

My father didn't look at all pleased to have his order refused. 'Very well, but do so quickly.' He turned his gaze back to me. 'You've always wanted to play the hero, Kellen. Ever since you were a little boy, you wanted to be the great warrior who sacrifices all to save those he loves. I think you're still that little boy. So let this be my gift to you: stay where you are, say nothing and accept your fate. In doing so you will save thousands upon thousands of lives.'

He removed the crown from his head and set it upon the fingertips of the wooden stand. The lines on the card slowly settled until they were completely still. The red mage gestured and the card flew to his hand.

'You will not chain me,' Nephenia said, tearing off her gloves. The stumps of missing fingers on each hand still sent a chill through me, but already she was forming somatic shapes. 'I may not be able to perform all the high magics any more, but I'll die before I let you bind me.'

'Yeah,' Ferius said, making steel cards spin and turn around her fingers. 'I've never been partial to chains either.'

The red mage held up his hands. 'I will not bind any of you,' he said.

'You won't?' I asked.

He shook his head. 'There is another way. You and the Argosi woman will allow yourselves to be captured. I will take the girl with me. Her life will be the assurance that you hold your silence when the Gitabrians come for you. Keep your promise to me, and once my business is done, I swear I will get her out of the country and set her free.'

'You think I'll abandon my friends?' Nephenia asked. 'You're even more stupid than you look in that preposterous outfit.' She took a step towards him, her fingers forming a simple ember blast spell. I doubted it would get past his shield.

'You have made a hundred bad choices already, Neph'aria. I beg you not to make one more.'

'She won't,' Ferius said, interposing herself between them. 'He's right, girl.'

'Stop calling me "girl"! You don't call Kellen "boy"!'

That seemed a somewhat less than relevant issue right now, but Ferius nodded nonetheless. 'You're right . . . kid.' She put her hands on Nephenia's shoulders. 'But you gotta be smart now. Me and Kellen, well, we set ourselves on a path. This is where it ends.' She nodded to me, and I knew what she wanted me to say.

'Please, Neph. If I have to die, I want to do it knowing it meant something. Besides, Ishak needs you. Reichis will too. Keep your valuables hidden under your pillow at night, though.'

Nephenia, for all the toughness I'd seen in her these past weeks, looked as if she were about to break. 'Who will I be if I let the two of you die for me?'

Ferius smiled. 'Anyone you want. Maybe even an Argosi.' She took her hands off Nephenia's shoulders and hugged her close. It was an oddly affectionate gesture, given how the two of them had never seemed to get along all that well. That's why I noticed when Ferius slipped the card depicting the mechanical dragon into the pocket of Nephenia's coat.

The faint sound of boots crunching leaves drifted out from the forest behind us. Lots of boots.

'We go now,' the red mage said to Nephenia. 'Either by your choice or mine.'

She let go of Ferius and ran over to me and kissed me on the cheek. 'No goodbyes between us, Kellen. Not for long, anyway.' She turned and walked towards the red mage. He made a series of somatic shapes with both hands and uttered a spell I barely recognised other than it blended silk and ember magic. A moment later the two were invisible to my eyes. Ferius and I were left alone just as the Gitabrian secret police came for us.

'That was right brave of you, kid,' Ferius said.

'Thanks,' I said, though until that moment I'd just assumed Ferius had some clever ploy worked out to escape our pursuers and that she'd wanted Nephenia out of the way in the very unlikely case that things didn't work out.

Sometimes I'm a little more optimistic than my life history warrants.

Over the ridge a dozen men and women came, about half armed with fire lances, a few with spell-shields. Two carried long poles with loops of wire on one end that looked suspiciously like they were meant to go around one's throat. At the head of the pack came Servadi Zavera té Drazo. She looked happy to see us.

'You *do* have a plan, right?' I asked Ferius.

She dropped to her knees and put her hands behind her head. 'Nope.'

'Oh.'

Crap.

53

The Noose

I was right about the purpose of the wire loops at the end of those seven-foot-long poles.

I managed to wheeze, 'Damn it . . .' before I could no longer get enough air to speak.

The devices had an ingenious design to them: about a third of the way from the bottom end, the wooden poles had a piece of brass wrapped around them, maybe eight inches long. Once the noose was around your neck, all the person holding the pole had to do was twist the brass piece and the wire tightened, enabling them to decide just how much to let you breathe. If at all.

The handcuffs binding our wrists behind our backs were similarly inventive. The braided strands of copper wire were joined together by a little steel disc. Through a mechanical process I couldn't quite figure out, any time you pulled against the cuffs, the wire tightened around your wrists.

I was starting to really dislike the Gitabrian infatuation with clever inventions.

Spots appeared in my vision as the lack of air in my lungs became problematic. My tongue tasted bitter from the fear, though an entirely different emotion was taking over.

I was pissed off.

It wasn't the sheer number of times we'd been betrayed lately or the constant lies. It wasn't the fact that these insane secret police had been hiding war machines from their own people or even that I was, at best, a few painful minutes from being executed. No, what really made me angry was what Zavera was doing to Ferius.

'Look at her!' she gloated, yanking on the wire noose around Ferius's neck, parading her before the officers before twisting the bronze apparatus to choke her mercilessly. 'Witness the pride of the Argosi!'

Laughter, all around me. A stupid, juvenile part of my brain counted each chuckle and chortle, fully intending on making them pay for each one if I ever got the chance.

Zavera drove the butt end of the pole into the ground, steadying it with her foot. She wrapped her hands higher up the shaft and with a strength that belied her size, hauled back, hoisting Ferius up until she was on tiptoes, practically dangling from the wire noose around her neck. I was forced to watch as her face turned purple and a gurgling sound escaped her lips.

Zavera made some stupid joke in Gitabrian that I didn't understand. The guy holding my pole lightened up on the noose momentarily. With a brief gasp of breath I shouted, 'Stop!' and then sucked in more air before the guy holding me could tighten the noose again. A dozen threats went through my mind, but none got past my lips. *Arta tuco*, I reminded myself. The Argosi talent of subtlety. *Zavera's got you bound with a wire noose. You have to bind her with words. No . . . Not words. With a question.* 'Why do you hate her so mu—'

A sudden yank on the noose cut me off.

Zavera turned to look at me, letting Ferius drop gasping to the ground. 'What did you say?'

I couldn't speak of course. She gave a signal to my captor and he eased the tension so I could repeat my question. I didn't. That would be too obvious. If Ferius and I were to have any chance at all, we needed a miracle. That was a problem for two reasons: first, my people don't *believe* in miracles. Second, the only sort of miracle I *could* hope for would come in the form of a two-foot tall conniving ball of fur. Since even Reichis isn't arrogant enough to believe he could take on twelve trained warriors, I had to give him more time.

Time was the problem.

I needed to somehow string along the spymaster of Gitabria like she was some dumb rube about to get swindled in a poker game. Since Zavera was clearly *not* a dumb rube, this was going to take subtlety. Arta ancestors-be-damned tuco subtlety. So when I spoke again, it was to casually say, 'Nothing. Just coughing is all.'

A little arta valar can't hurt, right?

Zavera smiled at my brazenness. She handed the end of her pole to one of her officers and went to kneel in front of Ferius, who was trying with only moderate success to get air into her lungs. 'You asked why I hate the Argosi, no?' She reached out a hand to stroke Ferius's cheek. 'It is because—'

'No,' I said, cutting her off. 'You must've imagined it.' Talking when you're only getting a fraction of the air necessary to make your vocal cords vibrate is hard work. I breathed in as slowly and deeply as I could before adding, 'Besides, I already know why you *resent* Ferius so much.'

Yeah. 'Resent' was the word I needed. Not 'hate', which would simply have made Zavera give her reasons. I didn't give a damn about those. My only job was to keep her interested in me.

She glanced over, eyes narrowed. 'Really? To what do you attribute my supposed "resentment"?'

Good question. I closed my eyes. I think better when I'm not staring at people who plan to kill me. 'You fight better than she does,' I began.

'That hardly seems cause for resentment, does it?'

'Shut up, I'm not finished,' I said. That got me a yank on the noose that made my throat seize. It was necessary though. Zavera was too smart. I had to keep her off balance by saying things that would frustrate her even as they sparked her interest.

That's right: I was turning into Ferius Parfax.

'You have a position of power,' I went on. 'Of prominence among your people. She's nothing but a wanderer.'

'Perhaps I misunderstand your use of the word "resent"?' Zavera suggested.

I didn't bother to reply. I knew she'd give me one more sentence at least. Ferius says that human beings are often bound by arbitrary habits – like the way most people will give three points when they're trying to make a convincing argument. Not two, not four. Three.

Of course Ferius was currently halfway to being choked to death and at the mercy of a lunatic.

Okay, I thought. *Make this last one good. Only, what do you say to surprise a Gitabrian spymaster?* I closed my eyes tighter, shutting out the world as I put together everything I knew about Zavera. It was kind of funny actually, because for all her hatred towards Ferius, she kind of reminded me of . . .

Oh hell.

I opened my eyes, and looked at her properly for the very first time. What I saw was something even Ferius herself had missed. 'You're an Argosi.'

Apparently that was a rather rude thing to say because the guy holding my pole yanked on it hard. I was dragged all the way back until I fell flat on the ground, choking as I looked up at a cloudless sky. The sound of Zavera's footsteps was followed by the woman herself. She stood over me, filling my vision like some Berabesq god come to judge me once and for all. She spread her hands out and then, very slowly, clapped.

54

The Argosi

Arta precis is the Argosi talent for perception – for seeing what others do not. Until that moment in the forests outside of Cazaran, I'd never really shown much promise at arta precis. *Nice that I got to show off before Zavera kills me,* I thought.

She knelt down closer to me. 'I was wrong about you,' she said. 'When I first met you inside that cell in Notia Veras, I wondered why any Argosi would make a teysan of a bumbling, self-centred little boy. I thought perhaps this was some act of defiance on her part. The Path of the Wild Daisy is known for her delight in mocking our training.' She reached down and grabbed a handful of my hair. With the index finger of her free hand she tapped my forehead. 'But there is something in there that is not entirely without potential. I could have made a fine spy out of you, I think.'

'Teach me,' I said. 'Let Ferius live and I swear I'll be yours.'

She raised an eyebrow. 'You would be *my* student?'

'From now until death.' It was true actually, because the second my hands were free I was going to pull powder from the pouches at my belt and blow a hole through her bigger than the one I'd left in that tower.

She patted my cheek. 'Alas, your arta tuco is not quite up

to the job.' She leaned closer and whispered in my ear, 'It is in the eyes where lies must first be told. Yours betray your lips at every turn.'

Ancestors. Do all Argosi really talk this way?

Zavera stepped away from me. 'Get him up,' she commanded the man behind me.

He did – by tilting the pole until I had to scramble to my feet to keep the wire from slicing through my throat.

Zavera returned to Ferius. 'The Argosi have lied to you, Teysan Kellen fal Ke.' She signalled to the man holding the pole. He spun Ferius around so her back was to Zavera. Then the spymaster smashed her fist into Ferius's back at the precise spot where she'd been injured before.

'No!' I shouted. All pretence of arta tuco or arta precis or anything else fled as I realised what Zavera planned to do. She'd *wanted* us to figure out who she was – wanted Ferius to know her secret so it would mean that much more when she beat her to death with her bare hands.

'The Argosi delude themselves that with a few tricks here – a few clever ploys there – they can avert war.' She turned and drove her elbow into the exact same spot. 'That is a folly the world cannot abide.'

Zavera's third punch was even more brutal than the first two. Ferius's legs went out from under her. The only thing holding her up was the noose. Blood seeped through the back of her shirt. 'Ah, there we are. Not long now. One final blow will rupture her kidney. An unpleasant way to die, but well deserved, I promise you.' She patted Ferius on the shoulder. 'I followed the Way of Wind once, you know. I found the signs. But they weren't in the discordances. No, the truth wasn't to be discovered in one or two stray cards.

It was in the concordances. The entire deck. I told the other Argosi, warned them that the nations of this continent could not help but fall into war. It was only a matter of time.' She shook her head. 'I *begged* them to take action.'

'What sort of action could the Argosi take?' I asked, desperate to keep her talking – to keep her from hitting Ferius again. 'What did you want them to do?'

'To choose a damned side!' Zavera swung an arm towards the city in the distance. 'The Gitabrians are a good and noble people! They seek only to send out their ships, to explore, to invent. Not once since they arrived on this continent have they attacked their neighbours. But the Argosi *never* take sides.' She clenched her fist and slammed it against her own chest. '*I* chose a side. *I* chose to stand with those who love peace, to protect them from the Jan'Tep arcanocracy and the Berabesq theocracy and the Daroman empire. Manipulators and madmen. Thugs and brutalisers.' She turned her head up to the sky. 'When our mechanical dragons soar high above their heads, when they strike deep into their territories, destroying their palaces and their temples and their sanctums, only then will these warring nations learn to love peace.'

She turned back to Ferius and raised her fist. 'Tell me where the girl is. I know there were three of you. I must keep the secret of the dragons a little longer. Tell me where the charm-caster has gone and I will give you a death that will be a mercy compared to the one you deserve.'

So much for the red mage's brilliant plan. I should've realised it was stupid in the first place. Zavera had *met* Nephenia. Of course she knew there'd be another threat to deal with.

Ferius mumbled something unintelligible. The spymaster

grabbed her by the shoulder and spun her around. 'What is that?'

Ferius coughed. Blood dribbled from her mouth. 'I said . . . she's long gone. You'll never find her. Oh, and she's got my card. *Sister.*'

Without a word, Zavera turned her back around, exposing her wounded side. She didn't hit her, but instead – with cruel and deliberate slowness – bunched her fingertips together and pushed them against the wound. Ferius moaned in agony.

I struggled in vain against the noose around my neck. What do you do for your friend when she's about to die? What would Ferius want? 'You've lost,' I taunted Zavera. 'Before long Nephenia will find the other Argosi. They'll know what you've done. You wanted the Argosi to take a side? Guess which side they'll take once they see the card she's carrying!'

Zavera's jaw clenched in anger, but it didn't stop her from pressing ever harder into Ferius's back, taking her life a fraction of an inch at a time.

Something small flew through the air. I only saw that it was a rock when it struck Zavera in the right temple. The spymaster spun around, eyes blinking as a trickle of blood dripped from the wound. 'Who threw that?'

A voice called out from the forest behind us. 'Lady Ferius! We've got to run!'

Zavera's gaze turned to me. She smiled as we both recognised the voice.

55

The Way of Fools

Zavera almost seemed grateful as she called out, 'Bless you, Magiziera Nephenia! You have helped to save a wondrous nation!' She signalled to a group of her soldiers. 'Six of you, go find her. Take the spell-shields. She will try her Jan'Tep tricks on you.'

Damn it, Nephenia. Why did you have to be so rash, impetuous, reckless . . . I stopped. There wasn't much point wasting my anger coming up with insults that all meant the same thing. Neph had thrown away the one hope we had of the Argosi learning what Zavera had done.

'You surround yourself with careless, pampered children,' she said to Ferius. 'What did you expect to happen?' She paused. '*Sister*.'

Far off in the forest, Nephenia called out again. 'Lady Ferius!'

The expression of despair on my mentor's face proved once and for all that even *her* arta valar – her swagger – had its limits. 'They ain't just children!' she shouted. Like a drunk in the street she swung a kick at Zavera that went wide, nearly pulling both her and the soldier holding the pole attached to the noose around her neck off balance. Then she grinned. 'A couple of them are animals.'

The rush of leaves came from somewhere high up in the trees. The man behind me screamed. I was yanked backwards as he fell under what I guessed was a very painful series of gashes delivered by a maniacal squirrel cat. The pressure on the noose disappeared. Air tastes a lot sweeter when you can get enough of it into your lungs.

'The nets,' Zavera shouted at the men and women around her. 'Do not waste your fire lances on the animal – he's too fast. Use the nets to capture him first.'

Ferius called out to me. 'Hey, kid, I ever show you this trick?' She threw herself backwards, using the back of her neck to push the pole. The guy holding it, not wanting to let go, found himself tripping on a tree root and bashing his head against a low-hanging branch.

Something tickled my wrists behind my back. 'Stupid Gitabrian handcuffs,' Reichis muttered. A moment later, they came loose. The little bugger really does have a knack for knots and locks.

My relief at having my hands free was short-lived since two of Zavera's soldiers came at me and a third aimed her fire lance in my direction just in case I tried to move. Ferius though – with her hands still cuffed behind her back – spun around, pulling the now free pole along with her. The men coming for me got their feet tangled up in it and went down hard. Unfortunately, they took Ferius with them. I took advantage of the momentary distraction to launch myself away from where the fire lance was pointed. By the time the woman holding the weapon had readjusted her aim, I was already in the air, my hands throwing powders from my pouches. I've practised firing my spell from every position imaginable, so even before my shoulder hit the ground, the red and black powders had begun to collide with each other. '*Carath*,' I intoned, my fingers forming the somatic shapes.

Two explosions thundered almost simultaneously, shaking leaves from the trees, turning them to ash as they fell all around us. For a second I wasn't sure who'd got who, but while my ears were ringing painfully, my opponent was rolling on the ground trying to put out the red and black flames on her left side.

My hearing was almost gone. Sounds were muted, as if I was underwater. I smiled though, as I heard first one then a second of Zavera's troops scream in that distinctive way people do when a squirrel cat's teeth tear off part of their ear. Closer to the ground, Ishak raced like a demon, disappearing into the foliage before the secret police could aim their fire lances at him, reappearing a moment later to leap up and bite an arm or leg. Anytime one of them tried to fight back, Reichis would glide down from a tree, grab onto their head and kick with his hind legs, tearing the skin at the back of their neck to shreds.

Once I managed to regain my footing, I got off two more shots. The first hit the target, knocking down a fire lancer. The second missed entirely. Considering my hands were still numb from the handcuffs, I was lucky not to have blown off my own fingers. 'Where's Nephenia?' I called out to Reichis.

Ishak looked up from where he stood on the back of an unconscious man and barked, 'Lady Ferius! We've got to run!' Only then did I recognise they were exactly the words Nephenia had said as we'd fled the cave.

Reichis giggled. 'Man, I can't get enough of that trick.'

She's not really here. She can still get the card out of Gitabria!

Our luck ran out when the six soldiers Zavera had sent

in search of Nephenia returned. They aimed their fire lances in our direction. Once again we were at a disadvantage. You'd think Zavera would've been relieved.

'Games!' she screamed.

I turned to see her holding Ferius, one arm around her neck, squeezing.

'You play games while the good and decent see their future put at risk!' The spymaster shook her head. 'But you will fail. The Argosi have always failed when it mattered most. The final flaw in Credara Janucha's designs is being solved even as we speak.' Zavera wrapped her free hand around Ferius's jaw. With one twist she would break her neck.

'Stop!' I shouted. 'You said you've already won! What good will killing her do?'

Zavera didn't even seem to hear me at first, but then she said, 'It will make me feel better.' She swatted idly at something on the side of her own neck. I hadn't noticed any insects, though I probably had bites of my own by now. Zavera returned her hand to Ferius's jaw. 'Yes. I believe this will make me feel much—'

She was cut off by a figure leaping from the shadows of the forest. Fingers curled like claws grabbed at the side of Zavera's head as the figure went past. Zavera screamed in pain, her hand going to the bleeding wound on the side of her scalp. The sound of fire lances boomed, but as the smoke cleared, the assailant stepped out to face Zavera. She held a piece of the spymaster's ear in one hand. 'I begin to see the appeal,' she said.

'Damn right,' Reichis chittered.

'You?' Zavera asked, almost laughing. '*You* have come?'

The old woman's voice was like the first crackle of ember

magic right before the blast. 'Touch my daughter again,' Enna said, 'and I'll drag you through every hell there is until I find one that'll have you.'

Ferius, barely conscious from her exertions and the beating she'd taken, looked up from the ground, blinking through tears. 'Momma?'

Enna smiled. It was a fierce, wild thing to behold. 'I'm here, love. Just gotta do a piece of business.'

Three of the fire lancers started to reload their weapons even as two others came for the Argosi. 'Stop!' Zavera said. She approached Enna and gave a short bow. 'I feel foolish that I did not know you the last time you came to Gitabria. I take it you are the Path of the Rambling Thistle? My maetri spoke of you as the greatest Argosi he had ever known.'

Enna returned the bow. 'Your maetri was an idiot. Otherwise he would never have allowed you to become the Path of Oak and Steel.'

'I have not been called that in a long time.'

'That's just as well, child. It was a fool's path.' She stepped into a guard position, one hand out in front of her, the other in a tight fist just over her head. 'See what trouble it's brought you?'

Zavera looked at the old woman in wonder. 'You think to duel me? However legendary your arta eres tricks may once have been, I'm afraid those years are long behind you.'

'True,' Enna admitted. 'But here's something you may not have seen before.' She waved her hands in the air theatrically. 'By the mighty power of sea and sky, of earth and flame, of sour wine and flat beer, let my enemy fall!'

Zavera's eyes narrowed. A second later she fell flat on her face.

Ferius rose unsteadily to her feet. 'You still usin' that old trick?'

'Sometimes the old ways are best.' Enna turned to the fire lancers, who'd finished reloading their weapons and were now taking aim at her. 'Poison thorn,' she explained, miming a slap to her neck. 'Got your boss with it before I came out of the trees. Got each of you too. You're gonna feel pretty awful any second now.'

The six soldiers looked at each other, searching for signs of the poison's effects.

Enna sighed. 'Ain't you taught that boy the signals?' she asked Ferius.

'He's still learnin'.'

Oh, right. I pulled powder and fired my spell. The three fire lancers had their backs to me and were close enough together that the blast sent them flying. Two more went down when steel cards sliced into their hands and chests. Durral came walking out of the forest, the cards flying from his hands so fast I couldn't even see him throw them. Reichis and Ishak drove down the last of our enemies, then proceeded to growl at each other over who got to eat what. The pair of them had taken injuries in the fight though, and eventually sank down to sleep on top of their intended meal.

'Damn, Pappy,' Ferius said, getting her hands out of the cuffs. 'You ain't lost your aim.'

'Keep tellin' you it's in the wrist,' Durral replied. 'You always put too much shoulder into it.'

She grinned at him. 'I'd be happy to argue that point, but I've got to . . .' She stumbled a bit, then felt at the back of her neck. Her fingers came back holding what I guessed must be a tiny thorn. 'Aw, now why'd you go and—'

Enna caught her in her arms. She eased her to the ground, seating herself and placing her daughter's head in her lap. 'We'll take care of her,' she said to me. She unslung a pack from her back and tossed it over. 'There's food for the journey and some healing ointments in there. You go on now. You know what you've got to do.'

I nodded, though my heart sank a little. I guess in those fleeting moments of watching a family reunited, I'd forgotten that such things weren't for me.

56

The Murderer

It was twilight before I reached the Gitabrian capital, and fully dark by the time I descended the wooden platform to Janucha's cliffside home. Reichis had been furious at being left behind, but he was injured, and I was too ashamed of what I was about to do to bring him with me.

I crept onto the stone veranda, removing my boots so my footsteps wouldn't be heard once I was inside. I used my sotocastra coin to pick the lock on one of the windows and entered the building with black and red powders in my hands and murder in my heart.

I used to wonder about the hextrackers and bounty mages who so willingly killed for money. What would it take to make you give up that last shred of decency – that most basic element of humanity – that stops one person taking the life of another? I was only seventeen, and yet I'd come face to face with dozens of men and women only too happy to kill for the right price. I'd even asked a few of them about it. Their answers, whether glib or stern, justified by some greater good or damned by their own greed, never satisfied me. It was all just nonsense. To kill? To *murder*? There had to be something more – some terrible instant in which their lives had changed, like when lightning strikes desert sand and turns it to blackened glass. I understood now that no such grand or ghastly event was needed. Killing was simply a matter of steps.

I had come to this country hoping to be a hero like Ferius. I would leave as an assassin.

I wished I could blame the Gitabrians. For all that they spoke eloquently about the innocent pursuit of beauty and invention, they kept their enemies locked away in secret prisons. Their spymaster, Zavera, swore she only did what was necessary to protect her homeland, yet she had laughed while choking and beating Ferius Parfax to the brink of death.

Or maybe my father had done this to me, with his unwavering conviction that one man had the right to determine the life and death of all those around him. Could I blame Enna for convincing me that the only way to protect my mentor was to commit the very crimes she abhorred?

The simple truth was that I'd done this to myself.

When I'd seen the torment inflicted on Cressia – when I'd hunted the mages to where they hid in that tower – Ferius had asked me if I was willing to kill whoever was behind that door without giving them a chance. I hadn't been then, not really. If it weren't for Shalla being there, no doubt I'd have ended up dead. I couldn't afford that now. So somehow during that long run back from the mountain I'd built inside myself all the gears and springs, pistons and wires needed for killing another human being. Like the Gitabrians, I was a contraptioneer now, and I'd invented a murderer.

The inside of Janucha's home was dark, the only light that of the moon and stars coming in through the tall windows.

I walked barefoot on the cold marble floors to the doors outside the contraptioneer's workshop. My fingers trembled. My whole body vibrated, not with trepidation but simply from exhaustion. I would have to be quick.

'Kellen?'

I spun around. Cressia was standing a few feet behind me. She was wearing some sort of nightdress and blinking away the sleep from her eyes. 'What are you doing here?' she asked.

Fumbling, I thought in response. *Tripping over myself. Trying so hard not to make any sound that I forgot to listen to everything else.* There was something oddly amusing about the fact that, for all my deadly determination, I was still pretty bad at sneaking into places.

'He's here for me,' another voice said, as the doors to the workshop opened. Janucha held a lantern in one hand, her customary leather apron with its dozens of pockets filled with tools covering her plain linen garments.

I wasn't sure how to play this. If I blasted Janucha now, I'd be killing a mother in front of her daughter. I doubted Cressia would let me get away with that, which would leave me an even more troubling dilemma than the one that had brought me here.

I guess there are two types of murderers. Now I have to decide which kind I am.

Suddenly Janucha changed the game. 'I asked him to come.'

Cressia approached, eyes narrowed both from the glare of her mother's lantern and from suspicion that she was lying. 'You *asked* him to come? In the middle of the night?'

'It's complicated, my darling.' The inventor gestured and a pair of guards exited the workshop behind her.

'Hejandro and Ruis are going to take you somewhere safe,' Janucha informed her daughter.

'Safe? What do you mean? What's—'

'Do as I say, daughter,' Janucha commanded, but Cressia's obedience or lack thereof became moot as the two men picked her up and took her bodily from the house, ignoring both her outraged protests and the blows she rained down on them.

'Why did you send her away?' I asked, though I was pretty sure the answer was, '*So she doesn't have to watch as my other guards kill you.*'

Janucha motioned for me to follow her into the workshop. With her back turned to me, there was no reason why I couldn't simply blast her then and there. Apparently she knew it too. 'I know what you've come to do, Kellen. I only ask that you allow me to reveal the truth to you first.'

'You said the sacred alloys were all but gone, but I've seen the alción mistivae inside the volcano. I've seen the mechanical dragons.'

She halted in her steps. 'Would you believe me if I swore to you that I myself only learned of their existence a few hours ago?'

'I might.'

I could almost hear the smile in her voice as she asked, 'But that wouldn't make any difference now, would it?'

I reached into the pouches at my sides, my hands shaking worse than ever. 'I'm sorry, Janucha. I can't let this go on. If you were to find the flaw in your designs . . .'

Something sharp pressed into the back of my neck. For the third time that night someone had snuck up on me. The voice close to my ear was quiet. 'My wife already knows the flaw,' Altariste said. Further down the hall came the sound of more footsteps. They had a distinctly military cadence. His next words were spoken with such indignation and outrage that it took a moment before I realised his fury was directed not at me, but at Janucha. '*She's* the one who put it there.'

57

The Inventor

Altariste's companions led us out the door and onto one of the wooden platforms that travelled up the cliffside before pushing us onto the Bridge of Wonders. This late at night we were the only ones crossing. The six men and women who pushed and prodded us wore regular Gitabrian street clothes, but both their weapons and demeanour marked them as secret police. Janucha seemed as surprised as I was to find them taking orders from her husband.

'Altariste, how could you betray me like this?' she asked.

He spun on her, forcing the two men escorting her to stop suddenly. 'Betray *you*?' His fists clenched. 'All these years together, a life *built* together. Yet all the while you lied to me, pretended you loved me!'

'I do lov—'

'No. Do not dare say those words to me again!' His jaw tightened and his breathing came in heavy gasps as if he'd been running up an endless hill. 'I was devoted to you, Janucha. I set aside my own inventions to be your assistant, always believing that I was the luckiest of men to have the most brilliant, daring woman in all of Gitabria choose me over all others.'

She looked at him as if a stranger had taken his place. 'Husband, you speak as if I were unfaithful to you.'

He grabbed at one of the front pockets of her apron, pulling out the mechanical bird. He held it up to her face, moonlight glistening down on its metal wings. 'You claimed it was an accident. Impossible to repeat. But you knew the secret all along. You had me sketch your plans for you, document your formulas over and over and over. Every one of them a trick, a scheme meant to deceive the lords mercantile into believing you were trying to solve an undecipherable problem.'

With everyone's attention on the bird, I tried to break away from the guards. Before I took my first step, two of them had fire lances aimed squarely at my chest. The mechanical bird squirmed frantically in Altariste's hand. He only gripped it tighter. Janucha tried to take it from him, but two of the guards grabbed her arms. 'Husband, please, you will break it.'

Altariste glared at the contraption and squeezed until it let out a pained cheep. He slackened his grip and shook his head. 'Even now I can't do it.' He handed it back to her. 'I can't bring myself to destroy this wonder you have created.'

Janucha gently placed the bird back in the pocket of her apron. 'Then, husband, let us—'

Altariste turned on his heel and set off across the bridge. The guards forced us to follow. 'Together we could have been heroes to our people, Janucha. Legends. They would have sung our names for a thousand years.'

'It would have been a song with a bitter end,' she said. 'There is a reason why I could not bring myself to repeat the experiment.'

Altariste didn't reply at first, but when we reached the far side of the bridge he stopped for a moment and chuckled. 'All these years, Janucha, you told me I was the sentimental one, but it's you who've allowed your heart to rule your head.'

'Husband, where are you taking us?'

The guards ushered us down the wide avenue and I saw our destination: the great amphitheatre where Janucha had first revealed the mechanical bird. Altariste held up a key more complex than any I'd ever seen before, and unlocked the front gate. He signalled to the guards, who pushed us inside. We were led around the circumference of the building to a thick iron door. Again Altariste produced his key. 'All my life I dreamed of standing upon the stage of the Grand Exhibition, or better yet, standing hand in hand with my wife, the *Maedra Bellegenzia*, the mother of beautiful invention, as the world marvelled at some wonder we had created together.'

He unlocked the door and pushed it open. The guards prodded us to enter and then walked us past rows of stone benches to the centre of the amphitheatre. Altariste gestured to the stage. 'Today could have been that day.'

It was Janucha's expression I saw first, a mixture of dread and sorrow that not even her intellect could master. 'My love, what have you done?'

Altariste's creation was so much larger and more terrifying than it had appeared when I'd looked down on it from a hundred feet above. I found myself holding my breath, trying not to make a sound for fear of waking the beast. This close, I could see the perfect circles of the metal scales along its wings, the copper tubes hidden within its fanged jaws. Would they spew fire down upon its victims? Acid? Or was there something even worse this Gitabrian inventor had devised?

Would the two-foot-long claws attached to its mechanical limbs be able to tear only flesh, or could they rend stone and steel as well? And when men and women saw this monstrosity dive down from the skies, would any of them dare to fight? Or would they simply kneel and wait for death?

'I have done that which you failed to do, my love,' Altariste replied.

Then he had the guards lead us up the stairs to the stage, and revealed that the iron dragon was the least of the horrors we were to witness that night.

58

The Perfect Flaw

It was the smell that got to me first. The dry, smothering odour of ashes and the cloying stench of burnt flesh. Instinctively my eyes went to the dragon, expecting to see death within its jaws, but that was stupid. No matter how frightening the mechanical beast appeared, it was still just an assemblage of parts, of gears and pistons, armatures and metal plates. Having spent my life around spells, I could feel the tingle of hundreds of charms that had been placed on individual pieces, but the result was still a lifeless contraption – a device like any other save Janucha's mechanical bird. What I smelled had come from Altariste's efforts to remedy that flaw.

'Why?' I asked, staring at the dozens and dozens of dead animals littering the stage. Dogs, birds, cats – it was as though Altariste had gathered every stray beast in Cazaran, only to destroy them. Behind the dragon, connected to it by copper cables six inches thick, was a steel cage, roughly four foot square, blue sparks running along its length. Instruments and tools like those I'd seen in Janucha's workshop lay carefully arranged on long wooden tables.

Altariste took a coin from his pocket. 'As a boy I marvelled at the castradazi and their antics. I always assumed it was the composition of the metals that made the coins special, but there's more. The alloys come to life when the vibration of a spirit matches that within the coin. But to find that perfect match?' He tossed the coin onto one of the piles of dead animals. 'The odds are nearly impossible.'

'Oh, my husband,' Janucha said, staring at the death all around us. 'What insanity brought you to this?'

Altariste strode to one of the workbenches and grabbed several rolled-up sketches. He threw them at her. They fell at her feet, opening to reveal strangely beautiful designs. 'The only insanity was yours, Janucha. For months I have slaved over your designs, trying to help you find success, but you took steps to prevent me from doing so. I am your *husband*, but you couldn't stand to see me prove that my intellect could compare with yours!'

Janucha shook her head. 'I have always known your potential, Altariste. I kept the flaws hidden from you above all others because I knew if I didn't, you'd one day solve the riddle. Because I knew you could not stop yourself from giving the secret police what they asked for.'

'Can you not hear the madness in your words? We are contraptioneers! It is our role – no, our *duty* – to devise new creations for the good of our people.' He knelt down in front of her and placed both his hands over the front pocket of her apron reverently as though she carried their child within. 'You devised the miracle of our generation, yet you would have kept the secret to yourself. Why? To sell to some foreign master?'

A palpable sorrow overtook Janucha's features as she met her husband's gaze. 'So I could take the secret with me to my grave.'

'Liar!' he cried, rising to his feet. 'If this were true, why did you wait so long? Why not simply kill yoursel–'

'Cressia,' I said, the truth suddenly so obvious that I wondered why it had taken me so long to figure it out. '*The great work of a mother's life*' Janucha had called her. 'You were waiting for her to come home, weren't you? That's why you held out so long, pretending to try new experiments, to try to find the flaw in the design. But you *put* the flaws there.' I pointed to the mechanical dragon. 'You figured out the true nature of your so-called "miracle" – that it involved the imprisonment of an unwilling spirit inside your machines.'

Janucha took the mechanical bird out once again, allowing it to perch on two of her fingers. A tear slipped from her cheek to drop on one of its metal wings. 'I . . . I had no idea at first.' She stroked the bird's chin. The creature tilted its head in response. 'In the old texts, our forebears spoke of the experiments of the first alchemists. They believed that life could be found in the sacred metals, in the alloys of the castradazi coins. We had long ago lost the means to make those alloys, but I believed that they were the key to bringing life to my creations. What I didn't know was the mechanism by which the alloys accomplished this: that their unique composition could bind spirits to them.' Again she stroked the bird. 'Cressia's pet, Thasassa, used to keep me company in my work. When I first attempted to chemically recreate the alloys, she was . . . She died. Then when the bird came alive, I thought . . . I fooled myself into believing I had achieved that which only our ancestors had accomplished before. And I had. But it wasn't a miracle. It was an abomination.'

'An abomination?' Altariste asked. 'Are you mad? It is power!

Power that will mean our people no longer need to bow and scrape before the other nations of this world. No, we will rule them! With the mechanical dragons, we will—'

'Start a war,' I said, cutting him off.

'A war my people can win!' Altariste said. 'Your Argosi friends fear bloodshed? Then they should be helping us! With a fleet of living dragons, the other nations will realise there is no point in resisting us.'

A chuckle escaped my lips, empty of humour but thick with disgust. 'You damned fool. You think the Jan'Tep will *ever* submit? The mages from my country will spread out, hiding everywhere, using spells to assassinate every powerful man and woman – and their children – that they can find, in hopes of weakening their enemies. You think the Daroman empire, which has *never* known defeat, will suddenly drop their weapons because of some new machine of war? They have their own inventors, their own war masters. They'll find new ways to fight and kill your dragons.'

'They, like everyone else, will soon see the futility of resisting,' Altariste said.

'Have you met the Berabesq?' I asked. 'They'll be convinced this is a holy war their God *wants* them to fight.'

'Give it up, husband,' Janucha pleaded. 'This path leads to nought but destruction.'

'Wrong. It leads to creation.' He went to the cage and swung open the door. 'The flaw you hid in your designs, my love, was that the castradazi coins require the right kind of spirit to come to life, one attuned to the alloys.' Altariste looked over at me, and mixed with his insanity was a genuine sympathy. 'Forgive me, Magizier Kellen fal Ke. I would not choose this were there any other alternative.'

Two pairs of strong hands took hold of my arms and began dragging me towards the cage. Altariste pulled down on a lever next to it, and the hiss and roar of captive lightning began to shimmer along the copper wires that travelled to the mechanical dragon. 'Don't think of it as death,' the inventor said, 'merely a different kind of life.'

59

The Sacrifice

I resisted, for what it was worth. I fought tooth and nail – literally – biting and scratching at the two men hauling me over to Altariste's cage. Reichis would have been proud. Actually that's not true. He would've scolded me for being a feeble skinbag who never learned how to tear out a human's throat with my teeth. He'd have been right, too.

In the end I simply let them carry me. Maybe it wouldn't be so bad, I thought. Being human hadn't worked out all that well for me. Could I do any worse as a mechanical dragon? First thing I'd do, of course, was grab Altariste in my claws and drop him in the Cazaran Gorge.

'Husband, you must stop this!' Janucha screamed. She too tried to fight for my release, but her guards were no more courteous than mine. 'This is murder! The bonding doesn't unite the spirit to the machine, it destroys it. All that is left is a servant, a child-like creature that follows commands but has no true will of its own!'

So much for my big revenge plan, I thought.

'You laugh, that is good,' Altariste said to me. I hadn't realised I was. 'Let us begin this journey bravely togeth—'

An explosion echoed through the amphitheatre. The guard

holding my right arm let go of me and fell to the ground, probably due to the smoking hole in his back. The guard on my left spun around to see what had happened, dragging me with him. At the centre of the aisle leading to the stage stood Cressia, holding a spent fire lance. She dropped it to the ground and picked up one of the other four she'd brought with her.

'Daughter, no!' Altariste shouted.

One of the other guards rushed down the stairs towards her. Without so much as flinching, Cressia aimed her second lance, twisted the tubes, and fired again. 'I am Étuza Cressia fal Ghassan,' she said. 'And I will kill the next man who lays his hands on my friend.'

As rescue attempts went, it was pretty impressive. Unfortunately, by now two of the three remaining secret police had their own lances trained on her. Janucha tried to get in their way but the woman holding her knocked her down.

'Heed me child!' Altariste called out to his daughter. 'These men and women will not hesitate to kill you if you attack again, no matter what your name. I swear to you, the boy's sacrifice is necessary for the future of our people.'

For a moment it looked as if Cressia might try to grab another of her fire lances, which would almost certainly have been the end of her. But then she looked up defiantly and walked to the stage. 'He saved my life, Father. You saw him take the worm from my eye. It nearly consumed him and yet he risked himself for me.' She walked up the stairs to stand before her father. 'If your foul experiments are so vital for our nation, then surely my life will serve as well as his.'

Janucha tried to rise to go to her daughter, but the woman

guarding her put her boot against her back. 'Husband, listen to the simple logic of Cressia's words. You cannot justify murdering Kellen any more than you could our daughter.'

'Has my whole family gone mad?' Altariste demanded, shaking his fists in the air. 'No! No, I will have no more of this! Put the boy in the cage. Now!'

'I'll show you who's going in a cage!' a screeching voice called out from high up in the air. To everyone else it would've sounded like the chittering of some animal crawling around the upper galleries of the amphitheatre. That's why no one but me looked up to see a two-foot-tall squirrel cat, limbs outstretched and glider flaps catching the wind as he dived down from the open roof.

Reichis crashed into the guard hanging onto my arm with the force of . . . well, a small but very angry animal. But the squirrel cat's claws tore into the man's cheek, tearing strips of flesh away and ripping a scream from his lungs. I threw myself at one of the other guards, who was trying to aim her fire lance at him. We landed hard on the stage floor, but she was more agile than I was and got out from under me, slamming her elbow into the side of my head. I struggled to get up, my vision blurry from the blow. By the time I could see straight again, it was already over.

Reichis had very nearly done the impossible: with an injured leg and a half-dozen other wounds, he'd run all the way here from the forests outside Cazaran, climbed up the side of the amphitheatre and leaped down from the roof to attack my enemies. He'd taken out one of the guards and left Altariste's scalp bleeding down his face. If life had been at all fair, that kind of courage would have been enough to win the day.

But the first thing you learn as an outlaw is that life is anything but fair.

Only two of the secret police remained, but one wore heavy gloves and was strong as an ox. She held Reichis so tightly even he couldn't squirm out of her grip. With a sneer on her face she began crushing him. I ran to him only to find myself back on the floor, my legs knocked out from under me by the other guard's fire lance.

'Please,' I said to Altariste. 'Don't let her hurt him.'

The inventor didn't seem as if he'd heard me. He stared wide-eyed at Reichis. 'Incredible.' He put a hand on the guard's arm. She loosened her grip and the squirrel cat took in gasps of air. Altariste, still bleeding from the top of his head, leaned over to peer at Reichis. 'It came all this way to save you, didn't it? This creature . . . When you first brought it into our home, I thought it was some kind of pet.'

'Pet?' Reichis wheezed. 'I'm going to kill you twice once I deal with this dumb mutt holding me.'

'He speaks, doesn't he?' Altariste asked. 'What does he say?'

A chill went up my spine as I realised why the inventor was now so fascinated with Reichis. 'He's just a dumb animal,' I said. 'Nothing more than that.'

Undaunted, the inventor reached out a hand and petted Reichis's head. 'He is truly intelligent. I see it now.' He smiled. 'Were I to believe in signs, surely this would prove our endeavour was fated to be.' He turned to Janucha. 'Don't you see, my love? The animal's etheric affinity to Kellen means we can bind it to the sacred animals. There is no longer any need to sacrifice the boy!'

'No,' I said. 'Don't do this!'

The woman holding Reichis walked over to the cage and threw him inside, slamming the door behind him. The captive lightning running through the metal bars enveloped him as the squirrel cat screamed my name.

60

The Mechanical Dragon

I was on my feet and running for the cage before anyone could stop me. If I'd taken even a second to think about it, I would've realised what a bad idea that was. The moment my hands touched the bars the shock threw me backwards. I landed hard on the floor. The guard who'd been holding me before pointed his fire lance at me, but by this point nobody was paying attention to Janucha or Cressia.

The contraptioneer took a long metal screwdriver from her apron and with remarkable efficiency and brutality drove it into the meat of the guard's shoulder. Cressia grabbed the fire lance from his hands and aimed it at the woman who'd thrown Reichis into the cage. The guard looked like she was trying to decide whether she could bridge the distance before Cressia fired. Apparently she figured wrong, because a second later she had a burning hole in her leg.

I ran back to the cage. No one had bothered to take my pouches from me, so I pulled powder, tossed it in the air and spoke the incantation as my hands directed the blast at the locked door. The twin red and black fires erupted in a deafening explosion, only to disappear as they hit the bars.

Reichis screamed again, all the fur on his body sticking out as the lightning passed through him.

I tried a second blast against the cage, using even more powder and burning my fingers, but it did nothing. The guard with Janucha's screwdriver in his shoulder, apparently offended by my attempts, grabbed a fire lance and aimed it at me. I drew a pair of steel cards Ferius had given me a while back and flung them at him. The first caught him in his good shoulder and the second sliced a line of blood across his cheek. Before he could recover, I ran over and grabbed his arm, twisted the fire lance from his grip and bashed his head with it. He collapsed to the floor and I drew powder a third time.

'The power of the lightning creates an energy field that fire cannot penetrate,' Janucha warned. She put a hand on my shoulder. 'I'm sorry, Kellen. This will be over soon.'

'Can you not see?' Altariste shouted, running over to his mechanical dragon, stroking the metal plates along one of its wings as they shook and shimmered into life. 'This is not death, it's creation!'

'Kellen!' Reichis screamed, struggling to rise, futilely searching for some way out of the cage. 'Kellen, please! I promise I won't steal any more. I promise!'

I went over and grabbed Altariste by the collar. He was heavier than me but I managed to swing him around. 'Tell me how to stop the process!'

'You cannot,' he declared proudly. 'No more than any man can stand in the way of—'

I punched him in the face and threw him down on the floor before turning to Janucha. 'There has to be a way, please!'

She got that look in her eyes that I'd seen once before, when Cressia was being tortured by the mages – shedding her emotions so she could work through the problem. 'The field is a reaction of the lightning with the alloys on the plates inside the cage. To break the connection, you'd have to change the geometry of . . . Ah, I fear the complexities are far too—'

'Actually, I understand geometry just fine,' I said, pushing past her. I reached inside my coat and took out the five coins Savire had given me. The castradazi had said the secret was in making the coins dance. I flipped one at the lightning field. It shot back at me, but I grabbed it out of the air. I stared at the five of them in the palm of my hand.

'The alloy isn't enough,' Janucha said. 'It is a matter of distance and spatial relationships. It requires perfect calculation of the—'

'Shut up, please,' I said, still staring at the coins. She was wrong. Sure, you could create the alignments with mathematics, but there was another way to do it: the way Savire had shown me. I touched one to my forehead, then to my heart, and finally tapped my hand again. A prayer, I guess, which was odd since I've never been religious. I walked closer to the cage. The energy from the lightning tickled the hairs on my hands and arms. I tossed one coin in the air lightly, then a second and a third. I juggled them around and around, then added the fourth. Each time one landed in my palm, I felt for the weight of it, the way it either dropped quickly or hesitated. That pause, that hesitation, was from it coming close to its natural distance from the other coins. So I adjusted each time, not trying to think my way out of it but instead letting my hands work instinctively as they searched for the perfect distance between each coin in the air, spinning them as I went.

'They must be in perfect alignment,' Janucha said behind me.

'I'm on it.' It was incredibly difficult to keep the coins going, and I had to close my eyes to stop being distracted by the lightning and the cage and, most of all, by my business partner's spirit being stolen from him.

'Kellen,' Reichis chittered, this time softly. I couldn't resist opening an eye and seeing him slumped against the floor of the cage, the sparks dancing around his fur that was now a uniform dull grey. 'I think I'm done, Kellen. I think I'm . . .'

Wind came from behind me, nearly knocking me down. 'Look!' Altariste said, crawling along the floor towards the dragon whose wings were now beating. 'Look upon the future of Gitabria!'

Suddenly the dragon launched itself from the stage, flying into the centre of the amphitheatre, climbing towards the open ceiling.

'No!' I screamed. I lost control of the coins for an instant and they tumbled down. I barely managed to catch them all. *Don't fight*, I told myself. *You can't win with force. Let the coins feel your spirit. They want to dance.* I closed my eyes again and tossed the coins into the air. By sense of touch alone I juggled them until I could feel them almost in alignment, and then, my fingers moving faster and smoother than they ever had before, I gently tapped each one to make it spin.

'By the first principles,' Janucha breathed close behind me.

I opened my eyes. The five coins floated in the air, turning slowly around an invisible axis as each one spun on its end. Inside the space left between them was a gap where the lightning couldn't touch. Reichis was flat against the bottom of the cage now, becoming ever more lifeless as the mechanical dragon circled higher and higher into the air. *I'm too late*, I thought. *No. You don't know that!* I drew powder from my pouches a third time, tossed them into the gap between the coins, formed the somatic shape with my hands and said, '*Carath*.'

The twin fires roared through the empty space, smashing into the apparatus powering the lightning and holding the cage door shut. The sudden blast of light blinded me, then, just as quickly, everything was dark.

'What have you done?' Altariste screamed. I turned to see him racing down the stairs. In the sky above the amphitheatre, the dragon's wings had stopped beating. The stars disappeared from view as the metal beast came falling back down to earth, smashing into the centre of the amphitheatre. Stone benches shattered under its impact, sending dust and debris into the air. Broken gears and pistons erupted from the beast's outer shell. The creature tried to rise, the whine of its battered and twisted metals parts like the beginning of a scream. It teetered for a moment, then toppled and fell at the feet of its creator. 'No,' Altariste said. He repeated the word over and over as he knelt down and stroked the mechanical dragon as though love might bring it back to life.

I ran back to the cage. With the lightning gone, the stage was dark and I fumbled blindly for the cage door. My hand hit one of the coins, knocking it out of alignment, and all five scattered to the ground. I managed to find the latch and opened it. Reichis's fur was cool to the touch. I couldn't feel his heart.

'Oh no,' I said. 'No, no. Please. Please, Reichis!'

A match was struck and dim light brought his still form into view. 'Quickly,' Janucha said, grabbing my coins from the ground and placing them in my hand. 'You must make the coins dance again, draw what is left of the animal's spirit back from the dragon.'

I did as she commanded, sending the coins spinning in the air above my palm. Blue shimmering sparks drifted up from the broken remains of the mechanical dragon. They came towards me, pulled, it seemed, by the coins. They floated like fireflies around Reichis's limp body, dancing there as if uncertain whether to come together or fly apart.

Janucha brought her hand down on the coins, flattening them against my palm. 'What do I do now?' I asked.

'There is nothing you can do,' the inventor replied. 'Either his spirit is strong enough or else—'

'There's no "or else",' I said. 'There's no creature alive with more spirit than Reichis.' I picked him up in my arms, whispering in his ear. 'You hear me, you mangy little thief? You rotten, uncouth son of a bitch? You murdering, eyeball-eating little *varmint*? Nobody breaks your spirit apart. Nobody.'

As I spoke, the dancing blue sparks spun around each other, much as the coins had done. They shimmered and shook, as if everything in the universe was intent on pulling them apart, then, just as suddenly, they disappeared. 'No,' I said, stroking the fur of his muzzle. 'No, please don't go, Reichis. I can't do this without—' I howled in pain as something sharp – no, several somethings – pierced the skin of my hand. When I pulled my hand away, tiny drops of blood welled from four little punctures.

Reichis opened one eye. 'Oh, hey, Kellen. What's going on?'

I put him down on the floor. 'You bit me, you little bastard!'

Slowly he rolled over to get his feet under him and pushed himself up. 'Really?' He gave a little snicker. 'Sorry. Instinct.'

Despite how badly I wanted to make him pay for that, and despite the shaking in my hands, I grabbed him and held him to my chest. For once he let me, and I could feel him trying to get warmth from me. 'Kellen?' he asked.

I barely trusted myself to speak without turning into a crying mess. 'Yeah?'

'Two . . . Two things . . .'

'What is it?'

'First, I was kidding about never stealing again.'

A sob escaped my lips, which was embarrassing, but at that precise moment I didn't care.

'And second . . .' He made a small motion with his head, his nose pointing towards Altariste, who was very slowly walking up the stage stairs towards us. 'Would you mind killing that guy for me? I think I need a nap.'

I held the furry little monster close for a moment more before gently setting him down and turning my attention to the guards. I was going to need both hands for what came next.

61

Deaths of Necessity

I'd thought maybe Altariste intended on trying to kill me for having destroyed his grand invention, but I guess not everyone's a murderer at heart. 'Please,' he wept, holding his hands out to Janucha. 'Please, wife, help me rebuild him.'

I had already resolved in myself that if he got any closer I was going to beat him unconscious and then wait until he woke up so I could beat him again. I felt Janucha's hand on my arm. 'This is a family matter,' she said.

I was surprised to see the mechanical bird back in her hand. She whispered to it for a moment, and it took flight, circling above Altariste. He gazed up at it in wonder. 'It is so beautiful, Janucha.' He reached out a hand towards it. The bird glanced back briefly at Janucha, as if seeking permission. The contraptioneer nodded, and the bird landed on the proffered perch. 'How can something so miraculous be a sin?'

'I don't know,' Janucha said. 'But it is.' She gave a small whistle and the bird's claws dug into the flesh of Altariste's hand. He gave a shout of surprise and pain, and shook it off. The bird flitted away, and he sucked at the tiny bleeding wounds. 'Such a small thing,' Janucha said sadly. 'Barely more than a pinprick.' She reached into her apron and withdrew a thin glass vial half-filled with a green oil.

Altariste's eyes narrowed in confusion, then he removed his hand from his mouth. The slightest hint of green intermingled with the red of his blood. He fell to his knees.

Cressia gave a cry and ran to her father. 'Mother, what have you done?'

'What I would have died to prevent, were the choice still left to me,' Janucha replied. The bird came to land on her shoulder again. She went to kneel beside her husband. 'You understand now, my love? Even something so delicate can be deadly when it is controlled by the will of fools.' Altariste started to gag. Green foam escaped from his lips. Janucha put her arms around him and wept. 'This is the means by which miracles become abominations.'

It didn't take more than a few minutes for him to die, and, as these things go, it didn't seem very painful – not physically at least. He lay in the arms of his wife and daughter. As the light left his eyes, though, I saw a sorrow so profound that it made me hate myself for having been willing to murder him myself. It made me hate the world in which I lived all the more.

For a long time I just stood there, waiting. Janucha spoke to her daughter. They argued, and cried, and finally held each other awhile before Cressia turned and walked away, pausing only to wave at me once before she left the amphitheatre. Janucha stared after her. 'Of all the wonders I have seen, none confound me more than my own daughter.'

'Where will she go?' I asked.

'A ship awaits her in the harbour to take her across the waters to lands untainted by the madness that plagues our own continent. Cressia always wanted to be an explorer. She will travel to places beyond the reach of the secret police.

'They won't stop trying to find her,' I said. 'The lords mercantile, the secret police . . . They've invested too much, risked too much. They'll do whatever it takes to force you to reproduce the experiment, and if you keep failing, eventually they'll find someone else.'

Janucha came to stand next to me. 'You are a clever young man, Castradazi Kellen té Jan'Tep, but the world is full of clever young men.' She gestured towards the front of the amphitheatre where it led out to the city. 'My country is full of clever men.'

'But you aren't simply "clever", I take it?'

She gave a weary smile. 'Would it sound presumptuous if I were to tell you that what Altariste kept shouting to anyone who would listen was, in fact, true? That mine is a once-in-a-generation intellect?'

'No, but couldn't Altariste have made the same claim? You said you worried he would figure out how—'

'I walked a thousand steps up a mountain of complexity to uncover the secrets of the alloys. Standing there, at the very summit, one step from the answer, Altariste was able to make the final leap.' She knelt down to pick up one of the sketches he'd strewn on the floor of the stage. 'Without my work? He could have lived for a thousand years and never found the answer.' She placed the sketch back among the others, then took another vial from her apron and spread its contents over all of them. Within seconds they had dissolved into nothingness.

The bird came and landed on her shoulder. 'You must return to my home and use that clever little powder spell of yours to destroy my workshop. There must be no trace of my experiments for others to follow.' She reached up a hand and stroked the bird's metal feathers. 'There is one last thing I must ask of you. Would you . . . I cannot bring myself to destroy her.'

'I'll . . . I'll do what has to be done,' I said, hating myself at the thought of ending the life of even a mechanical being, which I guess is how you're supposed to feel.

Janucha took my hand in hers. 'Goodbye, young man. Leave no trace of our passing, and forgive me the enemies my actions have brought you.'

'I'm getting used to enemies,' I said, but I don't think she heard me. She gave a soft whistle to the bird and, as it had done to Altariste, it dug its claws briefly into her flesh.

'Fly,' she said softly, and the bird rose up to flitter about the stage. Janucha lay down on the floor and gazed up at her creation flying overhead, and smiled at the bird's antics, even as her eyes closed a final time.

I picked up Reichis and went down the stairs to where one of the guards had left my pack. I slipped the strap over my shoulder and gently placed the squirrel cat inside. It was only then that I realised I wasn't alone.

62

The Red Mercy

My enemy was facing away from me, standing next to the remains of the mechanical dragon. The red silks of his garments glinted as they reflected the lights from the stars above the open roof. The effect was oddly beautiful.

'Hello, Kellen,' he said. His voice was spell-masked with breath magic, as it had been in each of our encounters. I couldn't say whether it was deep or high-pitched, or even whether his diction was clear or mumbling. How long he'd been out here I couldn't know, but with the world being the way it is, I had no doubt he'd heard everything that had transpired.

'Where is Nephenia?' I asked.

'On the Bridge of Dice. She's with another of the Argosi. Seems this city is filthy with them.'

His casual, almost conversational words threw me. 'You let her go, just like that?'

'Just like that. She shouldn't have to be part of this.'

I thought about that for a moment and decided I agreed. 'In all the old stories,' I said, 'the great mages were said to duel three times. This is our third meeting.'

He turned to face me, the crimson lacquer mask showing an expression of cold determination. 'And our last.'

My hands were relaxed at my sides, as were his. Neither of us were amateurs, and neither of us so much as let our fingers twitch despite the urge to run through the somatic forms for the spells we'd use against each other. No, all the preparation was inside. This was something I'd never really understood before – that what really happens before a duel is what Janucha had saved me from a few minutes earlier: preparing to commit a murder.

'I don't want to kill you,' I said. 'I'm so sick of death now that I'd almost rather you kill me first.'

'Easily arranged.'

'But I can't,' I said. I removed my pack and placed it gently on the floor a little way away. Reichis, who claims to have a sixth sense for danger, was still dead asleep. 'The squirrel cat is my responsibility. So are Ferius and Nephenia and even the hyena. So are all the people I care about. And if there's one thing you've made perfectly clear, it's that you'll hurt them if I let you get past me.' I flipped open the tops of my powder pouches, though I wasn't planning on using them. I'd already let one of the coins slip down from my cuff into the palm of my right hand. I'd use it as a distraction and then duck left before I . . . It really didn't matter. The only preparation that mattered was the one that had already happened in my mind. I'd decided I was ready to kill now. Or at least I thought I had, which, unfortunately, isn't the same thing at all.

'You're so stupid, Kellen. You always have been.'

He moved so fast and so fluidly then that in that brief instant before the ember spell erupted from his fingertips, I knew without a doubt that he could easily have killed me in either of our previous encounters. The explosion that accompanied the strike was so loud I threw my palms against my ears, even though losing my hearing would be the least of my problems. The light was so bright I couldn't see, and then a second burst, this one even louder, was followed by me being thrown several feet away onto one of the stone benches. I landed hard, the air knocked out of my chest. It took me a moment before I was prepared to consider that I might not actually be dead.

I got up on my elbows and even that made my head swim. I turned to see red and white flames dancing on the stage. The machines, Janucha and Altariste's bodies, the dead and dying guards, all of them were gone.

'Where is the bird?' he asked. My ears were still ringing. I gestured to the stage. 'You destroyed something beautiful that the world will never see again,' I lied.

'It's better this way,' the red mage said, and turned to walk out the doors of the amphitheatre.

Slowly I rose to my feet. I went to check on Reichis. He was unharmed and, somehow, still asleep. I picked up the bag and ran after the red mage. 'Your blast was too powerful to be an experiment gone awry. They'll know this was Jan'Tep magic.'

'Maybe. Probably. But they'd expect us to have done it anyway, given the tensions between our nations. You should be happy. Their secret police won't suspect you of destroying their great invention now, given they must know your own magic is too weak to cause this kind of damage.'

'So this is what? All part of the cost of doing business?'

He stopped outside the doors. I saw the slight shift in the

lines of his lacquer mask. He was smiling. 'You really are naive, you know that?'

'Maybe, but I'm not stupid. You can take the mask off now,' I said, then added, 'Panahsi.'

He didn't move at first, but then reached up and touched his fingers to the mask. It collapsed into the same red silk as the rest of his garments. He unwound the fabric from his head. 'Pan'erath,' he corrected me. His face was thinner than I remembered it, his strong jaw more clearly defined. He was leaner, too, which was why I hadn't recognised him before. 'How did you know?'

I shrugged. 'The little things. You didn't just want to kill me, you wanted to beat me. No, that's not it: you wanted me to *know* that you could beat me. Then you had the chance to kill Nephenia, but you—'

'It's your fault,' he said.

'What is?'

'What Neph's become. What you turned her into.'

The way he said it bothered me. 'There's nothing wrong with Nephenia.'

A kind of fury took over his features. 'You *ruined* her, Kellen. She was bright and beautiful and could have had a great future with our people, but you poisoned her. You turned her feral.'

Feral. What an odd choice of word. 'She made all her own choices, Pan. Her father—'

His hands clenched. 'I could have protected her! I told her she just had to put up with it a little while longer, then once we were married, I'd—'

'"Put up with it a while longer"?' I asked. 'Is that what you tell yourself?'

Red and blue light began to slither and wind itself around his forearms. I don't think he could stop himself from drawing on the magics now. 'You ruined everything, Kellen. Can't you see that?'

However enraged he might be with me, I think I was angrier. Part of me was ready to test my speed against his and the hells for the consequences. But that wouldn't help anyone, and besides, the only reason I was in such a rage was that I knew he was right. 'I never meant to hurt anyone. I just wanted to be left alone, to try to make a life for myself. Why is that so wrong?'

The movement of the raw magics around his forearms slowed and then dissipated. 'Because that's not how the world works, Kellen.' He looked away from me, to the northwest, where, hundreds and hundreds of miles away, the lords magi of our clan were probably plotting their next move. 'They'll kill them to get to you, Kellen. Nephenia. That Argosi woman. Anyone who tries to defend you. You've evaded them enough times now and they know it's because you're so good at getting people to protect you.'

'We protect each other,' I said.

He snorted. 'What was it you asked me earlier? "Is that what you tell yourself?"' He turned back to me. 'Your enemies won't stop coming. When I go back and say I failed, they'll send someone else. It won't stop until your friends are dead. They want you alone.'

'Why?'

He pointed a finger at my face. I didn't have to guess what he was aiming at. 'The shadowblack. The lords magi . . . Kellen, it was your father who ordered me to kill you.'

Those words struck me like a blow. I didn't even accuse

him of lying, so sure was I in that moment that he was telling the truth.

'The other clans, they've agreed to elevate him, Kellen. Your father is going to be mage sovereign of the Jan'Tep people. But they had one condition.'

'He had to be willing to kill me.'

Pan nodded. 'And he will too. No matter what else happens, so long as you have the shadowblack, they'll believe your existence will mean the destruction of our people.'

'Is that what you believe?'

'I don't know. But it doesn't matter. Unlike you, I know what it means to be Jan'Tep – to be loyal to my people.'

'Then why not kill me?'

He began re-wrapping the silk around his head. When he completed the last turn, the silk suddenly took shape and became the crimson lacquer mask. Panahsi – Pan'erath – was the red mage once more, and when he spoke next, it was with that distant, ethereal voice. 'Because she would never forgive me.'

The bands on his forearms gleamed, his hands twitched in the somatic shape I'd seen him use before. He disappeared, and I was left alone.

63

The Shadows

By the time I got to the Bridge of Dice, Ferius was there with Nephenia and Ishak. Apparently Enna and Durral had managed to find horses belonging to the secret police posted near the mountain. What was more surprising was that they were still in Cazaran.

'It's done?' Enna asked me.

I nodded.

'And the discordance? The bird . . .'

'Destroyed,' I replied. 'There's nothing left of it. The metals themselves were melted to slag.' I let the lie hang between us. The Argosi might be wiser than me, but I refused to be part of ridding the world of such a tiny marvel. The bird was the only one of its kind, and none would ever come after it. Let the creature find what joy it could for whatever time it had. To distract Enna, I added, 'Janucha is dead.'

The Path of the Rambling Thistle took my hand and kissed it. 'I'm so sorry, Kellen. No one should be asked to do what I asked of you.'

I took the card she'd given me – the 'Path of Shadows' – from my pocket and handed it to her. 'I won't be needing this any more,' I said.

Enna hesitated, but then accepted it. She smiled. 'Durral always says the mark of a true Argosi is never letting anyone choose their path for them.'

'Guess you'll be heading out?' Ferius asked her father.

'It's called the Path of the Rambling Thistle for a reason,' he replied.

For a man who clearly loved his daughter, he really was an ill-tempered bastard. He offered Enna his arm and the two of them started along the bridge. But then he stopped. Without turning back he asked, 'Unless you'd like to have that drink? I hear the booze in this town is terrible, but the company's not so bad once you get used to it.'

I don't know that I could ever describe the look on Ferius's face. It's not like she lit up or even cracked a smile. Outwardly she looked as if maybe she hadn't heard him. But if there was one true thing Zavera had said to me, it's that lies start in the eyes. It turned out Ferius wasn't that good a liar. 'Well, I suppose I ain't got nothing better to do,' she said.

Under a crescent moon, in a city where our names would no doubt be listed among Gitabria's most reviled enemies, we celebrated. Even after the hour had grown late, and Enna and Durral had finally taken their leave, the rest of us walked across every one of Cazaran's eight bridges and sampled just about every delight we could find.

And why shouldn't we?

Ferius, Nephenia, Reichis, Ishak and I had helped stave off a wave of horrors. The five of us had dared to defy the most powerful and devious rulers of two different nations, stared them in the face and brought their plans crumbling down around them. Didn't we deserve to revel in our victory? To spend a little too much coin, to drink a little too much wine, to stop every once in a while and look at one another and share that very special smile that said that we'd been braver than anyone could ask and luckier than anyone had hoped?

Of course we deserved to celebrate.

So we did.

Gitabria not being the safest place for us any more, we finally made our way out of Cazaran and rode for a travellers' saloon near the border. Despite the fact that none of us had slept for at least two days, we went on celebrating. I danced with Nephenia, staring at her all the while like I'd only just met her, which was in many ways true. When I stared a little too long, she winked at me as she turned on the dance floor and ran a hand through her hair. 'Still think it's too short?'

'It's perfect,' I said.

It was too. I understood that now. I'd been blind before, unable to see the . . . What was it Ferius likes to call it? The incomparable beauty of imperfection? It wasn't just her hair either. The sunburned skin, the scars, and even the missing fingers . . . These weren't flaws or failings. They were chapters in Nephenia's story, they were . . . her.

So I danced, and I stared, and I said stupid things because they didn't seem stupid at the time. I danced with Ferius too. It's even possible that somewhere in there I found myself dancing with Reichis, who was drunker than any of us – even Ishak, who turned out to have quite the taste for booze – and, being a squirrel cat, managed to turn even that into a boast.

'You all right, kid?' Ferius asked me, when she found me sitting by myself a while later.

'Couldn't be better,' I lied.

She held my gaze a moment longer, as though she were

trying to peer through the haze of a sandstorm, but soon she nodded and reached out a hand to pat me on the shoulder. I think it was her way of saying that I was allowed my secrets.

The weather was fine that night, so we decided to ride away from the saloon and make our beds under the stars for what little darkness was left. Ferius went to sleep first, resting with her hat over her face and snoring preposterously as if to tell us she wouldn't hear anything. Nephenia smiled at that, and while we both laughed, her fingers lingered in mine just long enough to be an invitation.

'Early start tomorrow,' I said, pulling away.

She didn't miss a beat. 'Gotta get busy savin' the world, kid.'

It was a passable Ferius impression, but I think Reichis does it better. At that precise moment, however, he was locked in a duel with Ishak to see who could snore loudest, and I think he was winning.

'Sleep well, Kellen,' Nephenia said as she went off to her bedroll.

'Not if I have to listen to all this racket,' I replied, and made a show of taking my own pack a few yards away from the cacophony.

I waited an hour or so until I was sure they were all asleep, then quietly collected my things and strapped them to my horse's saddlebags. I walked him about a hundred yards away, and he obliged me by being about as silent as you can ask a horse to be. In fact, I was making more noise than he was on account of the way I kept sniffling like a lost child. I'd got far enough away from the campsite to ride off, but I couldn't bring myself to mount up. So I did something then that I never thought I'd do again – not by choice anyway. I walked in shadow.

Darkness fell on darkness, as if black itself wasn't black enough for shadow. The stars faded away, one by one. The distant glow of the fire disappeared, leaving me with no light at all, and yet I could see with almost painful clarity. In silence I walked back to our camp to stand before my sleeping friends, a ghost without form or substance, made only of longing and regret. Being lost in shadow was different this time. I could still see Reichis curled up on a patch of brush, his face buried in the thick fur of his tail. But another Reichis raced around the campsite from one spot to another, his eyes frantically searching for threats, his teeth bared to snarl at invisible enemies. He was so full of fear – not for himself, but for the others. He knew there were monsters in this world, but they would not get by him to hurt his pack. Not again.

'Goodbye, squirrel cat,' I said, though he couldn't hear me. 'You were the best business partner I ever had.'

Ferius tossed and turned even as another version of her stood a few feet away, staring off at the horizon. She looked utterly alone, as she had been for a long time, as she always would be. This was the path she had chosen for herself, the gamble that her life would be worth more to the world as an Argosi wanderer, regardless of the cost to herself.

'I hope you're right, Ferius, and that all those sacrifices you keep making are worth it. Just don't forget that the Path of the Wild Daisy is also the path of joy.'

Ishak, for his part, looked remarkably similar both in the real world and that of shadow. Maybe hyenas just don't keep as many secrets as other beings. Somehow I doubted it, though.

I turned to Nephenia last, because I'd needed as much time in shadow as I could so that the growing sense of distance, of isolation, would make walking away from her possible. Her body lay by the fire, shivering despite the heat. I only realised then that she wasn't used to the cold nights that came with a life on the road, and yet not once in our travels had she complained about it. Her hands twitched as she slept, mirroring the movements of her phantom self, who knelt staring into a pool of water as she cut her hair over and over again with a pair of scissors. Even as each lock of hair fell to the ground, another took its place, and Nephenia kept cutting it. Part of me worried that this was some kind of compulsion. But the longer I watched, the more I understood that this wasn't mania, but rather an act of defiance – an insistence that Nephenia would be who she chose and never again be controlled by others. Cutting her hair was her way of saying she would be the person *she* wanted to be and never someone else's pretty little doll.

Her physical body shifted in her blankets, pulling them up closer to her chin, then she settled back into deep sleep.

'Goodbye, Nephenia,' I said at last. 'I hope you and Ishak will stay with Ferius and Reichis. They could use a good charmcaster to keep an eye out for them.'

I felt myself fading a little more, and it became harder to see the others. Each time I'd come out of shadow before, it had seemed as if people had forgotten me. When they woke up in the morning, would these strange individuals who'd become my family remember me at all? If they did, I hoped they'd understand why I left. Because they *were* my family. And like Reichis, I would do anything to protect them. Ferius had taught me that doing the most important thing you can do means making sacrifices, so I'd leave them behind, because, like Nephenia, I could not live with someone else pulling my strings. Pan had been right: as long as I had the shadowblack, the people I loved most would be in danger.

So I had to find a way to rid myself of it once and for all.

Alone.

I stepped out of shadow and stumbled to my knees. I was facing away from my horse, as though my body had started to walk back towards the campsite without me.

'Will you hurry up?' a chittering voice said from behind me. 'I'm getting bored here.'

I turned to find Reichis in his customary spot on my horse's neck, staring up at the sky with his front paws crossed over his furry belly. 'How did you—'

'Squirrel cat, remember?' he said. 'We don't fall for any shadowblack nonsense. Besides, you and me are business partners.' He reached a paw behind his head to prod the little velvet bag holding his trinkets. 'The way I figure it, you still owe me three heists before our contract is up.'

'Reichis, I . . .'

'Hey,' he said, tilting his head to stare at me with those beady little eyes of his. 'You remember that time I bit off a chunk of your ear and we ended up having to go get Ferius to sew it back onto your head?'

'Um . . . No. That never happened.'

'Really? Because I'm pretty sure I remember it.' He hopped up from the horse's neck and then took a couple of quick steps across its back before jumping onto my shoulder. He whispered in my ear, 'It was right after that time you tried to leave me behind with two – *two* – skinbag females and a hyena. A *hyena*, Kellen!'

'Reichis . . . where I'm going . . . I mean, I don't even *know* where I'm going, but I know it's going to be someplace bad. I can't—'

'You reckon there's going to be danger?' he asked.

'Definitely.'

'Dark and powerful mages?'

'Probably.'

'Maybe even a few demons?'

'I—'

He swivelled his head towards me and gave me an evil grin. 'Because I haven't murdered any demons yet, and I really think it's time I gave it a try, don't you?'

I hesitated for a long while as he kept his eyes locked on mine. Usually I can win a staring contest with the little bugger, but not tonight. Then it occurred to me that I really didn't want to. I walked over and mounted our horse, Reichis still perched on my shoulder. I gave the horse a gentle squeeze and we set off at a slow walk towards the main road.

'This'll be fun,' Reichis said after a little while.

'Fun?'

'Yeah. I mean, now that we've got rid of those other three. They were really slowing us down. Well, *you*, mostly.'

'How do you figure?'

The squirrel cat gave a little chortle. 'Because of the way you keep drooling around Nephenia.' He wrinkled his nose. 'Bad enough the way you smell normally, but do you have any idea what kind of a reek you put out when you were trying to get her to mate with you?'

'I didn't—'

'Besides,' he went on, ignoring me entirely, 'this makes for a better story: the young, noble warrior, setting out on a righteous quest, accompanied by his faithful – if a bit dense – human sidekick.'

'You're a little monster sometimes, you know that?'

The squirrel cat gave me a snarl. 'Hey, I'm the biggest monster the world's ever seen, and you better not forget it.'

I loosened my grip on the reins and let the horse pick up the pace as we made our way down the long, dark road towards whatever was waiting for us out there. 'I'm starting to pity those demons,' I said.

Acknowledgements

I get lost in shadow all the time. You'd think after having six novels published I'd get the hang of this writing thing, but I haven't. People ask me about my 'process', and all I can say is that it's a winding mess and without the help of patient and insightful guides, I'd stay lost forever. In that spirit, I thought you might like to know the path this book took to get to your hands.

Charmcaster got its title when Jane Harris, the brilliant publisher at Hot Key Books, informed me that 'Hextracker' just wasn't as good a title as the others in the series. I responded by telling her to come up with a better one. She did.

Gitabria, along with its eight bridges, contraptioneers and coin magic, were brainstormed and debated with the help of my fellow novelists in the writing group of which I am privileged to be a member: Wil Arndt, Stephanie Charette, Brad Denhert, and Kim Tough.

The discordances, with their mechanical birds and crowned mages and other enigmatic details, were devised with the help of my editor, Felicity Johnston. The beautiful illustrations found in the book were drawn by Sam Hadley under the art direction of Nick Stearn. The amazing cover design (along with Reichis finally getting the prominence he deserves), is their creation as well.

Nephenia, one of my favourite characters, appears in this book in part because Matilda Johnson, my first editor at Hot Key, challenged me in *Spellslinger* to give her more voice and agency. In doing so, Nephenia went from a side player to someone who doesn't let anyone but herself decide her own fate.

The mechanical dragons got short shrift in the earlier drafts of the books. It was my fellow novelist Eric Torin who warned me I was taking the easy way out – as he does with all my books. Oh, and if you like Shalla, you should know that she came into being years ago when Eric suggested there needed to be someone in the books that Kellen could never outwit.

Conspiracies, assassins, coin magic, Jan'Tep plots, deadly inventions, shadowblack paths, masked assassins . . . I swear there was a point where I thought it would be impossible to fit them all into one book. The truth is, it *wouldn't* have been possible if Fliss (aka Felicity Johnston) hadn't helped me work through the problems over innumerable trans-Atlantic Skype sessions. I couldn't have gotten through the changes without the help of Kim Tough, who read countless versions, and my wife, Christina de Castell, who, when she says it's good, I can finally breathe easy again.

Well . . . there's one other voice who must be obeyed on the subject of squirrel cats getting their due: thanks, Simone Hay.

Of course, once the story was sorted out, then the real work began: Jim Hull of narrativefirst.com let me argue with him about story structure, Sarah Fuller spotted problems in the first act, Melissa Hyder graciously copy-edited the book faster than anyone should ever have to, and Jade Craddock and Talya Baker are fixing my no doubt thousands of typos and grammatical errors as I write this.

That *Charmcaster* found its way into your hands is thanks to my agents, Heather Adams and Mike Brian of HMA Literary, and Mark Smith, CEO of Bonnier Zaffre, who took a gamble on the series and who I still owe a private jet. Jane Harris, Publisher of Hot Key Books, put together an amazing team including Jamie Taylor who turns it into an actual book, Nicola Chapman who markets it, Tina Mories who gets people to talk about it, and the fantastic sales team at Bonnier Zaffre for getting stores to carry it. If you're reading this in a language other than English, it's because Ruth Logan and Ilaria Tarasconi got publishers around the world excited about it and, of course, thanks to the translator of this particular edition.

If that sounds like a lot of people, that's only the start. Remember that there's a very good chance you heard about *Charmcaster* from a review by a kind, dedicated and likely unpaid blogger writing about books out of love for the genre. Your local booksellers fight to keep stories like these on the shelves so that you get the chance to enjoy them. Or maybe you borrowed this particular one from a library staffed by some of the best humans out there. Even Reichis likes librarians.

Oh, and the reason authors keep writing? It's the readers – who don't just accumulate books but talk about them, write letters and emails to authors and give meaning to our literary meanderings. Your enthusiasm means more to me than I can find the words to express. I'll keep trying though.

If you'd like to write to me, you can find me at www.decastell.com or follow me on Twitter @decastell

Turn the page for a preview of Kellen's next adventure . . .

SOULBINDER

Hope is a wondrous island upon whose shores we all wish to tread. Be wary though, that when you find your eyes drawn to that distant horizon, you remember to look down once in a while . . .

– Stupid Argosi proverb

1

The Problem with Sand

The desert is a liar.

Oh, sure, from a distance that endless expanse of golden sand *looks* inviting. Standing at the top of a sand dune, warm breezes soothe the scorching sun above, beckoning you to the wonders awaiting below. Whatever you desire – treasure beyond imagining, escape from your enemies, or maybe even a cure for the twisting black lines that won't stop growing around your left eye – some fool will swear it's waiting for you across the desert. A *dangerous journey? Perhaps, but the rewards, boy! Think of the rewards . . .*

Look closer, though – I mean, really close – say, an inch or so from the sand itself. This is easy to do when you're face down in it waiting to die of thirst. See how each and every grain of sand is unique? Different shapes, sizes, colours . . . That seamless perfection you saw before was just an illusion. Up close the desert is dirty, ugly and mean.

Like I said: it's a stinking liar.

'*You're* a stinking liar,' Reichis grumbled.

My head jerked up with a start. I hadn't even realised I'd spoken out loud. With considerable effort I turned my head to see how my so-called business partner was faring. I didn't get very far. Lack of food and water had taken their toll on me. The bloody bruises inflicted by the spells of a recently deceased mage whose foul-smelling corpse was rotting in the heat a few feet away didn't help either. So was I going to waste what life I had left to me just to glare at the ill-tempered, two-foot-tall squirrel cat dying by my side?

'*You* stink,' I replied.

'Heh,' he chuckled. Squirrel cats don't have a very good sense of their own mortality. They do, however, have an acute penchant for assigning blame. 'This is all your fault,' he chittered.

I rolled over, hoping to ease the stiffness in my spine, only for the wounds on my back to scream in protest. The pain drew a rasping moan from my parched throat.

'Don't try to deny it,' Reichis said.

'I didn't say anything.'

'Yes, you did. You whimpered and I heard, "But, Reichis, how could I possibly have known that I was leading us into a death trap set by my own people? I mean, sure, you warned me that this talk of a secret monastery in the desert where monks could cure me of the shadowblack was a scam, but you know me: I'm an idiot. An idiot who never listens to his smarter and much better-looking business partner."'

In case you've never seen a squirrel cat, picture an angry feline face, slightly tubby body, unruly bushy tail and strange furry flaps connecting their front and back limbs that enable them to glide down from treetops to massacre their prey. 'Good-looking' isn't exactly the phrase that comes to mind.

'You got all that from a whimper?' I asked.

A pause. 'Squirrel cats are very intuitive.'

I drew a ragged breath, the heat off the sand burning the

air in my lungs. How long had the two of us been lying here? A day? Two days? My hand reached for the last of our water skins, dragging it closer. I steeled myself for the fact that I'd have to share what was left with Reichis. People say you can live three days without water, but that's not factoring in the way the desert robs the moisture from you like a . . . *like a damned squirrel cat*! The water skin was bone-dry. 'You drank the last of our water?'

Reichis replied testily, 'I asked first.'

'When?'

Another pause. 'While you were asleep.'

Apparently the desert wasn't the only liar I had to contend with.

Seventeen years old, exiled by my people, hunted by every hextracker and bounty mage with two spells and a bad attitude, and the last of my water had just been stolen by the closest thing I had to a friend out here.

My name is Kellen Argos. Once I was a promising student of magic and the son of one of the most powerful families in the Jan'Tep territories. Then the twisting black markings of a mystical curse known as the shadowblack appeared around my left eye. Now people call me outlaw, traitor, exile – and that's when they're being polite.

The one thing they never call me is lucky.

'Sure, I know the place,' the old scout had said, her mismatched hazel and green eyes glued to the dusty leather bag of copper and silver trinkets on the table between us. We had the ground floor of the travellers' saloon to ourselves, with the exception of a couple of passed-out drunks in the far corner and one sad fellow who sat on the floor by himself, rolling a pair of dice over and over as he sobbed into his ale about having the worst luck in the whole world.

Shows what you know, buddy.

'Can you take me to it? This monastery,' I asked, placing a card face up on the table.

The scout picked up the card and squinted at the shadowy towers depicted on its surface. 'Nice work,' she observed. 'You paint this yourself?'

I nodded. For the past six months, Reichis and I had crossed half a continent in search of a cure for the shadowblack. We'd pick up clues here and there, brief scrawls in the margins of obscure texts referring to a secret sanctuary, rumours repeated endlessly by drunks in taverns like this one. The Argosi paint cards of important people and places, imbuing them with whatever scraps of information they collect in hopes that the resulting images will reveal otherwise hidden meanings. I'd taken to painting my own. If I died in my search for a cure, there was always a chance the cards would find their way into Argosi hands, and then to Ferius Parfax, so she'd know not to bother looking for me.

The old scout tossed the card back down on the table as if she were placing a bet. 'The place you're looking for is called the Ebony Abbey, and yeah, I *could* take you there . . . if I were so inclined.' Her smile pinched the crags of sun-browned skin on her forehead and around her eyes, her face like a map of some long-forgotten country. She had to be well into her sixties, but her sleeveless leather jerkin revealed rope-like muscles on her shoulders and arms. Those, along with the assortment of knives sheathed to a bandolier across her chest and the crossbow strapped to her back, told me she could probably handle herself just fine in a fight. The way she kept staring at the bag of trinkets on the table without paying much attention to me made it plain that I hadn't made a similar impression on her.

Searching for a miracle cure hadn't been a particularly profitable enterprise so far. Every coin I earned as a spellslinger during my travels had been wasted on snake-oil salesmen peddling putrid concoctions that left me sick and vomiting for days at a time. Now my travel-worn linen shirt hung loose on my skinny frame. My face and chest still showed the bruises and scars from my last encounter with a pair of Jan'Tep bounty mages. So I could understand why the sight of me didn't exactly fill the scout with trepidation.

'She's thinking of beating you up and taking our money,' Reichis said, sniffing the air from his perch on my shoulder.

'That thing ain't rabid, is it?' the scout asked, sparing him a wary glance.

Other people don't understand the chitters, snarls and occasional farts Reichis uses to communicate. 'I'm still trying to figure that out,' I replied.

The squirrel cat gave a low growl. 'You know I can just rip your eyeballs right out of their sockets and eat them while you sleep, right?' He hopped off my shoulder and headed towards the two drunks passed out in the corner, no doubt to see if he could pick their pockets.

'Ask them that know the tales,' the old scout began in a sing-song voice. 'They'll tell you naught but seven outsiders have ever been inside the Ebony Abbey's walls. Five of them are dead. One's a dream-weed addict who couldn't find his own nose with both hands, never mind a secret monastery hidden in the desert.' She reached for the little bag that contained everything I still had of any value. 'Then there's me.'

I got to the bag first. I may not look like much, but I've got fast hands. 'We haven't agreed terms yet.'

For the first time the old scout's mismatched eyes locked on mine. I tried to match her glare, but it's unnerving to have two different-coloured eyes staring back at you. 'Why you want to mess with them Black Binders anyway?' she asked. Her gaze went to my left eye, and I could tell she'd picked up on the slight discolouration where the edges of the skin-coloured mesdet paste met the top of my cheekbone. 'You ain't got the shadowblack, do ya?'

'Shadow-what?' I asked. 'Never heard of it.'

'Well, I hear there's a posse of Jan'Tep spellcasters who'll pay plenty for one o' them demon-cursed. There's a particular fellow they've been hunting a while now, or so I hear.'

'I wouldn't know about that,' I said, trying to lend my words a hint of a threat. 'Like I told you before, I'm just writing a book about obscure desert monks.'

'Lot of money for that bounty. Maybe more than what's in that bag of yours.'

I removed my hands from the bag and let my fingers drift down to open the tops of the pouches attached to either side of my belt. Inside were the red and black powders I used for the one spell I knew that always left an impression. 'You know what?' I asked casually. 'Now that you mention it, I think maybe I *have* heard about this shadowblack bounty you mention. Word is, a lot of dangerous folk have tried to collect on it. Have to wonder what happened to all of them.'

One corner of the scout's mouth rose to a smirk. Her own hands, I saw now, had managed to make a pair of hooked knives appear. 'Met plenty of dangerous men in my time.

None of them impressed me much. What makes you any different?'

I returned her smile. 'Look behind you.'

She didn't, instead angling one of her knives just a touch until the blade caught the reflection of a certain squirrel cat who'd surreptitiously made his way up to the top of the coat rack behind her and was now waiting for the cue to pounce.

Yeah, the little bugger makes himself useful sometimes.

I counted three full breaths before the old scout slowly set her knives down on the table. 'Sounds like a mighty fine book you're writing, my young friend.' She snatched up my bag of trinkets and rose from the table. 'Best we load up on supplies in town before we make the trip.'

I waited a while longer, doing my best to make it appear as if I hadn't decided whether to hire her as my guide or blast her into ashes. Truthfully though, I was waiting for my heart to stop racing. 'How far away is this abbey?' I asked.

She adjusted the strap of her crossbow and slid her knives into their sheathes. 'A long ways, as these things go, but don't worry; you'll enjoy the journey.'

'Really?'

She grinned. 'Folks say the Golden Passage is the gentlest, most beautiful place you'll ever see.'

2

The Virtue of Corpses

Faint scratching sounds returned me to my current predicament. I opened one eye a fraction, groggily expecting to be blinded by the reflection of sunlight against the shimmering golden sand. Instead I was greeted by twilight and a bitter chill. You'd think a place as blisteringly hot during the day as the Golden Passage would be temperate at night. But no, the temperature goes from scorching to freezing with barely an hour of warmth in between. I shivered and tried to go back to sleep.

The scratching continued though – so close that for a second I batted at my ear, fearful that some insect was burrowing inside. When that failed to solve the problem, I forced my head up enough to turn towards the source of the incessant noise. Reichis was wearily dragging himself along the sand.

He's trying to get to me, I thought.

Fondness broke through the cold and despair. For all our quarrelling, the squirrel cat and I had saved each other's lives more times than either of us could count; now he wanted to die beside me.

I reached out a hand, only to discover he wasn't getting any closer. He was actually crawling *away* from me.

Have I mentioned that squirrel cats are ungrateful little wretches? My so-called business partner hadn't been expending his last ounce of strength so that we could meet our end together; this wasn't some final moment of friendship between us. No, instead the furry monster was slowly working his way to the war mage's corpse.

'What are you doing?' I asked.

No reply. Reichis just kept crawling inch by inch to his destination. When he finally lay next to the corpse's head, panting and exhausted, I worried that perhaps the squirrel cat's mind was so far gone from thirst that he'd mistaken the dead man for me. With a trembling paw, he reached for the mage's unblinking eyes that stared blindly up at the darkening sky. That's when I finally understood what Reichis was up to.

'Oh, for the sake of all my dead ancestors,' I swore, 'tell me you're not planning to—'

With the deftness that comes from practice – a *lot* of practice – Reichis used one of his claws to dig out the man's eyeball. He then opened his jaws wide, dropped the disgusting, squishy sphere into his maw, and bit down. 'Oh . . .' he said, moaning rapturously, 'that's tasty.'

'You're repugnant, you know that?' I'm not sure the words actually came out of my mouth. At that precise moment I was using what little strength of will I had left to keep myself from vomiting.

'Yummy,' he mumbled between chews, then swallowed noisily.

What few people know about squirrel cats is that the only thing more revolting than the way they devour their food is their insistence on rhapsodising about it afterwards. 'You know,' he began with a contented sigh, 'you worry that it'll be overcooked, on account of this guy's face having caught fire and all, but it turned out perfect. A little crispy on the outside; soft and warm on the inside.' He reached a paw over to the other side of the dead mage's face. 'You want the left one?' he asked, adding a slight snarl to convey that the offer wasn't entirely sincere.

'I'll pass. Doesn't it just make you more thirsty? We're likely to die from lack of water a lot sooner than we'll expire from hunger.'

'Good point.' Reichis hauled himself closer to the mage's chest, where a massive wound from our duel had left a pool of blood. The squirrel cat began lapping it up. He paused when he caught me staring at him in horror. 'You should probably drink some too, Kellen. Must have *some* water in it, right?'

'I am *not* drinking blood. I am *not* eating eyeballs.'

The squirrel cat served up a sarcastic growl. 'Oh, right, because your culinary hang-ups are so much more important than our survival.'

I couldn't think of a suitable retort. He might've been right, for all I knew, though I had no idea if human beings could actually get enough moisture from blood to make a difference, or if it would just make me sick. Either way, I couldn't bring myself to find out, so I just lay there for a few minutes with nothing to do but listen to the sound of Reichis's enthusiastic slurping. When he was finally done, he lay back down on his side and called to me. 'Kellen?'

'Yeah?'

'I know this is kind of a sensitive topic, but . . .'

'What?'

'Well, when you're dead, is it okay if I eat your corpse?' Hastily he added, 'I mean, it's better if one of us lives, right?'

With what little strength I had left, I rolled away from him onto my back, ignoring the pain that exploded from my injuries. I didn't want the last thing I saw in this world to be the blood-soaked face of a squirrel cat as he pondered which to eat first, my eyeballs or my ears.

High above, beyond the petty concerns of mortals, the stars began to appear, thousands of tiny sparks coming to life. Though the Golden Passage was an arid, unlivable hellhole, the night sky out here could really put on a show. I took in a breath, only to have my throat spasm painfully – a reflex that I guess must be the result of going too long without water.

I'm going to die here. The words invaded my thoughts as suddenly and as forcefully as an iron binding spell. *I'm really going to die tonight, killed by some arsehole Jan'Tep bounty hunter and my own stupidity.* I felt myself starting to cry, and with trembling fingers reached up to wipe at tears that weren't there.

I must've let out a sob, because Reichis groaned. 'Oh, great, cos bawling your eyes out is really going to help conserve water.' Squirrel cats aren't exactly known for their compassion.

Usually when I get myself into trouble, my survival depends on the timely arrival of a certain curly red-haired gambler by the name of Ferius Parfax. There I'll be, on my knees, begging some lunatic who happens to have a thing against shadowblacks, waiting for the blade (or mace, or crossbow, ember spell, or . . . you get the idea) to come crashing down on me, when all of a sudden *she'll* turn up.

'Well now, don't you two look as fussy as two feisty ferrets fightin' over a fern,' she'll say. Actually, she's never used those exact words, but it's usually something equally nonsensical.

'Do not dare interfere, Argosi,' the mage (or soldier, assassin or random irritated person) will shout back.

Ferius will push that frontier hat of hers a half-inch higher on her brow, reach into her waistcoat to pull out a smoking reed, and say, 'Far be it from me to interfere, friend, but I've grown somewhat accustomed to that skinny fella you seem intent on carvin' up. Gonna have to ask you to kindly back off.'

After that? Well, fight-fight-fight, clever remark, certain death, near-impossible daring feat, enemy goes down, one last clever remark – usually at my expense – and then I'm saved. That's how it's been ever since I left my homeland on my sixteenth birthday.

Only now everything's different. Six months ago I'd abandoned Ferius, my mentor in the ways of the Argosi, and Nephenia, the charmcaster I once loved, on account of I'd learned that my people were never going to stop hunting me and anyone with me, so long as I had the shadowblack. Since the swirling black marks around my left eye showed no sign of fading away, that meant leaving the two people I was closest to behind or risk them being killed by enemies intent on getting to me. As painful as my departure had been, at least it had felt kind of noble.

For about six minutes.

The problem with being noble and self-sacrificing is that when you get into a jam – say, like, when the tattooed metallic bands on a Jan'Tep hextracker's arms are glowing from all the magic he's summoned to kill you – there's nobody to get you out of it.

'Hey, Kellen . . . ?' Reichis asked with an uncharacteristic hesitation in his voice.

'Yes, you can eat me when I'm dead. Happy now?'

Silence for a moment, then, 'No, I was just wondering if you think that mage was telling the truth.'

'About what?'

'When he said he killed Ferius.'

Thank you for choosing a Hot Key book.

If you want to know more about our authors and what we publish, you can find us online.

You can start at our website

www.hotkeybooks.com

And you can also find us on:

We hope to see you soon!